**Praise for #1 *New York Times* bestselling author
Sherryl Woods**

"Sherryl Woods always delights her readers—
including me!"
—#1 *New York Times* bestselling author
Debbie Macomber

"Sherryl Woods gives her characters depth,
intensity and the right amount of humor."
—*RT Book Reviews*

"Woods…is noted for appealing, character-driven
stories that are often infused with the flavor and
fragrance of the South."
—*Library Journal*

**Praise for *New York Times* bestselling author
Maisey Yates**

"Yates's thrilling…contemporary proves that
friendship can evolve into scintillating romance.…
This is a surefire winner not to be missed."
—*Publishers Weekly* on *Slow Burn Cowboy*
(starred review)

"This is an exceptional example of an opposites-
attract romance with heartfelt writing and solid
character development.… This is a must-read that
will have you believing in love."
—*RT Book Reviews* on *Seduce Me, Cowboy*
(Top Pick)

With her roots firmly planted in the South, #1 *New York Times* bestselling author **Sherryl Woods** has written many of her more than one hundred books in that distinctive setting, whether it's her home state of Virginia, her adopted state, Florida, or her much-adored South Carolina. Now she's added North Carolina's Outer Banks to her list of favorite spots. And she remains partial to small towns, wherever they may be.

Sherryl divides her time between her childhood summer home overlooking the Potomac River in Colonial Beach, Virginia, and her oceanfront home with its lighthouse view in Key Biscayne, Florida. "Wherever I am, if there's no water in sight, I get a little antsy," she says.

Sherryl loves to hear from readers. You can visit her on her website at www.sherrylwoods.com, link to her Facebook fan page from there or contact her directly at Sherryl703@gmail.com.

Maisey Yates is a *New York Times* bestselling author of more than thirty romance novels. She has a coffee habit she has no interest in kicking, and a slight Pinterest addiction. She lives with her husband and children in the Pacific Northwest. When Maisey isn't writing, she can be found singing in the grocery store, shopping for shoes online and probably not doing dishes. Check out her website, www.maiseyyates.com.

#1 *New York Times* Bestselling Author

SHERRYL WOODS

JOSHUA AND THE COWGIRL

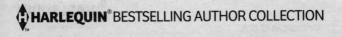

HARLEQUIN® BESTSELLING AUTHOR COLLECTION

ISBN-13: 978-1-335-08151-3

Joshua and the Cowgirl

Copyright © 2018 by Harlequin Books S.A.

The publisher acknowledges the copyright holders of the individual works as follows:

Joshua and the Cowgirl
Copyright © 1991 by Sherryl Woods

Seduce Me, Cowboy
Copyright © 2017 by Maisey Yates

Recycling programs for this product may not exist in your area.

This edition published by arrangement with Harlequin Books S.A.

For questions and comments about the quality of this book, please contact us at CustomerService@Harlequin.com.

Printed in U.S.A.

www.Harlequin.com

CONTENTS

JOSHUA AND THE COWGIRL

Sherryl Woods

CHAPTER ONE

WHEN HE STEPPED out of his car, placed his three-hundred-dollar Italian loafers into a foot of fresh snow and found himself face-to-face with an inquisitive cow, Joshua knew deep in his gut that Wyoming was not going to be one bit better this time around. The sophisticated world of international financial consultant Joshua Ames did not include cows. At the globe-trotting pace he lived, it didn't even include tame little kittens or rambunctious puppies.

Admittedly his life had taken a certain predictable turn these last few years, but he found comfort in that. He lived in a world of fast sports cars, like the flashy red convertible he'd rented at the airport in Cheyenne before he'd realized that Indian summer was not a concept with which Wyoming weather was acquainted. With so much of his life spent in five-star hotels, he felt settled only in the luxury of exclusive skyscrapers—like the oceanfront tower he'd reluctantly left behind in Florida or the cozy pied-à-terre he kept that overlooked Central Park in New York. Joshua's life, even on the rare occasions when he bothered with breakfast, even included thick cream for his fresh raspberries. However, in all of his thirty-seven eventful years his world had never, ever included a face-to-face encounter with the source of that cream.

Until now.

The creature had ambled close enough that he could

feel its hot breath. Images of the pageantry and violence of the bullrings in Spain flashed through his mind with untimely clarity. His own breath caught in his throat. Good Lord, surely this was a gentle milk cow, *not* a bull! He nervously checked for some sign of ferocity and impending threat in its limpid brown eyes, but saw only vague curiosity. He wasn't about to get intimate enough to investigate for more positive identification of its gender.

Joshua took a cautious step backward, butted into a strand of barbed wire, yelped and muttered a string of colorful obscenities, most of them directed at his client and best friend, Cal Rivers. Scratch that. *Former best friend.* Joshua was never going to forgive him for this or any of his other myriad sins, which seemed to be stacking up like old newspapers now that marriage had turned Cal's previously razor-sharp brain to lovesick mush.

Retaliation held a certain rapidly growing appeal. Maybe he'd just bungle Cal's corporate books so thoroughly that an entire team of accountants working around the clock wouldn't be able to untangle them by tax time. Maybe he'd help him choose a few highly questionable junk bonds for his steadfastly risk-free portfolio. Maybe he'd triple his usual fees and take that long-delayed vacation in Paris at Cal's expense.

Or maybe he'd just shoot him. Yeah, that was it, Joshua decided with enthusiasm. There had to be a shotgun someplace on this godforsaken ranch. He would load it and then track down his former best friend. When he found Cal, he'd blow him to smithereens for dragging him away from civilization for the second time in the year and a half since Cal had been reunited with his family. To think that he had actually encouraged the reconcili-

ation! Joshua should have known better. He should have
realized that sooner or later a happily settled Cal would
insist that he come back to this place that reminded him
all too vividly of a time in his life he'd spent years trying to forget.

Not that Joshua hadn't tried to protect himself from
such an eventuality. Joshua had warned Cal way back
then that he would not ever set foot on this desolate ranch
again. He had sworn to die first. He was not interested in
dust. He did not appreciate wide open spaces. The sun-
sets in Florida were quite enough, not that he paid much
attention to them. Joshua had clients far less intractable
than Mrs. Caroline Whitfield McDonald, Cal's maternal
grandmother. He was not a bookkeeper, which was what
Mrs. McDonald sorely needed. Those were all good reasons, solid, self-protective reasons.

Joshua had rarely admitted, even to himself, that the
real reasons went much deeper. Behind the excuses were
the memories. Dredged up from the depths of the past,
the memories recalled the scared, overprotected boy he
had once been; a boy who had been thoroughly, painfully out of his element in a rough-and-tumble environment much like this.

Now that he was standing up to his ankles in snow, he
realized he should have mentioned that, as well. Snow
was meant for ski slopes in winter. There wasn't a mountain in sight in this empty, dreary part of Wyoming. To
top it off, it was barely September. He'd left ninety-degree
temperatures back home. He shivered in the harsh, blus-
tery air and wondered if he'd be taking his life in his
hands to try maneuvering around the cow to reach the
jacket in the car. Since it was only a suit jacket, he decided it wasn't worth it. He'd still be freezing his butt off.

Okay. Cal had made a mistake in not mentioning the snow. But Joshua was sure he had stated emphatically that he absolutely, positively was not interested in getting up close and personal with livestock unless he was betting a financial bundle on cattle futures.

Cal, damn him, had laughed at each and every protest. Hooted, in fact. He'd bided his time, then lured Joshua out here by reminding him of their years of friendship, their long business association. He'd thrown in a healthy suggestion of desperation. Right now, with that cow staring him in the face, Joshua knew all about desperation. As far as he could tell, Wyoming was fraught with it.

"I see you've met Jezebel," a husky feminine voice, threaded with all-too-familiar gloating laughter, said just when he was contemplating the precise details of murder and mayhem. Desperation took a new twist as his thoughts veered dramatically and predictably.

Garrett. Traci Maureen Garrett, to be precise—and Joshua was the kind of man who insisted on being precise. Working with numbers—huge numbers—required it. Surviving around Garrett, he'd discovered, also demanded a similar degree of attentiveness.

Traci Maureen Garrett had very nearly driven him nuts when they'd met nearly a year and a half ago. Her smug attitude, sharp tongue and sly humor had stung. If the slam-bang, ready-for-combat pace of his heartbeat right this second was any indication, she was going to do it again. He considered it yet another black mark against Cal. A mere eighteen months ago he had been a serene, contented man. Now he was one inch from another jab of barbed wire, six inches from a fire-breathing cow and laughing distance from a know-it-all female who was obviously delighting in his fix.

Above all, though, Joshua Ames was a proud man. No cow—or cowgirl—was going to see even the faintest hint that he was intimidated. He mustered his most confident smile and turned slowly, never letting that creature out of his line of vision.

"Jezebel?" he said. "Is there much room for wickedness in the bovine world?"

"Let's just say that Jezebel always manages to find trouble."

A fascinating, dimpled smile, that also meant trouble, met his gaze. That never forgotten, daring, tempting smile kept him from lingering too long on the thick braid of sunlight-blond hair, blue velvet eyes and long—endlessly long—slender legs encased in snug denim. Not trendy denim, he noticed with a faint sigh of regret, but faded, hard-working jeans meant to withstand life on a cattle ranch.

His gaze settled on her smile, the curve of generous lips, and stayed there—reluctantly. The punch-in-the-belly impact of that smile hadn't diminished one bit. Unfortunately. It had been yet another reason to steer as far away from this ranch as possible. Traci Maureen Garrett, who had a spark of sheer mischief in her eyes, was *not* the woman of his dreams. *She* couldn't be. Surely God wouldn't be cruel enough to let him fall for a woman who managed a cattle ranch!

"I see," he said, adopting what he hoped was suitable nonchalance for a man who felt as if he'd been pole-axed for the second time in his life. The first time had been a year and a half earlier. The unlikely, impossible Garrett had figured heavily in both incidents.

"Is she a family pet?" he inquired.

"Nope. Actually she's about one step away from being

sent to market. My personal hunch is that she knows it and is trying to ingratiate herself around the house."

The concept of this cow being someone's dinner appealed to Joshua in a perverse way that told him a lot about his overall mood with regards to this latest assignment. From the indulgent expression in Garrett's eyes, however, he decided he'd best keep his bloodthirsty opinion to himself. She was obviously fond of this cow, which made her contradictory willingness to send it off to slaughter a little chilling.

That was part of what troubled him about Garrett. One minute he was totally and completely enthralled by her careless, untamed beauty and captivated by her quick mind. Then, in less time than it took to saddle a horse, he was reminded that she was tough as nails, and as uncompromising and mule-headed as one of those self-made millionaires with whom he occasionally had to tangle over financial policy. Maybe this time, if he could catch his breath around her, he'd be able to figure her out.

Maybe, if he was very, very lucky, he'd be able to get her out of his system. To his regret, all these months and the clever efforts of innumerable beautiful, sophisticated women hadn't accomplished it. Maybe proximity would…if it didn't get him into a hell of a lot of trouble first.

GARRETT WAS NOT proud of herself. She knew she was enjoying Joshua Ames's discomfort a little too much. A kind, generous woman would take pity on him and send the perfectly harmless Jezebel fleeing back to the pasture the cow had escaped from. Unfortunately some crazy quirk in her psyche kept her from feeling much pity for this city slicker who obviously felt so much disdain for her beloved world of blue skies and wide open spaces.

The man's attitude was the pits. Only her fondness for her boss, Mrs. Caroline Whitfield McDonald, had kept her from telling him exactly what she thought of him the last time he'd breezed in here with his slightly crooked nose poked in the air. Mrs. Mac, as she was known around the ranch, obviously needed him—or thought she did. It was Garrett's personal opinion that Mrs. Mac had run the ranch quite capably and successfully without interference from a know-it-all financial genius from the east. Her grandson, however, had thought otherwise. He'd appeared out of the blue, taken one look at the admittedly haphazardly kept books and sent for the cavalry. No doubt he feared for his inheritance. Garrett hadn't quite dared to suggest as much to Mrs. Mac.

"I'm surprised you came back," Garrett said, taking a no-trespassing stance that worked especially well on the cowboys around town.

"No more than I am," Joshua admitted with disarming candor.

"Why did you? Surely you have more important things to do than balance the accounts around here. Isn't your forte spending other people's money?"

"Actually, it's increasing their money," he said, amusement lurking in the depths of his eyes. There was no hint of false modesty, no suggestion that he ever dared to lose any of their cash.

"Since I doubt that Mrs. Mac lets you near her capital, why are you here?"

"Cal insisted."

"And everyone jumps to do his bidding, don't they?" Garrett couldn't keep the resentful note out of her voice.

"Friends do," Joshua said softly. "What's Cal asked you to do?"

"I don't take orders from him."

"I can imagine," he said, grinning suddenly. "I don't suppose that's kept Cal from giving them. Has he been throwing his weight around? Asking impertinent questions? Stepping on your managerial toes?"

She shrugged. "Cal can make all the suggestions he wants to Mrs. Mac. It's his ranch or will be soon enough."

Joshua's gaze narrowed. "And that really infuriates you, doesn't it? Were you hoping to get it for yourself?"

The too-close-to-the-mark dig irritated her. "Not the way you mean. I was hoping for a chance to buy into it," she said.

His features instantly softened with apparent understanding. The suggestion of pity only angered her.

"I'm sure Cal would work a deal with you," Joshua said. "I don't think he's interested in keeping the place for himself. Cal's got enough on his hands with that horse farm down in Florida. Now that he's won a couple of races, he's more convinced than ever that raising Thoroughbreds is the life for him."

Joshua's aggrieved tone told her what he thought of that idea. If he'd meant to reassure her, though, he'd missed the mark. Cal's disinterest wouldn't help her situation a bit. Mrs. Mac had her mind set on giving this place to her grandson. Her legacy, she said. His birthright. She'd been trying her damnedest to manipulate him into accepting it. Knowing Mrs. Mac, sooner or later she'd have her way. Then, even if Cal were willing to sell someday, Garrett wasn't likely to have the kind of cash it would take to impress him.

"It'll be years before I can pay Cal what it's worth,"

she told Joshua honestly. "He'll probably sell it off long before that." She hoped Joshua Ames couldn't tell just how much that hurt. Garrett had been so darned close for the first time in her life to getting what she wanted, and now it was slipping away. It was all but certain the ranch was going to a man who didn't give a damn about it and was likely to sell it to strangers at the first opportunity.

"Maybe I could talk to him."

The offer sounded so sincere and was so totally unexpected that Garrett found herself staring at him in astonishment. "Why would you do that?"

"Beats me," Joshua said. "Maybe it's your charming personality."

Garrett flushed, taking the pointed barb square on the chin. The man hadn't been here five minutes and she was taking out all of her anger and frustration on him. It wasn't Joshua's fault she was going to lose her dream. It wasn't even his fault that he was a greenhorn. She surveyed the thick blond hair, the stubborn chin, the wreck of a nose that ruined the perfection of his face but created interest. Everything about Joshua Ames shouted money and glamour, *except* that nose. It spoke of street-tough masculinity. She wondered who had dared to bloody it and under what circumstances. Then, perversely, Garrett wondered why she cared.

She was still wondering that when he said, "Do you suppose we could get inside before I freeze to death?"

Snug in the warmth of her sheepskin jacket, she couldn't resist taunting him. "It's mild out here. You should be here in January."

He shuddered visibly. "God forbid!"

Garrett grinned. "Go on in. Mrs. Mac's waiting for you."

"And Cal?"

"He's flown back to Florida," she said, enjoying the quick blaze of fury that swept into his eyes before he could discreetly mask it.

"He's gone where?" Joshua bellowed so loudly that Jezebel took flight and headed back to the pasture.

"Left just as the snow started. Should be landing back there about now," she confirmed cheerfully.

"I'm going to kill him."

"Seems to me you're going to have to catch up with him first."

He appeared torn between the desire to flee and resignation. "You don't have to enjoy this so damned much," he muttered.

"Why not? We get so little entertainment out here in the boondocks."

Joshua winced, but his guilt was apparently fleeting. Then a wicked, dangerous gleam filled his eyes. That glint, hot enough to melt snow, warmed her as no sheepskin jacket ever had. His gaze raked over her from head to toe. Very slowly. "Perhaps I can find other ways to change that."

Garrett's cheeks flamed at the deliberate taunt. She knew how to handle the straightforward passes thrown by hopeful cowboys. She was less sure how to deal with sly, flirtatious comments meant to rattle her. Garrett knew instinctively, though, that she couldn't allow Joshua to see that his seductive remark bothered her in the slightest. Poking her hands into her pockets, she looked him straight in the eye and declared with bold impudence, "I doubt you're man enough."

Instead of the stunned outrage she'd expected, the insult merely drew one of his devastating killer smiles. "I guess we'll just have to see about that, won't we?" Joshua challenged, running a finger along the line of her jaw. Deep inside her something responded to that deliberate touch, something that scared the daylights out of her.

"When hell freezes over!" she retorted, swiping his hand away and trying to ignore the spine-tingling effect of his low chuckle of amusement.

He glanced around meaningfully at the endless snow-covered vistas and smiled. A distressingly masculine expression of smug satisfaction spread slowly across his face, finally reaching his eyes. Those sexy, fascinating blue-green eyes, Garrett decided, were going to be her undoing. His gaze locked on hers and no matter how hard she willed it, she couldn't seem to tear her gaze away.

"Looks to me like it already has," he said, more laughter threading through his rich voice.

"Hmm?" she said blankly.

Joshua gestured at their surroundings. "Hell, sweetheart. Looks to me like it's already frozen over."

CHAPTER TWO

GARRETT BLISTERED THE blue skies with every epithet she could think of to describe Joshua's character and his heritage. She was still muttering under her breath when she charged into the barn at full throttle.

"Whoa," Red Grady said, catching her by the elbows and steadying her as she plowed into his solid, barrel chest. "Who lit a fire under you?"

"That man," she said, as if that would be explanation enough.

"At last check we had about a dozen men on the premises. Care to be more specific?" the ranch foreman inquired, barely containing a grin.

"Joshua Ames."

"Ah," Red murmured knowingly. "He does have a way of getting under your skin. Why is that, do you suppose?"

"Because he is an obnoxious, know-it-all jerk." Garrett grabbed the saddle soap and went to work on her saddle. Red propped a booted foot on a sawhorse and watched her.

"If you rub much harder, you're going to wear out the leather," he observed finally. "Want me to beat the man up for you?"

Garrett's gaze shot up to meet his laughing eyes. "You'd do it, too, wouldn't you?" she said, more grateful than ever for Red's enduring friendship.

It had been nearly fourteen years since Red had found her waiting tables in that roadside diner halfway between Cheyenne and the ranch. He'd befriended her over eggs and grits and a stack of pancakes that still awed her. Garrett had been seven months pregnant, exhausted and lonely. An uncomplicated, caring man, Red had stood by her, listening to her fears and her dreams. A month before her daughter had been born, he'd brought her to meet Mrs. McDonald. The job interview had gone smoothly. She had known that Red had stuck his neck out for her and that, very likely, Mrs. McDonald had invented a job for her. He'd wanted to see her settled before the birth. She would never forget Red for that. Nor would she ever take advantage of him.

"I can handle Joshua Ames," she told him now, though she hadn't the faintest idea how.

He tucked a finger under her chin and tilted her head up. "You know I'd do anything for you, though. That's a given. You need, you ask, okay?"

Garrett wrapped her hand around his larger, callused one and pressed it to her cheek. "Thanks, Red."

His cheeks turned a shade of red very nearly as bright as his curly, untamed hair. He backed off a step and shoved his hands into his pockets. "No need for thanks. As far as I'm concerned, you and your daughter, Casey, are family and families stick together." He grinned at her. "Besides, I wouldn't mind taking a punch at the competition on my own account anyway."

The offhanded remark was made cheerfully enough, but it troubled Garrett just the same. She knew Red was fond of her. In his own stumbling way he'd told her more than once that he'd be pleased to share a future with her. If she was ever going to trust a man, Red would be the one, but something had always held her back. Today, encountering Joshua again and feeling her blood race hot and wild at his slightest touch, she recognized what had kept her from that commitment to Red. Garrett didn't want the kind of danger Joshua represented, but settling for less wasn't in the cards for her, either. She'd rather go through life alone, accountable only to herself and to Casey. It was a choice she'd made years ago. Until the day she'd met Joshua Ames, she'd never questioned it.

That alone told her far too much about the threat he posed. With any luck, though, he would be gone in a day or two and she would survive this second attack on her senses unscathed. If there was even the most remote chance of it happening any other way, well, there was always Red's offer to punch the man out for her.

JOSHUA PACED FROM one end of the cluttered parlor to the other, dodging musty, old-fashioned furniture and cursing Cal as he went. A fire blazed, which should have made the room welcoming. Instead the house felt stuffy and overheated, making it especially oppressive after the icy air outside and Garrett's equally chilly reception.

Joshua's temper, usually slow to rise, was leashed so tightly that the slightest irritation was likely to set him off. It was his experience that Mrs. McDonald could irritate the dickens out of him in less than ten seconds flat. He could hardly wait for her to waltz in here in that imperious way she had and try to explain why he was here and Cal was basking in the Florida sun. He heard the sharp tapping of her cane and prepared himself for a royal battle.

"Mr. Ames, it's so lovely to have you back with us again," she greeted him in a voice that rang with a strength belied by her slow, obviously painful approach. Joshua found himself moving swiftly to grasp her elbow as she eased herself onto a Victorian chair covered in faded brocade. Though the chair looked miserably uncomfortable, she sat in it regally. Her back was not quite as ramrod straight as he'd remembered, but her still coal-black hair was swept up in a crowning braid that added to the impression of stature and quiet dignity. He might have been fooled had he not seen her enter the room or looked closely at her face.

Filled with compassion, Joshua pulled up a chair and sat opposite her. He'd heard about her osteoporosis, but this was the first evidence he'd seen of its devastating effect. His anger died in the face of her valiant struggle to brave a pain that shadowed the snapping blue of her eyes and drained the color from her cheeks. The disease had clearly worsened since his last visit.

"Can I get you something?" he offered.

A faint smile tugged at the grim set of her mouth. "I can still manage to ring for the help, young man. Tea will be served shortly."

Joshua sat back, chastened yet amused. Obviously nothing had weakened her spirit. In that instant his reluctant respect for the gritty, eighty-two-year-old rancher grew tremendously. He vowed to do nothing more to undercut her bravery. This was one situation in which chivalry was most likely to be deemed pity and refused out of hand.

"Where's Cal?" he asked far more mildly than he'd intended.

Her mouth turned down. "Home, I expect. He said something about those infernal horses of his, then took off."

"Even though he knew I was coming?"

"I suspect his sudden hurry might have had something to do with my offer to build him his own place out here, so I could watch my great-grandbabies grow up."

Joshua grinned reluctantly. "That would do it."

"I don't know why the man's so stubborn," she grumbled. "It makes perfect sense for him to live out here. I know I could convince Marilou, if he'd just give me a little time to work on her. She likes the sense of family continuity here."

"And you're perfectly willing to use his wife's weakness for family ties to manipulate Cal. No wonder he's run for his life. I'd be surprised if he ever brings Marilou and the baby back again."

Mrs. McDonald scowled at him impatiently. "I might have known you'd stick up for him. Can't any of you see that this place will all be his one of these days? He needs to know how to run it."

"Cal certainly doesn't need it and he says he doesn't want it."

"Stubborn fool. He's ignoring reality. I am not about to change my will at this late date. If nothing else, he should think of his children."

"He can provide for his children well enough and I suspect he comes by the stubborn need to do so naturally."

The observation drew a nod of reluctant satisfaction. "I expect he does at that. I suppose I ought to count it as a blessing that he's not some namby-pamby sort I can push around."

"You certainly should," Joshua agreed, though less than ten minutes ago he'd been wanting to shove Cal around a little himself. "So, why am I here? Are you hoping I'll be more amenable to your whims?"

She chuckled. "That's not a label I'd pin on you, young man. You're worse than that grandson of mine. Cal insisted on dragging you out here, though. Took one look at the books and nearly went into cardiac arrest. He snuck off to call you right after that."

"I set up a very simple bookkeeping procedure for you the last time I was here. Didn't you use it?"

She waved a gnarled, bejeweled hand indifferently. "More or less."

Joshua groaned. "What about the accountant in Cheyenne I contacted for you? Why didn't you call him?"

Her chin rose. "I didn't like him."

"Why?"

"He was too young."

"He was nearly sixty."

"I didn't like that awful after-shave he used. Smelled all prissy to me. How can you trust a man who douses himself with scent like that?"

Joshua muttered an oath, forgetting that Mrs. McDonald's hearing was sharp as ever. She stiffened. "Young man, I do not tolerate language like that in my house."

"Sorry," he said automatically. "I don't suppose it crossed your mind that you're looking for excuses to keep Cal around and involved in things?"

She sniffed indignantly. "Well, of course I am." She sighed. "Not that it's doing me any good."

"How'd he convince you to let me come back?"

"He didn't ask."

"I could leave," he offered, possibly a shade too enthusiastically. She settled a sharp gaze on him and shook her head.

"You might as well stay, now that you're here. I've put you in the same room at the top of the stairs. If you need anything, just ask Elena. You should be comfortable enough there for the next few weeks."

An immediate knot formed in the pit of his stomach. "Weeks?" he repeated.

"According to Cal, that's how long it's likely to take

to straighten out the mess we've made of things. Garrett tries, but she has too much to do around here as it is. We both sort of figured if there was money in the bank accounts at the end of the year we'd done okay."

Joshua listened to the casual tone and detected the false note at once. Mrs. McDonald had not survived all these years as a widow in this hard, unforgiving environment with an attitude like that. She'd probably counted every penny, then squeezed the last cent of value out of each and every one.

He met her gaze head on. "You're an old fraud, you know that?" he said.

Flustered by the direct challenge, she feigned a coughing fit, then finally shrugged and winked at him. "Maybe so. Maybe not. You'll know better once you've seen those books."

"I wouldn't put it past you to keep a duplicate set, all nice and tidy, locked away in your bedroom."

"What if I do? You won't find it."

"Maybe I will," he warned. "It'd mean a lot to me not to come here again."

"Enough to sneak in there and risk getting shot with the rifle I keep by my bed?"

Joshua thought of the danger Garrett represented to his equilibrium and those acres and acres of snow-covered land just crawling with cattle. "Could be," he told her. "I guess we'll both just have to wait and see."

"POR FAVOR," ELENA pleaded as Garrett edged anxiously toward the kitchen door. "The *señora* wishes you to dine with her and her guest tonight. The little *señorita*, as well."

"I promised Casey I'd make pizza tonight," Garrett improvised, a trifle desperately. She did not want to sit

at that oversized dining-room table and make small talk
with a man whose gaze heated her blood as Joshua's did.
It had been incredibly disconcerting this afternoon to discover that she was not nearly as immune to men as she'd
believed all these years. It was particularly distressing
that it was Joshua Ames who'd awakened her senses from
a fourteen-year slumber.

"I cannot tell the *señora* that," Elena said. A crafty
note crept into the housekeeper's voice. "You will have
to tell her," she said triumphantly.

"Tell me what?" Mrs. McDonald said just then, putting an end to the test of wills.

Garrett sighed. "I was just explaining to Elena that I'd
promised Casey pizza tonight. I'm sorry. I won't be able
to join you for dinner."

"Casey is already in the parlor entertaining Joshua."

Garrett's spirits sank. "Oh."

Mrs. McDonald nodded victoriously. "That's settled
then. Hold dinner for a half hour, Elena. Mr. Ames and
I will have a sherry in the parlor, while we wait for Garrett to change."

Garrett looked down at her dirt-smeared jeans and
muddy boots. She was achingly tired. If Mrs. Mac was
determined to drag her to this dinner, she could just take
her as she was. For an instant she was childishly tempted
to tell her just that. In the end, though, her fondness for
Mrs. Mac, as well as a streak of determined pride, kept
her from doing it. "I'll only be a minute," she promised
wearily.

It was a full half hour before she reappeared, but judg-
ing from the approval in Joshua's eyes, her attempts to
downplay her femininity had been wasted. His slow ex-
amination took in the bulky, shapeless blue sweater that

fell below her hips, as if he were imagining every concealed curve. His gaze lingered appreciatively on the stretch pants below, then rose again to settle on her face. The only makeup she wore was a pale pink lipstick, but he seemed fascinated by it. Finally, as if he, too, felt disconcerted, he jerked his gaze away, moved toward the silver tray set on the desk and poured himself another glass of sherry from the crystal decanter. He drank it down in one gulp.

To Garrett's dismay Mrs. Mac's curious gaze was fixed on him the entire time. Garrett recognized at once the spark of interest that flared in her eyes at the scene before her. The old woman was an inveterate matchmaker. She'd made Garrett's marital status her pet project years ago. Garrett's stubborn refusal to go along with any of her schemes had finally dimmed her hopes, but obviously the last few minutes had rekindled the old fervor.

"Hey, Mom," Casey said. "Mr. Ames said he'd teach me to play chess. Isn't that great?"

Garrett didn't like the idea of her daughter getting chummy with Joshua. It would be just one more reason why she'd have to be nice to him and at the moment she wanted to put up as many hostile barriers as possible. "Between your schoolwork and your chores, I don't know when you'll have time."

"Perhaps Casey could be excused from her chores while Joshua is here," Mrs. McDonald suggested with sly innocence.

"Absolutely not," Garrett protested.

Casey's face fell. "Oh, Mom, please. You know I've been wanting and wanting to learn. You don't know how and Mrs. Mac says he plays much better than she does.

Besides, it won't be for long. I deserve a vacation. All the other hands get one."

Garrett grinned despite herself. She ruffled her thirteen-year-old's unruly golden curls. Casey prided herself on being one of the cowboys. Since she'd been old enough to sit in a saddle, the men had tolerantly allowed her along on their roundups, teaching her everything they knew about ranching and probably more than she needed to know about the world. It had made her precocious, but it had also given her a sense of responsibility. She handled more chores than most children her age and she did it without complaint.

"How long a vacation do you figure you deserve?" Garrett asked.

Casey turned adoring eyes on Joshua, who in turn was watching Garrett's reaction. "How long will you be here?" Casey asked him.

He hesitated as if waiting for guidance from one of the women. "Long enough to teach you what you need to know to beat Mrs. Mac," he promised finally.

"I can almost do that now," Casey scoffed.

"Then maybe you ought to save that vacation for something else," he said.

Casey shook her head adamantly. "No. It's my vacation. I get to choose what to do during my vacation. I really, really want to learn how to play chess."

"I suppose it won't hurt if you take a few days to hone your skills," Garrett conceded finally, unwilling to rob her daughter of a few hours of excitement and special attention. Besides, if Joshua was occupied at the chessboard, he'd have far less time to trouble her with his penetrating glances.

Mrs. Mac rose just then. "Shall we go into dinner, ladies? Joshua? Elena has made one of her Mexican specialties, I believe."

Garrett watched closely as Joshua moved at once to her boss's side. His touch on her elbow was polite, a courtly gesture that the independent woman couldn't possibly interpret as pity. The thoughtfulness behind his action pricked Garrett's conscience. Her own rudeness grated in the face of his good manners. She sighed as she watched Casey follow them into the dining room, chattering like a magpie until Mrs. Mac, chuckling, hushed her. "You're making my stomach hurt with your tall tales, girl. Elena will have our hides if we don't do justice to her dinner."

With Elena hovering, they sat down to enchiladas crammed with spicy chicken and doused liberally with sour cream. Refried beans and Spanish rice completed the main course. Garrett picked up the bowl of green chili salsa and spooned it sparingly on her food. Mrs. Mac shook her head when it was offered to her. Garrett turned to Joshua.

"Salsa?" she asked innocently.

"Of course."

He ladled on a generous portion that left Casey wide-eyed and Garrett chuckling to herself. He lifted the first forkful of food to his mouth. Garrett waited for him to grab for his glass of water. But even though the hot sauce brought tears to his eyes, he grinned. "Wonderful," he said with obviously genuine pleasure as Elena beamed, her face a roadmap of wrinkles. "This is the best Mexican food I've had since I lived in Texas. Most restaurants are real wimps about the seasonings."

"You lived in Texas?" Casey asked. "Did you have oil wells?"

"Afraid not."

"Cattle, like us?"

"No. My dad was a banker, first in ranching country, then in Dallas. I guess I developed my fascination with numbers and money from listening to him. When banks all around us were failing, his stayed solvent."

Casey seemed awed. "I'm flunking math," she admitted. "Numbers don't make any sense to me at all, especially algebra."

Joshua grinned at her. "Sounds to me like that's what we ought to have you studying on vacation, instead of chess," he said. "Numbers are great. You can always count on them to do the same thing."

There was an oddly sorrowful note in his voice that drew Garrett to ask, "What about people, Mr. Ames? Don't you trust them?"

He turned the full force of his gaze on her. She could feel the impact all the way to her toes and regretted drawing his attention to her. "Actually, I find certain people fascinating," he said in a low, seductive tone that made her pulse scamper like a newborn filly. "Tell me, how did you happen to end up on a Wyoming cattle ranch? Were you born around here?"

Garrett's mouth seemed to go dry under the intensity of his gaze. Fortunately her irrepressible daughter chimed in. "I was," she said. "But Mom moved here from Chicago before I was born. She worked in a diner as a waitress until Mrs. Mac hired her."

"Oh, really," he said, his eyes sparking with increased curiosity.

Garrett knew that look was about to lead to more questions. She tried to forestall them. "When did you and Cal meet?"

"When we were barely teenagers. My family moved into his neighborhood."

"So you roared through adolescence together."

"Cal roared. I grew up at a more sedate pace."

"Why was that?"

He shrugged as if the reason escaped him, but Garrett thought she detected a faint trace of some old hurt in the depths of his yes. "Were you rivals for the same girls?"

"No one was Cal's rival when it came to girls. They flocked to him."

"Don't be so modest," Mrs. Mac chided. "I imagine you had more than your share of feminine attention."

He grinned. "I have few complaints *now*, especially with Cal settled down and out of the running."

Garrett found the thought of Joshua Ames being pursued from coast to coast by glamorous women all too likely. He was probably the sort of rich, thoughtful, attentive lover who would appeal to any woman set on snagging a husband and challenged by his elusiveness. She wondered if any particular woman had the lead in capturing his heart. Because it infuriated her that the thought had even crossed her mind, there was a snap in her voice when she said, "Isn't it rather arrogant to assume you can take your pick of the remaining available women?"

Innocent blue eyes pinned her. "Is that what I said?"

"That's what it sounded like to me."

"Perhaps your hearing was affected by your own jealousy."

"It must be remarkably comforting to have an ego the size of yours, Mr. Ames."

Casey's gaze shot from Garrett to Joshua and back again. Even Mrs. Mac seemed taken aback by her sharp tone. Joshua simply laughed. "So I was right," he said. "You are jealous."

"I am not jealous," she said through gritted teeth. "Your love life is absolutely no concern of mine and I don't see that it's a fitting topic for conversation at the dinner table."

"You brought it up. Would you rather talk about your romantic conquests?"

"No, I would not."

Mrs. Mac appeared to be having trouble controlling a smile. "Now children," she said. "That's enough."

"Perhaps I'd better take my inflated ego back into the parlor, so I can get to work on those books," Joshua said.

"I wouldn't think of letting you work on your first night here," Mrs. Mac protested. "There will be plenty of time for straightening out those books tomorrow. Join us in the parlor for a nightcap."

Garrett very nearly groaned aloud when he blithely accepted the invitation. Still, to his credit, Joshua put on a polite facade for the next half hour. It seemed only Garrett was aware of the tension in the room. When she could stand it no longer, she excused herself.

"Casey and I really must be getting home. It's a school night."

Casey looked disappointed. She always enjoyed the chance to spend an evening with grown-ups. "But, Mom, I don't have any homework. Couldn't we stay a little longer?"

"Not tonight."

"Joshua, why don't you walk Garrett and Casey home?" Mrs. Mac suggested.

Garrett stared at her as if she'd suggested they fly to

Acapulco together. "Really, that's not necessary," she said hurriedly.

"But it would be my pleasure," Joshua said, that spark of mischief back in his eyes. "I'll get my coat."

As soon as he'd left the room, Garrett whirled on Mrs. Mac. "It is less than a hundred yards to our house. I walk it alone every single night. Why did you suddenly decide we needed an escort?"

"It's always lovely to make a man think he's needed, Garrett. You really should remember that."

"This man is *not* needed," Garrett said, her voice strained.

Mrs. Mac regarded her with barely suppressed amusement. "Interesting," she observed.

After nearly ten years of working for the perceptive, outspoken cattlewoman, Garrett knew exactly what was going on in her head. "What's interesting?" she inquired reluctantly.

"The way you two get along."

"We don't."

"Exactly my point. Why is that, I wonder? You always get along with everybody. You're the most even-tempered person I've ever known. That's why you do so well with the hands. Not every woman could overcome the hands' natural distrust of female leadership, but the hands know they can count on you to be cool and objective under the worst kind of pressure."

Garrett squirmed under the penetrating gaze. "I guess I was due for a change."

"Hmm."

"Don't start with me, Mrs. Mac."

Mrs. McDonald looked as innocent as it was possible for an eighty-two-year-old maverick to look. "It was just an observation, my dear. There's no need to get huffy. Besides, it just proves my point," she said complacently.

"I am not getting huffy."

"Uh-huh."

Garrett scrambled to get into her coat. Half dragging Casey, she was almost at the door when Joshua reappeared.

"Leaving without me?" he inquired lightly.

Garrett sighed. "Of course not."

He beamed and an unwelcome shiver of anticipation zipped through her. When his hand settled in the middle of her back, it took everything in her to keep from jerking away. She would not give him the satisfaction of knowing that his touch affected her in any way. Nor would she create another scene in front of her highly impressionable daughter. As it was, Casey would be asking far too many discerning questions the instant they were alone.

Outside, with the crunch of snow under their feet, she took some satisfaction in the thought that the walk was ruining those expensive shoes of his. By the time they'd reached the door of the cozy house she and Casey shared, she had almost relaxed, lulled by the clear, starry beauty of the night and by Joshua's undemanding silence.

"Thank you," she said grudgingly.

His eyes twinkled. "Aren't you going to invite me in?"

Casey's mouth opened and slammed shut at a quick prod from Garrett's elbow. "Some other time," Garrett said.

Casey, who apparently had a greater sense of discretion than Garrett had ever had any reason to believe, slipped inside, leaving the two of them alone on the stoop.

Before she realized his intention, Joshua's hand was snug against her neck and his lips were against hers. The feather-light caress was undemanding and as potent as wine. Garrett's senses reeled, even as her anger rose. She opened her mouth to tell him just what she thought of his arrogant presumption, but he cleverly silenced her with yet another persuasive touch of his lips.

This time, lost to the hunger of the kiss, there was no denying the warmth that spread through her, the undeniable invitation in the way her body swayed toward his. For one tiny, fleeting moment she allowed herself the pure, feminine enjoyment of that greedy, demanding, thoroughly masculine possession.

Then she slugged him.

CHAPTER THREE

JOSHUA HAD NEVER been more startled in his life. His jaw stung from the impact of Garrett's well-aimed blow. Watching as acute embarrassment edged out fury in her eyes, he began to chuckle. It had been years since anyone had caught him off guard like that. He gave her an admiring glance.

"Nice shot," he observed, rubbing his still-smarting flesh.

"I'm sorry," she stammered, poking her hands into her pockets and staring at the ground.

"Are you really?"

At his doubtful tone, her chin rose a defiant notch and her eyes clashed with his. "No," she admitted. "You deserved it."

"For kissing you?" he wondered. "Or because I made you want me?"

He was certain that not all of the sudden color in her cheeks could be attributed to the night air. "Don't flatter yourself," she snapped, but her heart obviously wasn't in it. They both knew she had wanted that kiss just as much as he had, and had probably been wondering about it every bit as long as he had.

He reached over and gently tapped her nose. "Remember the story of Pinnochio—terrible things happen to people who fib, especially when they lie to themselves."

Before she could respond, he turned and left. "Pleasant dreams," he called over his shoulder. He was all the way back at the main house before he heard the emphatic slam of her front door. He was laughing as he went inside.

By morning, he regretted being quite so cavalier. Nor was he quite as sure who'd had the last laugh. Overnight he had found himself giving the intriguing Traci Maureen Garrett considerable thought.

At midnight, he'd advised himself to cut his losses and ignore her.

At 1:00 a.m., he'd acknowledged that was impossible. He told himself she was like a burr that clung and irritated, then admitted she was more like pure temptation. The sweet hunger she'd tried so hard to hide was enough to lure a man to hell and hold him there.

By 3:00 a.m., he'd decided to take the first flight back to Florida, only to decide an hour later that he would not take the coward's way out. He'd left once before, when he should have stayed.

At five, he'd decided to spend the next few weeks pursuing her with every bit of all-out fervor at his command. The wickedly devilish scheme, admittedly, was dangerous. It was also the only plan likely to get her out of his system once and for all. Garrett was, no doubt, not the sort of woman who would wear well. He'd tire of her feisty, independent streak in no time. It never occurred to him to wonder what would happen if he didn't.

The decision rationally considered and made, he fell asleep at six, only to have her pester him relentlessly in his dreams. If her seductive behavior in that lone hour of sleep was any indication, he was about to embark on a suicide mission. Even so, he set out to find her first thing in the morning.

Seated in the parlor with Mrs. Mac, Garrett's cheeks were still pink from the wind and cold. Strands of golden hair had been tugged free from her braid to curl rebelliously about her face. She looked softer and more accessible than he'd ever seen her. Then she caught sight of him and that icy disdain that she used to distance herself wiped the smile from her lips.

"Good morning," Joshua said cheerfully, pointedly choosing the place next to her on the old love seat. Crowded beside her, he saw to it that their thighs brushed. Garrett's whole body stiffened, but she managed to resist her apparent desire to move away from his deliberate provocation.

Mrs. McDonald observed the subtle byplay closely, then beamed at him. "Good morning, young man. If you've decided to stay with us, you really must get warmer clothes. That shirt might do very nicely for an office in Florida, but out here you'll have pneumonia by the end of a week." She turned to Garrett. "Dear?"

Garrett blinked, as if her attention had been very far away—or perhaps mere inches, if she dared to be truthful. "Ma'am?" she said vaguely.

"I'd like you to go into Cheyenne with Joshua today. Show him where to get appropriate clothing. Put it on my account." She grinned at him. "I can charge that off as a business expense, can't I?"

"Not if I have anything to say about it."

"Then consider them an early Christmas gift."

"Really, it's not necessary."

"It is," she insisted, seemingly oblivious to the sudden strain in his voice. "Otherwise, you'll end up in the hospital and I'll have to come visit. This cold air is terrible for my old bones. You wouldn't want to put an old woman through all that pain, would you?"

"I suppose not," he said, unable to hold off the rush of familiar resentment at her kindly fussing. The reaction was all out of proportion to the gesture, but it was as ingrained as the multiplication tables. Echoes of his mother's voice resounded in his head. He started to protest, then saw the expectant gleam in Garrett's eyes and decided to remain silent. It was cold. The clothes he'd brought were inappropriate. Did it really matter who pointed it out or who paid for a couple of flannel shirts?

"Thank you," he said finally.

As if in some way she'd understood his internal struggle, Mrs. Mac didn't gloat. She merely nodded. "Good. Then that's settled."

"Not quite," Garrett said, obviously scrambling for an excuse now that he'd failed to provide her with a more convenient out. "I can't possibly drive into Cheyenne today. I have work to do."

Mrs. Mac waved aside the objection. "You have a dozen men out there who can do the work. I pay you to give them orders, which I'm sure you did at the crack of dawn as usual."

"You also pay me to see that they're carried out. What if there's a crisis?"

"There were crises on this ranch long before you arrived, my dear. I handled them. I suppose I can manage to rally for a few more."

Garrett immediately looked guilty. "I didn't mean..."

Mrs. Mac smiled. "I know you didn't, dear. We'll call Red in before you leave and you can give him any last-minute instructions." She waited for Garrett's reluctant nod, then moved briskly ahead. "Now that we're all agreed, why don't we have one last cup of coffee before you leave and I'll explain what else has to be done in Cheyenne. You might as well take care of a little business for me."

"Yes, why don't we do that?" Garrett said, her expression grim but resigned. She kept her gaze studiously fixed on her boss, ignoring Joshua. It was probably just as well, he thought. If she'd seen the blatant look of anticipation in his eyes, she probably would have slugged him again.

To stave off another blow, Joshua kept his own attention on Mrs. Mac's list of errands. Though he wouldn't have put it past her to contrive them, he had to admit they all sounded legitimate. She promised to write out careful, detailed instructions, along with appropriate notes for her banker and her attorney, guaranteeing that Joshua would get all the cooperation he needed to fully investigate the state of her business holdings.

"As long as you're here, I might as well take advantage of your expertise," she told him. "Garrett, there are one or two things you might want to take care of, as well."

The list went on and on. "Don't expect us back for dinner," Joshua said when he'd heard the last of her orders.

Garrett's startled gaze clashed with his. "We'll be back," she said with expected contrariness.

He placed his hand on her knee. "You really must let me thank you for all your trouble by taking you to dinner," he said emphatically.

"No thanks are necessary," she insisted, her teeth clenched.

"We'll discuss it on the way."

"The matter is settled."

"We'll see."

It was Mrs. Mac's chuckle that finally ended the debate. "Don't rush back. Enjoy yourselves," she said.

"Oh, I intend to," Joshua replied, his gaze lingering on Garrett's scowling face.

"You are impossible," she informed him twenty minutes later when they met outside. "Do you have to have everything your own way?"

"I'd be happy to accommodate your wishes," he said.

"Then leave me alone."

"This trip wasn't my idea."

"You could have told her no."

"She's my boss."

"Who are you kidding? You don't need her business. You're only here as a favor to Cal."

"I can't very well be rude to his grandmother, though, can I?"

"You'd be rude to God himself, if it suited your purposes. That must mean that this trip into Cheyenne suits your purposes. Would you mind telling me how?"

"I wanted to spend some time alone with you," he said bluntly.

She regarded him with frank skepticism. "Why?"

"You fascinate me."

Hands on her hips, obviously seething with indignation, she faced him. "Maybe we ought to get something clear now, Mr. Ames. I may live a simple life, but I wasn't born yesterday. I've met men like you before, rich men who think the whole world should be at their beck and call, callous men who don't give a damn about the feelings of the people they hurt. I am not about to become your personal toy while you're in town. If you're bored without your usual bevy of adoring women, then get your work done and go home."

Joshua might have been stung by her analysis of his personality and integrity, but he was more intrigued by the story behind her anger. It was apparent to him that some man had hurt her deeply and for a surprising instant, he wanted to find him and beat him to a bloody pulp. The thought of trying to avenge Garrett's honor, when she had made it quite clear she could take care of herself, was amusing. It was made all the more ironic as he recalled all those infuriating years in his youth when he'd been too frail even to stand up for himself, and it had been Cal who'd come to his rescue more times than he cared to remember.

He owed Cal more than he could say for his staunch defense and for ultimately teaching him to defend himself. By the time he'd eventually rallied from the recurring childhood bouts with illness, he might have been resigned to being an unathletic weakling, but a fiercely protective Cal had seen to it that hadn't happened. He'd taught him to stand up to his overly protective mother and given him the skills to fend off bullies. Now, with regular workouts at the gym, he took his physical strength for granted. He'd be almost glad of the chance to use it to slay dragons for the woman who hid her vulnerability behind a facade of tough talk.

Instinctively wanting to help, he reached over and caressed her cheek. "Who hurt you?" he asked gently.

For a fraction of a second she seemed to be lost, caught up in the tenderness of his touch. Then she blinked away a faint sheen that might have been the start of tears and backed away. "We'll take the truck," she said matter-of-factly. "I'll drive."

"We'll take my car. I'll drive."

Garrett scowled. "Mr. Ames, this isn't some test of

wills here. We're expecting more snow today. Your car won't be able to handle it." She directed a scathing glance at the convertible. "What on earth possessed you to rent something so unsuitable?"

"I like convertibles." He dropped his voice to a seductive murmur intended to play across her senses. "Haven't you ever ridden in one with the top down and the wind blowing through that long blond hair of yours, whipping it into your face?"

For an instant she looked almost wistful, then she said dryly, "Not when the windchill factor sets the temperature twenty degrees below freezing and there's snow in the air."

He shivered at the reminder. "You have a point. Okay. We'll take the truck, but I'll drive."

"It's straight shift."

"That's the only kind we rich playboys drive," he mocked, finally getting a smile from her.

She handed him the keys. "You win, hotshot, but when the blizzard starts, don't beg me for help."

"I wouldn't dream of it. Besides, the prospect of a blizzard raises all sorts of interesting possibilities for tonight."

"You must have a really rich fantasy life, Mr. Ames."

He smiled. "It's getting better all the time."

THEY SAVED THE shopping for last. It was probably just as well. Garrett wasn't at all certain she was going to survive the impact of seeing Joshua emerge from a dressing room in jeans, a Western shirt and boots. It didn't seem to matter that the boots had a spit-polish shine or that the jeans were still stiff. If the man had been perched on a barstool in Angel Dawson's saloon, she'd have labeled him a cowboy. A devilishly handsome cowboy, she admitted ruefully, as whipcord lean and hard as any one of the hands at the ranch.

"What do you think?" he asked.

"You'll do."

"That's the best you can come up with?" he retorted, sounding genuinely disappointed.

Garrett found herself grinning. He reminded her of the five-year-old Casey dressed in one of Garrett's fancy Sunday dresses, lipstick smeared across her face, her tiny feet tucked into Garrett's high-heeled shoes. That same hopeful expression had been in her eyes when she'd said, "Mommy, how do I look? Am I as pretty as you?"

Remembering that, she patted Joshua's arm. "You're very handsome," she conceded. "There's just one thing missing." She walked over to a display of cowboy hats, picked out a black one and brought it back.

"I thought the good guys wore white," he responded.

"They do," she said, standing on tiptoe to settle the black one on his head at a rakish angle. As she leaned into him, her breasts brushed his chest and her breath snagged in her throat. Breathless, she felt herself trapped by the intensity of his gaze and the utter stillness that fell over him. Expectation pulsed between them. With the hat in place, she suddenly seemed unable to figure out what to do with her hands. As if they had a will of their own, they dropped to his chest, lingering for no more than a heartbeat, just long enough to feel the thudding of his heart, to take in the vitality and warmth his body promised.

As if she'd taken a dare, only to discover that the price was way too high, she jerked her hands away. "We'd better be going."

Regret shadowed his eyes, but he nodded agreeably.

She was so busy being thankful because he didn't argue that she wasn't prepared to have him hurry her from the store straight down the sidewalk and into a restaurant they'd passed earlier. She balked at the door, but the scent of spices, the cozy warmth of a fireplace and Joshua's hand firmly on her back propelled her inside.

"We should leave now, before the snow gets any worse," she said.

It was a sensible suggestion, but she delivered it so mildly she couldn't really blame him for ignoring it. The real truth of the matter was that she didn't want to go. The air of anticipation that had been flirting with her senses ever since Joshua's arrival the previous afternoon was having an odd effect on her. After all these years, she was remembering what it was like to have her blood run wild and feverishly. She was rediscovering the thrill of being desired. And, she admitted, she wasn't ready for it to end quite yet. A nice restaurant seemed like the perfect place to indulge herself in Joshua's attention without any threat of an intimacy she couldn't handle.

She flirted outrageously, watching the flare of heat in his eyes with feminine satisfaction. When his fingers skimmed across hers, she tried to analyze why such an innocent touch could make her pulse race, then gave up and simply enjoyed the effect. With every sip of wine, she became less cautious. It had been so long since Garrett had played with fire, she'd forgotten the risks of getting burned. They were halfway home when it came to her exactly what kind of trouble she'd gotten herself into by permitting the lingering, provocative dinner. The wind was howling. The snow was falling in billowing, blinding whirls, coating the road with windblown drifts. It might have been beautiful, if it hadn't been so dangerous. Tension immediately replaced her mellow mood.

"Have you ever driven in snow like this before?" she asked, noticing that Joshua's knuckles were white as his hands gripped the steering wheel.

"No."

"Then let me drive the rest of the way."

For an instant she thought he'd say no just to prove how macho he was, but he glanced over at her and nodded. "You're probably right. You know more about handling a truck in this stuff than I do."

He pulled to the side of the road and traded places with her.

"Thank you," she said.

"For what?"

"For not being a jerk about this."

"I'm not interested in getting the two of us killed just to prove some ridiculous point."

Just then the truck skidded wildly. Garrett fought against every instinct and turned into the skid. Once the truck was under control again she risked a glance at Joshua. He looked perfectly calm.

"No sarcastic comments?" she asked disbelievingly.

"We're still on the road, aren't we? I'd have had us in the ditch."

"Don't give me too much blind trust. We're still twenty-five miles from home and this storm is getting worse by the minute."

Joshua peered out the fogged-over windshield. "I don't see how you can tell where the hell we are. It all looks the same to me."

"That's because you're used to watching for street signs instead of landmarks." She pointed toward a faint shadow on the left. "That's Bear Claw over there. Just up ahead you'll be able to see a stand of cottonwoods. They're right alongside Horse Creek."

"All I see is white."

To be perfectly honest that was nearly all Garrett could see, as well, but she figured there was no sense in both of them panicking. If she could make it another three miles or so, they'd be within hiking distance of an old line cottage on the edge of Tom Rutgers's ranch. If they had to, they could stay there for the night. It wouldn't be fancy, but it would be stocked with provisions and wood for a fire. They'd survive. With the snow this bad, no one at home would be expecting them anyway. If she hadn't been so muddleheaded with wine and other distractions, she would never have left Cheyenne in this weather.

Just then, she noticed the headlights bearing down on them, coming far too fast for a road this slick. She pressed lightly on the brake as she steered toward the shoulder of the road, trying to give the idiot room enough to pass. For an instant she thought they'd be just fine.

Then, suddenly, the truck lost traction. They hit a rut and skidded straight toward a ditch.

"Hang on," she warned tightly. "It's going to be a bumpy ride."

She heard Joshua's low chuckle. "Seems to me Bette Davis once said that."

"Yes, but she wasn't about to crash into a ditch."

Garrett struggled with the steering wheel, but it was apparent that the truck wasn't going to stay on the road. She eased up on the brakes, figuring the best she could hope for now was to lessen the jolt when they skidded to a stop. Fortunately they were in no real danger of smash-

ing into anything. Nor was the ditch so deep that they
were likely to flip.

With one last jarring bounce, they rocked to a stop.
Her arms tense and aching from trying to maintain control of the truck, she leaned forward and rested her head
against the steering wheel.

She felt Joshua's fingers against her cheek, the touch
gentle and comforting. "Are you okay?"

"Just embarrassed."

She risked a glance in his direction and discovered he
was grinning. Either he was oblivious to their plight or
he was just plain nuts. Maybe he'd hit his head.

"If I'd known how badly you wanted to spend the
night alone with me, I'd have suggested a room in Cheyenne," he teased.

"This is no time to be joking. We're in a mess of trouble. People freeze to death in weather like this."

"Surely not cowgirls."

"I'm serious, Joshua. We're a long way from the nearest shelter. We can't stay in the truck with the heater on.
That's a good way to suffocate, too."

"Maybe help will come along."

"The only people on the road tonight are idiots, like
that guy who ran us off."

"Or like us."

She frowned. "Like I said, idiots."

"Hey, we made a bad call. Now we're stuck in a ditch.
Moaning about it won't save our necks. Maybe we can
get the truck out. I'll check it out."

Garrett didn't want to admit that she was impressed
with his totally unflappable attitude. It might be fool-
hardy, but it was certainly better than the hysterical accusations he might have been flinging in her face. As

he climbed out of the truck, Garrett shivered in the blast of icy air. She knew what he was going to find, but if it made him feel better to see that they were well and truly stranded, so be it. It was no time at all before the door opened again. Joshua's expression was grimmer now.

"Can you find your way to that shelter?"

Garrett nodded halfheartedly, realizing that she'd been hoping against hope that she was wrong about their plight. "I can try." She took a deep breath, then added somberly, "If we get lost, Joshua, we could die of exposure. That's a very real risk on a night like this."

"And the odds of us dying right here?"

"Depends on how long the storm lasts or whether somebody finally does come along."

"I vote we try to make it to the shelter. You?"

Still amazed that he wasn't casting blame, she decided if they ever got out of this fix she might have to re-evaluate her impression of his gumption. "Let's go. There are flashlights and blankets in the back. I'll leave a flare in the snow, so if anyone does come along and see the truck they'll call for help."

"Too bad this truck doesn't have a radio. I'd think anyone driving the distances you all do out here would find that a necessity."

"We do," she admitted ruefully. "This one's in for repair. There's probably one in Rutgers's shack, though. Once we get there, we'll be able to let everyone know where we are."

She saw him smiling at her. "What's so amusing?"

"Not amusing. Impressive. Now that we've made the decision, you have no doubts at all that we'll make it, do you?"

She turned the bravest smile she could manage on

him. "With what we've got ahead of us, doubts could be a real killer."

Joshua held out his hand. "Then let's go for a hike in the snow, sweetheart. I can't think of anything more romantic."

Garrett scowled. "Doesn't your mind ever veer away from sex?"

"Doesn't yours?" he challenged. "I was talking about romance, not sex."

"Sure you were."

The argument might have gotten even more heated if they hadn't needed every single whisper of breath just to go on.

CHAPTER FOUR

THE KILLER WAS the bitter, biting wind. It cut through all their layers of clothing, aided by the dampness of the snow that clung to their faces, to their hair, to their coats. Drifts, some already hip-high, hampered their slow, tedious, slippery progress along the roadway.

They'd been walking for nearly an hour and it was virtually impossible to tell how far they'd gone. Surrounded by endless whiteness, they could barely see to take the next step. By staying carefully on the road, they'd cut the risk of getting lost or wandering in circles. However, with fresh snow filling their tracks almost the instant they'd moved on, it was as if they'd gone nowhere, as if they'd never been at all. Joshua had to wonder if anyone finding the truck would even be able to track them.

"You look like a snowman," Garrett observed with a thready laugh that hinted she was near hysteria.

Joshua stopped and drew her into a tight embrace meant to comfort and warm, if only slightly. Surprised that she didn't resist, he gazed into her eyes. Almost at once he became caught up in the unexpected vulnerability he found in the blue depths in that one unguarded instant. The woman in his arms at this moment was a woman he could love, a woman he could cherish and protect always. The realization stunned him.

Drawn to Garrett as never before, he pressed his lips

to her cold, wet cheek, to her forehead, her eyelids, then her cheek again before settling inevitably on her trembling mouth. She tasted of snowflakes, but the heat that raged through him felt as if he'd stirred the embers of a dying fire. Though only temporary, he prayed it would be enough to keep them both going.

"You look beautiful," he whispered, staring into eyes now shining with unshed tears.

"I'm sorry," she said, her gloved fingers against his face.

"For what? Dumping us into a drift?"

"No. For thinking…" Her teeth chattered uncontrollably. "For thinking you were a jerk."

"Sometimes I am."

She shook her head adamantly. "No."

"Something tells me you won't think quite so kindly of me once you've had a chance to get warm again and come to your senses. If it weren't so damned cold out here, I'd be tempted to take advantage of your attitude while it lasts."

She shivered, but managed a faint smile. "Once a lecher, always a lecher," she said with a sigh that feathered against his cheek.

"If you wanted a gentleman out here with you, you came with the wrong guy."

She tilted her chin and examined him thoughtfully. "Mrs. Mac thinks you're a gentleman."

"Hey, no fair," he said, tucking her arm through his and beginning to move ahead again. "Women always throw around compliments like that just to trap a man into behaving the way they want him to."

"What?"

"You know exactly what I mean. *I know how much you respect me; I just know I can trust you.* What man would dare to try seducing a woman who's just said that? It would make him into the worst sort of sleeze."

"I'll have to remember that," she said softly, the words slurring slightly.

She stumbled over a thick branch buried deep in the snow and fell to her knees. Joshua lifted her up and prodded her on. The weariness in her voice terrified him. Surviving in a blizzard was beyond his experience, but he knew he didn't dare let her fall asleep. "Come on, lady. We have miles to go before we sleep."

"But I'm so tired," she protested. "Couldn't we rest for just a minute?"

"I'm tired, too, but I don't relish a snowbank for a pillow. Look around. See any of those famous landmarks you recognize? We've been following the road for over an hour now. On a good day that would mean about four or five miles at least. Tonight it's no more than a couple. Is there anything closer than the shack you mentioned?"

She shuddered so hard, her whole body shook. "No-o-o. No-o-thing."

"Then we'll keep going. Why don't you tell me about Chicago? I've always liked it there. Why on earth would you ever leave?"

Her expression altered at once. An unforgiving chill turned her eyes as icy as their surroundings. "I—I h-hated it."

Sensing that he'd touched on a nerve that could stir her blood with anger, he pushed. "Why?"

Her gaze skittered away evasively. "I—I just did."

"But the drive along Lake Michigan is beautiful. There's so much to do—theater, art, restaurants, shopping in the Loop or Watertower Place. All women love to shop. You left that behind for this?" He waved his hand at the snowy spread of lonely emptiness.

She glared at him and to his relief he could practically feel the heat rising inside her.

"Mind you, I'm not thrilled with the fix we're in right now," she said, "but I'd take this over Chicago any day. The skies are endless washes of blue. There's no crowding, no city crime, no deep-down dirt. Life here is so uncomplicated. The people are honest and decent and hardworking. When I was a little girl, I used to dream of places like this. I couldn't wait to come."

"Casey said you worked in a diner when you first got out here."

"I waited tables, did a little cooking until the customers rebelled at my burnt toast. The couple who owned it were kind. They didn't ask a lot of questions about my past."

He heard the hint of censure in her voice, but it only spurred his curiosity. "What kind of past could an eighteen-year-old girl possibly have had that she'd want to hide?"

She didn't reply for so long that he thought he'd gone too far. Finally, her voice faint but defiant, she said, "I was sure you'd guessed by now. I was pregnant."

Left unspoken was the fact that she'd obviously been unmarried, as well, and that she was still deeply ashamed. He wished with everything in him that he'd been around to protect her back then, to claim her and Casey as his own.

"You aren't the first woman to make a mistake," he reminded her gently.

"Casey was not a mistake," she said fiercely. "I love her. She's the very best thing in my life."

He squeezed her hand tightly. "Sweetheart, I know that. Anyone seeing the two of you together would know it. But at eighteen you were alone and scared. It must have been hard for you."

"It was hard and it was lonely, but it was heaven compared to what I'd left behind."

She pulled her hand free and lurched on ahead, obviously desperate to put distance between them. Questions raced through Joshua's mind, but this time he wisely kept them to himself. Probing Garrett's secrets, understanding how she had become the pricklish, solitary woman she was today were not on tonight's agenda. Tonight was all about survival, getting the two of them to that cabin before this hateful blizzard froze them to death. If nothing else, he had touched a nerve so sensitive that the fire of her anger would keep her going awhile longer.

GARRETT HATED REMEMBERING. She had spent too many years forgetting, setting up a dam against the inevitable tide of hurt. Yet no matter how hard she tried, the memories always flooded back. Every time they did, they were just as fresh, just as painful as they'd been on the day she'd caught the bus west from Chicago. Right now, hip-deep in another drift of snow, she hated Joshua for making her remember. She wanted to get as far from his penetrating questions as she could.

It was only when she'd covered another half mile or so with him trudging silently behind her that she realized he'd purposely goaded her. He'd given her the incentive to keep going when her whole body had wanted to sink into nothingness.

The irony, of course, was that the farther she went, the closer she came to the time when they would be alone in that cabin with no way left for her to avoid the probing questions about her past. She could retreat into stubborn, defiant silence, but she had a feeling Joshua knew exactly how to get around a woman's resistance. If she didn't want to talk, he'd suggest occupying her time with something far more intimate and dangerous. Every kiss they'd shared told her that she'd be far better off talking, gabbing until she was blue in the face. She'd be wise to tell him about the cattle, about Casey, about Wyoming, even about the past, if only it would keep the undeniable, growing attraction between them safely at bay.

Realistically, though, she knew there weren't enough words in the world to do that. As miserably cold as she was, she had only to look into his eyes to feel a stirring of heat. She had only to feel the strong clasp of his gloved hand around her own to feel warmth spreading through her. His kisses exploded into welcome fire.

And that meant trouble. She knew it as well as she knew that another hour out in this weather and she'd have more to worry about than the effect of a few stolen kisses. It was unbearably cold. In all the years she'd lived in Wyoming, she had never been exposed for this long to the bone-chilling iciness. Her feet and hands were dangerously numb, probably close to frostbitten.

Still, they trudged on, Joshua keeping up a running patter of nonsensical, one-sided conversation. At least she assumed it was nonsensical. She couldn't seem to concentrate on what he was saying. She only wanted to sleep, to hibernate like a bear until this awful storm ended and spring emerged to turn the prairie grasslands an undulating green.

"Garrett. Garrett! Come on, sweetheart. You have to pay attention."

Joshua's words seemed to reach her through a thick fog. "Pay attention to what?" she said finally, because he seemed to expect her to say something.

"The landmarks. What should we be looking for?"

"Trees. Cottonwoods. The creek. It'll be frozen now." She tilted her face up to catch a snowflake on the tip of her tongue. For a moment she forgot to be afraid, forgot that she was with the man who threatened her peace of mind. She was a child again and the world was a beautiful, magical fairyland. "Do you skate, Joshua? We could go ice-skating on the creek."

"If you ask me, we're already skating on thin ice. This is about as dangerously as I care to live."

"I could teach you to do a figure eight. Mrs. Mac taught me."

He regarded her incredulously. "You and Mrs. Mac went ice-skating?"

"It was the first year I was at the ranch. Casey was only a baby, so it must have been..." She tried to make the calculations, but the numbers seemed to be elusive. "A long time ago. Mrs. Mac loved to skate. She said it reminded her of when she and her husband were courting. He drank himself to death. Did you know that? Then her daughter, Cal's mother, ran away and married a man Mrs. Mac didn't approve of. It was very sad."

She felt the sting of sympathetic tears in her eyes. "Did you know she's been running this ranch by herself for nearly fifty years? She's even been president of the cattlemen's association. Isn't it nice the way women are respected in Wyoming? They always have been, you know. They got the vote here really early. It's probably because men saw how well they coped with the hard life here. Women are much tougher than men think."

She cast a curious gaze in Joshua's direction, wondering what his reaction would be to that declaration. "Well?" she insisted. "What do you think?"

"About what?" he said distractedly.

"About women?"

"I'm rather partial to them." An unmistakable gleam lit his eyes.

"That is not what I asked you. I asked if you agreed that we're tougher than men think we are?"

"I think you are very tough."

She smiled. "Thank you."

"Of course, I think your brain is freezing."

She regarded him indignantly. "It is not."

"Then explain to me why we are having this ridiculous conversation, when I need you to help me find that line shack."

"I am helping."

"How?"

That was a tough one. So far, he was the one who'd kept them moving. "I'm watching for the trees."

"Any sign of them?"

"No," she admitted dejectedly. "Actually, I'm really tired, Joshua."

"I know you are, sweetheart, but it's bound to be close. Is it on the road?"

"No. It's a few hundred yards to the east."

Joshua groaned. "Then how the hell are we supposed to see it from the road?"

"I keep telling you about the trees. Aren't you listening?" she replied testily.

"I don't see any damn trees."

Challenged, Garrett peered through the blinding, whirling snow. She could barely see Joshua, much less anything at a distance. His doubts, however, had given her the incentive to keep going. She would prove to him, prove to all of them that women were tough, that *she* was tough. She'd been trying to prove it her whole life.

Drawing on her last reserves of energy, she plowed on through the snow, knowing that they had to be close, fearing that if they didn't find the cabin soon, she and Joshua would become one of those tragic cases of people who died of exposure only a few feet from warmth and protection.

Now it was Joshua who was lagging behind, dispirited. It was up to her to save them now. He had gotten them this far by badgering and cajoling. The tactics had been underhanded but clever. Once again she admitted she was going to have to revise her initial impression of Joshua. He might be a greenhorn, but he had a streak of inventiveness and determination in him she had to admire. She wondered if he would be equally as resourceful as a lover. She flirted with the idea for several minutes and decided the possibilities were fascinating. Wasn't it odd, how he'd started her thinking about sex? She'd studiously avoided thinking about it for a long time now. Garrett glanced sideways and caught his bleak expression. This was no time to be indulging in impossible fantasies, she reminded herself sternly.

"I think I see the trees," she lied, using hope as an incentive.

"Where?"

"Just ahead. Come on, Joshua. We're almost there."

"There are no trees."

"Damn it, I see them," she insisted. "Walk."

"I am walking."

"Faster. It'll keep your blood circulating."

"I wonder if the stories are true," he said.

"What stories?"

"About people who've frozen to death coming back to life once they've thawed out."

"I will not allow you to think like that," she said furiously. "We are not going to freeze to death. We are not going to require thawing out."

He turned a silly, endearing grin on her. "I'd enjoy thawing you out, Garrett."

She moaned at his craziness, but she couldn't deny that the mere suggestion had sent a gentle wave of heat washing through her. Definitely a resourceful lover, she decided, intrigued again by the thought. If the image stirred her blood, maybe it would do the same for his.

"What is the first thing you're going to do when we find the cabin?" she said.

"Build a fire."

"And then?"

"Get out of these wet clothes."

That aroused some provocative images. She was getting warmer by the second.

"And then?"

He regarded her intently. Heat was definitely flaring in his eyes. She congratulated herself as he asked, "Are you deliberately leading me on here?"

"Leading you on?" she repeated innocently.

"Planting seductive little notions in my mind just to turn up my thermostat?"

"Would I do that?"

"You would if you thought it would motivate me to keep going."

"Is it working?"

"It's working, sweetheart. If my body ever gets as hot as my thoughts, you're in a whole pile of trouble."

The prospect might have daunted her but just then she saw the landmark they'd been watching for, the stand of trees and the creek just beyond.

"Joshua," she breathed softly, reaching out to clasp his hand.

He went absolutely still beside her. "What?"

"We've found it!"

"The cabin?" he said doubtfully, peering through the curtain of snow that fell before them.

"The creek, but the cabin won't be far now." Impulsively she threw her arms around him. "We made it, Joshua! It's okay. In no time we'll be in front of that fire."

She looked up then and caught the blaze in his eyes. Suddenly reality caught up with seductive fantasy. She realized what she had done by planting all those provocative possibilities in his head...and in her own. He'd pretty well summed it up, in fact. She was in a whole pile of trouble.

CHAPTER FIVE

NEVER IN HIS life had Joshua been so relieved to see a primitive little snowbound shack in the middle of nowhere. Half buried in snow and totally unprepossessing, it was as welcome as any suite in any five-star hotel he'd ever visited in some exciting world capital.

The last hour had been pure hell. He'd been terrified that Garrett was going to give up before they reached safety. Then he'd been struck by a sudden inspiration. He'd guessed that she would rally if he challenged her, if he made it a test of her fortitude against his. For some reason she seemed to feel a deep need to prove herself to him, to declare her independence and strength at every turn. Discovering why could prove to be fascinating, if only he could stop this violent shivering long enough to put his mind to the task.

"We're going to have to break in," he said, already looking around for something heavy to use on one of the narrow windows. They'd have to patch it later to keep the cold out.

"No, it'll be unlocked. It's left that way specifically for emergencies like this. We just have to get to the door."

Even that appeared a daunting prospect with drifts blocking their way. "I don't suppose you have a folding shovel tucked in your back pocket?" he asked.

"Afraid not."

"Then let's get to work."

With stiff hands that would barely do his bidding, he scooped away snow that was piled halfway up the cabin door. Garrett worked silently beside him until at last they were able to get to the handle and push the door open. Snow trailed in behind them and the vicious gusts of wind made closing the door again almost impossible. They both put their weight against it to slam it closed.

Only when it was shut did he think to ask, "Is the firewood outside?"

Her shoulders sagging with fatigue, Garrett nodded. "Probably buried in that drift. There should be some in the fireplace, though. Let's get a fire started and warm up some before we bring in more." Her gaze turned hopefully toward the stone hearth.

Joshua shook his head. "I'll get it now. Once I settle down, I'm not going to be the least bit interested in braving that weather again before morning."

"You won't have long to wait. It's nearly morning now."

"It can't be. It was barely midnight when the car went into that ditch."

She glanced at her watch. "And it's 4:00 a.m. now. By all rights we should have frozen to death in that time." She shuddered. "If you hadn't kept us going…"

He shook his head and clasped her hands. His eyes met hers. "I'd say we're even." The tension that had sprung to life every single time they'd touched crackled through the air again, until at last he said softly, "Why don't you start a fire and see if there's coffee or some brandy? I'll get more wood."

Bracing himself against the wind, he went back outside. As Garrett had suspected, there was a supply of logs just outside, covered with snow. He carried three loads inside and would have gone back for a fourth if Garrett hadn't suggested with a wry expression that they had enough for the next twenty-four hours.

"I want a big fire."

"You'll warm up quickly enough," she promised as she knelt before the hearth and touched a match to the kindling. The first spark held the promise of a blazing warmth that drew him to her side. He held his still-gloved hands toward the flames and felt the tingling pain that came as his circulation was restored.

"You can lose the gloves," she teased. "Now they're just keeping the heat out." She reached over and removed them for him. Again, her gaze caught his and held. Her fingers, every bit as stiff and icy as his own, skimmed over the back of his hands. He captured them and held on.

"Your hands are frozen," she said.

"So are yours." He touched his lips to her fingers. "Does that help?"

Slowly she nodded.

He placed her hands inside his jacket, against his chest. "And that?"

A faint tremor swept through her, but again she nodded.

"What about the rest of you? How do you feel?"

"I can't even feel my feet."

"Let's take a look," he said, releasing her hands. "Sit right here in front of the fire." She huddled on the braided rug, her shoulders hunched over her knees as he reached for her boots and tugged them off. "Wiggle your toes."

She stared at her feet, an expression of consternation on her face. Nothing happened. "I think they're too stiff to wiggle," she said finally.

Joshua picked up one icy foot and began to rub, trying

hard to ignore the effect that touching her was having on him. For a man who was half frozen, he was having decidedly overheated thoughts. Since those thoughts were about as out of place tonight as he was in this cabin, he concentrated instead on Garrett's poor, icy feet.

Think of it as a medical emergency, he told his straying libido. The truth of that had absolutely no impact. Instead he found himself fascinated by the incongruity of a woman who ran a cattle ranch and prided herself on tough, fiery independence wearing a frosty-pink toenail polish. Sexiness hidden by rawhide, vulnerability protected by cactus prickliness. It seemed to sum up her whole intriguing personality.

As if she sensed the direction of his thoughts, Garrett drew away from him. "They're better now," she said. "Why don't you check to see if there are some dry clothes we can put on, while I make that coffee?"

The last thing Joshua wanted to do right that second was put on clothes. With an intensity that rocked him, he realized he was much more interested in getting the rest of Garrett's clothes off. He wanted her with a blaze of raw desire that could have heated the whole damned cabin. The force of his yearning was compounded by the certainty that he shouldn't take her, not tonight, maybe not ever. There were too many complications, too many unanswered questions. He'd discovered the depths of his own feelings tonight, but he had no idea what he should do about them. As for Garrett, he couldn't even begin to guess what she was thinking, what she was feeling.

Oh, she wanted him. He had few doubts about that. But she would have regrets in the morning and even deeper ones after he'd gone. Some instinct warned him that she'd been left once too often in the past. Joshua wouldn't be the one to do it to her again and until he'd given it a lot more thought, he couldn't promise her that wouldn't happen.

To take his mind off the needs his body had expressed in plain, masculine language, he looked around the single room and decided that calling it a shack was a serious misnomer. Though it was small, it was well equipped for emergencies or for those times when cowboys were chasing cattle far from the bunkhouse. A lone, narrow bed, made up with white sheets and layers of colorful wool blankets, was pushed against one wall. A sofa, which likely converted to a bed, had been placed in front of the fire and a small kitchen area included a refrigerator, well-stocked cupboards, a stove and a rough-hewn table with two chairs. A well-used deck of cards on the table was testimony to the late-night pursuits of the last occupants and curtains at the windows suggested a woman's touch in this man's domain. There was no sign of a telephone or radio. The cabin's one other door led, he hoped, to a bathroom.

Before investigating that, he opened a trunk at the foot of the bed and found several flannel shirts, neatly folded, along with a pair of jeans. He held the pants next to his body and decided they were probably an inch or two short, but they'd do. He went into the bathroom, took a shower in surprisingly hot water, dressed and then took another of the shirts to Garrett.

"Go change. I'll watch the coffee."

While she was gone, he found cups, then hunted in the cupboards for a can of soup. It had been hours since dinner and they needed to get something more into them besides caffeine. He dumped the chicken noodle soup into a pot and turned on the heat. He'd just gotten bowls out when he sensed that Garrett was back in the room. He turned and saw her standing in front of the fire and suddenly his breath turned ragged.

Her hair was no longer braided and the golden waves fell halfway down her back like a splash of sunlight. The flannel shirt skimmed over curves to end just above her knees, leaving a provocative amount of slim, bare legs to tempt a man. Deliberately turning his back on her, he said in a choked voice, "Maybe you ought to wrap yourself in one of those blankets."

"I'm fine. It's plenty warm in here now."

Warm. It was maybe five degrees cooler than hell itself. All of Joshua's good intentions had been shot down with one glimpse of those heavenly, long legs. Those legs could wrap around a man and hold him prisoner until he drowned in a sea of wild sensations. Images, dangerous images, flashed through his mind, lingered, tempted and then were determinedly banished. Only to return again. And again.

A smart man would go outside and fling himself face-down in the snow. A wise man would sit down at this kitchen table with a cup of coffee and a bowl of soup and forget all about temptation, if he had to methodically count noodles to do it. Joshua told himself all about being smart and wise as he crossed the room and stood beside her. When she turned to face him, her cheeks flushed from the fire, her hair shimmering, his heart slammed against his ribs. God, she was gorgeous, desirable.

"Even after everything we've been through tonight, you look beautiful," he said, his voice husky.

She lifted her head and hesitant, troubled eyes met his. She took a deep breath, then blurted, "Joshua, I've been thinking."

"About?"

"We're stuck here for the rest of the night, maybe even longer."

"Yes."

"I don't want you to think… I mean, just because we're alone here…"

"I'm not going to do anything you don't want me to do," he said, brushing a strand of still-damp hair from her face, his fingertips lingering against the flushed, soft-as-silk skin.

"No. Of course not," she said hurriedly. "It's just that I think things should be clear."

She was being so serious, so intent. His lips twitched in amusement. "Absolutely."

"So I'll sleep on the sofa," she announced firmly.

"You'll sleep in the bed."

"You can't possibly sleep on that sofa. It's too short."

"It probably converts to a bed."

"It doesn't."

"I'll manage." He grinned. "Unless, of course, you could be persuaded to share."

Her expression clouded over. "Didn't you hear a word I just said?"

"All of them, as a matter of fact. Soup?" He went back to the kitchen area and began ladling the soup into the bowls, telling himself it was a damned good thing one of them had some willpower. He sure as hell didn't.

"We really need to talk about this," she insisted.

"Why? It's all settled. You sleep in the bed. I sleep on the sofa. It's only one night, after all. I've slept on worse." He couldn't actually recall when. "Eat your soup."

"I don't want the damned soup. I want to discuss this."

"Why? Is there some reason you're obsessed with our

sleeping arrangements? If you want, I could put a cord down the middle of the room and drape a blanket over it. They did that in a movie once. Of course, it was back in the thirties or forties."

"If you're implying that I'm being old-fashioned and prudish—"

"If the shoe fits."

"I just think it's better to spell things out from the beginning, so there are no misunderstandings."

"The winner of the National Spelling Bee couldn't have done it any better. Your soup's getting cold."

Glaring at him, she sat down at the kitchen table and began to eat. The silence throbbed with tension, a sexual awareness that all of his glib words and her rules hadn't cooled one whit. Damn it! In her attempts to warn him off, she'd only succeeded in making him want her more. Whatever happened between now and morning, he could not sit by and watch her crawl into that lonely single bed. It would be such a terrible waste. It would also be sheer torture.

He picked up the deck of cards and shuffled. Suddenly he was propelled back thirty years, to the endless days when he'd been confined to bed with nothing more than a game of solitaire between him and awful, mind-numbing boredom. With a glint in his eyes, he dealt the cards.

"Five card stud," he announced tersely.

"Joshua, I'm exhausted."

He glanced significantly across the room. Her gaze followed his, saw the now-controversial bed and returned to the cards before her. Picking them up, she glanced over them, chose two decisively and dropped them on the table.

His eyebrows rose. "Just two?"

"Two," she confirmed, her expression grim.

They played until the cabin began to fill with the first muted light of dawn. Garrett yawned, glanced at the score sheet she'd insisted on keeping and announced, "You owe me four thousand, seven hundred and twenty-six dollars." She squinted at the paper. "And thirty-two cents."

"You cheat."

A smile teased at the corners of her mouth. "Joshua, you do not tell a cowboy he's cheating at cards unless you have proof or a gun."

"Then it's a good thing you're a girl, isn't it?"

She frowned at once. "A *cowgirl*," she corrected. "And I may not have a shotgun with me, but I would hate to have to tell Mrs. Mac that you're the kind of man who welshes on his debts. She has a shotgun."

"By her bed. Yes, I know. She told me. You realize, of course, that I wouldn't be a bit of use to her if she shot me."

"Her aim's pretty good. You'd still be able to add and subtract."

"I'm not so sure that's all she has in mind for me."

"Meaning?"

"I think she has plans for the two of us."

Pink stole into Garrett's cheeks. "I can't imagine what gave you that idea, but you're absolutely wrong."

"I don't think so. She'll probably be waiting for us with that shotgun, but not for the reason you think. She'll probably insist on my marrying you now that I've besmirched your honor by spending an entire night alone with you in this cabin."

"I'm sure you'll be the first to correct her impression."

He grinned. "I don't know. My masculine pride's at stake here, too."

She tossed her cards on the table and stood up. "Go to hell," she said with feeling.

He got slowly to his feet and leaned across the table until he was within mere inches of her delectable mouth. "But this is so much more fun," he said, his gaze locked on her lips. His breath snagged. "Damn it, I want you, Garrett," he said, his voice a mixture of regret and yearning.

"It's not me you want," she said, but she didn't back away.

He was touched by the haunted look in her eyes. He told himself that she needed proof, longed for it, but would never in a thousand years admit it.

"It is you I want," he said emphatically. Cupping her chin in his hand, he proved it by touching his lips to hers. "So soft," he murmured. "So sweet."

Her mouth trembled and her eyes suddenly lit with a flare of pure longing. In one swift move he shoved the table aside and drew her to him, claiming her mouth with a hunger that raged through him like wildfire. All the fears of the previous night fueled him with desperation. He could have lost her, lost himself without ever knowing the sweetness of her, without ever savoring the way she was melting in his arms.

By the time his fingers looped under the hem of the flannel shirt, she had abandoned herself to the feelings she'd kept banked through the night. Shyness and self-denial seemed to vanish on a wave of passion that took them both by surprise with its primitive force of raw need.

"Hurry," she told him when his fingers found her heat at last. She arched her back, moving against his hand, pleading with him. "Joshua, please hurry. Please."

With slow deliberation, he pulled back. "Not yet. Not yet."

Not until he could strip away the shirt that hid her from his gaze. Not until he could take the rosy tip of each full breast into his mouth, thrilling at the responsiveness, the faint gasp of pure pleasure. Not until he could caress the taut flesh of her belly, the gentle curve of her hip, the silky flesh of her thighs. Not until his own body was hard and throbbing with need as her hesitant fingers became bolder and bolder. Not until he could banish the last, lingering doubt about the consequences of what was happening between them and give himself over to the wild sensations that made his blood pulse with pure fire.

With one last shred of sanity, Joshua found protection and slipped it on, telling her with that instinctive, caring gesture that there would be no repeat of her past, no lingering regret for her to manage in the years to come. Whether she understood all that was beyond him. He knew only that he needed her in some elemental way that was both wonderfully simple and terrifyingly complex. Those were things he would have to sort out later, after he'd made love to her, after he'd gentled her like a skittish filly and made her his own.

Damn, he thought as he lowered himself to the bed beside her. It was going to be Garrett, after all. There didn't seem to be a damn thing he could do to stop the loving, the unexpectedly sweet emotion that crowded his heart. Not tonight. Maybe not ever.

With slow, deliberate kisses he stirred her again, his own body responding instantly, this time demanding fulfillment. Eyes locked on hers, he entered her with one slow, tormenting stroke. As her silken heat closed around him, a deep sigh of astonishing contentment shuddered through him. Then he was moving, each thrust binding them together, sealing their fate in a way that should have terrified him, but instead filled him with a sense of completeness he had never known.

Watching her, he saw the excitement build in her eyes,

felt the tension in her body as it strained toward that moment of pure ecstasy that lurked again and again just beyond them. Then with one final, deep stroke, he felt her control shatter, heard her exultant cry. His own body splintered into a million sparks of dazzling light. He cried out her name and then, as they floated slowly back to reality, he murmured it again.

"Garrett, my love," he whispered with a sigh. "Oh, baby, I love you."

He felt her go absolutely still beneath him.

"What is it?" he asked at once. "What's wrong?"

Propping himself on an elbow, he studied her face, still glowing with the thrill of their lovemaking. There was no missing the troubled expression, the tiny flicker of panic that sprang to life in her eyes. Guessing at the cause, he said gently, "I do love you, you know."

"You can't," she said matter-of-factly, avoiding his gaze.

"Oh, but I can."

"You and I would be a disaster together."

"You call the last hour or so a disaster?"

She flushed. "It was a release, that's all. It could have happened between any two people who'd been through what we'd been through tonight."

"That hardly qualifies as a disaster, then, does it?" he said, barely tempering his anger.

"No, but I'd say the description fits all the other hours since you and I have known each other." She said it flatly, as if emotions could always be fit into tidy little compartments, separated as black or white. Didn't she know about the grays? Didn't she understand anything at all about the power of love?

"Okay, I'll admit we have a few little differences we'll need to work out," he conceded.

"That's like describing the Rockies as a couple of puny little hills."

"The pioneers made it across the Rockies. We can get past our differences."

Uncertainty seemed to replace rock-solid conviction. The wistful expression in her eyes made his heart ache.

"I'll prove it to you, Garrett. Give me time and I will prove it to you."

"There are not enough years in a lifetime for you to prove that to me," she said, her tone utterly bleak.

This defeated attitude threw him. Where was the woman who was certain she could conquer the world and do it alone if she had to? Or was that the problem? he thought with sudden insight. Was she convinced that she had to go it alone? He tangled his fingers in her hair and pressed kisses to her cheeks, her bare shoulders, stopping just short of the temptation of her breasts.

"Who made it impossible for you to believe in love? Was it Casey's father?"

Her eyes closed, but not before he'd seen the pain. "He didn't help," she admitted finally.

"Then who?"

"I don't want to talk about it."

"Why?"

"Because I don't like remembering."

"Sometimes that's the only way to banish the memories once and for all."

"My God, now the man thinks he's Dr. Joyce Brothers," she said with forced levity, rolling her eyes heavenward. "Where did you get your degree in psychology, Dr. Ames? Did it come with your business degree? Or was it in a cereal box?"

"Your sarcasm only proves I'm right."

Glaring at him, she jumped out of the bed and grabbed for her shirt. Holding it protectively in front of her with one hand, she reached for a blanket with the other.

"Where are you going?"

"To the sofa to sleep. It's what I should have done hours ago."

Joshua snagged a corner of the blanket and reeled her back, tumbling her down on top of him. She sat up fighting mad. "I am not sleeping in this bed with you."

His gaze pinned her. "Why not? Sleeping with me seems pretty innocuous compared with what we were doing in this bed a few minutes ago."

"A gentleman would not remind a lady of indiscretions she'd rather forget."

"I told you long ago that I'm no gentleman."

"I can see that."

Her irritation amused him. Taming her would be a delightful challenge. Capturing her heart would require all of his ingenuity and charm. Understanding her might be the most complicated—and rewarding—test of all.

With one final glare in his direction she lay down on the bed, turned her back to him and pulled the blankets up to her chin. Defiantly, Joshua lifted the blankets, fit himself to the curve of her, lowered the covers and draped an arm over her waist. He waited, then, for the inevitable explosion. Instead she merely sighed, a tiny whisper of sound that could have been resignation or exhaustion. And then she was asleep.

"Round one," he murmured victoriously, then wondered what the hell he was going to do if he actually won the fight.

CHAPTER SIX

GARRETT COULDN'T FIGURE out why she couldn't move. Irritably she kicked at the blankets and felt them give, but only slightly. She tried again to roll over and realized she was pinned between the wall and some equally immovable object. A warm, breathing object. An object that seemed to draw her like a magnet.

Joshua!

Oh, Lord, she thought with a muffled moan. She really had done it this time. She had violated the single rule that had guided her life for the last thirteen years. With her hormones whizzing like an adolescent's, she had tumbled into bed with a virtual stranger. Why? Why after all this time? Why this man? It must have been the fear, the dangerous night they had survived. Surely it had been no more than a desperate need to reaffirm life. Wasn't that exactly what she'd told him as dawn had stolen into the cabin?

Unfortunately she seemed to be the one who didn't quite buy that. Garrett knew deep inside that she had responded to some inner yearning for the promised comfort of his arms. That need she'd felt last night for the first time in years was ultimately far more dangerous than the passion. It warned her that her defenses were weak. She was not immune to Joshua's rare combination of strength and gentleness. She needed to get out of this bed, into her clothes and back to the ranch where she'd have the protection of Casey, Mrs. Mac and a dozen cowboys to keep her from making yet another dreadful, weak mistake.

She would do just that, too…in a minute. First, she wanted to take one last, lingering, intimate look at the man whose touch had filled her with life. His dark blond hair was mussed in a way that would probably have appalled his barber. The line of his jaw was shadowed with stubble, giving him a rakish, sexy look. Even in repose, his muscles were taut and well defined. The mat of hair across his chest arrowed down, narrowing to a faint line as it disappeared below the sheet that was tangled provocatively low on his hips.

Lord, he was gorgeous, she thought with a sigh. She tried to drag her gaze away but couldn't. She was fascinated by the textures of his skin, by the play of light across his body. Maybe it wasn't just Joshua. Maybe she would have been equally fascinated by any masculine form. It had, after all, been a very long time since Casey's father had taken her to bed. Her eyes followed the line of Joshua's out-flung arm, ending finally at his hand, a hand that she knew from experience could caress with daring, bold strokes or tease with utmost subtlety. Just the thought of those expert touches filled her again with dangerous yearnings.

Irresistibly drawn to him, she reached out a hand, but when her fingers were no more than a hairbreadth from his chest, she jerked away. No. Maybe, if she'd been capable of viewing this as no more than a casual fling, she could indulge in one caress, but her defenses warned her against that much at least. Joshua had changed the rules by declaring his love. Such declarations weren't worth the breath wasted on them, but the temptation to believe, to trust, was always there. Garrett had learned the danger of that the hard way and it was a lesson she was never likely to forget.

Convinced that she dared stay no longer, she tried to slither through the nest of blankets toward the foot of the bed. Keeping one watchful eye on Joshua, she moved inch by inch to safety. As she crept, he turned restlessly, reaching for the space where she had been. She heard a softly muttered curse, just before she felt his fully alert gaze on her back.

"Going someplace?" he inquired, stretching lazily.

Evading his eyes, she said, "I thought I'd add some wood to the fire."

"If you'd crawl back up here, I'd keep you warm."

The seductive offer alone fulfilled that promise, she thought as flames instantly heated her blood. "Thanks, but I think I'll stick to my original plan."

"Any special reason why you chose that particular route to leave?"

"I was hoping not to wake you."

"How thoughtful," he said skeptically, just when she was congratulating herself on her inventiveness.

Since it was too late to sneak away undetected, Garrett jumped out of bed, grabbed the clothes that had been hung in front of the fire to dry and raced for the comparative safety of the bathroom.

"Garrett," Joshua said softly just as her feet hit the icy tile.

She hesitated, her hand on the doorknob.

"I'm ninety-nine percent certain that I didn't store the wood in there."

She scowled at him and slammed the door behind her. The man was so damned smug and he had the uncanny knack of reading her thoughts, which meant it was more essential than ever that she get them off of him and back on practical matters such as getting back to the ranch, where she could put acres and acres and maybe a thousand head of cattle between them.

She stood under a steaming shower, hoping to wash away the memory of Joshua's caresses, but the slickness of the soap and water on her sensitized flesh had exactly the opposite effect. It was as if his hands were sliding over her again, reminding her, in the very core of her being, of what it meant to be a woman. She'd spent so long in what was predominantly a man's world that the rediscovery came as something of a shock. It was an awakening that could only lead to disaster, especially if she counted in any way on Joshua to keep that feeling alive on a permanent basis.

For one wistful moment she tried to imagine him staying, tried to envision a lifetime of powerful sensations such as those he'd stirred in her last night. No matter how hard she tried, though, the picture wouldn't stay in focus. He wouldn't mean to hurt her by leaving, but he would leave. There was no question in her mind about that. Getting back to what he thought of as civilization had been on his mind from the instant he'd put those fancy, impractical shoes of his into ankle-deep snow.

That meant there could be no repeat of what happened during the night—no more smooth-as-silk kisses, no more innocent touches destined to lead to something more intimate. Celibacy was something with which she'd been familiar for a long time now. There was no reason to believe she couldn't embrace that life-style again after such a brief lapse in judgment.

As Garrett brushed and braided her hair, she studied

her face in the foggy bathroom mirror. Her eyes seemed wider and brighter than usual, her mouth softer and more vulnerable, her skin a healthy pink. Like a woman in love! No, more like a woman who'd lost the last of her sanity. She yanked her hair tighter, as if to tame the emotions that had caused the changes in her appearance. She stiffened her spine resolutely and curved her lips downward. Better, she decided. Unfortunately there was nothing she could do about the glow of her complexion or the defiant sparkle in her eyes.

Reminding herself that her entire future hinged on her ability to impress Joshua with her intention to pretend that nothing untoward had happened between them, she opened the bathroom door and stepped back into the cabin's main room.

While she'd been gone, Joshua had added wood to the fire. Now he was in the kitchen, humming cheerfully as he poured pancake batter onto a griddle. He glanced at her over his shoulder and smiled.

"Breakfast's almost ready. Want some coffee?"

"Sure," she said, pleased with the brisk response. Unfortunately she couldn't control her hesitant steps as well. An intuitive man would sense at once that she was running scared. As she'd already noted a dozen times in recent days, Joshua was uncannily intuitive where she was concerned.

He was also too damned attractive, she noted regretfully. With stubble darkening his cheeks, his feet bare and his flannel shirt hanging open to the waist, he promised untold masculine delights. She was caught off guard by the suggestion of intimacy that still lingered, by the captivating web of domesticity that surrounded them. She had never, in all of her adult life, shared such a morning ritual with a man, not unless breakfasts from the back of a chuckwagon during roundup counted. Not once during all of those roundups had she felt the slightest temptation to kiss the back of the cook's neck, as she did now. Drawn across the room, she was within inches of doing just that. Then she stopped, horrified by how easily her good intentions vanished in Joshua's tempting presence.

"The snow's stopped," he informed her, turning a stack of perfect, golden pancakes onto a plate and handing it to her.

She blinked in bemusement, barely grabbing the plate before it tumbled from her uncooperative fingers. "Terrific," she said aloud, but a startling shaft of disappointment speared her. If the storm had passed, it would be only a matter of time before they could return to the truck. The idea did not seem nearly as appealing as it had mere seconds earlier.

As if he'd guessed her mixed reaction, Joshua regarded her intently. "Going back won't be the end of it, you know."

"The end of what?" she said, ridiculously pleased even as she evaded his meaning.

"Us."

"There is no us," she said automatically.

"We'll see."

His tone of certainty finally snapped her back to reality. If she'd had all her wits about her, she would have smacked that smug expression from his face. Instead she hurriedly tried to inject a note of steel into her voice when she declared, "When we get back to the ranch, I expect you to steer clear of me."

"Not a chance in hell, sweetheart."

"I won't have my daughter or anyone else getting the idea that something's going on between us."

"We can always sneak out to the barn at midnight," he suggested. "Or maybe we could just steal a few kisses..."

"No barn! No kisses!" she warned him. "Or..."

A dangerous spark of defiance flashed in his eyes. "Or what?" he asked evenly.

"Or I'll have you ridden out of town on a rail," she vowed recklessly.

Joshua chuckled. "To do that, sweetheart, you'd have to tell everyone what it is I've done. You'll never do that."

She lifted her chin. "Try me."

"I already have. That's what this is all about." He straddled the chair across from her and regarded her seriously. "Garrett, I'll be the first to admit that what's happening between us is damned inconvenient. It's also probably misguided as hell. We're like oil and water, cactus and silk. But I've been around long enough to know that there's something special between us that doesn't come along all that often in a lifetime. It would be a damned shame to ignore it."

She heard the determination in his voice, but she also thought she heard a hint of wistfulness. Startled, she studied his face, trying to see some faint sign of vulnerability. If it was there, he'd covered it well. She saw only resolve in the depths of his clear gaze, stubbornness in the set of his jaw. Oddly, it was what Garrett didn't see, the longing, that terrified her the most. She could withstand Joshua's direct attacks on her senses. She could fend them off with glib sarcasm and studiously kept distance. The vulnerability, however, evaded her defenses and went straight to her heart.

Fortunately, Joshua was not a man likely to reveal his weaknesses too often. In the end, his own show of strength would be her greatest protection. Secure in that knowledge, she finished the pancakes with enthusiasm and sipped her coffee, aware that Joshua continued to watch her intently. When his attention began to unnerve her, she gathered the dirty dishes and stacked them in the sink.

"Since you fixed breakfast, I'll clean up."

"You wash. I'll dry," he countered.

"Maybe you should go shovel a path out of here for us."

Even as the words came out of her mouth, she caught him grinning at her. "Man's work and woman's work, huh?"

"Something like that," she agreed, hiding the fact that what she'd really wanted was to put distance between them. A lot of distance. It wouldn't hurt if he wore himself out, either. Then, even if they were stranded overnight again, he'd be too exhausted to want her.

"It won't work, you know."

"What won't work?"

"I'll still want you, no matter how tired I am." Chuckling at her incredulous and no doubt guilty expression, he reached for a towel. "Start washing, lady. Then we'll both go shovel the snow."

It was less than fifteen minutes before they were both bundled up and outdoors. The stark winter landscape had been softened by drifts of snow. The sun scattered diamond chips of light across the endless blanket of white. The cloudless sky was the purest azure. As beautiful as it was, though, Garrett knew the danger it represented to the cattle. They could freeze to death in a blizzard like last night's. The hands needed to be on the lookout for strays at once. The counterpointing of urgent danger with the spectacular beauty of the snowfall was one of the harsh realities of life on the ranch.

"We need to get back to the truck," she said, her sense

of duty restored. "If we take the shovels along, we should be able to dig it out of the ditch and get back on the road."

Joshua turned her slowly until she was facing him. With the tip of his finger, he tilted her chin until she could no longer avoid his gaze. "Don't run away from this, Garrett."

"I'm not running," she denied heatedly.

"You are. You've been running ever since I told you last night that I was falling in love with you."

"What if I have? Isn't that what you're going to do? Aren't you going to walk away from this eventually and go back to Florida? I'm just trying to save us both a lot of heartache."

"But you're also costing us the time it would take to get to know each other."

"For what? So that we can be ripped apart inside a few weeks or months from now when we finally have to admit that we will never belong together."

"How can you predict the ending, when we haven't even begun?"

"Men like you do not end up with women like me. That's a fact, Joshua."

His jaw clenched. "What the hell is that supposed to mean? Men like me? What exactly does that mean?"

"It means that you live a certain kind of life, back in civilization, as you call it. You're rich. You can buy anything you want. Well, you can't buy me. My price tag is way too high."

Joshua ignored the rising fury in her voice. His fingers stroked her cheek, the pad of his thumb following the generous curve of her bottom lip. Despite herself, Garrett was mesmerized.

"I don't want to buy you, sweetheart," he said gently. "I just want to love you."

"No," she responded stubbornly, backing away. She had to get away from the feel of his hands on her, away from the warm glint of desire that lit his eyes and lured her like a beacon. "Absolutely not. Not again."

"You take everything too seriously," he told her, stalking her through the snow.

The sudden spark of devilment in his eyes and the lazy, flat-out amusement in his voice made Garrett very, very nervous. She held out a warning hand. "Joshua!"

"Hmm?" He stepped closer, reaching for her.

Garrett ducked under his arm and started to run, floundering through the drifts. "Stay away from me, Joshua Ames!"

"I can't," he said, gaining on her.

Garrett caught sight of him over her shoulder, turned unexpectedly and tripped him. He fell, sprawling face-down in the snow. She paused long enough to gloat, then took off, laughing at the startled expression on his face.

"Okay, that does it," he muttered, trying to keep a smile from ruining the murderous tone of his voice. "When I get my hands on you, Garrett..."

"*If* you get your hands on me," she taunted as she rounded the side of the cabin and headed for the road.

"*When*," he repeated, gaining on her.

It was a little like being chased by the Abominable Snowman. Clumps of snow clung to his clothes and hair. He'd grabbed handfuls of the stuff, too, and was forming a gigantic snowball that she knew was destined for her. She hit the frozen creekbed running, her laughter trailing behind.

Suddenly her feet shot out from under her and she

tumbled face-first into the snow on the opposite bank. Before she could even roll over, Joshua was on the ground beside her, pulling her into his arms, tumbling with her like playful kids in the season's first snowfall. The teasing attack took her back in time. Once, just once, she'd crept out of her parents' crowded, dirty apartment to see the first snowfall. Blanketed in purest white, the world for that brief, fragile moment had indeed been a wonderland, spread out before the eyes of a seven-year-old who'd seen too much of harsh reality. She had lain down on her back and made snow angels, then built a snowman, thrilling to the magical winter world she was creating. She felt the magic again now. That same innocent joy was stealing over her.

Because of Joshua. Joshua, who was trying to sneak a handful of snow down her back. Laughing, Garrett formed her own snowball, ready to retaliate. He grabbed her hand. "Oh no, you don't," he warned, his gaze locked on hers.

"No?" she questioned softly.

"No."

She let herself go limp in his embrace. "Okay," she said agreeably.

He smiled. "That's better." He shifted until he had her pinned to the ground. "Better yet," he said, his eyes blazing.

"You like this?" she inquired innocently.

"Having you under my control? Absolutely."

"There's just one thing you should remember."

"What's that?"

The hand that he'd mistakenly freed came up and jammed a fistful of snow down his shirt. As he yelped, she scooted free. "You're in the West," she reminded him sweetly. "You really should remember to watch your backside."

"And you really should watch who you challenge," he countered. He was on his feet in an instant, covering the distance she'd put between them far faster than she could increase it. Expecting to be tumbled back into the snow at any second, she gasped with shock when arms suddenly scooped her off her feet. The next thing she knew she was dangling headfirst over his shoulder.

"Joshua Ames, put me down this instant!"

"Sorry. You can't be trusted."

"And you can be?"

"Absolutely. I always do exactly what I say I'm going to do. Didn't I warn you that you couldn't run from me? Didn't I vow to stick with you like glue?"

"Where exactly are you taking me?"

"Where else? Back to my lair, so I can ravish you."

Garrett slammed a defiant fist into his back. Considering the thickness of the sheepskin coat she'd insisted he buy the previous day, the punch had no more impact than a pesky fly landing on him. Okay, she thought in resignation and an undeniable flaring of anticipation, for the moment she was going to have to concede his physical superiority. That meant relying on her wits.

The incentive was fairly powerful. If she didn't escape his clutches, she was very likely to stop listening to her head and go with her hormones, which apparently weren't the slightest bit daunted by the icy temperatures. Apparently she wasn't nearly as far removed from the cavewomen as she would have liked to believe. There seemed to be a primitive appeal to being dragged off by a chest-thumping man. There was something astonishingly heady about a man wanting her enough to make such a public declaration. She indulged in the feminine satisfaction of that for a few brief seconds before reminding herself forcefully to extricate herself from this predicament.

"Now!" she muttered aloud, in case the message wasn't getting through her hormone-induced stupor.

"Did you say something?"

"No. You know, though, since you seem to have all this energy, it would probably be a very good time for us to get to the truck. The snowplow should be along anytime. It could help dig us out."

Joshua opened the cabin door and stepped inside before he responded. Slowly he let her slide down his body until her feet reached the floor. Though he'd loosened his embrace, Garrett found she couldn't bring herself to take that one step that would have ended the contact between them. Even through the layers of clothes, her body throbbed with awareness, the tips of her breasts chafing against the warm flannel of her shirt.

"Are you so sure that's what you want?" he said softly, lowering his mouth to hers. The touch was a thrilling blend of fire and ice. He tasted of snow and to her deep regret she couldn't remember anything ever being any more delicious, any more tempting. With the tip of her tongue she tasted snowflakes as they melted on his lips, on his cheeks and finally on his forehead. Beneath her kisses, Joshua remained perfectly still, but there was a slow flaring of passion in his eyes, a faint hitch in his breathing.

Before she could stop herself, her hands came up to cup his face, her thumb imitating his earlier gesture, rubbing against his bottom lip, tracing the shape until suddenly he drew it into his mouth in one slow, utterly provoking movement that turned her insides to liquid fire.

"Damn you," she murmured as she stood on tiptoe to claim his mouth.

"I don't want this," she whispered, immediately confirming the depth of the lie by returning again and again to steal kisses that she knew would bind her to Joshua more tightly than ever.

"If you truly don't want this, stop now," Joshua warned raggedly.

"I can't," she breathed, hating the helpless rush of feelings that came over her in his arms, only in his arms.

With a groan, Joshua scooped her up again and carried her to the still-mussed bed. Hurriedly he stripped away her clothes, and then his own. As it had the night before, the fire between them raged fast and hot, consuming her with its powerful, demanding embrace. Maybe someday there would be time to linger and savor. Now there was only this violent, urgent claiming, this deep-down hunger that overwhelmed her, easing only when Joshua was buried deep inside her, when their bodies were joined in hot, elemental sex.

Shaken by the storm that swept them to the top countless times, Garrett was near tears when the sweet, devastating explosion finally rocked through her. Joshua was with her through it all, his own cry mingling with hers.

Dragging in deep, gasping breaths, she couldn't seem to keep from whispering, "It's never been like that for me. Never."

"Not for me, either, sweetheart. Never for me, either. Now do you see why I can't let you go?"

Garrett's protest died on her lips as Joshua's arms tightened around her again. Snug against his damp chest, a deep, satisfying contentment stole over her.

Later would be time enough to let go. Later, when this wasn't so new, it would be easier to see that it could never last. Now, though, with everything in her, she wanted the feelings to go on forever.

CHAPTER SEVEN

LYING IN BED with Garrett warm and yielding in his arms, Joshua was convinced he'd tasted forever and it was the sweetest, most uncomplicated thing he'd ever known. Garrett possessed strength and vulnerability in equal measure. With her unpredictable blend of serious maturity and childlike wonder, she would always continue to surprise and delight him. He needed that, responded to it in a way that was all the more remarkable because she was unlike any woman he'd ever met, yet it was as if he'd been searching for her.

Knowing how she felt, though, he was tempted to keep the two of them stranded here indefinitely, or at least until he could convince her they had a future. Though he was stunned himself that he was contemplating a lifetime commitment, he was not a man to waste time when faced with the inevitable. He wanted Garrett, needed her, and he was going to have her.

Unfortunately those happily-ever-after, forever thoughts lasted less than twenty minutes before being disrupted by the pounding on the door and a chorus of frantic shouts. Complications suddenly abounded.

"What the hell?" he said, dragging on his pants. "Who's out there? The folks who own this place?"

Garrett groaned. "No. It's Red. Mrs. Mac must have discovered we didn't stay in Cheyenne and sent him on a rescue mission. If he found the truck, he'd guess where we headed."

Joshua had his doubts about Mrs. Mac being behind Red's untimely arrival. From the speculative gleam he'd seen more than once in Mrs. Mac's canny eyes, he guessed she'd leave them right where they were. He wasn't quite so sure about the ranch foreman. On the few occasions when they'd crossed paths, he'd suspected Red had his own plans for Garrett. He'd probably initiated this rescue attempt all on his own.

"Mom?" Casey yelled just then. "Mom, are you in there?"

"Oh, dear Lord," Garrett moaned, turning dismayed eyes on Joshua.

He squeezed her hand. "It's okay. I'll go out. You get dressed."

"But she'll know," she said, yanking on a shirt and fumbling with the buttons as she leapt out of the bed.

Joshua put his hands on her shoulders and regarded her intently. "Slow down, sweetheart. Maybe, *maybe*, she'll guess. She won't *know*. And even if she does, would that be so horrible?"

Garrett broke free and began snatching up sheets and clothes that had been scattered every which way. "How can I teach her about morals and being responsible, when I go and do something like this?"

Joshua removed the pile of laundry from her arms and tossed it on the sofa. "There's nothing more moral than love. I love you."

"You do not," she countered furiously. "Joshua, could we debate this some other time? It sounds as if they're about to break the door down."

"I'll take care of it. Just settle down and get dressed."

He noticed with regret that his promise didn't wipe the worried expression from Garrett's face. They really were going to have to work on the trust angle, he thought as he swung open the door and stepped outside, pulling on his jacket.

"Hey, angel," he greeted Casey, warming at the smile that instantly spread across her face. "What are you doing here?"

"You're okay," she said, flinging her arms around him with obvious relief. "Is Mom inside? Is she okay, too?"

"Everybody's fine. She's getting dressed," he said, turning his gaze on Red, who was regarding him warily.

"I think I'll just check on her," Red muttered, stepping toward the door.

Joshua's hand gripped his arm. He could feel the tension that spread through Red's body and prayed the man wouldn't decide to turn their test of wills into a brawl. "I said she was getting dressed," he said quietly. "She'll be out in a minute."

"And I said I want to check on her," Red repeated, his jaw clenched, his massive shoulders squared. The glint in his eyes seemed to take Joshua's measure. Under other circumstances Joshua might have been willing to give him the fight he obviously craved. It would have settled things between them once and for all.

Casey seemed to pick up on the faintly antagonistic byplay between the two men at once. "Is something wrong?"

"Nothing, angel," Joshua told her, returning Red's fierce gaze and daring him to hint otherwise.

Red's body finally relaxed, but the protective gleam in his eyes didn't dim. "I'm sure your momma's fine, honey.

I was just gonna see for myself, but I guess there's no need if she's on her way out."

Casey seemed to accept the explanation. She faced Joshua. "We found the truck in the ditch. Did you run it off the road? Mrs. Mac said you probably weren't used to driving in the snow."

"Danged fool thing, trying to drive in that blizzard," Red said accusingly. "Could have gotten the two of you killed. You'd think even a greenhorn would know better."

"Actually, Garrett was driving when the truck went off the road. Another driver nearly skidded into us and she had to swerve to avoid him."

The knowledge that it was Garrett who'd crashed the truck didn't seem to temper Red's irritation. "Still say you didn't have any business being on the road in the first place. Should have stayed in Cheyenne."

"You're probably right about that," Joshua agreed, though he wouldn't have traded the past twenty-four hours for anything in his previous experience. "The storm turned bad before we realized it."

Just then the door opened again and Garrett stepped out, a forced smile on her face. There were lines of strain across her brow. Joshua wished he could wipe them away, but he knew she would evade his touch.

Garrett opened her arms and Casey ran into them. Her eyes met Red's, then darted nervously away. Joshua nearly groaned. If the foreman had any doubts at all about what had been going on inside the cabin, her skittish demeanor would confirm his suspicions. Garrett's attempts to struggle for an air of nonchalance were downright pitiful. In a perverse way Joshua was almost pleased. It meant she'd had few, if any, previous occasions calling for subterfuge.

"I see the cavalry has arrived," she said too heartily. "Thanks, guys. How'd you know to come looking for us?"

"I got worried, Mom. Mrs. Mac said you were okay. She said you'd probably decided to stay in Cheyenne, but I called the hotel where you always stay anyway. They said you never checked in. I told Red and we came looking. We found the truck. Red says you're lucky you didn't break your 'danged necks,'" she added, obviously quoting the man precisely.

Red had too many *danged* opinions, as near as Joshua could tell. He scowled at the man, who was eyeing Garrett as if she were a plate of chow after a long day on the range.

With her hands poked into the back pockets of her jeans, Garrett was suddenly all business. The transformation was uncanny and a little irritating. Joshua wasn't quite sure what he'd expected when they first confronted the outside world again, but it wasn't this quick shedding of the vulnerability that had touched him.

"Red, are the men out checking on the cattle?" she asked when Joshua wanted her to go on being just a little flustered, just a little pink-cheeked with embarrassment.

"Went out at first light."

"Any problems?"

"None I'd heard about by the time we left our trucks back a piece. The hands have been in touch on the CB. No need to worry yourself. I've been through more of these blizzards than I care to recall. I know what to do."

"Of course, you do. It's just that…"

She turned toward Joshua. Before she'd even completed the sentence, he shrugged in resignation. "Go on back. I know you have work to do. I'll get back to the truck and bring it home."

"We can stop and tow it before we go back," Red offered grudgingly. "I'll leave it down by the creek."

"That'll be fine," Joshua told him, avoiding Garrett's gaze. "I'll clean things up inside before I go."

"I'll help," Casey offered. "I don't need to get back right away, do I, Mom? I can make sure Joshua finds the truck okay."

Garrett appeared reluctant, but she said only, "Are your chores done?"

Casey nodded. "There was no school, so I did 'em this morning. I even baked cookies with Elena until I got really worried about whether you were stranded someplace. I guess it's good that I worried, huh?"

Garrett's eyes met Joshua's for no more than a second before she nodded and said, "Yes, real good, sweetheart."

"Can I stay?"

"If Joshua doesn't mind."

"No, I'll be glad of the company, in fact." Even if it was the wrong company. Maybe he could use the opportunity to pry some information from Casey that would help him in his campaign to woo her mother.

He refused to be caught staring wistfully after Garrett as she left with Red, so he turned and headed back inside.

"Joshua."

Garrett's voice halted him. He looked back at her. "Bring the laundry on back to the house, okay?"

He nodded and closed the door. Casey was standing in the middle of the floor, studying the room curiously. "There's only one bed," she announced.

"Yep, that's right."

"Does the sofa open up?"

"No, it doesn't. Why the fascination with the sleeping arrangements?"

"Well, you and Mom were here alone all night. I mean, what did you do?"

"We played cards."

"I meant about sleeping."

He could feel a brick-red blush creeping up his neck. "I slept on the sofa," he claimed, thankful that the sheets had been dumped on top of it to lend a certain credence to the statement.

Casey regarded him disbelievingly. "You're too tall." Her gaze narrowed. "Did you and Mom sleep together?"

"Sleep together?" he repeated in a choked voice.

"You know, did you have sex?"

How in hell did anyone ever raise a teenage daughter? he wondered weakly. Struggling for composure, he asked, "Don't you think that's a rather impertinent question?"

Casey grinned. "Mrs. Mac says I'm precocious."

"Well, Mrs. Mac is right. Did she also mention that it's a trait you might want to keep in check?"

"I guess that means you did," she said, losing him completely.

"Did what?"

"Sleep with Mom."

"I never said that."

"When people don't answer you directly, it generally means they think you won't like the answer or that you're not grown-up enough to hear it."

Joshua caught himself grinning and carefully wiped the smile from his lips before he faced her. "And just where did you pick up that bit of insight into human nature?"

"Mrs. Mac and Mom. They never answer my questions."

"Maybe it's because you ask the wrong ones."

"You mean because they're personal."

"Exactly."

"But this one's not really personal," she said earnestly. "I mean, don't you think it affects me, too, if you're going to get involved with my mom? I mean, you could end up being my dad or something."

Sensing a mine field, he asked carefully, "And how would you feel about that?"

Casey looked thoughtful. "I guess it would be okay, as long as you didn't tell me what to do and stuff."

"Then we have a problem, young lady, because I most definitely would be inclined to tell you what to do."

She turned startled eyes on him. "You would?"

"Absolutely. I may not be up on the rules of parenting, but I think that's what dads do, even stepdads."

He couldn't mistake the flaring of hope in her eyes. "Does that mean you're really going to marry Mom?"

Joshua decided that Garrett would not appreciate learning of their impending engagement from her daughter. "Bundle those sheets and towels up in a pillowcase. It'll make them easier to carry."

"I guess that means you are," Casey said, grinning. "Great. I'd almost given up on her, you know."

"Given up?"

"On getting Mom to get married. Mrs. Mac had, too," she confided.

"Don't count your chickens before they're hatched."

She looked puzzled for an instant, then nodded. "You want me to keep my mouth shut until you can convince Mom."

He nodded. "It might be wise."

"You're probably right. She always hates it when I figure things out before she does."

"I'll bet she does," Joshua said with a laugh. "I'll just bet she does."

By the time they had straightened up the cabin and made their way to the truck, which Red had left on the side of the road near the frozen creek, it was already nearing dusk again. Joshua cast one last look in the direction of the cabin, aware that the last twenty-four hours had changed his life. If only Garrett would admit to the same thing, he thought. Instead he kept visualizing her going off with Red the first chance she got.

"What does your mom think of Red?" he asked Casey as they started home.

"She likes him, I guess." She regarded him closely, her eyes widening in sudden understanding. "Oh, you mean, like does she think of him as a boyfriend or something?"

Joshua winced. "Yes," he admitted reluctantly.

"Nah. She's known him forever and ever. He helped her get the job at the ranch. I think maybe he used to go in the diner where she was working when she first got here. He likes her a lot, but Mom's pretty picky. She doesn't date a lot."

"I'd think she'd be asked out all the time."

"Oh, she is, but she won't go unless Mrs. Mac puts up a fuss. Mom says there's no point in wasting her time and their money. She said she made up her mind a long time ago that she'd never get married. Why do you suppose that is?"

"Hey, kiddo, you're the one with all the answers."

"Well, it could be because she never got over my dad. She never talks about him or anything. I used to ask, when I was little, but she'd get all sad, so I finally stopped." Suddenly her expression turned wistful. "I wish I knew something about him. It's weird not knowing."

Joshua felt as if someone had sucker punched him. He'd sensed the hurt that Casey kept well-hidden behind her facade of precociousness, but it had never occurred to him that Garrett might still be carrying a torch for the man who'd fathered Casey, then left her alone. For all their sakes, he resolved to get some answers the minute he could get Garrett alone.

Unfortunately, Garrett seemed to have some very set ideas about handling what had happened between them in that cabin. Within minutes of his arrival back at the ranch, he could tell she planned to ignore it—and him.

It was another twenty-four irritating, thoroughly frustrating hours before he was finally able to corner her in the barn, where she was rubbing down a beautiful roan horse that looked far too big and feisty for her. He had visions of that wild-eyed beast spooking and taking off, tossing Garrett and leaving her lying injured in the snow.

The horse sensed his presence before Garrett did and began prancing restlessly in its stall. When the horse tossed it's head, ripping the reins from Garrett's hand, she said quietly, "Joshua, I think you'd better leave." She still hadn't turned around.

Joshua chuckled despite himself. "How'd you know it was me?"

"I know the effect you have on women," she retorted. "Apparently that extends to Bright Lightning here, too."

Bright Lightning? Good Lord! Couldn't she ride a horse named Old Dobbin or something? He knew better than to suggest it. He settled for saying, "My male ego tells me to take that as a compliment, but I have a hunch you didn't mean it that way."

She shrugged. "Take it however you like."

He edged toward the stall, where the horse was finally beginning to quiet down. Reaching into his pocket, he took out a sugar cube and held it in the palm of his hand. The huge roan whinnied in delight and took it, then nudged his shoulder for more. Garrett shook her head. "Tamed another one," she said dryly.

Joshua stayed silent, rationing out sugar cubes, while Garrett continued to curry the horse. When both were calmer, he said, "I'm not trying to tame you, Garrett."

"Aren't you?"

"Of course not. Your spirit is what makes you who you are."

"You know nothing about my spirit, Joshua. You know next to nothing about me."

"I know that your skin feels like satin." His voice dropped seductively. He tipped her chin up so he could look into her eyes. "I know that your eyes turn midnight blue when I make love to you. I know that your hair is the color of sunlight, that you can beat the daylights out of me at poker, that you have a hearty appetite…" His eyes locked on hers as he added, "For everything."

An unmistakable shudder swept through her and she closed her eyes to hide the fiery sparks that had turned them the rarest shade of sapphire. When she blinked them open an instant later, the heat in their depths had chilled. "That's only a part of me."

"A part you've ignored for far too long."

"Don't you think you're being a little presumptuous?"

"Maybe," he replied noncommittally, bunching his

hands into fists at the possibility he might be wrong. "But I don't think so."

"Okay, let's say for the moment that you're right. Let's say that I'm some love-starved cowgirl, stuck out here in the middle of nowhere. What makes you think I want anything more from you than a quick roll in the hay?" Flashing eyes echoed the challenge in her voice.

Joshua flinched at the crude statement. "If all you wanted was temporary gratification of your sexual urges, you could have turned to Red or any of the other men who no doubt lust after you all the time."

"But you're so much more convenient. You'll be leaving. There won't be any messy sentiment, no lingering complications involved."

"Just love," he said softly.

Her voice climbed. "You do *not* love me!"

Bright Lightning whinnied nervously.

"I'll prove it, if you'll let me."

Only a man as determined and intuitive as Joshua would have caught the wistfulness that swept over her face for no longer than a heartbeat. "No," she said firmly.

"Coward."

She whirled on him then. "I will not be some damned experiment for you, Joshua Ames. You can't goad me back into your arms."

"I will do anything I have to to get you back in my arms." He stepped closer and again lifted her chin with his finger. His voice dropped. "Consider it fair warning, Garrett. I will do *anything*."

He could feel her trembling, could tell that she was torn between fury and longing. As he anticipated, she went with the anger, aiming her open hand straight at his cheek. He caught it in mid-swing. Keeping his gaze on hers, he kissed the palm of her hand, swirling his tongue over the faintly callused flesh until he could hear her breathing quicken in the hushed air.

"Remember this, too," he warned. "There's nothing I like more than a good fight."

THE SNEAKY, LOW-DOWN DEVIL! The minute Joshua left her alone, Garrett turned the barnyard air blue with her opinion of him. Most of the obscenities ranked him somewhat lower than a snake's belly or took a stab at defining his parentage. She was pleased with the increasing range of her expletives, until she heard his laughter ringing out on the winter wind. The creep had heard every word. Worse, he found her outburst amusing. The patronizing son-of-a...

"Mom!"

She swallowed the rest of her diatribe. "In here, Casey."

Dressed in jeans that were frayed at the knees and a jacket that was exactly like Garrett's, Casey looked like an active, happy teenager. Garrett studied the glow on her cheeks and the sparks in her eyes and reminded herself that this was what her entire life had been about. All she wanted was for Casey to grow up surrounded by love and fresh air and an appreciation for hard work. She wanted Casey to take for granted the independence that her mother had had to fight so hard to attain. She wanted her to be strong enough to withstand whatever knocks came her way.

Casey swung herself up onto a saddle that was sitting astride a sawhorse. "How come you were using all those words you won't let me say? Are you mad at Joshua?"

"Yes," she said, knowing it would be useless to deny what Casey had already heard with her own ears.

"How come? I think he really likes you, Mom."

"I don't think so."

"But he told me..." she began, then choked off the rest of the sentence.

Garrett's gaze shot to her flustered daughter. "Told you what?"

"Nothing."

"Casey, don't lie to me."

"But I promised, Mom. You wouldn't want me to go back on my word, would you?"

Actually she would, but she knew she couldn't ask it. "No," she said wearily. "What do you want for dinner tonight?"

"Pizza," Casey said at once. "You've been promising and promising. Will you make it tonight?"

"How about you making it? We have all the ingredients."

"Sure. Is it okay if I ask Joshua?"

"No!"

Expecting Casey to protest the terse response, Garrett was startled to see that she was grinning. "I guess you're really mad at him, huh?"

"Look, sweetheart, I don't expect you to understand, but this is between Joshua and me."

"Grown-up stuff, huh?" Her grin broadened. "Great!"

"Great?"

"Yeah. He must be making progress."

"Progress?" Garrett repeated weakly.

Casey dismounted and ran for the door. "Gotta go, Mom. I'll have the pizza ready in a half hour. Don't be late."

"Hey, who's the mother here?"

"Sometimes I think it'd be better if I were," Casey

said, a mischievous glint in her eyes. "Then you'd listen to my advice."

Garrett chuckled. "When I want your advice, short stuff, I'll ask for it."

"I guess I shouldn't hold my breath."

"Probably not. Now go. I'm starved."

Dead tired and fueled by irritation, Garrett finally got back to the house an hour later. "Sorry I'm late," she called out as she dropped her coat over the back of a chair and headed toward the kitchen. The inviting scent of garlic filled the air, along with Casey's laughter. Since her daughter had become addicted to the telephone and boys almost simultaneously with her thirteenth birthday, she thought nothing of it. She tugged off her boots and padded toward the kitchen in her stockinged feet.

She had one foot through the doorway when she realized that Casey was sitting at the table and the phone was in its cradle. The hairs on the back of her neck rose.

"Hi, sweetheart," Joshua said cheerfully. "We saved you some pizza."

Garrett turned furious eyes on her daughter, but Casey ignored the glare. With a wink at Joshua, she stood up and headed for the door.

"See you guys later," the little traitor announced. "I have homework."

"You didn't even have school today," Garrett said, desperate to keep her from leaving. "Stay and have a soda with us."

Casey and Joshua exchanged a glance that was all too knowing.

"It's a report," Casey said. "It's due next week. I think it's going to take a lot of time, way more than I thought."

"Thanks for keeping me company, kiddo," Joshua said. "The pizza was great."

"Thanks. See you later."

Then she was gone and there was no place for Garrett to hide.

CHAPTER EIGHT

"WHAT ARE YOU doing here?" Garrett demanded, her fingers clenching the back of a chair. Deep inside she was aware of a brief flash of jealousy. Joshua and Casey were so comfortable together. An instantaneous bond had sprung up between them that somehow made her feel left out. She wanted to be a part of that easy camaraderie, even as she distrusted it.

Furious at the contradictory feelings raging inside her and blaming Joshua, she glared at him as she waited for an answer he seemed in no hurry to give. The kitchen, normally cozy and warm, suddenly felt stifling. With Casey's departure, she felt abandoned, left to face the danger of Joshua alone. The charged atmosphere pulsed with tension. She wanted to sit down, but knew that the minute she did she'd be giving him an edge, admitting to her nervousness.

"I just came calling, ma'am." One of his most beguiling smiles spread across his face.

Garrett's heart thundered. Her gaze narrowed. "Don't try some *aw shucks* routine on me. Didn't you hear a word I said to you earlier?"

His irritating grin broadened. "Quite a few words, as a matter of fact. Be thankful it wasn't Mrs. Mac who heard you. She'd be washing your mouth out with soap."

Garrett's lips twitched with impossible-to-contain

mirth. "She probably would," she admitted ruefully, then stiffened as she recognized how close the conversation was to veering off into something perfectly civil. She had no intention of being polite to a man who'd invaded her privacy, who'd plunked himself in the middle of her home when he knew very well that she didn't want him there.

"Let's stick to the point," she said. "You and I both know that Mrs. Mac has nothing to do with this."

"Sorry. I didn't mean to distract you."

"You didn't."

"Oh, really," he said softly, his eyes gently accusing her of the lie.

Garrett's gaze slid away, evading. "Damn it, Joshua, don't you take anything seriously?"

"I take you very seriously."

"Don't start with that again. Just tell me how you finagled your way in here."

"I knocked."

"Simple as that, huh?"

"Casey has very good manners."

"I don't suppose she invited you in the first place."

"Why? Did you tell her not to?"

Garrett flushed.

"I see that you did," he said wryly. "Oh, well, I won't take it personally."

"You should." Her expression sobered. "I don't want you here, Joshua. Not in my home."

"Because I represent a threat."

"Yes."

"To what?"

"To my life-style, my peace of mind."

His brows rose a fraction. "Just by stopping in to bring you a bouquet of flowers."

"Flowers?" she said blankly as he gestured toward the kitchen counter. An old-fashioned cranberry glass pitcher was filled with a huge, colorful assortment of fragile spring blossoms. Deeply touched and unwilling to admit it, Garrett's breath clogged her throat. She blinked against the damnable sting of tears. She wanted to touch them, to get close enough to smell the sweet aroma. Because Joshua was in her way, she didn't. She held her distance.

"Where on earth did you find them?" she inquired, carefully tempering her enthusiasm.

"I didn't go out and pick them, if that's what you were wondering."

Garrett couldn't take her eyes off of the blooms. No one except Casey had ever given her flowers and that was hardly the same. Casey's ragged bouquets of smushed wildflowers had been presented by grubby little hands. This array looked as if Joshua had plundered a vivid spring garden. No florist in Cheyenne could have come up with this spectacular, unseasonal arrangement. She lifted her gaze to his. "Where?" she repeated.

"I had them flown in."

"Flown in?"

He shrugged. "Even though you seem to think it's a crime, being rich does have some advantages."

Garrett's pleasure dimmed perceptibly. The casual explanation robbed the gesture of something that a moment before had seemed so special. The flowers, the extra effort, meant nothing to a man like Joshua. He could have imported the entire orchid population of Hawaii, if he'd been so inclined. It was probably part of his regular seduction timetable, listed on some computer index along with his appointments and handled by an efficient secretary. In her case, the romantic gesture had come after the fact, but he struck her as a man who would veer only so far from his routine.

"They're very nice," she said flatly.

She saw the faint puzzlement creep into Joshua's eyes, the quick flare of anger. "What's wrong?"

"Nothing. They're lovely. Thank you."

"Enough of the polite good manners. What the hell's wrong now? Two minutes ago you looked as if I'd presented you with diamonds. All of a sudden it's as if they've turned into garden worms or something. Is it what I said about being rich?"

Before she could form a denial, he shook his head. "That's it, isn't it? What the hell is wrong with having money?"

"Stop cursing."

"Why? I'm not using any words you haven't flung about today."

"Lower your voice. Casey will hear you."

"Don't you want her to know what a stubborn, pig-headed woman she's got for a mother?"

Garrett sighed regretfully. "I'm sure she's already aware of that."

"Well, it can't be my language. She's sure as hell heard worse."

"Joshua!"

He leaned forward intently. "Talk to me, Garrett. Tell me what's wrong with having money."

She dragged her fingers through her hair, tugging strands loose. He was pushing her back to that *other* time again, forcing memories she didn't want to face. "It's not the money exactly."

Joshua refused to settle for the weak evasion. "Then what? It's legal. I don't pedal drugs or export arms to the enemy, so what's the problem? Talk to me, Garrett. We need to get past this."

"We don't need to do anything. I'm sure you earn your money perfectly legitimately. I'm sure you're wallowing in it. I just don't want any part of it."

He leaned toward her until his hot, angry breath whispered across her cheek. "Why, Garrett?"

Something finally snapped in her. "It's what you do with it, okay? What all men with money do."

His eyes turned suddenly cold. "Let's leave other men out of this for the moment," he suggested, his tone frosty. "What precisely do I do with my money that you find so offensive?"

Memories flooded in, crowding out the image of the man across from her and replacing it with the man she hated, the man she despised. Tears streamed down her cheeks as she accused him, "You use it to control people, to buy and sell them, to get your own way no matter the cost."

As if it came from far away, she heard Joshua's sharp, furious intake of breath. Dragging herself back to the present, to this moment and this man, she watched with a sinking sense of dismay as his shoulders tensed and a dull red color crept into his cheeks.

"When did you come up with this particular insight into my personality?" he said tensely. "Was it the flowers? Forget the damned flowers."

With one violent sweep of his arm, he reached back and knocked them off the counter, sending them crashing to the floor. Pink and apricot tulips and bright yellow daffodils mixed with shards of cranberry glass and water. Holding back a gasp, Garrett had to resist the desire to reach out and rescue the precious, broken blossoms.

"Maybe it was earlier," he accused. "Maybe it was the minute I arrived here eighteen months ago."

Garrett winced in guilt.

He sighed sorrowfully. "I'm right, then. You made up your mind about me way back then and nothing—not even making love with me—nothing that's happened since has done anything to change it. Do you know how pathetic that is? Are you going to spend the rest of your life shutting people out based on some crazy first impression of how they squander their bank account?"

"No. Yes." Her own fury kicked in then, renewed by his derision. "Yes, I am. If that's what it takes to keep us safe, that is exactly what I'm going to do."

"Safe?" Joshua asked, his expression suddenly troubled. "What is that supposed to mean? I'm no threat to you."

She shook her head wearily. "Yes, you are."

"I think you'd better explain."

"I can't." She looked up, wiping furiously at her tears. "I just can't."

She heard his sigh of defeat, knew precisely when he got to his feet. Her breath held, her heart aching, she waited for him to leave. Finally, to her astonishment, he leaned down and kissed the top of her head.

"You may be stubborn and pigheaded, Traci Maureen Garrett, but so am I," he said softly. "So am I."

THE WALK BACK to the house cooled some of Joshua's anger. For a full minute in that kitchen he'd wanted to shake Garrett until her teeth rattled for making such horrible judgments about him. The tears had held him back, shaken him in fact. With a sudden flash of insight he'd known with absolute certainty that her response was based on the past, not the present. Her own past. It had nothing to do with him at all. If he was going to understand her, he had to find out what had happened to her years ago to rob her of her ability to trust. Unless he could do that, he might as well return to Florida and forget all about her.

He went back into the main house through the kitchen and found Elena polishing the silver.

She looked up at his entrance and smiled. "Señor Ames. You missed dinner. Are you hungry? I could make you something. There are enchiladas."

"Thanks, Elena, but I ate with Casey."

"Ah," she said, beaming. "And Garrett, *si?*"

"Afraid not."

"She was still working? It is too late. She works too hard, that one."

"Yes, she does." Picking up a rag and a beautiful silver coffee carafe, he began to polish. The mindless task soothed him, giving him pleasure as he watched the soft sheen replace the tarnish. Was that what it would take with Garrett, a gentle touch to wipe away years of built-up hurt?

"Were you here when she first came, Elena?"

The housekeeper gave him a sharp look. "*Si*, I was here. The *niña* was just a baby. They came here from the hospital."

"Did Garrett ever talk about the baby's father?"

Mrs. Mac stepped into the kitchen just in time to hear the question. "If you want to know something about Garrett's past, don't you think you ought to be asking her?"

Joshua wasn't fazed by the rebuke. "Every time I broach the subject, she shuts up like a clam. Even Casey hasn't been able to get anything out of her."

Mrs. Mac looked startled. "The child told you that?"

He nodded, his expression grim. "She finally stopped asking. It can't be healthy for either one of them to keep this veil of silence thrown over the past."

"No," Mrs. Mac agreed slowly. "I've suspected for some time that there was more to the story than Garrett has ever revealed to me."

"What has she told you?"

Mrs. Mac looked troubled. "Joshua, I understand your need to know, perhaps even better than you do yourself."

"I love her, if that's what you mean."

Elena burst into excited Spanish, kissing him on both cheeks. Mrs. Mac nodded thoughtfully. "You surprise me."

"Didn't think I was capable of love, huh?"

Something that might have been a smile tugged at her normally stern lips. "No, young man. I wasn't sure you had the guts to admit it."

"I don't like to waste a lot of time and energy ignoring the inevitable. I'm going to win her over, Mrs. McDonald. Will you help me?"

"Yes," she said without hesitation. "I think our Garrett has finally met someone worthy of all she has to offer and man enough to make her see it. It could take time, though. Promise me you won't give up on her. It could be a bumpy ride."

He grinned. "She warned me of exactly the same thing, only in a slightly different context. I don't scare easily. I guess if I did, I'd never have made the trip out here, no matter what Cal did to persuade me. Something told me eighteen months ago I was lost when it came to Garrett. I managed to persuade myself that the feelings would diminish with time and distance and sanity, but they haven't," he concluded with a shrug. "I guess the only thing left is to come up with a battle plan."

"I can see to it that the two of you are thrown together," Mrs. Mac offered, her eyes snapping with excitement at the prospect of matchmaking. "We could have a party. This old house hasn't seen a wonderful, romantic ball in many years."

"The party might be good, but forget the rest. I think Garrett's had her fill of being maneuvered. What she may have missed is a simple, old-fashioned courtship." A chagrined expression crossed his face. "Come to think of it, so have I. This could be fun." He met Mrs. Mac's sparkling gaze. "Any suggestions? What worked on you? I heard you were a softie when it came to ice-skating. I'm not sure I have the ankles for that, but I could try."

A dreamy look came into her eyes. "So Garrett told you about that, did she? Skating under a full moon certainly sets the right mood for romance. In the meantime, though, you could start with flowers, lots and lots of flowers."

Joshua threw back his head and laughed. "I've already tried that one. They wound up on the kitchen floor."

Suddenly the memory of the scene just a short time before came back to him.

"Of course, I was the one who put them there," he admitted thoughtfully.

Before he'd sent them crashing, before the fight had erupted, he'd seen the wistfulness in Garrett's expression, seen the shimmering tears of delight in her eyes before the gift had been somehow spoiled. Maybe what she needed rather than lavish bouquets was one single rose.

CHAPTER NINE

GARRETT FOUND THE SINGLE, perfect rose lying on her saddle when she went to the barn at dawn a few days after her fight with Joshua. She'd been so successful in avoiding him that she'd actually convinced herself he'd given up on her. Soon he would finish his work and return to Florida where he belonged. Now with the sweet scent of the white bud counterpointing the more familiar earthy aroma of hay and horseflesh, she realized he had only been giving her room to breathe.

"Oh, Joshua," she murmured as she touched a finger to the velvety softness of the petals. The man was definitely sneaky, sliding through her defenses just when she thought she was immune to his charms. Anger had been her best defense so far, but how could she possibly get angry over something as beautiful and unexpected as this?

The barn door squeaked on its hinges just then and she looked up, fully expecting to find Joshua. Her traitorous pulse hammered at the prospect. Filled with a mixture of anticipation and dread, she slowly turned, only to find Red stomping his boots on the ground and shaking the snow from his jacket. Deep inside her, relief warred with disappointment.

"You riding out with us today?" he asked when he saw that she was saddling Bright Lightning.

"I thought I would."

He nodded, his expression turning thoughtful. Garrett recognized the look. He was worried. Instantly she was all business.

"Red, is something bothering you? Is there something happening around here that I should know about?"

He glanced pointedly at the rose. "You tell me."

"Meaning?"

"You've been jumpy as a June bug these last few days. You're standing here clutching a rose and now you want to take off to check the fence in the northwest section. I'm just trying to figure if any of that has anything to do with what's going on between you and this Ames fellow."

"There is nothing going on between me and Joshua. Nothing," she said too quickly, too emphatically. Her gaze skidded guiltily away from his, then determinedly returned to see Red's eyes narrow consideringly.

"Well, now, I might have believed that if I hadn't seen the two of you coming out of that cabin the other day. The tension was thicker than a morning fog in the Tetons. Just now you jumped about a foot in the air when I opened that door. Unless I miss my guess, you was expecting him."

She shook her head. "Not really."

"Hoping for him, then."

"Absolutely not."

Again he nodded slowly. Garrett was busy congratulating herself on the success of her deception when he said, "Maybe, just maybe, you can fool yourself, woman, but you can't fool me. I've known you too long. I've seen the way you keep a man at arm's length and do it with a smile, so's he never knows he's been flat-out rejected. Lord knows, you've done it enough to me and the other cowboys around these parts. If you'd been shut up in that cabin with any one of us overnight, you'd have walked out of there in the morning just as cool as you pleased. Instead your face was all flushed like you'd been riding lickety-split over the back forty."

Garrett felt a renewed blush creeping into her cheeks. "Red, this really isn't any of your business," she reminded him.

"Maybe. Maybe not. But I know what I saw. If the man did a thing to hurt you, I'd expect you to tell me about it. I'd take care of him so he wouldn't bother you again. You and Casey are pretty special to me and to all the men. Either of you ever need anything, all you have to do is ask."

The sweet satisfaction of being cared for brought fresh tears to her eyes. "Thanks. I know I can count on all of you, but there's nothing to worry about. I'm a grown woman. I can handle Joshua."

"If you say so," he said doubtfully. "He the one who gave you that flower?"

"Yes."

"Means a lot, a man giving a woman a flower like that, wouldn't you say?" Red commented shrewdly.

She thought of all the flowers Joshua had delivered to her house a few nights before and the way they'd ended up all over the kitchen floor. "It's just a rose."

"You ever found one waiting for you out here in the barn before?"

"No."

"Then I got one last thing to say and I'll stay out of it till you come askin' for advice. You watch your step around a man like that. You ain't used to his slick, big-city techniques. Before you know it a man like that'll have you all mixed up, doing something you're likely to regret. You'll wind up getting hurt. None of us around here wants to see that."

Garrett sighed. She knew more than Red could ever imagine about slick, big-city techniques and a whole lot about regrets. She recognized a practiced seduction technique when she saw it and certainly knew better than to believe that a single rose meant anything. Regretfully she let the flower slide from her fingers and drop to the barn floor, its significance as faded as its petals were likely to become.

"Let's get going," she told Red, taking Bright Lightning's reins and following the still-troubled foreman outside. Ominous gray clouds scudded by overhead. As she closed the barn door she glanced inside and saw that the rose had been trampled. Blinking back tears, she mounted her horse and turned toward the north, into the cold that suddenly seemed crueler than ever.

JOSHUA FOUND THE crushed rose late that afternoon. A swift fury swept through him, followed by a growing sense of resignation. This wasn't going to follow the quick battle plan he'd envisioned. Winning Garrett was obviously going to require an all-out campaign. Maybe he could get Mrs. McDonald to speed up plans for the ball. He very much needed to hold Garrett in his arms again and he doubted she'd let him do it except on a dance floor.

He went back to the main house and found Mrs. McDonald in the parlor going over the books he'd just finished working on. "Checking to see if my addition's okay?" he inquired.

"Looking to see what you've embezzled," she taunted right back. Shrewd blue eyes assessed his mood and her tone softened. "Did you find Garrett?"

He didn't even bother to ask how she'd known that's where he'd gone. "No. There's no sign of her."

"It's my guess that she rode out with Red and the men. There have been problems with the fencing."

"Is that part of her job?"

"No, but she likes to ride when she's thinking about something. My hunch is that you've given her a lot to think about the past few days."

The thought of her out there with Red grated on his nerves. For the first time in his life he was afflicted with a nasty streak of pure jealousy. "Any idea which direction they were heading?"

"I know exactly."

He glanced at her and found that her gaze was studiously fixed on the columns of figures in front of her. "Would you care to share that information with me?"

"No."

"I thought you told me you were going to help me."

"That's what I'm doing. Chasing after her like a man who has the right to won't win her over." She looked up at him then. "Don't threaten her independence, Joshua. She'll only come to resent you."

He sighed as he recognized the wisdom in her advice. "What should I do, then?" he said, wandering around the room, picking things up and putting them down.

"Wait and while you're at it, you might take a look at my personal checkbook. It doesn't seem to match the statement I got last month from the bank. Hasn't for some time now," she added.

"How do you expect to find signs of embezzlement, if you can't even balance your own account?" he teased.

"Gut instinct, boy. Don't you dismiss that so easily."

"I wouldn't dream of it."

"Joshua, seriously, if you're starting to get restless here already, maybe Garrett's not the woman for you."

"Meaning you don't think she'll ever be a whither-thou-goest sort of wife."

"Precisely. She went through a lot to get to Wyoming in the first place and as far as I can see, it's given her something she very much needed. She'll fight to keep it."

Suddenly he was afflicted with the unexpected and confusing sense that he was in a situation in which he was absolutely helpless. He didn't like not being in control. He hated the uncertainty. "Why does love have to be so damned complicated?" he growled, thumping an original Remington bronze back onto its pedestal.

"It's not the loving that's complicated," Mrs. Mac told him. "It's the details. If you think of it that way, the two of you should be able to work out anything. Now I think I'll go take my nap."

"If you can rest easily that must mean the books are okay."

"So far," she retorted. "So far."

She struggled to her feet. Holding herself erect, despite the pain that was reflected in her eyes, she crossed the room and patted his hand. "Use this time that Garrett's away to think things over carefully. Don't start something that you can't live with. It wouldn't be fair to either one of you."

"I'm not sure how much thinking I'll be able to get done between now and dinner," he told her. "It could take me longer than that just to decipher what you've scribbled in this checkbook."

"There's no rush. Garrett's not likely to be back tonight. Chances are they won't make it back for a day or two, especially if we get another snowfall tonight."

Joshua's eyes widened and thoughts of his own snow-bound night with Garrett sent a dozen provocative memories racing through his mind. "A day or two," he repeated, more disgruntled than ever. "I'm supposed to relax while she's out on the range for a day or two with a bunch of cowboys?"

"If you can't do it now, it won't get any easier," Mrs. Mac warned him. "That's just something more for you to think about."

"Well, hell," he muttered when she'd left the room.

"I heard that," she called back.

Chuckling ruefully, he shouted, "Sorry."

When she'd gone, he continued to prowl the cluttered room restlessly, unable to rid himself of the image of Garrett riding off with Red. Again. Once more she'd chosen the company of the ranch foreman over him. Maybe it was a losing battle after all. He allowed himself ten minutes of thoroughly dispirited thinking, then snapped himself out of it. He picked up the phone and started making calls.

By the time Mrs. Mac came down to dinner, he'd had a fax machine and his own phone line installed. In the morning some of his most critical files would arrive by overnight express. If he was going to stay here and fight for Garrett, then he might as well stay busy. It was entirely possible that three-fourths of his jealousy problem resulted from not having enough to occupy his own time.

Mrs. Mac took in the new equipment and nodded in satisfaction. "Settling in, I see."

"I hope you don't mind."

She grinned at him. "Not a bit. I was worried you might leave. I take it this means you won't."

"Not until she orders me away."

"I thought she had."

"Okay, not until she really means it."

Mrs. Mac chuckled. "That's the spirit," she said, thumping her cane on the floor in approval. "Why don't you go over and get Casey? I expect she's doing her homework so she can play chess with you tonight. She'd probably like to help us plan that party, too. I think it's time we got busy on that, don't you?"

"Absolutely."

"Then get a move on, boy. These things don't just happen, you know."

When Joshua went outside he was surprised to discover that the night had turned foggy as a warm front moved in to push away the Arctic air of the previous days. Instead of more snow, it seemed they were in for a bit of Indian summer. Fortunately he had a solid sense of direction. He made it to Garrett's house with only one slight detour into the side of a truck.

Still rubbing his bumped shin, he tapped on the door. "Casey, it's Joshua. Mrs. Mac says dinner's almost ready."

The door opened wide and Casey greeted him with a grin. "Hi. I'll be ready in a minute. I'm having trouble with my math."

"Bring your books along. Maybe I can help you with that after dinner."

"That would be great. Then we can play chess, okay? I was reading the book of rules you gave me today."

"When did you have time to do that?"

"In study hall."

"Maybe you should have been doing your math then."

"Why, when I knew you could help me tonight?" she said, tugging on her jacket and gathering up a stack of books.

"What if I'd said no?"

"You wouldn't," she said confidently. "You're trying to get on Mom's good side."

He certainly couldn't fault her logic, except for one tiny thing. "Your mother isn't so crazy about the idea of you and me spending time together."

"That's just what she says," she said dismissively. "Don't you know anything about women?"

"Apparently not. Would you care to enlighten me?"

"Well, I probably don't know about all women, but I sure know Mom. She, like, says a lot of stuff she doesn't really mean, when it comes to men."

"Why would she do that?"

"I figure it's because she's scared. If she chases them away, then she can keep things just the way they are."

"And how do you feel about that? Are things okay the way they are?"

Casey's hesitation and the brief sadness that flickered in her eyes were answer enough. "Sure," she answered loyally.

"Really?" he pressed.

"Well, they're okay for me, I guess, but I'm pretty nearly grown up. I won't be around here forever. What'll happen to Mom then? I mean, sometimes I think she gets pretty lonely now. She doesn't say anything. It's just the way she looks." She stared up at him hopefully. "She hasn't looked that way as much since you came. Now she just looks scared."

"And that's better?"

She seemed to puzzle over her answer before finally saying, "I think so. Don't you?"

"I think we'll just have to wait and see."

She snuck her hand into his and held on tight. Joshua wasn't exactly sure who was reassuring whom.

DURING DINNER JOSHUA was struck by the sense of family that crept over him. Here he was with a woman who wasn't his own grandmother and a teenager who wasn't his own daughter, yet he felt a contentment he hadn't felt in years. If only Garrett were at the table with them, he was certain he would feel complete.

His own childhood had taught him the value of family and the warmth that came from shared meals like this. His mother had been the kind of woman who'd insisted that everyone be at the dinner table at the same time night after night. It had been the one time of the day set aside for catching up on everything from schoolwork to international politics. Even when he'd been sick, she had seen to it that he came to the table. On the rare occasions when he hadn't been able to, she had insisted that the family gather in his room so he wouldn't feel left out of the warmth and camaraderie. Tonight he realized how much he'd missed it.

That realization also gave him his first clue about why his relationship with other women had never felt right. Most of them had had active careers of their own. Dinners had been catch-as-catch-can affairs, sometimes coming at midnight and consisting of Chinese take-out. Maybe he was more old-fashioned than he'd ever realized. He really enjoyed long, lingering conversations over a home-cooked meal. The affectionate bantering between Mrs. Mac and Casey amused him and in no time at all the two of them had drawn him into it.

"Okay, you two, uncle. It's not fair ganging up on me," he accused.

"Sure it is," Casey protested. "You just have to fight back."

He rolled his eyes. "Whatever happened to showing respect for your elders?"

Mrs. Mac waved a finger at him. "That's the last thing I expected to hear from you, young man. You haven't given me a shred of respect since the day you arrived."

"Deep down I respect you," he countered.

Chuckling, she retorted, "Maybe you could get it to the surface a little more often."

"I'll work on it," he promised. "Now what about this party? How can I help?"

Casey's eyes lit up. "We're having a party?"

"I thought we might," Mrs. Mac said. "Let's get Elena in here and talk about food."

"Can I invite my friends?" Casey asked.

"I don't see why not. That's the fun of a party around here, seeing all the generations together under one roof."

"Will there be square dancing? I went to the party over at Rutgers's last year and they had square dancing. It was fun."

Joshua groaned as he saw his plans to hold Garrett close vanishing in a flurry of whirling and bowing. "I was kind of looking forward to an old-fashioned waltz," he muttered.

Mrs. Mac's eyes sparkled with mischief. "The last dance at my parties is always a waltz."

"The last dance," he repeated weakly. How the hell would he ever make it through an entire evening without taking Garrett into his arms? How would he be able to bear watching her with men like Red, who were bound to be more adept at the lively square dances he'd never tried?

"Seems to me there's something to be said for anticipation," Mrs. Mac said.

"If I anticipate any more, it'll make me crazy," he said just as the door leading to the kitchen burst open. He took one look at Red's anxious expression and his heart plummeted.

"Where's Garrett?" he said at once, his voice barely under control and only because he didn't want to upset Mrs. Mac and Casey.

"There's been an accident," Red said, meeting his gaze head-on.

"Where the hell is she?" Joshua repeated, gritting his teeth together to keep from hurling accusations in the foreman's face.

"At the hospital. She's fine, really. It's just a broken ankle."

"Sit down," Mrs. Mac ordered, casting a warning look at Joshua. She shouted for Elena. "Bring Red some coffee and a plate." She turned back to the man who was sitting uneasily on the edge of his chair, warily watching Joshua. "Now tell us what happened."

"Her horse stumbled. Must've been a hole under the snow. Won't be able to tell for sure till the snow melts. Anyway, she was thrown. The snow cushioned her fall, but her ankle got caught in the stirrup. That's what did it, I suspect. She's got a few other bruises and a scratch or two, but she'll be out in the morning, according to the doc. He put a walking cast on, but said she ought to stay off her feet as much as possible. He warned her if she didn't, he might have to put on a hip-high cast and keep her on crutches. You should have heard her when he suggested that." He shook his head. "Didn't know she knew that many ways to cuss a man out."

Casey was listening, her eyes wide. "I want to see her."

"No need for that, honey," Red said. "There's no need to be driving in this fog. You call her on the phone if you want. She'll be home first thing in the morning. I'll get her myself."

Joshua saw the worried look in Casey's eyes and was certain it reflected his own. Deep in his gut he was convinced that Red was telling them everything, that if Garrett was blistering the air, she would be just fine. Even so, he knew he'd never rest until he'd seen her for himself.

"I'll take you," he told Casey.

"Let the woman get her rest," Red argued, but fell silent at Joshua's fierce expression.

"Come on, Casey. Get your coat."

The drive to the hospital was the longest of his life, made worse by the thick blanket of fog that was every bit as treacherous as Red had suggested. Casey kept her eyes open for landmarks and was every bit as responsible for their safe arrival as he was.

"Thanks," she said to him when they finally reached the door to Garrett's room. "Thanks for bringing me."

"I wanted to be here, too, sweetheart. Just remember, if your mother's asleep, don't wake her."

Casey nodded and pushed the door open, then tiptoed in. Joshua stepped inside behind her. Garrett was lying on her back, her eyes closed, her hair spread across the pillow. With her cheeks almost as pale as the crisp white sheets, she looked beautiful and vulnerable. There was a faint scratch across her forehead and a bruise that shadowed the tender skin along the inside of her elbow. A white-hot rage churned inside of Joshua and he wanted to take Red and the horse responsible apart, bit by irresponsible bit.

Garrett's left leg, with its cast up to her knee, was propped on top of a pillow. She had balled a fistful of blanket into one hand and tugged it up under her chin, like a child might hold a security blanket.

Casey went to the chair beside the bed and sat down, her shoulders finally relaxing as she reached for her mother's free hand. Joshua pulled a second chair up beside her.

"They've probably given her something to make her sleep," he told Casey.

"That's okay. I just want to be here. Mom's never been hurt before." She turned a beseeching look on him and for the first time since he'd met her, he could see the little girl's uncertainty that she usually kept well hidden. "We can stay, can't we? I mean until morning, in case she wakes up. We'd be here to take her home, then."

He reached over and squeezed her shoulder. "I wouldn't want to be anyplace else, sweetheart. Of course, we'll stay."

With a sigh, Casey inched her chair closer to his and leaned against him. Before he knew it, she was asleep, still clinging to Garrett's hand. He put his own hand over theirs and whispered a prayer of thanks that Garrett's injuries hadn't been worse.

For hours he sat without moving, his eyes on Garrett, watching the soft rise and fall of her chest, listening for any hint that she might be in pain, damning Red for letting this happen to her. Over and over he warned himself to hold his temper once she woke. She wouldn't appreciate his accusations, nor would she take kindly to any of his protective instincts.

Joshua knew from his own experience that hovering over Garrett would only be interpreted as an attempt to break her spirit. He'd felt the same about his mother's smothering concern more than once, even though rationally he'd known she was only worried about him. Now he began to see how difficult it was to allow someone he loved to have the freedom to take risks. The true depth of love was letting go. It had always seemed so simple to him, but it wasn't, not when it filled his heart with this terrible, aching fear.

Maybe loving Garrett was going to teach him a thing or two about his own past, he decided as he drifted to sleep. Maybe she wasn't the only one with something to learn about love.

CHAPTER TEN

GARRETT WOKE UP feeling grumpy and sore as hell. Her mouth was dry. Her shoulders and back ached from slamming into the ground and from sleeping in the same uncomfortable position all night. Her ankle was throbbing and her ego was seriously bruised. Of all the idiotic, stupid things to happen. She was an experienced rider. Losing her seat when Bright Lightning stumbled and getting tangled in that stirrup had been silly, greenhorn mistakes. She'd be lucky if any of the men ever showed her a lick of respect again.

She sighed deeply, indulging herself in a rare bout of self-pity. When tears threatened, she blinked them back and determinedly dragged herself back to the present. Berating herself now wasn't going to accomplish anything. The accident had happened. She ought to count her blessings that the injuries weren't worse. If Red hadn't chased down Bright Lightning and reined her in, they would have been. Once more, she owed him. A tear trickled down her cheek. She really hated owing anyone.

Enough, she told herself sternly. If she kept this up another five minutes, she'd wind up crying her eyes out. She'd be better off trying to figure out how the devil she was going to manage a ranch if she couldn't even get on a horse for the next few weeks. Not that Red couldn't be trusted to do whatever needed to be done with the cattle.

He'd been doing that long before she came on the scene. She was supposed to spend her time making management decisions. It was essentially an office job. She was the one who'd chosen to make it into something more. She was the one who'd insisted on riding out to see for herself what was happening, on working the roundups and the brandings, on surveying the fence lines and watching over repairs.

When she'd first arrived, she'd been expected to handle little more than the most basic record keeping and supply orders, but filled with hope and ambition, she had wanted to learn everything. Mrs. Mac had encouraged her. Garrett suspected she had reminded Mrs. Mac of her own early initiation into ranching. She had been generous in sharing her knowledge. Over the years they had come to work well together, even more so since Garrett had become Mrs. Mac's eyes and ears, doing all of the physically exhaustive tasks that the old woman had once relished doing herself. Garrett sighed at the prospect of giving all of that up, even for a short time.

"So, sleeping beauty, you're finally awake."

Startled by the low, husky voice, she turned her head and looked straight into Joshua's anxious eyes. She could read the exhaustion on his face, see it in the slump of his shoulders. Even so, his gaze caressed her and her breath caught in her throat. Despite all of her best intentions, she was very glad to see him. For an instant she was tempted to reach out to him, to draw on his strength and the comfort she knew he would offer all too willingly. Then she saw Casey sound asleep in the chair next to him and remembered the danger he represented.

"What on earth are you doing here?" she whispered, her tone guarded.

"Casey was worried about you." He reached for her hand and she felt his concern steal into her heart. It would be so easy, she thought, so easy to let this man into her life, to let him take care of her. He could give her everything she'd ever dreamed of.

He could also take it all away, leaving her far worse off than she was now.

"You scared the dickens out of me, too," he admitted, not taking his eyes off of her until he had looked her over from head to toe.

"I'm okay," she offered shakily. Afraid of the feelings that he aroused in her, she tried to pull away, but he only held tighter, then pressed his lips to her knuckles. The tenderness in his eyes, in his touch, tugged at her, made her long for all the things that they'd shared that one precious night, things that could never be again.

"You look like you've gone a couple of rounds with a nasty coyote," he observed.

She winced. She must look ten times worse than that for him to say it at all. "I think he won. Don't worry, though. I'm made of sturdy stuff. I'll just be a little wobbly for a while. How long have you been here?"

"Since last night."

"Last night? Why didn't you wake me?"

"You were dead to the world. You needed the rest."

"I'm sure I'm going to get more rest than I ever wanted over the next couple of days," she said wryly.

"Weeks," Joshua corrected with a smile that didn't quite reach his eyes.

"Days," she argued stubbornly. She caught her breath as she tried to shift her leg to a more comfortable position.

"Pain?" he said at once.

"A little."

"Which means it's just this side of unbearable, I suppose."

She grinned weakly. "Something like that."

"I'll get the nurse."

"Don't move," she ordered, gesturing toward Casey, who had shifted until she was leaning against him. "I'll ring for her. What time is it?"

"Barely six. You should try to get some more sleep."

"What about you? That can't be comfortable."

"The last time you said something like that, we ended up in the same bed." His gaze fell on the hospital bed. "It's possible, I suppose."

Her pulse lurched all too hopefully, but she shot an alarmed look at her daughter. "Joshua, Casey is…"

"Sound asleep. I'll stop teasing, though. Do you need anything besides the painkiller? Something to drink, maybe?"

"A toothbrush."

"I doubt the gift shop is open yet, but let me go check around." He squeezed her hand again and settled Casey more comfortably. "I'll hurry that nurse up, too."

"Thanks."

As soon as he left the room, Garrett saw Casey's eyes blink open. She suspected her daughter had been conveniently playing possum.

"Hi, Mom. You feel okay?" she inquired with a yawn.

"Probably better than you do after spending the night on that chair. You should be at home in your own bed. You have school today."

"If you hadn't gone and done something dumb like this, I would have been home."

As always, Garrett found herself grinning at her

daughter's fascinating mental gymnastics. "So, it's my fault," she concluded.

"You've got to admit that what you did was pretty silly. Weren't you concentrating or something?"

"I guess not."

"Were you thinking about Joshua?"

Since that was exactly what she'd been doing, Garrett could feel herself blushing. "Where would you get an idea like that?"

"Mom, it's not exactly a secret that you like him."

"Oh, really?" Oh, Lord. Why couldn't she have had a teenager who was oblivious to everything except clothes and boys? This was not a conversation she wanted to have with her daughter.

"Mom!"

"Okay, yes. I like him. Joshua is a very nice man." Her tone sobered and she forced herself to say something she probably should have said the minute she'd seen the bond beginning to form between Joshua and her daughter. "Honey, Joshua is only here for a short time. It wouldn't be wise for either one of us to count on him too much."

"He'd stay if you asked him to."

If only that were true, she thought wistfully. "No," she said firmly, the denial meant as much for herself as for Casey. "His life is in Florida. Please, sweetheart, don't get too close to him. He'll go away and I wouldn't want you to be disappointed when that happens."

"Joshua won't leave us," Casey protested, her expression turning mutinous. Garrett could tell she was shaken and for a minute she almost hated Joshua for coming into their lives and disrupting things. She'd wanted so badly to protect Casey from life's hurts, from the anguish of being left behind. Now it seemed inevitable that they were both in for heartache. She reached for Casey's hand.

"He will have to go back sooner or later," she said gently. "And that's okay. We're lucky to have known him as a friend."

"Mom, he wants to be more than our friend. I know it."

"Honey, even with the best intentions things don't always work out."

"But I know you love him, Mom. And he loves you."

The certainty in Casey's voice startled her. "Has he said that?"

"No. I mean, not exactly. Mom, I just know, okay."

"There are different kinds of love, sweetheart. Whatever Joshua said, I'm sure he meant it at the time, but there are things that just aren't meant to be," she explained flatly.

"But, Mom…" Casey protested.

Garrett winced against the pain. "Honey, that's enough. I don't want to discuss it anymore right now."

Casey opened her mouth to argue, but Joshua came back to the room just then, a nurse with him. By the time Garrett had been given a shot for the pain and had brushed her teeth, Casey had fallen completely silent. Garrett caught the suddenly distrustful look her daughter cast at Joshua and sighed with regret. In the long run, though, it was better that Casey not count on anything permanent. She had to learn that the only person a woman could ever really count on was herself.

JOSHUA COULDN'T IMAGINE what had happened during the short time he'd been gone from the room. Casey's mouth had turned down into a frown and she refused to meet his eyes. Garrett looked miserable and he suspected it had nothing to do with the pain since the shot she'd been given should have kicked in by now.

"What's up?" he asked cautiously. "You two have an argument?"

"No," they answered simultaneously, not looking at each other or at him.

"Then let's cheer up a little. I ran into the doctor out there and he said he's springing you, as long as you promise to follow orders. I told him that Casey and I would chain you down if we had to."

"That won't be necessary," Garrett mumbled. "One stupid mistake is all I can handle. I'll do whatever he thinks is best."

Joshua regarded her doubtfully. "That'll be a first. Casey brought you some clean clothes last night. I'll wait outside while you get ready to go."

Garrett nodded.

"Casey, you want to wait with me?"

She glanced at him, then just as quickly looked away. "Mom might need me."

He nodded. "I'll be waiting just outside, then."

In the hallway he tried to figure out why the tension in the room had suddenly been as thick as last night's fog. Maybe it had something to do with the fact that Casey had spent the night at the hospital, maybe Garrett was angry because Casey was going to miss school today. That would have been an easy enough explanation, but Joshua couldn't quite buy it. He'd seen the bleak expression in Casey's eyes. He'd noticed how she seemed to avoid meeting his gaze. Unless he missed his guess, they had argued about him.

When the door finally opened and Garrett hobbled out, she allowed him to take her arm. She protested only mildly over having to leave in a wheelchair. She thanked the nurses. She thanked the doctor. She even thanked him for being there to take her home. In fact, she was altogether too agreeable. She kept up a cheerful, non-stop monologue all the way to the car. The change in the weather seemed to fascinate her. She commented on it endlessly.

But all of Garrett's talking couldn't cover Casey's unnatural silence. He knew teenagers were prone to sulking, but he'd never seen any signs of it in Casey.

"Want to stop for breakfast?" he suggested as they drove out of the parking lot.

"I'm starved," Garrett admitted. Casey said nothing. "Any suggestions?"

"We could stop at Frank and Lena's diner, where I used to work. I haven't seen them in ages."

"Is that okay with you, Casey?" He glanced in the rearview mirror and saw rather than heard her mumbled response. He nodded. "Okay, then. You point the way."

Garrett guided him onto the highway, then to a turn-off just out of town. The diner, which was essentially a double trailer, sat by the side of the road, its red neon sign flashing hopefully against the gray sky. A handful of pick-ups lingered in the parking lot. Joshua pulled into the spot closest to the front door.

"You stay right where you are," he warned Garrett. "I'll get you."

"Joshua, I can walk a few feet."

"And get your cast soaked in the snow. Not a chance." He reached in and scooped her up before she could rally another protest. "Casey, lock up for me, okay?"

She regarded him sullenly, but did as he'd asked. Joshua opened the door to the diner and was instantly assailed by the aroma of fresh-baked muffins, bacon and coffee. A tall, lean woman wearing an apron glanced up from the grill and let out a whoop that was part joy and part dismay.

"Traci Maureen Garrett, what have you gone and done to yourself?" she clucked, rounding the counter to help with Garrett's coat.

"I took a spill from a horse," Garrett said.

"Well now, honey, that doesn't sound a bit like you," she said, regarding Garrett with concern, then turning to Casey and wrapping her in a hug. "Now, let me just look at you. I swear you've grown another five inches since the last time you and your mama were in here. Pretty soon you're going to be taller than your mama and twice as pretty."

Casey's mouth curved into a hesitant smile that faded almost before it began. She slid into the booth next to her mother, as if to protect her from Joshua.

Lena turned to him. "Now, just who are you, handsome? I don't recall seeing you around here before and I know all the good-looking cowboys. Can't say I blame Garrett for keeping you all to herself."

Joshua held out his hand. "Joshua Ames. I'm doing some work for Mrs. McDonald."

"Of course. You're that bookkeeper from back east."

He grinned ruefully. "Not exactly, but that's close enough."

"Well, I'm mighty glad to know you. Now what can I get you all to eat? Casey, honey, you want your French toast like always?"

"I guess," Casey mumbled.

Lena shot a penetrating look at her. "Then why don't you give me a hand over here. You always were a better cook than your mama. How about you, Garrett? Scrambled eggs and bacon?"

"Perfect. Potatoes and biscuits, too. I'm famished."

"And I suppose you want the works, too?" she said to Joshua. "Eggs sunny-side up?"

"How'd you know?"

"Lucky guess," she said with a wink. "I'll be right back with the coffee."

When Lena went back behind the counter, Casey went with her, clearly anxious for the escape. When she didn't return with the food, but remained with Lena, Joshua frowned. "What's up with Casey?"

Garrett looked momentarily guilty, then lifted innocent eyes to challenge him. "Nothing."

"Garrett, the girl hasn't said two words in the last hour. Now maybe for some kids that would be normal, but not for Casey. She's usually chattering a mile a minute."

"It's probably just a delayed reaction to the accident and seeing me in the hospital."

"Maybe," he said doubtfully. "I'll talk to her when we get back to the ranch."

For an instant, a look that might have been fear flashed in Garrett's eyes before she looked down at her eggs. "Leave her alone, Joshua. It's just the way teenage girls are, up one minute and down the next."

"Have you talked to her about what's bothering her?"

"Joshua, she is fine," she insisted, but he noticed that she suddenly seemed to have lost her appetite. She was pushing her eggs around on her plate and when she finally tired of that, she went to work on her toast, breaking it into inedible little pieces.

"What did you say to her?" he asked finally.

Her gaze shot up, met his, then skidded away.

"That's it, isn't it? You had a fight."

"Okay, yes. But I'm telling you it was just one of those mother-daughter things."

She might have been convincing, if her hands hadn't been trembling so badly.

"Did my name come up in this mother-daughter talk?"

"Joshua, not everything revolves around you."

"I'm well aware of that, but you'll have to pardon me for seeing two and two and coming up with four. It's the mathematician in me."

"Well, this time you've totalled wrong."

"You won't mind if I ask her that, will you?"

Her cheeks flooded with scarlet. "Yes, damn it. This is none of your business."

"It is if it involves me."

"You keep saying that and you have absolutely nothing to go on."

"I have the fact that Casey and I have grown very close since I came back to Wyoming. She has confided in me. As recently as last night, she seemed to trust me. Now she won't even look me in the eye. You add it up."

He could see that his words had hit the mark when her shoulders drooped and the color drained from her face. "Please leave it alone," she begged softly.

"I wish I could," he said with a deep sigh. "But I love the two of you every bit as much as if you were already my family."

He was ready to say more, but she cut him off. "We're not your family."

"Not yet."

"Not ever."

Suddenly he realized the toll the argument was taking on her. Her eyes were shadowed with fatigue. "Look, this isn't something we're likely to settle now. We'll discuss it later."

"There's nothing to discuss."

"You are an incredibly repetitive woman."

"And you are an exhaustingly stubborn man."

"An interesting match, don't you think?"

"Joshua!"

"Let's go get you into bed, sweetheart."

"In your dreams."

His eyes widened with feigned innocence. "What a wicked mind you have, my dear."

"Oh, go to hell," she muttered, but there wasn't much spunk behind it.

"Whatever you want," he said agreeably.

She glared at him.

"Ready to leave?"

"Do I have a choice?"

"Always. I can sit here sipping coffee all day long, if that's your preference."

"Then I'd like to go home, Joshua."

"I do so love it when you're docile."

"If I weren't loaded up with pain medication and immobilized by this cast, I'd show you just how far from docile I'm feeling right now," she informed him, her eyes flashing.

He grinned. "I'll take a rain check."

Her lips twitched and, though she fought it admirably, laughter bubbled out. "Oh, Joshua," she said with a sigh. "You are impossible."

"No, sweetheart, I am very possible." He dropped a kiss on her nose, then another on her lips. He might have lingered there for an eternity, tasting the sweetness, memorizing the shape, savoring the warmth, but Casey chose just that moment to join them.

Avoiding Joshua's eyes, she said stiffly, "I want to go home now."

"Your mother's tired, too. If you'll get her coat, we'll hit the road."

For an instant he thought she might not go. She cast a reluctant look toward her mother, but she went. Joshua figured he had just enough time for one last kiss, but Garrett thwarted that by hobbling away to say goodbye to Lena. Chagrined, he went after her. When he slid her coat around her shoulders, he leaned down to whisper in her ear, "Later."

She never once missed a beat in her conversation with Lena, but he felt the shudder that swept through her body. It wasn't much for an impatient man, but it was the most he was likely to get. It would hold him...for a time.

CHAPTER ELEVEN

GARRETT WAS A lousy patient. She had the temperament of a bear with a thorn stuck in its paw. Joshua had the devil's own time trying to get her to let him take care of her.

Over Garrett's strenuous objections, Mrs. Mac had insisted on settling her into the main house so that she could be properly looked after. The room she'd chosen, with a definite twinkle in her eyes, happened to be just down the hall from Joshua's. Garrett had warily gauged the distance, then retreated into silence.

Once left alone, she had stayed dutifully in bed for about two minutes. She had been halfway down the stairs when he'd caught her, scooped her up and carried her back. An hour later when he'd taken her a bowl of vegetable soup for lunch, she'd practically flung it in his face. Then she'd ordered him out of her room, out of the state, out of her life. She'd emphasized it by pointing the way.

Joshua crept back an hour later and found her asleep. He lingered in the doorway, unable to take his eyes off of her. The sight of her in that bed, even clad in a less than provocative nightshirt, did amazing things to his pulse. Guiltily—the woman was in pain, after all—he backed out the door. He was about to close it when her eyes blinked open. She sat bolt upright, stared around in momentary confusion, then sagged slowly back to the pillow.

"Feeling any better?" he asked, stepping inside but keeping a careful distance between himself and that all-too-tempting bed.

She groaned and turned her back on him. "Go away."

"Can I get you anything?"

"My files," she said, turning a hopeful look on him.

"How about a magazine?"

The counter offer drew a fierce scowl. "I have work to do. I want my files."

"How about a stockman's journal?" he compromised. "It wouldn't be my choice of leisure reading, but you might like it."

"I want my files."

"You have a decidedly one-track mind."

"So do you but I get paid for mine."

"You're on vacation."

"I don't take vacations."

"You do now."

"Says who?"

Mrs. Mac stuck her head in. "Says me. How are you?"

"I broke my ankle. That's hardly cause for all this fussing," she grumbled.

Mrs. Mac approached the bed far more bravely than Joshua dared. She plumped the pillows, ignoring Garrett's sour expression. "Maybe it's about time you let the rest of us fuss over you. You work too hard. The ranch won't collapse if you take some time off."

Joshua could tell from the suddenly fearful look in Garrett's eyes that Mrs. Mac's reassurance had exactly the opposite effect. "Just think what fun you'll have catching up," he taunted her. "Hours and hours of work piled up. You'll be able to feel incredibly noble."

Mrs. Mac regarded him oddly, then caught on. "That's

right. The work will be waiting. I don't know of anybody here who's likely to snatch it out from under you and see that it gets done. Now why don't you pretty yourself up a little and let Joshua carry you downstairs for dinner. I brought you a lovely new robe." She handed over some pink satin and French lace confection that set Joshua's pulse racing.

Fingering the satin cautiously, as if she feared the very femininity it suggested, Garrett said, "I can get down the stairs on my own."

"And spoil my fun?" he protested. "Not on your life. Need any help getting dressed?"

She shot an appealing look at Mrs. Mac, who was chuckling. She scowled. "Traitor."

Mrs. Mac drew herself up to her full, imposing height. "Humph! Some people don't see what's staring them right in the face."

"Which is? I'm sure you'll be happy to point it out to me."

Mrs. Mac shook her head. "Actually, I won't. I think I'll leave that to Joshua. Dinner is in forty-five minutes. If you'd like a glass of sherry, you'll need to hurry."

"From the look of things, I could use the whole damned bottle," she muttered, but she swung her legs over the side of the bed and hobbled into the bathroom. When Joshua repeated his offer of help, she slammed the door.

"Guess not," he said, and stood back to wait for her.

It was a pattern that was repeated for the next three days. Garrett's mood deteriorated with each passing day that she was confined to her room. She snapped at Elena. She had Casey fleeing the room in tears. Even Mrs. Mac was giving her wide berth by the end of the third day.

Only Joshua dared to venture into the room. He waved a white handkerchief first, then poked his head in.

"Don't shoot. I'm unarmed."

"Unfortunately so am I." She was sitting in bed, her arms folded across her chest, glowering at him.

"You have a nasty attitude."

"It's not getting any better being cooped up in here."

"Then I think I may have just the thing. Put on your warmest duds, sweet thing. I have a surprise for you."

Instantly her eyes flared with more excitement than she'd demonstrated since he'd made passionate love to her in that cabin. "You're taking me home?"

"Better than that."

"There isn't anything better than that."

"See if you still feel that way in an hour. Now, speed it up before I change my mind."

"Five minutes," she vowed. "Don't leave me."

His expression suddenly sobered. "Never. Haven't you figured that out yet?"

GARRETT SANK BACK on the bed in defeat. There was no way in hell to get her jeans on over that damned cast. And if she couldn't even get dressed, how could she go with Joshua? It was a measure of her boredom that she couldn't bear the possibility of missing this outing. Emotional dangers and pitfalls were the least of her worries. The unceasing sameness of these last few supposedly relaxing days was about to drive her out of her mind. She would have made a bargain with Satan himself to escape this tedium. Joshua pretty much fit into the same category.

She tugged on her jeans again, but they were hung up on that cast and no amount of coaxing was likely to solve the problem. She needed scissors.

"Joshua!"

He opened the door a crack. "Ready?"

"I need scissors."

His glance fell to the jeans that were sagging around her right ankle. Slowly his gaze worked its way from bare ankle to calf, from calf to dangerously exposed thigh. He swallowed hard as his gaze settled on the scrap of lace masquerading as panties.

"Scissors?" he repeated in a choked voice.

"My jeans won't fit over the cast."

"So I see." Laughing eyes that still smoldered with desire met hers. "Maybe I can help."

Now it was her breath that was snagging. "Scissors would be better," she said, but he was already kneeling in front of her, his fingers hot against her bare skin as he caught the cuff of denim and ripped. He tore it very, very slowly, his gaze studiously on the task, his fingers sliding along her leg. The feathery caress was sheer torment.

"Is that far enough?" he finally asked.

Tongue-tied, Garrett nodded, then glanced down. "There's just one thing," she said, unexpected laughter suddenly threading through her voice.

Joshua's dazed eyes met hers. "Hmm?"

"It's the wrong leg."

His glance shot to the jeans. As he took in the ripped right leg and the cast on her left leg, he rubbed his hand over his eyes. "It's your fault. When I touch you, I can't concentrate."

"Then don't touch me," she said.

"I can't do that, either," he warned, sounding helpless for the first time since she'd met him. His hands rested on the bed on either side of her hips. She sensed the turmoil raging inside him as he kept his hands away from her. With her own heart pounding, she knew she had to find some quick way to break the spell that was slowly weaving its way around them.

"Then at least do me one favor, okay?" she said, tangling her fingers in his hair.

"Anything."

"Stay away from the rest of my wardrobe."

She counted the heartbeats before Joshua finally chuckled and the tension snapped.

"Good idea," he agreed briskly. "Now do you have anything else to put on that doesn't require alterations or should I finish off these jeans?"

"I suppose you'd better finish them off. Maybe we can stop by my house for some more clothes while we're out."

Joshua draped a blanket around her this time, while he opened the left seam from ankle to knee.

"Try these," he said, handing them to her and scurrying for the door. If she hadn't known exactly how he felt, Garrett might have laughed at him. Unfortunately her own pulse continued bucking like a bronco.

Her heartbeat took another lurch when she saw Joshua's surprise waiting on the front lawn. An old-fashioned sleigh, sleek and black, the bright red reins dotted with silver bells, sat in the front yard. Two horses pranced in place.

"A sleigh ride," she said, her voice filled with wonder. "Where on earth did you find it?"

"Mrs. Mac thought she remembered it being in one of the outbuildings. There was a dust cover over it and boxes piled on top. The runners were rusty. I've been polishing the sleigh up the last three days. Do you like it?"

"I love it, but you hate being out in weather like this. Are you sure you want to do this?"

"Do you?"

"Oh, yes," she breathed.

Joshua smiled. "Then I'll love it."

He lifted her up and placed her carefully on the seat, then climbed up beside her. Red plaid blankets were quickly tucked around their legs. "All set? Is your leg comfortable? I put some pillows down so you could prop it up."

She reached over and impulsively kissed him. "You're wonderful."

"I keep telling you that," he said, but she could tell that he was pleased. Just for today, for these next couple of hours, she vowed to relax and say only what was in her heart. Somehow she would find a way later to live with the consequences.

Joshua snapped the reins and the tinkling sound of the bells rang out as the horses took off at a sedate clip. The sleigh glided across the snow, giving her an entirely new perspective. This was familiar territory zipping past, starkly beautiful in its own way. She had always loved it for the freedom and independence of spirit it represented, but today through fresh eyes, she viewed it as a place of romantic enchantment, as well. Icicles glistened on tree branches. The air was crisp again, the sky cloudless.

Eventually they stopped and Joshua poured steaming hot chocolate from a thermos into huge mugs, added a dollop of brandy and plopped a handful of marshmallows on top. Garrett took the first sip. "Delicious."

"Not half as delicious as you," he murmured, his gaze locked on her lips. "Your mouth is covered with chocolate and you have this tiny bit of marshmallow."

"Where?" She reached up with a napkin, but he brushed her hand away.

"Let me." His tongue slowly ran around the outline of her mouth, tasting, until Garrett was sure that the bottom would drop straight out of her stomach. There it was again, that strange, wonderful warmth that Joshua was able to generate deep inside of her. It was better than a bonfire. Snuggled cozily in his embrace, she felt a rare contentment steal over her.

She sighed. It was only the faintest of sounds, but it immediately drew a worried frown from Joshua.

"You okay?"

"Never better." She slid her hand into his. "How can I ever thank you for this?"

"Give me a chance. That's all I want, sweetheart. Just a chance to show you what our life together could be like. This is just a sample."

"Not every day can be like this."

"Maybe not, but we could give it a hell of a shot. There are so many things I'd like to do for you, so many places I'd like to share."

Warning bells rang dimly in the back of her mind, but for once Garrett pretended not to hear them. "Tell me about them, Joshua. Tell me about your life."

As they glided across the snow and day turned into dusk, he told her about a world filled with exotic, fascinating places she'd only read about, adventures she'd only dreamed of. It was an alluring world. The images he painted teased her mind, the way his touches teased her flesh.

"Have there been a lot of women in your life?"

"Millions."

"I'm serious."

"None to compare to you." He tilted her face up until her mouth was only a hairbreadth away. "None," he said again and fit his lips to hers. The velvet caress was convincing. The ragged pace of his pulse, when she touched her fingers to his neck, was even more so. A woman could believe in a man whose kisses heated like fire and tasted of chocolate. *She* could believe in *this man*.

But, dear Lord, how afraid she was. She looked into Joshua's eyes and saw love. She looked again and saw commitment. Then she looked into her own heart and the fear didn't seem nearly as real as his kisses and the promise in his eyes.

"A chance," he whispered. "Is that so terribly difficult for you?"

It was terrifying…or had been mere hours ago. Now it seemed possible. "I'll try," she vowed.

Joshua's arms stole around her in an undemanding hug that was far more compelling than the hottest passion. There was understanding in that hug and yet another promise. Garrett had rarely trusted promises. She had long since sworn off risks. Tonight it seemed her world was undergoing a change that was likely to affect the rest of her life.

THE SIGHT THAT greeted Joshua when he entered the kitchen brought laughter bubbling up from deep inside him. Wisely, he choked it off as he watched Garrett struggling to stir a lump of flour and milk into what he supposed was biscuit dough. She was scowling fiercely at the mess.

"Having an attack of domesticity, are we?" he inquired, probably a shade too cheerfully. She glowered at him.

"Elena's sick," she reported succinctly.

"So you're cooking dinner?"

"Don't sound so horrified."

"Horrified, no. Curious, yes. What exactly is that you're beating to death?"

"Biscuits," she said, confirming his original guess.

"Don't beat them," he suggested, keeping his voice bland. "They'll be tough."

"I suppose you could do better."

"I could."

She poked the bowl at him, which was no mean feat considering the size of the ceramic dish. "Be my guest."

"Ask nicely."

"I just did."

He grinned. "I don't think so. It sounded more like a challenge to me."

"And you don't rise to challenges?"

"Oh, I rise to most anything that intrigues me. In this instance, though, I think I'd prefer a small bribe."

She regarded him suspiciously. "Such as?"

"A kiss."

"Oh, no. Kisses with you have a way of leading into dangerous territory." A delightful blush crept into her cheeks.

He grinned. "Yes, they do, don't they? Be realistic, though. If I have to get dinner on the table for a dozen people, I won't have much time to follow through on that one little kiss."

Her eyes lit up and she asked thoughtfully, "You'll do the whole dinner?"

"Every course. Rare prime rib. Caesar salad. Mashed potatoes and gravy. Green beans almandine. Biscuits. Maybe even a cherry cobbler with cream." He drew the list out slowly, tantalizing her with the images. She was practically licking her very desirable lips when he added, "If I like the way you kiss."

She blinked and shook her head. "You'll do all that for one kiss?"

"Just think what I'd do if you threw in a hug."

She set the bowl on the counter with a decisive thud and crossed the room in three quick, decisive steps, her cast thumping on the tile floor. Before he realized what she meant to do, she'd pecked him lightly on the cheek, grabbed her jacket and headed for the door. "Thanks," she called over her shoulder, her expression very sassy and self-satisfied.

"Whoa!" He snagged a corner of her jacket and brought her to a halt.

Eyes wide, she stared back at him. "Yes?"

"That kiss won't even get the roast in the oven." He used her jacket like a rope to tug her closer. "Now, this is the sort of kiss I had in mind."

His lips slowly settled on hers, teasing, coaxing, re-kindling the quick velvet heat of desire. He lingered to learn the shape of her mouth, to rediscover the sweet, sweet taste of her. After one startled gasp, she fell vic-tim to his touch, melting in his arms, sliding her arms around his neck, threading her fingers through his hair. The temperature in the kitchen rose a good twenty de-grees. A few more and that lump of dough wouldn't need the oven to bake.

When he finally released her, she very nearly sagged into the nearest chair. "For that kiss you ought to cook for the next month."

"If you think I'm going to feed a dozen ranch hands, including the man who's half in love with you, for a month, you're crazy. You'd have to go for a lot more than one paltry, old kiss."

"That kiss was not paltry," she retorted, looking offended.

"I suppose you can do better?"

"Of course I can," she said before her eyes blinked wide. "I mean…"

"Oh no, sweetheart. You said it. Let's see you back it up." He stood nobly in front of her. "I'm ready."

She sniffed. "You look as if you're about to make some supreme sacrifice."

"I'll tell you after the kiss how much of a sacrifice it was."

"Joshua Ames, if you think you can goad me into kissing you again, you are out of your mind."

"Coward."

"Am not."

"Then let's see you pucker up, darlin'."

"I suppose you won't be satisfied until you get me into your bed again."

"Now that's an intriguing thought."

"One which I'm sure you never considered." There was the tiniest hint of sarcasm in her voice, but amusement danced in her eyes.

"Never," he said piously. "I am an honorable man. I will wed you."

He saw the quick flicker of fear, but she kept her voice emphatic. "Over my dead body."

"You would give up the chance to experience my culinary skills for the rest of your life?"

"I haven't even experienced them for dinner. Maybe you'd better get through this trial run. Then we'll see if we have anything to talk about."

"I have other talents deserving of a trial run," he offered generously.

Her gaze narrowed. "I've sampled those."

"And?"

"The jury's still out," she said sassily, ducking past him and heading for the door.

This time he let her go. If he hadn't, dinner would have been hours late and he'd have had a dozen ravenous ranch hands to fend off. Besides, it was more than enough that he'd planted the seductive notion in Garrett's mind. He knew it would nag at her for days now. Anticipation was sometimes every bit as sweet as the lovemaking.

CHAPTER TWELVE

JOSHUA AND MRS. MAC were up to something. Garrett watched their conspiratorial looks, their whispered conversations and grew increasingly suspicious. They had finally stopped hovering over her once the doctor had assured them that her ankle was healing nicely and would be in its cast no more than another week or so. They hadn't even objected too strenuously when she'd decided to move back to her own house. In fact, Joshua had barely seemed to react to the announcement at all. His suddenly disinterested attitude irked her almost as much as knowing he was just down the hall had previously provoked her.

"I'm going," she announced from the foyer, her small bag sitting by her feet. They barely even looked up. Joshua did manage a distracted wave.

"I'll be back next year," she said and waited for the flurry of commotion to begin.

"Okay," Mrs. Mac said mildly. Joshua never even glanced at her.

Thoroughly miffed now, Garrett stepped into the room, walked over until she was practically under their noses, in fact. "Okay, that's it," she announced. "What the hell is going on around here?"

Two pairs of innocent eyes stared up at her.

Mrs. Mac's face creased in a worried frown. "Garrett, dear, is something the matter?"

Hands on hips, she glared at the two of them. "You tell me."

They exchanged a look. "We're just making a few plans," Mrs. Mac said.

"Nothing that you need to worry about," Joshua added.

"What if I want to worry?" she countered, only one step away from a childish pout.

A grin tugged at Joshua's lips. "Feeling left out, are you?"

"I just think I have a right to know if something's going on. I am supposed to be the manager of this ranch."

"Oh, this isn't ranch business, dear." Mrs. Mac patted her hand.

Defeated, Garrett began backing toward the door. "Never mind, then."

Joshua grabbed her wrist and tried pulling her into his lap. She resisted. He tugged harder and finally tumbled her into his arms.

"Oh, for heaven's sakes," he said, amusement radiating from every rotten pore of him. "Let's just tell her."

Mrs. Mac looked thoughtful. "I suppose she will have to be told sooner or later, but I was hoping we could surprise her."

Garrett's eyes blinked wide and she pushed herself up from the awkward position in which she'd landed. It was not *really* intentional that she put her hand smack in Joshua's face for leverage. She addressed her questions directly to Mrs. Mac, who in the long run was a far more trustworthy source than the unscrupulous man holding her. "A surprise? For me? Why?"

"Well, your birthday is coming, dear. What do you think, Joshua? Should we tell her and spoil the surprise?"

Still rubbing his nose, which she'd mashed, he studied her intently. Finally he shook his head. "I don't think so."

Garrett tumbled out of his lap, grabbed a pillow from the sofa and threw it at him. Laughing, he caught in in mid-air. "Okay. Okay. You tell her, though. I need to focus all my attention on fending off another one of her sneak attacks. The woman can't stay away from me."

"You wish. Now talk."

"We're planning a party," Mrs. Mac announced.

Garrett blinked. "A party?"

Joshua rolled his eyes. "You know, one of those events where people get together, eat a lot of food, dance a little, tell jokes, put lampshades on their heads."

Mrs. Mac grimaced at Joshua's description. "My lampshades will remain precisely where they are," she warned.

"Don't tell me," he said. "I would never dream of doing anything so juvenile." His gaze shifted to Garrett. "But some of your guests might."

"Sometimes, you are thoroughly obnoxious," Garrett pointed out. It didn't seem to faze him. "Why are you having the party?"

"I told you, dear. It's for your birthday. It was Joshua's idea."

She regarded him suspiciously. "Why?"

His expression suddenly turned serious. The intensity of his gaze pinned her like a doe caught in headlights. His voice dropped to a husky whisper. "So I can get you into my arms on a dance floor and make love to you to the music all night long."

The provocative image ripped through her and left her knees trembling.

"Joshua," she objected weakly. She shot a look at Mrs. Mac to see how she was taking this blatantly sexual announcement. Instead of outright shock, she saw an unfamiliar dreaminess in those bright blue eyes.

"Oh, my," Mrs. Mac said finally. "Young man, you certainly know how to bring back memories."

She watched as Joshua reached over and gently squeezed a gnarled hand. "I expect you to save a dance for me, too," he told the older woman.

A spark of pure devilment crept into those old eyes. "Just watch where you put those wicked hands of yours, young man."

Garrett was able to pry very little additional information out of the two of them. Not even Elena, who was back to bustling about in the kitchen again, would reveal much. That night at dinner in her own house again, Garrett decided to see how much her daughter knew about the upcoming event.

"Casey, what have you heard about this party that Mrs. Mac is planning?"

Casey looked startled. "You know?"

"I know they're planning it. They wouldn't tell me any of the details."

"Did you tell them you wouldn't come?"

"No. Why would I do that?"

"I thought you didn't want to spend time with Joshua."

Garrett listened as her own advice came back to haunt her. "Sweetie, there's a big difference between going to a party and being involved with someone."

"What about the sleigh ride?"

"How on earth did you know about that?"

"Elena told me. I saddled up Bright Lightning and went for a ride to see if it was true." Accusing eyes glared at her. "Mom, you were kissing him."

She couldn't very well deny what Casey had seen with her own eyes, though she very much wanted to. "I know. I can't explain it, but it seemed like the right thing to do at the time."

A faint spark of hope flickered in Casey's eyes. "Does that mean you're going to date him, after all?"

Dating seemed an innocuous term for what had been happening lately between her and Joshua. Too cautious to label it more, she simply nodded. "While he's here," she was quick to point out. "I don't expect it to last once he's gone home again."

Although Garrett had made the claim aloud, she believed it the way an eight-year-old denied a belief in Santa Claus, with more hope of being wrong than certainty of being right. She did want it to last. She was beginning to dream of happily ever afters. She just wasn't going to admit it. If nothing else, she would salvage her pride when he'd gone.

Disappointment written on her face, Casey pushed her plate away. "May I be excused?"

"When you've finished your dinner."

"I'm not hungry. If I have to sit here a week, I still won't be hungry."

Since Casey was perfectly capable of making good on her claim through sheer stubbornness, Garrett sighed and waved her off. "See that your homework's done before you watch any TV."

Just then the back door opened simultaneously with a knock. Heart galloping, Garrett met Joshua's gaze. "Afraid to risk waiting for me to let you in?"

"Just saving your bad ankle. Hi, Casey, how are you? You haven't been around much the last few days."

Casey shrugged and stared at her uneaten meat loaf. "I've had homework."

"Want to take a break tonight and play a little chess with me?"

She shook her head and edged toward the door. "Too much homework," she mumbled and took off.

Joshua watched her go with troubled eyes. "Have you talked to her about this?" he asked Garrett.

"It'll pass."

He shook his head. "I don't think so. I think it's gone on long enough."

"Where are you going?"

"To talk to her."

"Joshua!" The protest was wasted. He was already through the door. She could hear his footsteps taking the stairs two at a time and winced. If Casey actually answered his questions, they would probably hear his roar of fury halfway to Montana. In fact, she wondered if there was any way to get safely across the state line in the next half hour.

Lines from *King Lear* about the sharp tongues of thankless children came to mind. She had a feeling she was about to discover exactly what Shakespeare had had in mind when he'd written them.

JOSHUA TAPPED LIGHTLY on Casey's bedroom door and waited. Finally he heard a very reluctant "Come in."

He cracked the door and saw that she was sitting at her desk, a wary expression on her face.

"Could we talk, kiddo?"

"About what?"

"Why you seem to be so mad at me?"

A sigh shuddered through her and her shoulders sagged. The look she directed at him was filled with guilt. "I'm not mad exactly."

"Then let's talk about what you are exactly." He sat down on the edge of her bed, faintly intimidated by the ruffled canopy and collection of dolls. He wasn't used to all these feminine frills. "Want to sit over here by me?"

Casey approached him cautiously and picked a spot near the head of the bed. She picked up one of the dolls, a well-worn baby doll with faded clothes and skimpy hair. Clutching it to her chest, she waited patiently. Joshua could see a whole ton of emotions in her demeanor—anxiety, caution, and an oddly grown-up calm. If she hadn't been clinging so desperately to that ragged doll or if he hadn't seen the storm raging in her eyes, he might have bought her serene facade. Suddenly faced with this girl, who was part child, part woman, Joshua grew nervous. He wasn't at all sure where to start.

"What's been happening with you lately?" he began innocuously enough.

She seemed relieved not to be asked a direct question about the cause of her anger. "You know, school, chores, stuff like that."

"You haven't been around the house much. I gather you've been eating your meals with the hands."

"Mom said it would be okay," she said defensively.

"Of course, it is. I just wondered why you didn't want to eat up at the house with us."

She shrugged and gazed at the floor.

"Okay, let's back up a minute. This goes back to that morning in the hospital, doesn't it?"

Her gaze shot to his, then skittered away. "I don't know what you mean."

"I think you do. You and your mother argued about something that day, didn't you? Was it about me?"

Joshua could hear the ticking of the huge, old-fashioned alarm clock sitting on the nightstand. It seemed an eternity passed before she nodded.

Biting back anger, he asked calmly, "Want to tell me about it?"

"Mom says you're going back to Florida," she mumbled.

With that single revelation, Joshua understood it all. Garrett had planted her own seeds of doubt in her daughter's fertile imagination. "You're afraid I'll leave you."

"And Mom."

"Casey, at some point, I will go back. I can't deny that. I have a business there."

A tear trickled down her cheek. With fingers that suddenly seemed all thumbs, he reached over and brushed it away. "No tears, okay. Casey, look at me."

Eyes shimmering with tears, she glanced up finally.

"Honey, I will always, *always*, come back."

"But you told me you wanted to marry Mom. You can't marry her and be gone all the time, can you? What kind of family would that be?"

He sighed and took her hand between his. "I don't have all the answers yet. I'm still not even certain if your mother wants me around on a permanent basis. Once she and I have worked that part out, I promise you, if it is within my power, we will be a family, all in the same place."

"Promise?"

"I promise."

"Are you going to ask her to marry you at the party?"

He grinned. "That is between your mother and me."

"Oh," she said, clearly disappointed.

"But I could use a little help in picking out her present. Want to go into Cheyenne with me on Saturday to find something?"

Her eyes lit up. "Really? You mean it? Just the two of us?"

"Just the two of us. We'll make a day of it. Shopping, lunch, the works."

"A movie?"

He grinned at her enthusiasm. "Why not?"

He reached across then and hugged her. "That's my girl. The next time you're worried about what's going on with me, you just ask, okay?"

"I'm sorry I doubted you."

"I'm just glad we worked it out. I've missed our chess games. You're the only competition around. Mrs. Mac really is lousy," he confided. "Just don't tell her I said so."

Giggling, she hugged him back. "I won't. I promise."

On his way downstairs it took everything in Joshua to keep his temper under control. The way Garrett had managed to twist things for Casey infuriated him. It was bad enough that she hadn't allowed any of his efforts to make a dent in her distrust, but to destroy Casey's faith in him was unconscionable.

He found her pacing the kitchen, limping back and forth on her walking cast and casting nervous glances toward the doorway. "You should be scared," he said mildly.

"What did she tell you?"

"The truth. She said you'd told her I was leaving, that she shouldn't count on me for anything."

Garrett's jaw set stubbornly. "I told her that for her own good. She can't count on anyone except herself."

"And me," he said furiously. "And Mrs. Mac and you. Or don't you believe you all qualify, either?"

"Of course, it's just that…"

"Just what? That I'm a man? That I don't live here? That I'm not her real father? Is that what this is really all about, Garrett? Are you still in love with the man who got you pregnant and then deserted you?"

"No-o-o." Her eyes wide with shock, she stammered over the too quick denial. "Of course not."

He shook his head. "I'm not so sure. There's a mighty fine line between love and hate. Maybe you ought to take a good, hard look and see which side your feelings for that man fall on. While you're at it, take a look at what you're feeling for me. I'm not a patient man, Garrett. You've stretched me just about to my limit. You sit on the fence much longer and I just might not be around when you decide to jump down."

On his way to the door he stopped just long enough to place a hard, bruising kiss on her suddenly vulnerable mouth. He wanted her to remember what was real, what was lasting.

He wanted her to remember him.

CHAPTER THIRTEEN

GARRETT HAD NEVER seen the house in such a state of chaos. Mrs. Mac had hired extra help to shine the floors, polish the chandeliers and help Elena in the kitchen in preparation for what seemed to be turning into an extraordinarily lavish birthday party.

All of the feverish activity only underscored Garrett's own restlessness. She couldn't concentrate. Memories of Joshua's warning taunted her day and night. He had been amazingly tolerant of her uncertainties. He'd even seemed to forgive her, if only barely, for upsetting Casey with dire predictions about his departure. The man was a saint, she thought crankily. All that generosity of spirit was tough to ignore, though she was certainly trying. The fact that her blood sizzled when he came into a room only compounded the problem she seemed to be having with her common sense.

Just then her pulse skipped a beat and she knew intuitively that Joshua had entered the room. Her whole body came alive in his presence, tingling, anticipating.

"Ready?" he asked, and again her heartbeat accelerated, though she knew rationally that the question was perfectly innocuous. The man was only taking her to the doctor to get her cast removed.

She should have been thrilled. She would finally be able to get around easily on her own again. Instead she had these crazy mixed feelings. Over the last weeks she'd grown accustomed to Joshua's gentleness. Though she'd fought him tooth and nail, deep down she'd enjoyed being taken care of. The breakfast and lunch trays in bed, the sleigh ride, the long quiet talks, all had finally bewitched her. She'd been able to justify her response by reminding herself repeatedly that it was just temporary, only until the cast came off. Now, perversely, she discovered she didn't want that incredible, cherished feeling to end. That was a dangerous, dismaying discovery for a woman who prided herself on needing no one.

"I'm ready," she said, turning around finally, praying that he couldn't read her confusion in her eyes.

"What is it?" he asked at once.

"What is what?"

"There's something wrong. You're crying."

Her fingers flew to her cheek. To her astonishment, she realized he was right. She really was coming unglued. Wiping the dampness away, she said, "Sorry, I didn't even realize."

At the tiny catch in her voice, he was across the room in three strides, pulling her into his arms. Nestled against his chest, that cherished sensation flooded through her again. Joshua represented strength and caring, two of the things most lacking throughout her entire life. Listening to the steady rhythm of his heart, feeling the power of its beat, a surprising reassurance swept over her. This wasn't Casey's father. This wasn't an immature boy who would walk out on her, leaving her heart in tatters. This was a man she could love through all eternity...if only she dared.

A sigh whispered through her and Joshua's arms tightened. "Garrett?"

"I'm okay," she said finally, stepping back. She saw the damage her tears had done to his shirt. "You, on the other hand, are a mess. Let me have that shirt and I'll get Elena to dry it and iron it for you."

A flicker of pure mischief dashed through his eyes as he reached for the buttons. "I think I like this crying stuff, after all."

Her gaze narrowed suspiciously. "Because?"

"You've never asked me to take off my clothes before."

"Joshua, I am not asking you to take off your clothes," she retorted even as she watched him dutifully unbutton his shirt. Her protest was entirely too weak. "I just meant…"

"Oh, I know what you meant. Normally you're just too shy to ask. Now you have an excuse." He stripped the shirt away and threw it over the chair, then reached for the waistband of his jeans.

"Don't you dare!" she ordered, but it was more whisper than command. Her eyes were locked on the breadth of his bare chest.

"But…" Joshua implored with all innocence.

Swallowing hard, she dragged her gaze up to challenge his. "If you even think about touching that zipper, I'm out of here."

Disappointment streaked across his face. "Too bad," he said, snapping the jeans closed just as Mrs. Mac came into the room and gasped.

"Oh, my," she said breathlessly. The starch was back in her voice in no more than a heartbeat. "Joshua Ames, put your clothes on right this instant. Garrett, I'm surprised at you. Casey could have been the one walking in here instead of me."

"It's…it's not the way it looks," Garrett explained hurriedly. "Joshua's shirt got wet. He was just taking it off so Elena could dry it."

"Humph!" Her expression was disbelieving.

"True," Joshua said. "Much to my dismay, our intentions were purely innocent."

"I doubt you were innocent the day you hit the cradle, young man. Wet or not, I suggest you put that shirt back on until you get another one from upstairs."

With a wink at Garrett, he put it back on every bit as slowly as he'd taken it off. To her dismay, she watched every bit as avidly as she had his disrobing.

"Come on, sweetheart. Let's get to that doctor. I can't wait to watch you taking something off."

"Joshua!" She shot a worried look at Mrs. Mac, but she was chuckling.

"The cast, darlin'. The cast."

"Oh," she said and could have kicked herself for not keeping the disappointment out of her voice. The man was entirely too smug without her giving him more to gloat over.

"I like you in pink," he noted. "What do you think, Mrs. Mac?"

"Very becoming."

Garrett glanced down at her red shirt and blue jeans. "Pink?"

"Your cheeks." His grin widened. "Fascinating. Now they match that shirt."

She glared at him. "I wonder if Red would drive me to the doctor."

Before she realized what he intended, she was off the floor and in Joshua's arms. He glowered fiercely. "Not likely. You and I have a date and I get real testy when a lady stands me up."

"Has anyone ever dared?"

He considered the question thoughtfully. "Not since the first grade Halloween party. Lynda Dixon."

"You still remember her name?"

"A man's not likely to forget a woman who rejects him."

"Obviously she was a very shortsighted woman."

"Exactly what I told her when she begged me to take her to the senior prom."

Laughing, she settled comfortably in his arms. "Okay. Okay. I get the picture."

He nodded approvingly. "I thought you might."

JOSHUA'S GRIP ON the phone tightened. This was the last thing he needed. After weeks of delicate maneuvers to assure Garrett of his feelings, he couldn't leave Wyoming now. She'd never trust him again. Now that she was out of that cast and on her own two feet, she'd take off on him like a shot at the first hint of what she perceived of betrayal. "Suzy, tell him I'll be back in a week or two," he told his assistant. "Reschedule the appointment."

"He's adamant, boss. You'll see him by the first of the week or he'll hire someone else."

Joshua wanted to tell the man to go to blazes, but he didn't dare. Not that he couldn't sacrifice this account and a dozen more. He didn't need their money. However, he did need to keep his reputation for reliability intact. That, every bit as much as his financial skill, was what kept him in business as an investment consultant. Obviously he'd put off this prospective client just as long as he could.

"Tell him I'll meet with him on Monday morning. I'll fly back late Sunday."

"I'll take care of it," Suzy said.

"Anything else?"

"Nothing I can't handle. Is everything okay out there? Are Mrs. McDonald's finances untangled yet?"

"As much as they're ever likely to be. I think she'd be content to keep her spare cash in a cookie jar, if she weren't so set on amassing a fortune to leave to Cal."

"A fortune he doesn't want or need. The only thing that man needs is family. Can't she see that?"

"Maybe if he'd stay out here for more than fifteen minutes at a time, she'd realize it. Instead, the harder she tries to bribe him into staying, the quicker he is to run."

"Maybe this time'll be different. Cal called this morning and said he and Marilou were leaving for the ranch at noon. He wanted to know if there was anything you wanted me to send along with him. I told him I'd just sent you half a dozen faxes and that anything else could wait until you got back."

"You didn't know I'd be coming back Monday."

"Sure I did," she said. "I can read you like a book. I'd already made your plane reservations, but Cal said you could fly back with them."

Joshua chuckled ruefully. "It's nice to know I'm so predictable."

"Not that predictable," she assured him. "For instance, I would have sworn you'd be back two minutes after you landed. Guess you hadn't gotten that cowgirl out of your system, after all."

"What do you know about Garrett?"

This time Suzy laughed. "Come on, boss. I can add two and two as well as you can. See you Monday."

"Yeah," he grumbled. "See you Monday. Maybe I'll surprise you and be late."

"That wouldn't just surprise me. It would send me into shock. Bye-bye."

Joshua would have growled something about the fate of disrespectful help, but she'd already hung up in his ear. Instead he simply sat and stared out the window. His fingers curled around the jewelry box in his pocket. He'd bought the engagement ring on his shopping trip with Casey. She'd helped him pick it out. The blue star sapphire shimmered like lights. The diamonds around it glistened like stars in a midnight sky. The ring had reminded him of the dazzle in Garrett's eyes when she had stared up at him in the heat of passion. He'd known at once that a simple diamond would never do. He planned to give it to her tomorrow night. With any luck the birthday party would turn into an engagement celebration. Now he wondered how much celebration he could hope for, once she learned that he was about to go back to Florida.

GARRETT STOOD IN front of the full-length mirror and slowly turned. She couldn't believe that the woman reflected in the glass was really her. The blue satin dress bared shoulders that were pale as cream. The hem skimmed her knees, displaying slender calves and well-turned ankles. She could barely tell that she'd just had a cast removed from one leg, though she had been forced to wear flat shoes rather than the heels that would have been more traditional with the gown. Over her objections, Casey had brushed her hair until it hung in a shiny wave below her shoulders. It was caught back from her face on one side by a rhinestone studded comb lent by Mrs. McDonald. The two of them had pronounced her *gorgeous* thirty minutes ago. She still couldn't quite get over the possibility that they might be right.

There was a tap on the door. Expecting Joshua, she called out, her gaze still fastened on her reflection. A soft, wolf whistle shimmered across her nerves. A thousand butterflies took flight in her stomach. She turned slow and found not Joshua, but Marilou Rivers, Cal's wife.

"Stay away from my husband," Marilou said, but her eyes were sparkling with amusement and there was an approving smile on her lips. "You look drop-dead gorgeous. Joshua won't know what hit him."

"Are you sure?" Garrett said, her voice filled with uncertainty. "It's not too much?"

"Maybe for a rodeo, but this is a party. You look perfect."

"Like a lady?" she said wryly. "That's what my daughter said. She sounded stunned."

"You know, Garrett, being a survivor and being a lady aren't incompatible. It's just a matter of balance."

"Maybe. Sometimes, though, I think what Joshua really needs is someone who's all woman."

Marilou chuckled. "I suspect you're as much woman as he could ever hope to handle. Just because you put on jeans and live on a ranch doesn't mean you can't be feminine underneath. Since Cal and I got married and I found myself living on a Thoroughbred farm, I've taken to wearing the frilliest lace underwear I can find. The first time he discovered that he almost had a coronary. Now every time he sees me in those pants, all he remembers is what I'm wearing under them. Believe me, he never forgets for one single second that I'm a woman."

Garrett wondered if Joshua always remembered her lace underwear and pink toenail polish when he discovered her in the barn with hay in her hair and dirt streaking her face. Maybe tonight she'd be able to give him new memories to cling to during those times when she was dusty and tired from a roundup. Maybe it was possible to give Joshua the lady he needed without losing her sense of self in the process.

Impulsively she hugged Marilou. "Thank you."

"For what?"

"For making a future for Joshua and me seem almost possible."

There was another tap on the door and this time it was Cal who stuck his head in and whistled. "Wow! Two of the prettiest women in town and they're hiding out upstairs. Joshua, come see the transformation."

Marilou gave him a mock glare. "I thought you said I was always beautiful."

"Oh, you are," he said hurriedly, winking at Garrett. "Must be that the color you're wearing is particularly flattering."

"Quick thinking," Joshua said approvingly as his gaze sought Garrett, who was still standing in the background. When he found her, his eyes widened. Cal and Marilou chuckled.

"Well, he's down for the count," Cal said. "Come on, wife. I think I hear our names being called from downstairs. We'd better get there before Grandmother hires an architect to build that house for us."

When they had gone, Joshua stepped into the room and held out his hands. "Come, let me look at you."

Garrett took his hands and held on tight.

"Scared?"

"A little."

"Sweetheart, these are your friends downstairs."

"But I'm used to running into them in a diner or maybe at the feed store. I'm out of my element on a dance floor."

"You wouldn't be out of your element at the White House. I'm very proud to have you on my arm. Now let's get going before Cal eats all the food."

"Cal and an entire army couldn't eat all the food Elena and the caterer have prepared."

"Elena? I thought the caterer was doing it all?"

"She wasn't convinced he'd make quite enough. Truthfully, I think she was feeling left out. Mrs. Mac wanted her to feel like a guest tonight, but she was still refusing to leave the kitchen last time I checked."

"How close did you come to refusing to leave the barn?"

"It crossed my mind, but I figured you and Mrs. Mac would have a posse out after me."

His gaze lingered on the bare curve of her shoulder, then drifted to the swell of her breast. "There is something to be said about the barn," he murmured, his breathing a little faster.

"Not on your life. I didn't get all dolled up to go tumbling into a haystack. Let's go, Mr. Ames." She tucked her arm through his and went with him downstairs. Halfway down she realized that the dozen or so early arrivals were all standing at the bottom, all eyes on their descent. It was a wonder she didn't trip and land in their midst. Joshua gave her fingers a reassuring squeeze.

"Showtime, darlin'. You're going to knock 'em dead."

The only impression Garrett really worried about, though, was the one she made on the man by her side. The fact that she cared so much worried her. Her gaze rose to meet Joshua's and found the sought-after approval blazing in his eyes. Her confidence soared.

"You're the most handsome man in the room," she

confided, lacing her fingers through his. "I'm very glad to be your date."

With his gaze locked on hers, he whispered, "We're going to make it a night to remember."

After that, everything became a blur. It was nearly midnight when the pace slowed and the band finally struck up the promised waltz. Garrett had sensed Joshua's increasing frustration with the lively square dances that had filled the evening. Every time the caller had insisted that he change partners, he'd done so with obvious reluctance. His possessive gaze had never strayed from her, especially when she'd been hand-in-hand with Red. Even now he still didn't fully realize that he had nothing to fear from the foreman. She thought of Red as a wonderful friend, an older brother almost, but nothing more.

Now, though, the first note of the waltz floated on the air and with a gleam in his eyes, Joshua held out his arms. "This is our dance, darlin'."

Garrett stepped into the embrace, her heart thundering in her chest as his hands settled on her hips and fit them snugly against him.

"Watch it," she whispered in his ear. "Mrs. Mac will be over here with a ruler in a minute to see that you keep a proper distance between us."

"She wouldn't dare. I've been waiting all night to hold you like this." He leaned back just enough to look into her eyes. "Happy?"

"Incredibly," she said and rested her head on his chest. "It's been an evening of magic."

"That's just what I promised. It could be like this always."

Oh, how she wanted to believe that. If anyone could convince her, Joshua could. "Always is a very long time."

"But I'm very good at making magic."

"You have an ego the size of Texas."

"It's not ego if it's fact."

"Then it's just plain old bragging," she teased, her fingers weaving through the hair that had grown long enough to brush the collar of his shirt. Heat flared in his eyes.

"You still enjoy taunting me, don't you?"

"As hobbies go, I'll admit I could find at least a dozen that would be far more boring."

"There's a real streak of vamp in you, did you realize that?"

"Is that good?"

He pulled her close again, until his very heat seemed to radiate around her. "Can't you tell how good that is?"

With a sense of shock, she realized exactly how aroused he was.

"I need you, Garrett. Come away with me."

"Now?" Longing and the sweet tension throbbing through her warred with duty. She couldn't disappear from her own party.

"Tomorrow."

Puzzled she stared at him. There was an unreadable look in his eyes. "Why tomorrow?"

For a moment there was only the rhythmic rise and fall of the music, the gentle sway of their bodies. She could feel his tension, though, and suddenly the worst fear she had ever known spread through her.

She pulled back and accused, "You're leaving, aren't you? You're going back to Florida tomorrow?"

Joshua's arms merely tightened around her.

"Joshua?"

He sighed deeply. "Yes. There's a meeting on Monday.

I have to be there. I have a responsibility to my other clients. I've neglected them for far too long."

"Then by all means go," she said tightly. "I wouldn't want to stop you."

She jerked free and ran through the house; Joshua was right on her heels. If it hadn't been for that damned ankle, she would have beat him. Instead he caught up with her just outside.

"Garrett, you have to listen to me."

Her whole body tensed when he touched her. Slowly he turned her around until she was facing him. Her chin rose a notch and she prayed he wouldn't see the way it quivered. "Why should I listen?" she demanded. "We all knew this moment was going to come. Go. You don't owe me a thing."

"No," he said softly. "I don't owe you anything, but I do love you."

"But you love your job more."

"More?" he said. "You think I love it more than you? More than this?"

He crushed her lips beneath his. Garrett's breath seemed to die in her throat as he plundered her mouth. She wanted to fight him. She even made one halfhearted attempt to push him away, but the blazing desire that fueled the kiss was persuasive. With a sigh, she gave in to the heat that swirled through her. She twined her arms around his neck and took all that he had to offer. A raging hunger made her needy. Fear made her desperate. He was going to go and there would be no more nights like this, no more kisses, no more gentle caresses or seductive touches. She would be alone again. In that instant of realization, she hated him. She hated him for giving her all of this and then taking it away.

She lifted her hands and touched his face, memorizing the faint lines, the purely male texture, that intriguing hint of some long-ago fight that marred the perfection. A great sadness settled over her.

"Garrett, marry me. Come with me to Florida."

For one heart-stopping minute the only thing that registered was the proposal. *Marry me. Marry me.* Joy began to build, chasing away the fear, chasing away the sorrow. Then the rest of his words sank in. He wanted her to leave this place, this haven. He was asking her to give up everything she had fought so hard for. How could he do that, if he truly loved her?

"No," she said. "I can't go to Florida with you. I love you, Joshua, but my life is here."

"Just think about it."

"There's no point," she told him flatly. "Everything I need is here."

"Not everything. Whether you're ready to admit it or not, you need me, too. One of these days, you'll have to admit that. I just hope it's before it's too late."

She shook her head. "I love you, Joshua, but I will never, *ever* need you. I won't ever need anyone again."

He smiled at her wearily. "Maybe one of these days, you'll see that the two go hand in hand." He pressed a chaste kiss on her forehead. "I'll say goodbye before I leave."

She nodded, then forced herself to stand perfectly still and watch him walk away. Only when he had gone did she allow the first sob to escape. She turned and fled to her house in search of the serenity it had always given her in the past. Tonight, though, the rooms seemed filled with ghostly reminders that she was losing something she might never find again.

CHAPTER FOURTEEN

The wind set up an eerie howling. It seemed like an eternity had passed since he'd watched Garrett go into her house. Joshua remained in the shadows, ignoring the freezing night air as he started after her. In his pocket, his fingers curled around the sapphire engagement ring. He should have given it to her. Maybe then she would have believed in him. Wasn't that what a ring was all about, a symbol of love, of commitment? Maybe it would have made a difference.

Then he recalled the bleak expression in her eyes, the shadow of pain, the accusing hint of betrayal. He sighed deeply and admitted that bits of glass and metal, no matter how precious, would be meaningless to a woman who wouldn't allow herself to trust anyone. If all these weeks had meant so little to her, there was nothing he could say now to convince her how much he loved her.

A faint whisper of cigarette smoke told him that Cal had joined him. Obviously, Marilou hadn't caught him or that cigarette would have been history.

"What's up, pal? Did Cinderella leave the ball?" Cal asked.

"Something like that."

Side by side, lost in their own thoughts, they stood silently for a time until Cal finally said, "You're in love with her, aren't you? Marilou thinks you have been for a long time."

Joshua sighed. "Since the first time I laid eyes on her, I suppose. I was planning to ask her to marry me tonight."

"But you didn't."

"The timing seemed all wrong. I have to fly home tomorrow and she thinks I'm leaving for good. I tried to get her to come along, but that only made matters worse."

"Could be that she thinks you expect her to give up her life here. Do you?"

"Would that be so wrong?" he asked angrily. "We could have a wonderful life in Florida. She'd never have to work another day in her life."

"With any other woman that might be the perfect gift. It might even be the case with Garrett, once you've given her some time to adjust to the idea of being idle. I don't know her well, but from what Grandmother has told me, she's a woman who very much needs to feel she's in control of her own destiny. There's nothing scarier to someone like that than trusting her fate to another person."

Joshua studied his friend's face. "Speaking from experience?"

"Absolutely. From the day we met, Marilou always knew what was best for me, how much I needed to feel a part of a family again. I was just too bullheaded to admit it. Once I did, life got a whole lot easier."

"How'd she persuade you?"

"Patience. Persistence." He grinned. "And the sweetest damned kisses I'd ever known." He squeezed Joshua's shoulder. "In fact, I think that little temptress is waiting for me now. If you have to leave tomorrow, fly back with us, okay? Play your cards right and I'll even let you hold the baby."

Joshua grinned at the totally bewitched tone in Cal's voice. "Is that supposed to entice me?" he teased. "Or scare me to death?"

"Trust me on this. You'll never experience anything like holding one of your own. I didn't think it was possible to feel an emotion that powerful. Maybe a sample will give you the patience and persistence you'll need to stick with Garrett for the long haul. You coming in now?"

"Not quite yet. Thanks for the talk, though."

"Anytime, pal. Anytime."

Eventually, when the chill reached deep into his very soul, Joshua went inside, but he didn't sleep. He spent the next hour prowling the house, hovering near the window that allowed him a view of Garrett's place and wondering if they were truly meant to be, after all.

When the waiting and worrying finally got to be too much for him, he began to pack. It didn't take nearly long enough. He carried his bags down to the foyer and placed them by the door. He would have left right then, but his promise to Garrett held him back. He had told her he would come by to say goodbye. If he failed even at that, she would convince herself that all the rest had been lies, as well.

At loose ends until the rest of the household awoke hours from now, he suddenly remembered the cabin. He and Garrett had shared only one night there, but they had been happy. It was the night he had discovered he was capable of love. It was the night Garrett had lost herself to passion, had dared to let him see her vulnerability. He needed to recapture that fleeting moment of trust, needed to remind himself of what he'd been fighting for. Recalling the provisions they'd used and the laundry that Elena had done, he went into the kitchen and stocked a box with new supplies. He found the neatly folded stack of clean sheets, towels and borrowed clothes in the laundry room.

A few minutes later he was on his way. With the roads no longer hazardously covered with ice, the trip took less than a half hour. He pulled the car onto the shoulder alongside the creek and set out on foot. The full moon made the path through the cottonwoods easy to follow.

It took two trips to get everything to the line shack. Once inside, with the door closed behind him against the bitter wind, he felt the cabin's peaceful spell begin to weave its way around him again. Memories came flooding back, images of Garrett's face glowing with passion, of her provocative touches, her sweet kisses. Joshua groaned as need rocketed through him. Damn the woman for captivating him! Any other woman on earth would have been less trouble. Any other woman would have meant less confusion, less heartache.

No other woman would have done.

Not ready to let go of the memories just yet, he started the fire and took off his jacket. He made a pot of coffee, then began putting the supplies away and remaking the bed.

When the cabin was once again as they had found it on that night that had sealed their fate so firmly in his heart, he sat on the sofa and stared at the crackling flames. He thought of his fancy apartments, his expensive furnishings and realized this simple place, after just that one night, felt more like home to him now. Because of Garrett. In his mind, on that night they had become a family, husband and wife in every way that counted. No ceremony would unite them any more meaningfully. If only he could make her see that.

He touched the flannel shirt she'd worn that night,

the one that had skimmed and revealed and taunted. The
fabric was softer now and smelled of something sweet,
something not nearly as sensual as Garrett. With a sigh,
he slid down and rested his head against the back of the
sofa. He rubbed a cuff of the shirt against his cheek and
wondered again how something so right could be turning
out so wrong. He still hadn't come up with an answer by
the time he fell into a fitful sleep.

GARRETT'S NERVES FELT as if they'd been rubbed raw.
Every noise, every creak of the house, every roar of the
wind made her sit up and stare around the room, looking for who knew what.

Hoping for Joshua.

Finally, after a restless, impossible hour, she gave up.
She dressed, went to the barn and saddled Bright Lightning. The horse was as eager as she to race the howling wind. It had been a long time since she'd ridden, a
long time since her thoughts had been uncomplicated and
her heart still her own. She would reclaim herself with
this night ride, free herself from the memory of Joshua.
She had no idea where she was going. She only knew
she didn't want to be here in the morning when Joshua
packed up his things and left. One goodbye was all she
could take.

The full moon spilled a silver path before her. As if
lured by the promise at the end, she gave Bright Lightning her head. The filly galloped at a fierce pace, flying
across the land until both horse and rider were breathless. The hard ride should have exhausted Garrett, but
she felt exhilarated. Her blood pounded. Her cheeks were
stinging, her muscles aching. She felt totally alive. The

last time she had felt quite this way had been in Joshua's arms, astride his supple body.

With a sigh she leaned forward in the saddle and rested her head against Bright Lightning's neck. "Damn," she murmured. She had chased away the blues but not the memories. If anything, with her heart thudding and the horse beneath her, thoughts of Joshua burned hotter than ever.

With a light touch of the reins, she found herself turning toward the Rutgers's line shack. Maybe if she confronted the past weeks head-on, she could put this mistaken interlude in her life to rest.

She approached the cabin from the east. Tethering Bright Lightning outside, she was almost to the door when she noticed that the snow around the front door had been trampled. A trail of footprints led back toward the highway. She followed them for a bit, until she caught a glimpse of that silly, impractical convertible of Joshua's. Her heart seemed to still.

"Why can't I get away from him?" she murmured to no one in particular. She started to go. She actually walked half a dozen paces toward her horse, giving the cabin a wide berth before being drawn back. She needed to know why he was here, why he'd sought refuge in this place. Was it for the same reason she had? Had he been seeking to banish memories once and for all? Or had he wanted to recapture them?

She found him asleep on the sofa, his head thrown back in a way that was bound to leave him with a stiff neck. His blond hair was mussed, his jaw shadowed with stubble. After only the faintest hesitation, she took off her jacket and sat beside him. It was only through sheer willpower that she confined herself to looking at him. She wanted desperately to touch, to soothe away the worried lines that creased his brow even in sleep. She wanted to know again the feel of his lips on hers. She wanted one last time to experience the wild joy of his caresses.

She denied herself all of that, telling herself it was wise, reminding herself that once imagined danger was now a painful reality. She curled her feet under her and watched the rise and fall of his chest. When she could finally bear it no longer, she dropped a light farewell kiss on that faintly crooked nose that reminded her of all the contradictions in his personality. She stood up and reached for her jacket again when his eyes blinked open.

"Garrett," he said, his voice husky with sleep. "I was just dreaming about you. I dreamed you kissed me."

Her lips curved just a bit. "I did. Just a peck, mind you."

He reached out a hand. "Would you kiss me again? I'd like to remember it while I'm gone."

She shook her head, heart hammering. "I don't dare."

"Why?"

"It would hurt too much. I ache inside, Joshua. I ache for what we're losing."

"Then hold onto it. Come with me in the morning. See how I live."

"You know I can't do that. I have responsibilities here."

A light seemed to go out in his eyes. He stood up and went to the fireplace, knelt down and stirred the embers until the dying sparks re-ignited. The action seemed fraught with symbolism. It made the ache even more painful to bear. Her nerves felt more raw now than when she'd lain alone in her bed only dreaming of Joshua.

"Maybe I should go," she said.

"No. Stay with me, please. Let's talk this out."

She shook her head. "If I stay, we won't talk."

Understanding flared in the depths of his eyes. He came back and sat beside her on the bed. "Maybe that's even better. Maybe that's the way we communicate best about what is really in our hearts."

"Making love is not an answer."

"Are you so sure of that?" he asked, his hand against her cheek. "Are you?" The back of his fingers rubbed against the hollow of her neck, then trailed lower until his hand stroked over her breast. The nipple tightened into a hard, sensitive bud. The shock seemed to cut all the way through her. He took her hand and pressed it to his lips. "Why did you come here tonight?"

"I can't explain it. Something drew me here."

"As it did me. Doesn't that tell you something, sweetheart?"

She stared at him helplessly. "I don't know. Maybe. Joshua, I don't know what to say to you anymore."

"And I don't know what to do anymore."

Their gazes caught and held. An eternity slid by...or maybe it was no more than a heartbeat.

"Just hold me," Garrett begged at last, not strong enough to deny herself this one simple pleasure. "Would you mind doing that? Suddenly I'm feeling very much alone and you haven't even left yet."

With a sigh, he drew her into his arms. With the fire crackling in the fireplace and his arms tight around her, Garrett felt safe and secure. If only the feeling would last, if only she could count on it being this way tomorrow and the next day and the next...

She stared up into eyes that had suddenly gone smoky with desire. His gaze lingered on her lips, then slowly he lowered his mouth to hers in a sweetly tender kiss.

Hunger exploded inside her like a flower bursting into full bloom. She was the one who deepened the kiss, who turned it from a gentle caress into an urgent claiming. All of the longing she had kept at bay over the last days went into that one lingering kiss. Fire leapt in her veins. Her pulse hammered. Somewhere deep inside, doubts fled, if only for this moment, this one last time.

Joshua's hands were gentle, too gentle. She wanted him to rush, to send her flying with all the brightness of fireworks in the night sky. He insisted on savoring, on lingering over each kiss, exploring with exquisite care. Her skin warmed under his touch, her blood pulsed to an excited rhythm. Each caress was a bittersweet reminder that it was the last time she would know this joy, the last time she would know the aching, deep-down pleasure of a kiss, the heart-stopping thrill of his heat deep inside her.

Ironically, when time speeded up, when each thrust of his body lifted them higher and higher toward a shattering climax, Garrett wanted him to wait, wanted this sweet joining to go on forever. Her body, slick with perspiration and desperate with need, betrayed her, arching into his, catapulting her over the edge, drawing him with her.

Joshua's hands cupped her face and he stared deep into her eyes. "I love you." Each word was spoken emphatically, convincingly.

"I know," she whispered. "I know."

He sighed and rolled away. "But it's not enough, is it?"

Suddenly chilled by his anger, she trembled. "I don't know. I just don't know anymore."

"Garrett, I don't know what else to say, what else to do."

"You sound as if you're blaming me, as if I'm the one

at fault because I can't give up everything to do this your way. That's not fair," she said.

"Not a damn thing about this is fair. And, yes, I'd like to know whose fault it is, if not yours. I've done everything I could think of to prove myself to you, to offer you a life that most women would envy."

The accusatory tone was still there and it filled Garrett with guilt. Uncomfortable with the emotion, she lashed back. "Maybe the bottom line is that you don't love me enough, either," she accused. "You're still trying to buy me."

"How can you say that? I've asked you to marry me. Isn't that proof enough?"

"No," she said. "No."

She climbed out of bed, away from the temptation of his body, away from the danger of her own responses. Grabbing her clothes, she jerked them on haphazardly. Unable to meet his condemning gaze, she stood in the doorway and whispered goodbye. Then, when it seemed certain he wouldn't respond, she closed it.

Only when she was safely on the other side, tears streaming down her face, did she dare to murmur, "I love you, Joshua. I really love you."

And then she ran.

CHAPTER FIFTEEN

GARRETT RACED FROM the cabin in a near panic. Suddenly she desperately needed the solace of home. She needed to remember what she was trying to protect, all that was important in her life. Riding back toward the ranch at a breakneck pace, she tried futilely to flee the power of the last stolen hour in Joshua's arms. Shaking and breathless when she arrived, she finally calmed as she curried Bright Lightning. Over and over she reassured herself that what had just happened didn't really matter, that she would survive Joshua's leaving in the morning and go on as before.

When the filly was bedded down in her stall, Garrett went outside. She leaned against the corral fence and stared at the night sky. The Big Dipper tilted clearly toward the North Star. Enthralled as always by the thick sprinkling of stars across the black-velvet backdrop, she barely heard the whisper of sound behind her, the faint crunch of ice-topped snow, yet she felt Joshua's presence. She supposed that in her heart she had known he would come after her, that he would never leave well enough alone. Tension crept through her as she waited, listening to his approaching footsteps, dreading another confrontation, another goodbye.

Then he was beside her, silent and still in a way that might have been comforting if his mere presence didn't so often set off such conflicting emotions. Irritation easily slipped into blazing anger. Fury too often slid into fascination and a pull so strong she was shaken by the implications. It had happened again tonight, even though he'd told her he was leaving, even though she knew it was over between them. Not since the night Casey had been conceived had she been so tempted to lose herself in the fool's-gold promise of a man's love. That had been a girl's misguided infatuation, though, while what she felt now was a woman's longing. The difference and her unwilling acknowledgment of it scared her to death.

Joshua was losing patience, losing the will to fight for her. She had heard the defeat in his voice. For weeks he had been content to let the heat build again, waiting until she shattered like a ceramic figure that had been fired too hot. Her resolve was close to shattering now and she hoped to God he didn't know it. She wasn't sure she could withstand the pressure he was likely to put on her.

"Have you ever had a dream?" she asked, breaking the silence.

"All the time."

The quick, easy response told her he didn't understand. "No, I mean a dream that consumes you, that determines who you are and what you'll become."

She caught the faint shake of his head and sighed. "Then I'm not sure you could ever understand."

"Make me understand. You said earlier that you ache. So do I. I see how much we have and I see it slipping away. Tell me about your dream."

"From the time I was a little girl I dreamed of nights like this. I read *Little House on the Prairie* and longed to live like that, on the edge of a frontier, in a land with clean air and vivid blue skies and endless horizons, a place of limitless possibilities."

"What about the hardships?"

"They seemed like nothing compared to the hell I was living in," she said simply.

"What hell?" he asked. "Can't you please tell me now? Can't you trust me to understand? If I have to give you up, at least I need to understand why."

Garrett wanted to do as he asked, but she was afraid it would be like unleashing a tidal wave, that once started, the hurt and anger would never cease pouring out of her. She lifted her gaze to meet his and saw the kindness that underscored everything Joshua did. More than that, she saw the love. Taking a deep breath, she began, drawing strength from the fingers that laced with hers.

"By the time I was five we were crammed into a one-bedroom apartment on Chicago's south side. Our view was an alley. I slept on a sofa in the living room, along with my sister. My brother slept on the floor. He would wake up screaming, terrified that the cockroaches were crawling over him."

A shudder ran through her. "God, it was awful."

"Surely there was someplace else..."

"Yes," she confirmed flatly. "There was someplace else, but it made that apartment seem like heaven. It was a room down the hall from a crack dealer. All of us in that one dreary room."

"Oh, baby," he murmured, his voice thick with emotion. "Your parents, didn't they...how could they..."

She recognized his struggle to grasp reasons that after all these years Garrett herself didn't understand. Parents were supposed to love. They were supposed to protect.

Hers hadn't. In a way they'd still been emotional children themselves, angry at life and totally self-indulgent.

Even though she had no valid explanation for the inexplicable, Garrett kept going, the words pouring out now. "After my father lost his job, he didn't give a damn about much of anything. My mother only cared about where her next bottle of booze was coming from. When I was eight, I was scavenging for food to keep my sister and brother alive. Every Christmas we'd get new clothes, cast-offs really, from the church down the street. I hated those clothes. I hated knowing that even the fanciest dress with the prettiest lace and ribbons could make me a laughing-stock because everyone would know that someone else wore it first. I wanted something new so badly it hurt. I did odd jobs, putting every extra penny I could get into a piggy bank, trying to save enough for a new pair of jeans. That's all I wanted, one damned pair of jeans." A bitter tear trickled down her cheek.

"Did you get them?"

"No. I came home from school one day and found my piggy bank shattered. My father tried to tell me we'd been robbed, but I knew better. Not even the most doped-up crack addict would bother robbing a dump like ours. Besides, there was a new bottle of liquor sitting on the table in front of my mother." She took a deep breath, then told him, "That was the day I vowed to get out. I stayed in school because it was the one place I could go and read. Books were my escape. The ones about the West were the best. The pioneers had such spirit, such determination. It seemed they could overcome anything. I wanted to be like that. I wanted to be strong."

Her voice dropped to a near whisper. "Then came Nicky."

"Casey's father?"

She nodded. "God, he was handsome. Thick dark hair. Midnight eyes. Strong features. He was gorgeous. And smart. And charming. He was twenty-two. I had just turned seventeen. We met in a restaurant, where I'd gotten a job as a waitress by lying about my age. He told me how beautiful I was. He bought me presents. He took me places I'd never been before, showed me a way of life I'd only imagined. I'd never felt so incredibly special in my entire life. It was just exactly like I'd read about in all the books. He was a real man, not like my father. Nicky was my knight in shining armor and I was being rescued. God, what a fool I was."

"You were seventeen years old, damn it."

"I should have known better, though. Men like that don't marry girls from the wrong side of the tracks."

"Men like me, you mean," Joshua said, his expression anguished.

She nodded. "Men like you," she agreed.

He winced at the accusation. She watched as he struggled for control. When he finally spoke, his voice was utterly calm. "What happened then?"

"I'm sure you can guess the rest."

"Tell me. I want to hear you say it."

It took every last bit of her bravery to admit, "Six months later I was pregnant and Nicky's parents were offering to buy me off."

She felt Joshua tense beside her, though his grip on her hand never wavered. His strength flowed into her. "What did he have to say about it?"

"He wouldn't see me. I was so sure they were keeping him away. God, it makes me sick when I think of the way I threw myself at him, begging him to talk to me, begging him…" Her voice caught on a sob. Drawing in a deep, calming breath, she went on. "When I finally realized that he'd never been in love with me, that I was only humiliating myself, I took their money and moved to Wyoming."

She lifted her gaze to Joshua's. "I came here with two things—a thousand dollars and the determination never again to be dependent on anyone. I've made a damned good life for Casey and for me."

"Yes, you have. You turned it around. Instead of letting what happened ruin your life, you made it the start of fulfilling your dream." He reached over and cupped her chin, turning her to face him. "Do you realize what kind of strength that took?"

She stared back at him unflinchingly and said quietly, "Do you?"

He held her gaze forever, then chuckled softly. "Message received."

"I hope so, Joshua. I truly hope so. I've worked damned hard for what I have. This beautiful place. My wonderful daughter. A rewarding job. I take none of it for granted and I won't give it up."

"I'm not asking you to give it up. I'm only asking you to share it."

"Oh, Joshua. It sounds so simple, but you know it's not that easy."

"Isn't it? Can't you do that much at least? Can't you let me become a part of the life you've created here? Marry me and let me replace all those painful memories with new ones, happy ones."

A beat passed, then another. When she didn't reply, he upped the ante. "I'll even move out here, if that's what it takes."

She wanted to believe in him, to grab at his offer to live here, but she could hear the reluctance in his voice. She wanted so much to accept his promise to be there for her always, but too many people had let her down. First her parents. Then Nicky. She didn't dare take a chance, didn't dare risk everything she had. And she couldn't ask him to give up a place he loved to live here with her. Finally she shook her head. "I can't. The past has a way of repeating itself."

"I'll never hurt you," he promised. "I won't let anyone hurt you again."

"I'm the only one who can do that."

"By keeping this wall around you?"

"Yes, if that's what it takes."

"And what about Casey?"

Garrett frowned at the question. "Casey is just fine."

"Is she? Then why does she have so many unanswered questions about her father? Have you ever told her what you just told me?"

"It would break her heart to know her father didn't want her."

"I'm sure she's already guessed as much. It's the uncertainty that really hurts her. Maybe that's none of my business, though. She's your daughter and you have to decide what she deserves to know. It is my business that the bond that was growing between Casey and me was deliberately broken. I will never understand why you felt the need to do that."

"Because she needs to know she shouldn't count on anyone."

"No," he said. "Casey knew she could trust me. In her heart, she believed in me from the very beginning. You're the one who planted the seed of distrust in her mind. Is that your way of protecting her? Will you let her grow into a lonely, frightened woman like her mother?"

As the harsh words sank in, Garrett shuddered. She thought of her lovely, beautiful, gregarious daughter living the kind of hard life she had chosen for herself.

As if he knew that he'd struck home, Joshua said, "Just think about it, Garrett. Think about how much you're robbing from Casey. Think of your daughter, if you won't think of yourself."

And then he walked away, leaving her with her bitter memories and her shattered dreams. Tonight, through Joshua's eyes, she had seen the two twisted somehow into one sad, painful vision of an endless, lonely future.

FOR WEEKS AFTER Joshua had gone, Garrett went around in a daze. She was moody and irritable. It was Red who finally snapped her out of her self-pity.

"Seems to me you're wasting time," he said, lounging in the big leather chair beside her desk.

They had spent the day going over reports and making decisions about marketing the cattle. There were fence repairs to be made, as well. Garrett's mind was on all of that, so it took a few minutes for her wandering attention to shift gears. "Sorry," she apologized. "I know I've been distracted lately."

"If you ask me, what you've been is lovesick. Ever since Joshua went back east, you've been looking like you've lost your last friend. Why don't you marry the man and put us all out of our misery."

"You know how I feel about marriage."

"Of course, I do. You told me every time I was fool enough to ask you. Course when it was me doing the asking, it made some sense. You never had a thing for me, the way you do for that greenhorn."

"Joshua is not a greenhorn," she defended automatically.

"About as close as a man can get. Never mind, though. That isn't the point. Why are you being so mule-headed, when you know it's what you want?"

"Habit," she said slowly, realizing as she said it that it was a good measure of the truth. The gut-wrenching fear that had kept other men at bay no longer applied when it came to Joshua. She knew in her heart he could be trusted. As he'd said, Casey had felt it instinctively and he'd proved it time and time again.

"A danged fool habit, if you ask me."

Her spirits suddenly began to soar. "It is, isn't it?" she murmured. Suddenly she was on her feet, flinging her arms around the startled foreman.

"Whoa," he said, setting her away from him. "You're hugging the wrong man."

"But you're the one who made me see what's been in front of my face all along. Now how the devil do I show Joshua that I'm ready to take the next step in our relationship?"

"You might consider calling him."

She thought of all the inventive ways he'd found to court her and shook her head. "Too boring."

"I doubt the man's looking for fireworks. A simple *I do* would probably suit him just fine."

She grinned as her plan began to take shape. "There's more than one way to get the message across."

Red's eyes narrowed. "You going to Florida? I could manage around here for a while, if that's what you've a mind to do."

"Thanks, I'd really appreciate it. I promise not to be gone long."

"Still say you could settle things mighty quick with a phone call. Let him foot the bill for the plane ride."

She grinned. "But what would the fun be in that? I'm going for something he'll remember for the rest of his life."

"Suzy, where the hell's the damned report?" Joshua shouted, prowling around the confines of his office. The wall-to-wall spread of glass facing the ocean did nothing to ease his claustrophobia or to soothe his frayed temper.

"Suzy?" he bellowed.

The door opened a crack and Cal stuck his head in. "Is it safe to come in or has this been declared a war zone?"

Joshua ran his fingers through his hair, then gestured Cal in. "I suppose Suzy would tell you to enter at your own risk."

"Having a bad day?"

"A bad month."

"Still no word from Garrett."

His gaze shot to Cal. "How did you know about that?"

Cal rolled his eyes. "You couldn't possibly be that dense. The phone lines between Wyoming and Ocala have been burning up since the minute you hightailed it away from the ranch with us. Marilou vowed if I didn't drive over here today to talk to you, she was coming herself. Having been the target of one of her well-intentioned campaigns, I thought I'd better save you the grief."

Joshua's irritation rose. "Are they all blaming this on me? I'm not the one who said no. I asked the woman to marry me, flat-out begged her, even if it meant having to give up all this and live in that godforsaken hellhole.

That sacrifice alone ought to tell you exactly how serious my intentions were."

"Were?"

"Are. Hell, I don't know anymore. The woman has the stubborn constitution of a mule. Maybe she's right. Maybe I am a lousy bet. Maybe all men are lousy bets."

"I take exception to that on my behalf and yours. You've avoided marriage for thirty-seven years. I seriously doubt that you're going to change your life-style on some whim. You must be in love."

"Tell that to Garrett."

"As a matter of fact, I have. So has Marilou. So has my grandmother. Apparently so has Casey. My grandmother says Casey's threatened to move to the main house if her mother doesn't marry you. She must be feeling pretty ganged up on by now."

Joshua sank into his chair. "See what I mean? The woman is hopeless."

"She loves you, though, right? There's no question in your mind about that?"

"She loves me. I'd bet my entire stock portfolio on it and you know how seriously I take that."

"Then get yourself back out there and wear her down. Prove it to her. Open an office and relocate your headquarters. Buy a house. Hell, buy some cattle."

Joshua's eyes widened in horror. "Are you out of your mind?"

Cal grinned. "I don't think so. Can you imagine a better wedding present for a woman who's always dreamed of owning her own spread? Put it in her name. Let her know that it'll be hers, no matter what happens between the two of you in the future, that she'll have her security and her independence."

"In other words, buy her."

"A cynic might see it that way. A romantic wouldn't."

"I have never, in my entire life, met anyone less romantic and more cynical than Garrett."

"Joshua, are you blind? Experience has taught her that. Give her new experiences. A little wining and dining. I thought you were an expert."

"She doesn't trust my motives."

"Because you haven't made the one, grand gesture that could convince her. Make the commitment to Wyoming and a life with her, a commitment she can see, and her doubts will vanish."

Joshua shook his head. "And if they don't?"

"If I know you, you'll turn the ranch into the biggest cattle operation in Wyoming and sell it at a tidy profit. You can't lose."

The idea began to hold a certain appeal. It was just quirky and dramatic enough to convince her. "Are you smart enough to dream this up on your own?"

Cal chuckled. "Are you kidding? No man thinks this deviously. Grandmother and Marilou say it's a surefire solution."

"I don't suppose your grandmother knows of a cattle operation that's on the market," he said wryly.

"As a matter of fact," Cal said, drawing some papers from his back pocket, "here's the prospectus on a place she thinks would be just about perfect. It came by express mail this morning."

As Joshua scanned the papers, his eyebrows rose in disbelief. "This is half the damned state."

"I think it's the part Grandmother doesn't already own."

"I don't suppose she has any advice on financing."

"Well..." He handed over a mortgage application with her banker.

"She doesn't miss a trick, does she?"

"You don't get to be one of the most powerful ranchers in the state by not going after what you want."

"Is there a message in there for me, as well?"

"Could be, my friend. Could be."

Joshua folded the papers and tucked them into his briefcase. "Suzy!"

The secretary peeked around the door, but refused to set foot in the room. "It's safe," he told her. "Book me on the first flight back to Cheyenne."

"Take my plane," Cal offered. "It's fueled and waiting."

"I hate your pilot. He still thinks he's flying war missions."

"He is fast."

Now that he'd made up his mind, speed was a consideration. And Cal's plane did have a phone in it. With any luck he could wrap up the negotiations for the land en route and present the deed to Garrett within a few hours after his arrival.

"Make sure there's plenty of Scotch on board," he told Cal. "I may need it, especially if there's another damned foot of snow on the ground."

"Done. Good luck, my friend."

"Something tells me I'm going to need it."

An hour later he was in the air and on the phone. The owner of the property was anxious to retire and get away to someplace warm. Joshua thought of his condo in Florida. If he was going to do this, there could be no looking back.

"I may have a solution for you there," he said. Twenty minutes later they had a deal.

"Damn, this better work," he muttered as the phone rang.

"Hey, boss, how's the weather up there?" Suzy inquired.

"Smooth. Anything happening I need to know about?"

"Does the fact that your office is filled with white roses mean anything?"

"White roses?" he repeated weakly.

"At last count there were twelve dozen and they're still coming. The florist seems a bit confused that he's not actually decorating a hotel ballroom for a wedding. Wait a sec. Someone new just came in and this one's not bearing flowers."

His head reeling, Joshua waited for more. The roses had to be from Garrett. No one else would understand the significance. But why so many? Why now?

"Boss, how do you feel about champagne?"

"Champagne?"

"A *lot* of champagne. Cases of champagne. Are we throwing a party that I didn't know about? Whoops, here comes a caterer."

Suddenly Joshua burst out laughing. The message was growing clearer by the minute. Somehow Garrett had finally realized that grand gestures and lavish gifts were only that, an attempt to please, an attempt to deliver a message that couldn't always be put into words.

"Boss, is this someone's idea of a joke?" Suzy asked.

"No, hon, I don't think it's a joke at all. I think it's deadly serious."

"Ohmigod!"

"What now?"

"There's a woman standing here in a wedding gown.

Boss, are you sure you didn't forget something really, really important?"

"Is she beautiful?"

"Breathtaking," Suzy confirmed. Her voice dropped. "She looks nervous, though."

"I can just imagine," he said with another chuckle.

"What should I tell her?"

"Tell her I'm negotiating a deal and I should be back in the office in an hour."

"An hour?" Suzy squeaked.

"Not even kamikaze Joe here can fly this jet any faster than that. Don't let her out of your sight, Suzy. And if there's not a preacher and a marriage license arranged for this surprise party, get 'em. Pull whatever strings you have to."

"Should I call Mr. and Mrs. Rivers and tell them to get over here?"

Still grinning, Joshua said, "Something tells me they'll already be on their way."

CHAPTER SIXTEEN

GARRETT FELT LIKE an idiot. From the minute she'd walked through the door to Joshua's office and had seen what twenty-five dozen roses looked like when amassed in one place, she wondered if she'd gone just the tiniest bit overboard. Mrs. McDonald, however, had urged her to go for broke. Over Garrett's objections, she had insisted on footing the bill, claiming that she'd foolishly missed out on her own daughter's wedding and had every right to make up for it with Garrett's. She'd taken over the arrangements with the logistical expertise of a military commander and the enthusiasm of a mother of the bride. Garrett hadn't had the heart to slow her down.

Now, though, with cases of champagne being opened and trays of food being displayed on any available surface, all adding to a distinct air of unreality, she wondered if she should have set some limits. The wide-eyed expression on Joshua's secretary's face confirmed that nothing quite like this had ever happened in this office before. Not that that was particularly astonishing, she conceded. Weddings didn't usually take the groom totally by surprise.

If there was a groom, she thought, suddenly filled with apprehension. What if Joshua had lost patience with her? What if he'd decided to get on with a life that didn't include her? Or, almost as bad, what if he was out of town?

"You must be looking for Mr. Ames," the secretary

said, following her hushed phone conversation. Though there was a definite twinkle in her eyes, her expression was outwardly impassive, as if brides turned up on the doorstep every day looking for her boss. "I'm Suzy Winters. You must be Garrett."

"How did you know?"

"I can't think of another woman he knows who would dare this. Can I help you?"

Garrett swallowed hard. "Is he here?" she asked, disgusted at the squeak in her voice. She certainly didn't sound very daring.

"Afraid not. He's at a meeting away from the office. He should be back within the hour, though. Could I get you something while you wait? Champagne, maybe?" A smile dashed across her lips, then retreated behind her businesslike facade.

Garrett chuckled. "It's a little too much, isn't it?"

"With a man as dense as my boss can be, you might as well hedge your bets."

Sensing an ally at once, Garrett nodded. "That was my thinking, too. Subtlety doesn't exactly sink in with him. Half the time I couldn't even get through to him with a direct hit."

"Are you expecting a minister? A few guests?"

Garrett nodded. "I told everyone to be here at three. I figured that would give me time to revive Joshua if he fainted dead away. It would also give me time to call it off if he told me to get lost."

"Somehow I don't think that's going to be his response. How'd you do it, by the way?"

"Do it?"

"Lasso him? Women all over the world have been trying for years. He's been resistant."

"I haven't the vaguest idea," she admitted, sinking down in a chair, the full skirt of her wedding gown spreading out around her. Mrs. Mac had personally picked out the dress, insisting that even an unorthodox wedding should observe some traditions. She'd spent an hour at the hotel fussing over the lace until Garrett had been ready to snap her head off.

Just then the florist, still clucking over the lack of suitable places to display his exorbitantly priced roses, came out of Joshua's office. He practically clicked his heels together as he presented her with his bill. Garrett looked at the total and swallowed a gasp. As she reached in her purse for her credit card, Suzy spoke up.

"Let me put them on Mr. Ames's account."

"One surprise today is probably enough," Garrett said, handing over the card. "I don't want the man to have a heart attack. Besides, my boss is taking care of everything and loving every minute of it. The woman is a closet romantic. I had no idea until I mentioned my plan to her."

"Given half a chance, I think most women are."

Moments later, inside Joshua's office, Garrett signed off on the bills for the catering and the champagne. Though the amount staggered her, it was mere pocket change to Mrs. McDonald. Garrett was uneasy with the sense of obligation implied, but for once in her life it didn't seem to matter. The only thing that mattered was showing Joshua how much she loved him. If it took a dramatic, outrageous gesture like this to do it, it was well worth the expense and the obligation.

She explored the office, studying what she could still see of the modern Scandinavian furniture. The crisp, clean lines and functional designs fit Joshua's no-nonsense personality. Buried under a sea of fragrant roses, however, the room had taken on a decidedly sensual personality that also fit. Hoping to calm her jittery nerves, she inexpertly popped the cork on a bottle of champagne sending a fizz of bubbles into the air.

The champagne tickled her nose, but did nothing for her nerves. She glanced at her watch. It was nearly three now. What if he didn't get back before the minister and the guests started arriving? Would he ever forgive her for putting him in the awkward position of having to give her his answer in front of witnesses, especially if that answer turned out to be no?

She heard the outer door open then close, and prayed it was Joshua. She clenched her hands together and waited. And waited. Maybe he'd been warned by the obviously loyal Suzy and had taken off again. Garrett opened the office door and peeked. A tall, red-faced man dressed in a suit and cowboy boots stood toe-to-toe with the diminutive Suzy.

"Where the devil is he?" he demanded, running his hand through a shock of prematurely white hair. "I've had this appointment for six weeks. First he was gallivanting around the country..."

"He was working on a client's account in Wyoming," Suzy corrected firmly.

"Whatever. All I know is I have a three o'clock appointment with the man and it's just about that now. Where the devil is he?"

"I've had to cancel all of his appointments for this afternoon, Mr. Schaeffer. I'm terribly sorry. I know Mr. Ames will want to see you as soon as possible, but something came up today that couldn't be helped. I did try to call you before you left your office to save you the trip. Perhaps, if you had checked for messages..."

Garrett grinned at the deft way in which Suzy had turned things around so that the man no longer seemed quite as certain that Joshua was the one at fault. His sunburned face turned one shade redder.

"I ain't gonna do business with a man I can't count on," he blustered. "I don't care if the recommendation came from the good Lord himself, it's no way to run an operation."

Garrett sensed that Mr. Schaeffer was about to bolt and it would be all her fault. Since she had no idea how valuable a client he might become, she threw open the door and stepped into the foyer. Startled, the man took a step back, his shrewd gaze taking in the wedding gown with an air of disbelief.

"Well, I'll be damned," he said softly. "Ain't you the prettiest little thing."

"Thank you," Garrett said, reassured by the compliment. Mrs. Mac had said the same thing, but she hadn't trusted it coming from her biased lips. "Forgive me for eavesdropping, Mr. Schaeffer, but I couldn't help overhearing about your cancelled appointment. I'm afraid it's my fault."

"How's that?" he said, obviously intrigued.

Garrett had met enough mavericks in her time to recognize one. Whatever business acumen Mr. Schaeffer might have, he was at heart an adventurer.

"I'm afraid I showed up without warning," she said, playing to that spirit of adventure.

"You running away from a wedding or something?"

"Actually, I'm here for a wedding."

"Here?" he said, looking around the reception area.

She gestured toward Joshua's office. "In there actually. I'm sure Mr. Ames would have given you more advance notice about changing your appointment, but he wasn't aware of my plans."

His gaze narrowed suspiciously. "You're gonna marry the man and he don't even know it."

She smiled. "That's about it."

"Well, I'll be. Mind if I stick around to see how things turn out? This'll sure be something I can tell the missus about. She thinks business is dull."

"As long as you don't hold it against Joshua for cancelling your appointment."

"Hell, no. In fact, if those contracts were ready, I'd sign 'em this minute. I'm gonna enjoy doing business with the two of you."

"Actually, I don't work here. I'm a cattle rancher."

"Well, don't that beat all. So am I. How about we just go inside and talk till that fiancé of yours gets here."

Roswell Schaeffer had a lot to say and talking made him thirsty. Garrett was very glad she'd ordered lots of champagne. In fact, she was beginning to feel less edgy by the time they'd started on the second bottle. Mr. Schaeffer was actually a very funny man. Or maybe it was the champagne. Her blood seemed to be singing with it. She was just thinking how agreeable the sensation was, when the door opened.

"What's this?" Joshua inquired.

To her amazement, his attention seemed to be riveted on Roswell Schaeffer, not the roses, the food or her wedding gown. "I can explain," she said.

"Could we have a little privacy?" Joshua asked the other man, never once looking at Garrett.

Mr. Schaeffer grumbled about missing out on all the fun, but he got to his feet and headed for the door.

"Please don't leave," Garrett said, suddenly feeling the need for an ally in case this didn't go at all the way she planned.

"I'll be waiting just outside," he promised her, then came back and leaned down to whisper, "A man'd have to be a fool to turn you down."

Her lips curved into a shaky smile. "Thanks."

When he'd gone, Joshua finally looked at her. At once his eyes darkened with familiar desire. "You look… stunning," he said in a low voice that slid over her nerves and set them aflame.

Clenching her hands together, she stared at him. "You're not surprised, are you?"

He shook his head. "I was on the phone with Suzy when you made your grand entrance. I was terrified you'd change your mind and leave before I could get back."

"Where were you?"

"In a plane."

"In the air?" she said incredulously.

He nodded. "Fortunately it was Cal's plane. The pilot turned it around."

"But where were you going? Was there some sort of emergency? Mr. Schaeffer had an appointment. Suzy said she'd cancelled it, that she'd had to cancel all of them. I thought it was because of me."

"No. Actually, something came up earlier."

"If it was that important, though, why did you come back?"

"I couldn't very well miss my own wedding, could I?" he said, smiling.

"We could postpone it," she offered, working to hide her disappointment. "I mean, if you were going someplace really important, I wouldn't want to interfere."

"Oh no you don't. I'm not about to risk having you change your mind again. Besides, how long can it take to say *I do?* We can go together."

"Combine your business with a honeymoon? Are you sure you won't mind?"

"Sweetheart, there is nothing, *nothing*, more important to me than marrying you. I'd almost given up on talking you into it. What finally convinced you?"

"I realized that I'd just gotten into the habit of saying no all these years and that all the things I'd worried about for so long didn't apply to the way we feel about each other. I spent too many years without anyone in my life. It didn't seem to matter before because I had Casey and Mrs. Mac and Red, but Red made me see that they would never be able to substitute for what you and I have together. I couldn't stand the thought of losing that feeling again, not just because I was being too bullheaded to take a chance."

"I owe this to Red, huh?"

She grinned at the note of possessiveness that had crept into his voice. "Maybe you'll be a little more civil next time you run into him."

"If this works out the way I want it to, I won't be running into him all that often."

Garrett's heartbeat slowed. Surely after all that he'd said, he didn't intend to ask her to leave Wyoming after all. As much as she loved him, she wasn't sure she could bear that. "What do you mean?" she asked.

Joshua's fingers brushed across her lips. "Stop frowning. It's not what you think."

"What do you mean, then?"

He drew a bundle of papers from his pocket and handed them to her.

"What's this?"

"Your wedding present. I was on my way to Wyoming to finalize the deal when Suzy told me you were here."

Garrett spread open the contract and started to read. "It's a ranch," she breathed softly.

"It's yours, if you want it. In your name, no matter what happens in the future."

Tears spilled down her cheeks as she threw her arms around him. "Thank you," she whispered as his arms closed around her.

"No, thank you," he said solemnly.

"But I haven't done anything for you."

"You came here. You arranged this wedding. That's the most precious gift you could have given me. Your trust."

She lifted shining eyes to meet his. "We're going to make it work, aren't we?"

"If you can figure out a way to warm up the winters in Wyoming, we'll do just fine."

She grinned at him, fitting her body provocatively to his. "Oh, I have a few ideas about that."

She heard his breath catch and felt his pulse begin to race. "Is it working?" she murmured.

"Working? In another ten seconds I'm going to have to adjust the air-conditioning or embarrass us both in front of our wedding guests."

Just then the intercom on his desk buzzed. Keeping Garrett pressed close, Joshua leaned over and punched the speaker button. "This better be important, Suzy."

"There are half a dozen people out here wondering if they should go or stay."

His gaze dropped until it locked with hers. "What do you think? Want to hold out for a church wedding with all the trimmings?"

Garrett glanced around the room. "That would be far too ordinary for the two of us, don't you think?"

"You're turning into a regular little daredevil on me, aren't you?"

She nodded slowly. "I think I like it, too. I never felt safe enough before. You've given me that."

"Then you want to go for it now?"

"Let's do it."

There were sparks of delighted amusement in Joshua's eyes as he gathered her into his arms and planted a kiss on her lips. "We are going to have one hell of an adventure, sweetheart. I promise you that."

Unconcerned with the sudden arrival of Casey, Mrs. Mac, Cal and Marilou, Garrett sealed their bargain with a sizzling kiss of her own. "I can't wait," she murmured in his ear.

"That's an even better vow than *I do*," he told her, laughing. "I can't wait, either."

"Then let's get on with it," Casey said impatiently. She tugged on the minister's hand. "Do it quickly, before they change their minds."

Garrett reached out a hand to her daughter, whose eyes were shining with happiness. "Would you be my maid of honor, baby?"

"Oh, wow," Casey breathed, taking her place beside Garrett. She leaned around her mother and winked at Joshua. "I told you we could pull it off."

He winked back and Garrett's heart sang. This was the real gift he was giving her, this intangible feeling of love and family and commitment. Even if the deal on the ranch were to fall through tomorrow, she finally knew deep in her heart she would have everything she'd ever dreamed of.

* * * * *

SEDUCE ME, COWBOY

Maisey Yates

To the whole Harlequin team.
This is the best job ever.
Thank you for letting me do it.

CHAPTER ONE

HAYLEY THOMPSON WAS a good girl. In all the ways that phrase applied. The kind of girl every mother wished her son would bring home for Sunday dinner.

Of course, the mothers of Copper Ridge were much more enthusiastic about Hayley than their sons were, but that had never been a problem. She had never really tried dating, anyway. Dates were the least of her problems.

She was more worried about the constant feeling that she was under a microscope. That she was a trained seal, sitting behind the desk in the church office exactly as one might expect from a small-town pastor's daughter—who also happened to be the church secretary.

And what did she have to show for being so good? Absolutely nothing.

Meanwhile, her older brother had gone out into the world and done whatever he wanted. He'd broken every rule. Run away from home. Gotten married, gotten divorced. Come back home and opened a bar in the same town where his father preached sermons. All while Hayley had stayed and behaved herself. Done everything that was expected of her.

Ace was the prodigal son. He hadn't just received forgiveness for his transgressions. He'd been rewarded. He had so many things well-behaved Hayley wanted and didn't have.

He'd found love again in his wife, Sierra. They had children. The doting attention of Hayley's parents—a side effect of being the first to supply grandchildren, she felt—while Hayley had…

Well, nothing.

Nothing but a future as a very well-behaved spinster.

That was why she was here now. Clutching a newspaper in her hand until it was wrinkled tight. She hadn't even known people still put ads in the paper for job listings, but while she'd been sitting in The Grind yesterday on Copper Ridge's main street, watching people go by and feeling a strange sense of being untethered, she'd grabbed the local paper.

That had led her to the job listings. And seeing as she was unemployed for the first time since she was sixteen years old, she'd read them.

Every single one of them had been submitted by people she knew. Businesses she'd grown up patronizing, or businesses owned by people she knew from her dad's congregation. And if she got a job somewhere like that, she might as well have stayed on at the church.

Except for one listing. Assistant to Jonathan Bear, owner of Gray Bear Construction. The job was for him personally, but would also entail clerical work for his company and some work around his home.

She didn't know anything about the company. She'd never had a house built, after all. Neither had her mother and father. And she'd never heard his name before, and was reasonably sure she'd never seen him at church.

She wanted that distance.

Familiar, nagging guilt gnawed at the edges of her heart. Her parents were good people. They loved her very much. And she loved them. But she felt like a beloved goldfish. With people watching her every move and tapping on the glass. Plus, the bowl was restricting, when she was well aware there was an entire ocean out there.

Step one in her plan for independence had been to acquire her own apartment. Cassie Caldwell, owner of The Grind, and her husband, Jake, had moved out of the space above the coffee shop a while ago. Happily, it had been vacant and ready to rent, and Hayley had taken advantage of that. So, with the money she'd saved up, she'd moved into that place. And then, after hoarding a few months' worth of rent, she had finally worked up the courage to quit.

Her father had been... She wouldn't go so far as to say he'd been disappointed. John Thompson never had a harsh word for anyone. He was all kind eyes and deep conviction. The type of goodness Hayley could only marvel at, that made her feel as though she could never quite measure up.

But she could tell her father had been confused. And she hadn't been able to explain herself, not fully. Because she didn't want either of her parents to know that ultimately, this little journey of independence would lead straight out of Copper Ridge.

She had to get out of the fishbowl. She needed people to stop tapping on her glass.

Virtue wasn't its own reward. For years she'd believed it would be. But then...suddenly, watching Ace at the dinner table at her parents' house, with his family, she'd realized the strange knot in her stomach wasn't anger over his abandonment, over the way he'd embarrassed their parents with his behavior.

It was envy.

Envy of all he had, of his freedom. Well, this was her

chance to have some of that for herself, and she couldn't do it with everyone watching.

She took a deep breath and regarded the house in front of her. If she didn't know it was the home and office of the owner of Gray Bear Construction, she would be tempted to assume it was some kind of resort.

The expansive front porch was made entirely out of logs, stained with a glossy, honey-colored sheen that caught the light and made the place look like it was glowing. The green metal roof was designed to withstand harsh weather—which down in town by the beach wasn't much of an issue. But a few miles inland, here in the mountains, she could imagine there was snow in winter.

She wondered if she would need chains for her car. But she supposed she'd cross that bridge when she came to it. It was early spring, and she didn't even have the job yet.

Getting the job, and keeping it through winter, was only a pipe dream at this point.

She took a deep breath and started up the path, the bark-laden ground soft beneath her feet. She inhaled deeply, the sharp scent of pine filling her lungs. It was cool beneath the trees, and she wrapped her arms around herself as she walked up the steps and made her way to the front door.

She knocked before she had a chance to rethink her actions, and then she waited.

She was just about to knock again when she heard footsteps. She quickly put her hand down at her side. Then lifted it again, brushing her hair out of her face. Then she clasped her hands in front of her, then put them back at her sides again. Then she decided to hold them in front of her again.

She had just settled on that position when the door jerked open.

She had rehearsed her opening remarks. Had practiced making a natural smile in the mirror—which was easy after so many years manning the front desk of a church—but all that disappeared completely when she looked at the man standing in front of her.

He was... Well, he was nothing like she'd expected, which left her grappling for what exactly she had been expecting. Somebody older. Certainly not somebody who towered over her like a redwood.

Jonathan Bear wasn't someone you could anticipate.

His dark, glittering eyes assessed her; his mouth pressed into a thin line. His black hair was tied back, but it was impossible for her to tell just how long it was from where she stood.

"Who are you?" he asked, his tone uncompromising.

"I'm here to interview for the assistant position. Were you expecting someone else?" Her stomach twisted with anxiety. He wasn't what she had expected, and now she was wondering if she was what *he* had expected. Maybe he wanted somebody older, with more qualifications. Or somebody more... Well, sexy secretary than former church secretary.

Though, she looked very nice in this twin set and pencil skirt, if she said so herself.

"No," he said, moving away from the door. "Come in."

"Oh," she said, scampering to follow his direction.

"The office is upstairs," he said, taking great strides through the entryway and heading toward a massive curved staircase.

She found herself taking very quick steps to try and keep up with him. And it was difficult to do that when she was distracted by the beauty of the house. She was trying to take in all the details as she trailed behind him up the stairs, her low heels clicking on the hardwood.

"I'm Hayley Thompson," she said, "which I know the résumé said, but you didn't know who I was... So..."

"We're the only two people here," he said, looking back at her, lifting one dark brow. "So knowing your name isn't really that important, is it?"

She couldn't tell if he was joking. She laughed nervously, and it got her no response at all. So then she was concerned she had miscalculated.

They reached the top of the stairs, and she followed him down a long hallway, the sound of her steps dampened now by a long carpet runner the colors of the nature that surrounded them. Brown, forest green and a red that reminded her of cranberries.

The house smelled new. Which was maybe a strange observation to make, but the scent of wood lingered in the air, and something that reminded her of paint.

"How long have you lived here?" she asked, more comfortable with polite conversation than contending with silence.

"Just moved in last month," he said. "One of our designs. You might have guessed, this is what Gray Bear does. Custom homes. That's our specialty. And since my construction company merged with Grayson Design, we're doing design as well as construction."

"How many people can buy places like this?" she asked, turning in a circle while she walked, daunted by the amount of house they had left behind them, and the amount that was still before them.

"You would be surprised. For a lot of our clients these are only vacation homes. Escapes to the coast and to the mountains. Mostly, we work on the Oregon coast, but we make exceptions for some of the higher-paying clientele."

"That's...kind of amazing. I mean, something of this scale right here in Copper Ridge. Or I guess, technically, we're outside the city limits."

"Still the same zip code," he said, lifting a shoulder.

He took hold of two sliding double doors fashioned to look like barn doors and slid them open, revealing a huge office space with floor-to-ceiling windows and a view that made her jaw drop.

The sheer immensity of the mountains spread before them was incredible on its own. But beyond that, she could make out the faint gray of the ocean, whitecapped waves and jagged rocks rising out of the surf.

"The best of everything," he said. "Sky, mountains, ocean. That kind of sums up the company. Now that you know about us, you can tell me why I should hire you."

"I want the job," she said, her tone hesitant. As soon as she said the words, she realized how ridiculous they were. Everybody who interviewed for this position would want the job. "I was working as a secretary for my father's... business," she said, feeling guilty about fudging a little bit on her résumé. But she hadn't really wanted to say she was working at her father's church, because... Well, she just wanted to come in at a slightly more neutral position.

"You were working for your family?"

"Yes," she said.

He crossed his arms, and she felt slightly intimidated. He was the largest man she'd ever seen. At least, he felt large. Something about all the height and muscles and presence combined.

"We're going to have to get one thing straight right now, Hayley. I'm not your daddy. So if you're used to a kind and gentle working environment where you get a lot of chances because firing you would make it awkward around the holidays, this might take some adjustment for you. I'm damned hard to please. And I'm not a very nice boss. There's a lot of work to do around here. I hate paperwork, and I don't want to have to do any form twice. If you make mistakes and I have to sit at that desk longer as a result, you're fired. If I've hired you to make things easier between myself and my clients, and something you do makes it harder, you're fired. If you pass on a call to me that I shouldn't have to take, you're fired."

She nodded, wishing she had a notepad, not because she was ever going to forget what he'd said, but so she could underscore the fact that she was paying attention. "Anything else?"

"Yeah," he said, a slight smile curving his lips. "You're also fired if you fuck up my coffee."

This was a mistake. Jonathan Bear was absolutely certain of it. But he had earned millions making mistakes, so what was one more? Nobody else had responded to his ad.

Except for this pale, strange little creature who looked barely twenty and wore the outfit of an eighty-year-old woman.

She was... Well, she wasn't the kind of formidable woman who could stand up to the rigors of working with him.

His sister, Rebecca, would say—with absolutely no tact at all—that he sucked as a boss. And maybe she was right, but he didn't really care. He was busy, and right now he hated most of what he was busy with.

There was irony in that, he knew. He had worked hard all his life. While a lot of his friends had sought solace and oblivion in drugs and alcohol, Jonathan had figured it was best to sweat the poison right out.

He'd gotten a job on a construction site when he was fifteen, and learned his trade. He'd gotten to where he was faster, better than most of the men around him. By the time he was twenty, he had been doing serious custom work on the more upscale custom homes he'd built with West Construction.

But he wanted more. There was a cap on what he could make with that company, and he didn't like a ceiling. He wanted open skies and the freedom to go as high, as fast as he wanted. So he could amass so much it could never be taken from him.

So he'd risked striking out on his own. No one had believed a kid from the wrong side of the tracks could compete with West. But Jonathan had courted business across city and county lines. And created a reputation beyond Copper Ridge so that when people came looking to build retirement homes or vacation properties, his was the name they knew.

He had built everything he had, brick by brick. In a strictly literal sense in some cases.

And every brick built a stronger wall against all the things he had left behind. Poverty, uncertainty, the lack of respect paid to a man in his circumstances.

Then six months ago, Joshua Grayson had approached him. Originally from Copper Ridge, the man had been looking for a foothold back in town after years in Seattle. Faith Grayson, Joshua's sister was quickly becoming the most sought after architect in the Pacific Northwest. But the siblings had decided it was time to bring the business back home in order to be closer to their parents.

And so Joshua asked Jonathan if he would consider

bringing design in-house, making Bear Construction into Gray Bear.

This gave Jonathan reach into urban areas, into Seattle. Had him managing remote crews and dealing with many projects at one time. And it had pushed him straight out of the building game in many ways. He had turned into a desk drone. And while his bank account had grown astronomically, he was quite a ways from the life he thought he'd live after reaching this point.

Except the house. The house was finally finished. Finally, he was living in one of the places he'd built.

Finally, Jonathan Bear, that poor Indian kid who wasn't worth anything to anyone, bastard son of the biggest bastard in town, had his house on the side of the mountain and more money than he would ever be able to spend.

And he was bored out of his mind.

Boredom, it turned out, worked him into a hell of a temper. He had a feeling Hayley Thompson wasn't strong enough to stand up to that. But he expected to go through a few assistants before he found one who could handle it. She might as well be number one.

"You've got the job," he said. "You can start tomorrow."

Her eyes widened, and he noticed they were a strange shade of blue. Gray in some lights, shot through with a dark, velvet navy that reminded him of the ocean before a storm. It made him wonder if there was some hidden strength there.

They would both find out.

"I got the job? Just like that?"

"Getting the job was always going to be the easy part. It's keeping the job that might be tricky. My list of reasons to hire you are short—you showed up. The list of reasons I have for why I might fire you is much longer."

"You're not very reassuring," she said, her lips tilting down in a slight frown.

He laughed. "If you want to go back and work for your daddy, do that. I'm not going to call you. But maybe you'll appreciate my ways later. Other jobs will seem easy after this one."

She just looked at him, her jaw firmly set, her petite body rigid with determination. "What time do you want me here?"

"Seven o'clock. Don't be late. Or else…"

"You'll fire me. I've got the theme."

"Excellent. Hayley Thompson, you've got yourself a job."

CHAPTER TWO

HAYLEY SCRUBBED HER face as she walked into The Grind through the private entrance from her upstairs apartment. It was early. But she wanted to make sure she wasn't late to work.

On account of all the firing talk.

"Good morning," Cassie said from behind the counter, smiling cheerfully. Hayley wondered if Cassie was really thrilled to be at work this early in the morning. Hayley knew all about presenting a cheerful face to anyone who might walk in the door.

You couldn't have a bad day when you worked at the church.

"I need coffee," Hayley said, not bothering to force a grin. She wasn't at work yet. She paused. "Do you know Jonathan Bear?"

Cassie gave her a questioning look. "Yes, I'm friends with his sister, Rebecca. She owns the store across the street."

"Right," Hayley said, frowning. "I don't think I've ever met her. But I've seen her around town."

Hayley was a few years younger than Cassie, and probably a bit younger than Rebecca, as well, which meant they had never been in classes together at school, and had never shared groups of friends. Not that Hayley had much in the way of friends. People tended to fear the pastor's daughter would put a damper on things.

No one had tested the theory.

"So yes, I know Jonathan in passing. He's… Well, he's not very friendly." Cassie laughed. "Why?"

"He just hired me."

Cassie's expression contorted into one of horror and Hayley saw her start to backpedal. "He's probably fine. It's just that he's very protective of Rebecca because he raised her, you know, and all that. And she had her accident, and had to have a lot of medical procedures done… So my perception of him is based entirely on that. I'm sure he's a great boss."

"No," Hayley said, "you were right the first time. He's a grumpy cuss. Do you have any idea what kind of coffee he drinks?"

Cassie frowned, a small notch appearing between her brows. "He doesn't come in that often. But when he does I think he gets a dark roast, large, black, no sugar, with a double shot of espresso."

"How do you remember that?"

"It's my job. And there are a lot of people I know by drink and not by name."

"Well, I will take one of those for him. And hope that it's still hot by the time I get up the mountain."

"Okay. And a coffee for you with room for cream?"

"Yes," Hayley said. "I don't consider my morning caffeination ritual a punishment like some people seem to."

"Hey," Cassie said, "some people just like their coffee unadulterated. But I am not one of them. I feel you."

Hayley paid for her order and made her way to the back of the store, looking around at the warm, quaint surroundings. Locals had filed in and were filling up the tables, reading their papers, opening laptops and dropping off bags and coats to secure the coveted positions in the tiny coffee shop.

Then a line began to form, and Hayley was grateful she had come as early as she had.

A moment later, her order was ready. Popping the lid off her cup at the cream and sugar station, she gave herself a generous helping of both. She walked back out the way she had come in, going to her car, which was parked behind the building in her reserved space.

She got inside, wishing she'd warmed up the vehicle before placing her order. It wasn't too cold this morning, but she could see her breath in the damp air. She positioned both cups of coffee in the cup holders of her old Civic, and then headed to the main road, which was void of traffic—and would remain that way for the entire day.

She liked the pace of Copper Ridge, she really did. Liked the fact that she knew so many people, that people waved and smiled when she walked by. Liked that there were no traffic lights, and that you rarely had to wait for more than one car at a four-way stop.

She loved the mountains, and she loved the ocean.

But she knew there were things beyond this place, too. And she wanted to see them.

Needed to see them.

She thought about all those places as she drove along the winding road to Jonathan Bear's house. She had the vague thought that if she went to London or Paris, if she looked at the Eiffel Tower or Big Ben, structures so old and lasting—structures that had been there for centuries— maybe she would learn something about herself.

Maybe she would find what she couldn't identify here.

Maybe she would find the cure for the elusive ache in her chest when she saw Ace with Sierra and their kids.

Would find the freedom to be herself—whoever that might be. To flirt and date, and maybe drink a beer. To escape the confines that so rigidly held her.

Even driving out of town this morning, instead of to the church, was strange. Usually, she felt as though she were moving through the grooves of a well-worn track. There were certain places she went in town—her parents' home, the church, the grocery store, The Grind, her brother's brewery and restaurant, but never his bar—and she rarely deviated from that routine.

She supposed this drive would become routine soon enough.

She pulled up to the front of the house, experiencing a sharp sense of déjà vu as she walked up to the front porch to knock again. Except this time her stomach twisted with an even greater sense of trepidation. Not because Jonathan Bear was an unknown, but because she knew a little bit about him now. And what she knew terrified her.

The door jerked open before she could pound against it. "Just come in next time," he said.

"Oh."

"During business hours. I was expecting you."

"Expecting me to be late?" she asked, holding out his cup of coffee.

He arched a dark brow. "Maybe." He tilted his head to the side. "What's that?"

"Probably coffee." She didn't know why she was being anything other than straightforward and sweet. He'd made it very clear that he had exacting standards. Likely, he wanted his assistant to fulfill his every whim before it even occurred to him, and to do so with a smile. Likely, he didn't want his assistant to sass him, even lightly.

Except, something niggled at her, telling her he wouldn't respect her at all if she acted like a doormat. She was good at reading people. It was a happy side effect of being quiet. Of having few friends, of being an observer. Of spending years behind the church desk, not sure who might walk through the door seeking help. That experience had taught Hayley not only kindness, but also discernment.

And that was why she chose to follow her instincts with Jonathan.

"It's probably coffee?" he asked, taking the cup from her, anyway.

"Yes," she returned. "Probably."

He turned away from her, heading toward the stairs, but she noticed that he took the lid off the cup and examined the contents. She smiled as she followed him up the stairs to the office.

The doors were already open, the computer that faced the windows fired up. There were papers everywhere. And pens sat across nearly every surface.

"Why so many pens?" she asked.

"If I have to stop and look for one I waste an awful lot of time cussing."

"Fair enough."

"I have to go outside and take care of the horses, but I want you to go through that stack of invoices and enter all the information into the spreadsheet on the computer. Can you do that?"

"Spreadsheets are my specialty. You have horses?"

He nodded. "This is kind of a ranch."

"Oh," she said. "I didn't realize."

"No reason you should." Then he turned, grabbing a black cowboy hat off a hook and putting it firmly on his head. "I'll be back in a couple of hours. And I'm going to want more coffee. The machine is downstairs in the kitchen. Should be pretty easy. Probably."

Then he brushed his fingertips against the brim of his hat, nodding slightly before walking out, leaving her alone.

When he left, something in her chest loosened, eased. She hadn't realized just how tense she'd felt in his presence.

She took a deep breath, sitting down at the desk in front of the computer, eyeing the healthy stack of papers to her left. Then she looked over the monitor to the view below. This wouldn't be so bad. He wasn't here looking over her shoulder, barking orders. And really, in terms of work space, this office could hardly be beat.

Maybe this job wouldn't be so bad, after all.

BY THE TIME Jonathan made a run to town after finishing up with the horses, it was past lunchtime. So he brought food from the Crab Shanty and hoped his new assistant didn't have a horrible allergy to seafood.

He probably should have checked. He wasn't really used to considering other people. And he couldn't say he was looking forward to getting used to it. But he would rather she didn't die. At least, not while at work.

He held tightly to the white bag of food as he made his way to the office. Her back was to the door, her head bent low over a stack of papers, one hand poised on the mouse.

He set the bag down loudly on the table by the doorway, then deposited his keys there, too. He hung his hat on the hook. "Hungry?"

Her head popped up, her eyes wide. "Oh, I didn't hear you come in. You scared me. You should have announced yourself or something."

"I just did. I said, 'hungry?' I mean, I could have said I'm here, but how is that any different?"

She shook her head. "I don't have an answer to that."

"Great. I have fish."

"What kind?"

"Fried kind."

"I approve."

He sighed in mock relief. "Good. Because if you didn't, I don't know how I would live with myself. I would have had to eat both of these." He opened the bag, taking out two cartons and two cans of Coke.

He sat in the chair in front of the table he used for drawing plans, then held her portion toward her.

She made a funny face, then accepted the offered lunch. "Is one of the Cokes for me, too?"

"Sure," he said, sliding a can at her.

She blinked, then took the can.

"What?"

She shook her head. "Nothing."

"You expected me to hand everything to you, didn't you?"

She shook her head. "No. Well, maybe. But, I'm sorry. I don't work with my father anymore, as you have mentioned more than once."

"No," he said, "you don't. And this isn't a church. Though—" he took a french fry out of the box and bit it "—this is pretty close to a religious experience." He picked up one of the thoughtfully included napkins and wiped his fingers before popping the top on the Coke can.

"How did you know I worked at the church?" she asked.

"I pay attention. And I definitely looked at the address you included on your form. Also, I know your brother. Or rather, I know of him. My sister is engaged to his brother-in-law. I might not be chummy with him, but I know his dad is the pastor. And that he has a younger sister."

She looked crestfallen. "I didn't realize you knew my brother."

"Is that a problem?"

"I was trying to get a job based on my own merit. Not on family connections. And frankly, I can't find anyone who is not connected to my family in some way in this town. My father knows the saints, my brother knows the sinners."

"Are you calling me a sinner?"

She picked gingerly at a piece of fish. "All have sinned and so forth."

"That isn't what you meant."

She suddenly became very interested in her coleslaw, prodding it with her plastic fork.

"How is it you know I'm a sinner?" he asked, not intending to let her off the hook, because this was just so fun. Hell, he'd gone and hired himself a church secretary, so might as well play with her a little bit.

"I didn't mean that," she insisted, her cheeks turning pink. He couldn't remember the last time he'd seen a woman blush.

"Well, if it helps at all, I don't know your brother well. I just buy alcohol from him on the weekends. But you're right. I am a sinner, Hayley."

She looked up at him then. The shock reflected in those stormy eyes touched him down deep. Made his stomach feel tight, made his blood feel hot. All right, he needed to get a handle on himself. Because that was not the kind of fun he was going to have with the church secretary he had hired. No way.

Jonathan Bear was a ruthless bastard; that fact could not be disputed. He had learned to look out for himself at an early age, because no one else would. Not his father. Certainly not his mother, who had taken off when he was a teenager, leaving him with a younger sister to raise. And most definitely not anyone in town.

But, even he had a conscience.

In theory, anyway.

"Good to know. I mean, since we're getting to know each other, I guess."

They ate in relative silence after that. Jonathan took that opportunity to check messages on his phone. A damn smartphone. This was what he had come to. Used to be that if he wanted to spend time alone he could unplug and go out on his horse easily enough. Now, he could still do that, but his business partners—dammit all, he had business partners—knew that he should be accessible and was opting not to be.

"Why did you leave the church?" he asked after a long stretch of silence.

"I didn't. I mean, not as a member. But, I couldn't work there anymore. You know, I woke up one morning and looked in the mirror and imagined doing that exact same thing in forty years. Sitting behind that desk, in the same chair, talking to the same people, having the same conversations... I just didn't think I could do it. I thought...well, for a long time I thought if I sat in that chair life would come to me." She took a deep breath. "But it won't. I have to go get it."

What she was talking about… That kind of stability. It was completely foreign to him. Jonathan could scarcely remember a time in his life when things had stayed the same from year to year. He would say one thing for poverty, it was dynamic. It could be a grind, sure, but it kept you on your toes. He'd constantly looked for new ways to support himself and Rebecca. To prove to child services that he was a fit guardian. To keep their dwelling up to par, to make sure they could always afford it. To keep them both fed and clothed—or at least her, if not him.

He had always craved what Hayley was talking about. A place secure enough to rest for a while. But not having it was why he was here now. In this house, with all this money. Which was the only real damned security in the world. Making sure you were in control of everything around you.

Even if it did mean owning a fucking smartphone.

"So, your big move was to be my assistant?"

She frowned. "No. This is my small move. You have to make small moves before you can make a big one."

That he agreed with, more or less. His whole life had been a series of small moves with no pausing in between. One step at a time as he climbed up to the top. "I'm not sure it's the best thing to let your employer know you think he's a small step," he said, just because he wanted to see her cheeks turn pink again. He was gratified when they did.

"Sorry. This is a giant step for me. I intend to stay here forever in my elevated position as your assistant."

He set his lunch down, leaning back and holding up his hands. "Slow down, baby. I'm not looking for a commitment."

At that, her cheeks turned bright red. She took another bite of coleslaw, leaving a smear of mayonnaise on the corner of her mouth. Without thinking, he leaned in and brushed his thumb across the smudge, and along the edge of her lower lip.

He didn't realize it was a mistake until the slug of heat hit him low and fast in the gut.

He hadn't realized it would be a mistake because she was such a mousy little thing, a church secretary. Because his taste didn't run to that kind of thing. At least, that's what he would have said.

But while his brain might have a conscience, he discovered in that moment that his body certainly did not.

CHAPTER THREE

IT WAS LIKE striking a match, his thumb sweeping across her skin. It left a trail of fire where he touched, and made her feel hot in places he hadn't. She was… Well, she was immobilized.

Like a deer caught in the headlights, seeing exactly what was barreling down on her, and unable to move.

Except, of course, Jonathan wasn't barreling down on her. He wasn't moving at all.

He was just looking at her, his dark eyes glittering, his expression like granite. She followed his lead, unsure of what to do. Of how she should react.

And then, suddenly, everything clicked into place. Exactly what she was feeling, exactly what she was doing… and exactly how much of an idiot she was.

She took a deep breath, gasping as though she'd been submerged beneath water. She turned her chair sideways, facing the computer again. "Well," she said, "thank you for lunch."

Fiddlesticks. And darn it. And fudging graham crackers.

She had just openly stared at her boss, probably looking like a guppy gasping on dry land because he had wiped mayonnaise off her lip. Which was—as things went—probably one of the more platonic touches a man and a woman could share.

The problem was, she couldn't remember ever being touched—even platonically—by a man who wasn't family. So she had been completely unprepared for the reaction it created inside her. Which she had no doubt he'd noticed.

Attraction. She had felt *attracted* to him.

Backtracking, she realized the tight feeling in her stomach that had appeared the first moment she'd seen him was probably attraction.

That was bad. Very bad.

But what she was really curious about, was why this attraction felt different from what she'd felt around other men she had liked. She'd felt fluttery feelings before. Most notably for Grant Daniels, the junior high youth pastor, a couple years ago. She had really liked him, and she was pretty sure he'd liked her, too, but he hadn't seemed willing to make a move.

She had conversations with him over coffee in the Fellowship Hall, where he had brought up his feelings on dating—he didn't—and how he was waiting until he was ready to get married before getting into any kind of relationship with a woman.

For a while, she'd been convinced he'd told her that because he was close to being ready, and he might want to marry her.

Another instance of sitting, waiting and believing what she wanted would come to her through the sheer force of her good behavior.

Looking back, she realized it was kind of stupid that she had hoped he'd marry her. She didn't know him, not really. She had only ever seen him around church, and of course her feelings for him were based on that. Everybody was on their best behavior there. Including her.

Not that she actually behaved badly, which was kind of the problem. There was what she did, what she showed the world, and then there were the dark, secret things that lived inside her. Things she wanted but was afraid to pursue.

The fluttery feelings she had for Grant were like public Hayley. Smiley, shiny and giddy. Wholesome and hopeful.

The tension she felt in her stomach when she looked at Jonathan…that was all secret Hayley.

And it scared her that there was another person who seemed to have access to those feelings she examined only late at night in the darkness of her room.

She had finally gotten up the courage to buy a romance novel when she'd been at the grocery store a month or so ago. She had always been curious about those books, but since she'd lived with her parents, she had never been brave enough to buy one.

So, at the age of twenty-four, she had gotten her very first one. And it had been educational. Very, *very* educational. She had been a little afraid of it, to be honest.

Because those illicit feelings brought about late at night by hazy images and the slide of sheets against her bare skin had suddenly become focused and specific after reading that book.

And if that book had been the fantasy, Jonathan was the reality. It made her want to turn tail and run. But she couldn't. Because if she did, then he would know what no one else knew about her.

She couldn't risk him knowing.

They were practically strangers. They had nothing in common. These feelings were ridiculous. At least Grant had been the kind of person she was suited to.

Which begged the question—why didn't he make her feel this off-kilter?

Her face felt like it was on fire, and she was sure Jonathan could easily read her reaction. That was the problem. It had taken her longer to understand what she was feeling than it had likely taken him. Because he wasn't sheltered like she was.

Sheltered even from her own desire.

The word made her shiver. Because it was one she had avoided thinking until now.

Desire.

Did she desire him? And if she did, what did that mean?

Her mouth went dry as several possibilities floated through her mind. Each more firmly rooted in fantasy than the last, since she had no practical experience with any of this.

And it was going to stay that way. At least for now.

Small steps. This job was her first small step. And it was a job, not a chance for her to get ridiculous over a man.

"Did you have anything else you wanted me to do?" she asked, not turning to face him, keeping her gaze resolutely pinned to the computer screen.

He was silent for a moment, and for some reason, the silence felt thick. "Did you finish entering the invoices?"

"Yes."

"Good," he said. "Here." He handed her his phone. "If anyone calls, say I'm not available, but you're happy to take a message. And I want you to call the county office and ask about the permits listed in the other spreadsheet I have open. Just get a status update on that. Do you cook?"

She blinked. "What?"

"Do you cook? I hired you to be my assistant. Which

includes things around the house. And I eat around the house."

"I cook," she said, reeling from the change of topic.

"Great. Have something ready for me, and if I'm not back before you knock off at five, just keep it warm."

Then he turned and walked out, leaving her feeling both relieved and utterly confused. All those positive thoughts from this morning seemed to be coming back to haunt her, mock her.

The work she could handle. It was the man that scared her.

THE FIRST WEEK of working with Hayley had been pretty good, in spite of that hiccup on the first day.

The one where he had touched her skin and felt just how soft it was. Something he never should have done.

But she was a good assistant. And every evening when he came in from dealing with ranch work his dinner was ready. That had been kind of a dick move, asking her to cook, but in truth, he hadn't put a very detailed job description in the ad. And she wasn't an employee of Gray Bear. She was his personal employee, and that meant he could expand her responsibilities.

At least, that was what he told himself as he approached the front porch Friday evening, his stomach already growling in anticipation. When he came in for the evening after the outside work was done, she was usually gone and the food was warming in the oven.

It was like having a wife. With none of the drawbacks *and* none of the perks.

But considering he could get those perks from a woman who wasn't in his house more than forty hours a week, he would take this happily.

He stomped up the front steps, kicking his boots off before he went inside. He'd been walking through sludge in one of the far pastures and he didn't want to track in mud. His housekeeper didn't come until later in the week.

The corner of his mouth lifted as he processed that thought. He had a housekeeper. He didn't have to get on his hands and knees and scrub floors anymore. Which he had done. More times than he would care to recount. Most of the time the house he and Rebecca had shared while growing up had been messy.

It was small, and their belongings—basic though they were—created a lot of clutter. Plus, teenage boys weren't the best at keeping things deep cleaned. Especially not when they also had full-time jobs and were trying to finish high school. But when he knew child services would be by, he did his best.

He didn't now. He paid somebody else to do it. For a long time, adding those kinds of expenses had made both pride and anxiety burn in his gut. Adjusting to living at a new income level was not seamless. And since things had grown exponentially and so quickly, the adjustments had come even harder. Often in a million ways he couldn't anticipate. But he was working on it. Hiring a housekeeper. Hiring Hayley.

Pretty soon, he would give in and buy himself a new pair of boots.

He drew nearer to the kitchen, smelling something good. And then he heard footsteps, the clattering of dishes.

He braced his arms on either side of the doorway. Clearly, she hadn't heard him approach. She was bending down to pull something out of the oven, her sweet ass outlined to perfection by that prim little skirt.

There was absolutely nothing provocative about it. It fell down past her knees, and when she stood straight it didn't display any curves whatsoever.

For a moment, he just admired his own commitment to being a dick. She could not be dressed more appropriately, and still his eyes were glued to her butt. And damn, his body liked what he saw.

"You're still here," he said, pushing away from the door and walking into the room. He had to break the tension stretching tight inside him. Step one was breaking the silence and making his presence known. Step two was going to be calling up one of the women he had associations with off and on.

Because he had to do something to take the edge off. Clearly, it had been too long since he'd gotten laid.

"Sorry," she said, wiping her hands on a dishcloth and making a few frantic movements. As though she wanted to look industrious, but didn't exactly have a specific task. "The roast took longer than I thought it would. But I did a little more paperwork while I waited. And I called the county to track down that permit."

"You don't have to justify all your time. Everything has gotten done this week. Plus, inefficient meat preparation was not on my list of reasons I might fire you."

She shrugged. "I thought you reserved the right to revise that list at any time."

"I do. But not today."

"I should be out of your hair soon." She walked around the counter and he saw she was barefoot. Earlier, he had been far too distracted by her backside to notice.

"Pretty sure that's a health code violation," he said.

She turned pink all the way up to her scalp. "Sorry. My feet hurt."

He thought of those low, sensible heels she always wore and he had to wonder what the point was to wearing shoes that ugly if they weren't even comfortable. The kind of women he usually went out with wore the kinds of shoes made for sitting. Or dancing on a pole.

But Hayley didn't look like she even knew what pole dancing was, let alone like she would jump up there and give it a try. She was... Well, she was damn near sweet.

Which was all wrong for him, in every way. He wasn't sweet.

He was successful. He was driven.

But he was temporary at best. And frankly, almost everyone in his life seemed grateful for that fact. No one stayed. Not his mother, not his father. Even his sister was off living her own life now.

So why he should spend even one moment looking at Hayley the way he'd been looking at her, he didn't know. He didn't have time for subtlety. He never had. He had always liked obvious women. Women who asked for what they wanted without any game-playing or shame.

He didn't want a wife. He didn't even want a serious girlfriend. Hell, he didn't want a casual girlfriend. When he went out it was with the express intention of hooking up. When it came to women, he didn't like a challenge.

His whole damned life was a challenge, and always had been. When he'd been raising his sister he couldn't bring anyone back to his place, which meant he needed someone with a place of their own, or someone willing to get busy in the back of a pickup truck.

Someone who understood he had only a couple free hours, and he wouldn't be sharing their bed all night.

Basically, his taste ran toward women who were all the things Hayley wasn't.

Cute ass or not.

None of those thoughts did anything to ease the tension in his stomach. No matter how succinctly they broke down just why he shouldn't find Hayley hot.

He nearly scoffed. She *wasn't* hot. She was… She would not be out of place as the wholesome face on a baking mix. Much more Little Debbie than Debbie Does Dallas.

"It's fine. I don't want you going lame on me."

She grinned. "No. Then you'd have to put me down."

"True. And if I lose more than one personal assistant that way people will start asking questions."

He could tell she wasn't sure if he was kidding or not. For a second, she looked downright concerned.

"I have not sent, nor do I intend to send, any of my employees—present or former—to the glue factory. Don't look at me like that."

She bit her lower lip, and that forced him to spend a moment examining just how lush it was. He didn't like that. She needed to stop bending over, and to do nothing that would draw attention to her mouth. Maybe, when he revised the list of things he might fire her for, he would add drawing attention to attractive body parts to the list.

"I can never tell when you're joking."

"Me, either," he said.

That time she did laugh. "You know," she said, "you could smile."

"Takes too much energy."

The timer went off and she bustled back to the stove. "Okay," she said, "it should be ready now." She pulled a little pan out of the oven and took the lid off. It was full of roast and potatoes, carrots and onions. The kind of home-cooked meal he imagined a lot of kids grew up on.

For him, traditional fare had been more along the lines of flour tortillas with cheese or ramen noodles. Something cheap, easy and full of carbs. Just enough to keep you going.

His stomach growled in appreciation, and that was the kind of hunger associated with Hayley that he could accept.

"I should go," she said, starting to walk toward the kitchen door.

"Stay."

As soon as he made the offer Jonathan wanted to bite his tongue off. He did not need to encourage spending more time in closed off spaces with her. Although dinner might be a good chance to prove that he could easily master those weird bursts of attraction.

"No," she said, and he found himself strangely relieved. "I should go."

"Don't be an idiot," he said, surprising himself yet again. "Dinner is ready here. And it's late. Plus there's no way I can eat all this."

"Okay," she said, clearly hesitant.

"Come on now. Stop looking at me like you think I'm going to bite you. You've been reading too much *Twilight*. Indians don't really turn into wolves."

Her face turned really red then. "That's not what I was thinking. I don't… I'm not afraid of you."

She was afraid of something. And what concerned him most was that it might be the same thing he was fighting against.

"I really was teasing you," he said. "I have a little bit of a reputation in town, but I didn't earn half of it."

"Are you saying people in town are…prejudiced?"

"I wouldn't go that far. I mean, I wouldn't say it's

on purpose. But whether it's because I grew up poor or it's because I'm brown, people have always given me a wide berth."

"I didn't… I mean, I've never seen people act that way."

"Well, they wouldn't. Not to you."

She blinked slightly. "I'll serve dinner now."

"Don't worry," he said, "the story has a happy ending. I have a lot of money now, and that trumps anything else. People have no issue hiring me to build these days. Though, I remember the first time my old boss put me on as the leader of the building crew, and the guy whose house we were building had a problem with it. He didn't think I should be doing anything that required too much skill. Was more comfortable with me just swinging the hammer, not telling other people where to swing it."

She took plates down from the cupboard, holding them close to her chest. "That's awful."

"People are awful."

A line creased her forehead. "They definitely can be."

"Stop hugging my dinner plate to your shirt. That really isn't sanitary. We can eat in here." He gestured to the countertop island. She set the plates down hurriedly, then started dishing food onto them.

He sighed heavily, moving to where she was and taking the big fork and knife out of her hands. "Have a seat. How much do you want?"

"Oh," she said, "I don't need much."

He ignored her, filling the plate completely, then filling his own. After that, he went to the fridge and pulled out a beer. "Want one?"

She shook her head. "I don't drink."

He frowned, then looked back into the fridge. "I don't have anything else."

"Water is fine."

He got her a glass and poured some water from the spigot in the fridge. He handed it to her, regarding her like she was some kind of alien life-form. The small conversation had really highlighted the gulf between them.

It should make him feel even more ashamed about looking at her butt.

Except shame was pretty hard for him to come by.

"Tell me what you think about people, Hayley." He took a bite of the roast and nearly gave her a raise then and there.

"No matter what things look like on the surface, you never know what someone is going through. It surprised me how often someone who had been smiling on Sunday would come into the office and break down in tears on Tuesday afternoon, saying they needed to talk to the pastor. Everyone has problems, and I do my best not to add to them."

"That's a hell of a lot nicer than most people deserve."

"Okay, what do you think about people?" she asked, clasping her hands in front of her and looking so damn interested and sincere he wasn't quite sure how to react.

"I think they're a bunch of self-interested bastards. And that's fair enough, because so am I. But whenever somebody asks for something, or offers me something, I ask myself what they will get out of it. If I can't figure out how they'll benefit, that's when I get worried."

"Not everyone is after money or power," she said. He could see she really believed what she said. He wasn't sure what to make of that.

"All right," he conceded, "maybe they aren't all after

money. But they are looking to gain something. Everyone is. You can't get through life any other way. Trust me."

"I don't know. I never thought of it that way. In terms of who could get me what. At least, that's not how I've lived."

"Then you're an anomaly."

She shook her head. "My father is like that, too. He really does want to help people. He cares. Pastoring a small church in a little town doesn't net you much power or money."

"Of course it does. You hold the power of people's salvation in your hands. Pass around the plate every week. Of course you get power and money." Jonathan shook his head. "Being the leader of local spirituality is power, honey, trust me."

Her cheeks turned pink. "Okay. You might have a point. But my father doesn't claim to have the key to anyone's salvation. And the money in that basket goes right back into the community. Or into keeping the doors of the church open. My father believes in living the same way the community lives. Not higher up. So whatever baggage you might have about church, that's specific to your experience. It has nothing to do with my father or his faith."

She spoke with such raw certainty that Jonathan was tempted to believe her. But he knew too much about human nature.

Still, he liked all that conviction burning inside her. He liked that she believed what she said, even if he couldn't.

If he had been born with any ideals, he couldn't remember them now. He'd never had the luxury of having faith in humanity, as Hayley seemed to have. No, his earliest memory of his father was the old man's fist connecting with his face. Jonathan had never had the chance to believe the best of anybody.

He had been introduced to the worst far too early.

And he didn't know very many people who'd had different experiences.

The optimism she seemed to carry, the softness combined with strength, fascinated him. He wanted to draw closer to it, to her, to touch her skin, to see if she was strong enough to take the physical demands he put on a woman who shared his bed.

To see how shocked she might be when he told her what those demands were. In explicit detail.

He clenched his jaw tight, clamping his teeth down hard. He was not going to find out, for a couple reasons. The first being that she was his employee, and off-limits. The second being that all those things that fascinated him would be destroyed if he got close, if he laid even one finger on her.

Cynicism bled from his pores, and he damn well knew it. He had earned it. He wasn't one of those bored rich people overcome by ennui just because life had gone so well he wanted to create problems so he had something to battle against.

No. He had fought every step of the way, and he had been disappointed by people in every way imaginable. He had earned his feelings about people, that was for damn sure.

But he wasn't certain he wanted to pass that cynicism on to Hayley. No, she was like a pristine wilderness area. Unspoiled by humans. And his first inclination was to explore every last inch, to experience all that beauty, all that majesty. But he had to leave it alone. He had to leave it looked at, not touched.

Hayley Thompson was the same. Untouched. He had to leave her unspoiled. Exploring that beauty would only leave it ruined, and he couldn't do that. He wouldn't.

"I think it's sad," she said, her voice muted. "That you can't see the good in other people."

"I've been bitten in the ass too many times," he said, his tone harder than he'd intended it to be. "I'm glad you haven't been."

"I haven't had the chance to be. But that's kind of the point of what I'm doing. Going out, maybe getting bitten in the ass." Her cheeks turned bright red. "I can't believe I said that."

"What?"

"That word."

That made his stomach feel like it had been hollowed out. *"Ass?"*

Her cheeks turned even redder. "Yes. I don't say things like that."

"I guess not… Being the church secretary and all."

Now he just felt… Well, she made him feel rough and uncultured, dirty and hard and unbending as steel. Everything she was not. She was small, delicate and probably far too easy to break. Just like he'd imagined earlier, she was…set apart. Unspoiled. And here he had already spoiled her a little bit. She'd said ass, right there in his kitchen.

And she'd looked shocked as hell by her own behavior.

"You don't have to say things like that if you don't want to," he said. "Not every experience is a good experience. You shouldn't try things just to try them. Hell, if I'd had the choice of staying innocent of human nature, maybe I would have taken that route instead. Don't ruin that nice vision of the world you have."

She frowned. "You know, everybody talks about going out and experiencing things…"

"Sure. But when people say that, they want control over those experiences. Believe me, having the blinders ripped off is not necessarily the best thing."

She nodded slowly. "I guess I understand that. What kinds of experiences do you think are bad?"

Immediately, he thought of about a hundred bad things he wanted to do to her. Most of them in bed, all of them naked. He sucked in a sharp breath through his teeth. "I don't think we need to get into that."

"I'm curious."

"You know what they say about curiosity and the cat, right?"

"But I'm not a cat."

"No," he said, "you are Hayley, and you should be grateful for the things you've been spared. Maybe you should even go back to the church office."

"No," she said, frowning. "I don't want to. Maybe I don't want to *experience everything*—I can see how you're probably right about that. But I can't just stay in one place, sheltered for the rest of my life. I have to figure out…who I am and what I want."

That made him laugh, because it was such a naive sentiment. He had never stood back and asked himself who the hell Jonathan Bear was, and what he wanted out of life. He hadn't given a damn how he made his money as long as he made it.

As far as he was concerned, dreams were for people with a lot of time on their hands. He had to *do*. Even as a kid, he couldn't think, couldn't wonder; he had to act.

She might as well be speaking a foreign language. "You'll have to tell me what that's like."

"What?"

"That quest to find yourself. Let me know if it's any more effective than just living your life and seeing what happens."

"Okay, now you've made me feel silly."

He took another bite of dinner. Maybe he should back down, because he didn't want her to quit. He would like to continue eating her food. And, frankly, he would like to keep looking at her.

Just because he should back down didn't mean he was going to.

"There was no safety net in my life," he said, not bothering to reassure her. "There never has been. I had to work my ass off from the moment I was old enough to get paid to do something. Hell, even before then. I would get what I could from the store, expired products, whatever, so we would have something to eat. That teaches you a lot about yourself. You don't have to go looking. In those situations, you find out whether you're a survivor or not. Turns out I am. And I've never really seen what more I needed to know."

"I don't… I don't have anything to say to that."

"Yeah," he returned. "My life story is kind of a bummer."

"Not now," she said softly. "You have all this. You have the business, you have this house."

"Yeah, I expect a man could find himself here. Well, unless he got lost because it was so big." He smiled at her, but she didn't look at all disarmed by the gesture. Instead, she looked thoughtful, and that made his stomach feel tight.

He didn't really do meaningful conversation. He especially didn't do it with women.

Yet here he was, telling this woman more about himself than he could remember telling anyone. Rebecca knew everything, of course. Well, as much as she'd observed while being a kid in that situation. They didn't need to talk about it. It was just life. But other people… Well, he didn't see the point in talking about the deficit he'd started with. He preferred people assume he'd sprung out of the ground powerful and successful. They took him more seriously.

He'd had enough disadvantages, and he wouldn't set himself up for any more.

But there was something about Hayley—her openness, her honesty—that made him want to talk. That made him feel bad for being insincere. Because she was just so…so damn real.

How would he have been if he'd had a softer existence? Maybe he wouldn't be as hard. Maybe a different life would have meant not breaking a woman like this the moment he put his hands on her.

It was moot. Because he hadn't had a different life. And if he had, he probably wouldn't have made half as much of himself.

"You don't have to feel bad for wanting more," he said finally. "Just because other people don't have it easy, doesn't mean you don't have your own kind of hard."

"It's just difficult to decide what to do when other people's expectations feel so much bigger than your own dreams."

"I know a little something about that. Only in my case, the expectations other people had for me were that I would end up dead of a drug overdose or in prison. So, all things considered, I figured I would blow past those expectations and give people something to talk about."

"I just want to travel."

"Is that it?"

A smile played in the corner of her lips, and he found himself wondering what it might be like to taste that smile. "Okay. And see a famous landmark. Like the Eiffel Tower or Big Ben. And I want to dance."

"Have you never danced?"

"No!" She looked almost comically horrified. "Where would I have danced?"

"Well, your brother does own a bar. And there is line dancing."

"I can't even go into Ace's bar. My parents don't go. We can go to the brewery. Because they serve more food there. And it's not called a bar."

"That seems like some arbitrary shit."

Her cheeks colored, and he didn't know if it was because he'd pointed out a flaw in her parents' logic or because he had cursed. "Maybe. But I follow their lead. It's important for us to keep away from the appearance of evil."

"Now, that I don't know anything about. Because nobody cares much about my appearance."

She cleared her throat. "So," she said. "Dancing."

Suddenly, an impulse stole over him, one he couldn't quite understand or control. Before he knew it, he was pushing his chair back and standing up, extending his hand. "All right, Hayley Thompson, Paris has to wait awhile. But we can take care of the dancing right now."

"What?" Her pretty eyes flew wide, her soft lips rounded into a perfect O.

"Dance with me, Hayley."

CHAPTER FOUR

HAYLEY WAS PRETTY sure she was hallucinating.

Because there was no way her stern boss was standing there, his large, work-worn hand stretched toward her, his dark eyes glittering with an intensity she could only guess at the meaning of, having just asked her to dance. Except, no matter how many times she blinked, he was still standing there. And the words were still echoing in her head.

"There's no music."

He took his cell phone out of his pocket, opened an app and set the phone on the table, a slow country song filling the air. "There," he said. "Music accomplished. Now, dance with me."

"I thought men *asked* for a dance, I didn't think they demanded one."

"Some men, maybe. But not me. But remember, I don't give a damn about appearances."

"I think I might admire that about you."

"You should," he said, his tone grave.

She felt… Well, she felt breathless and fluttery, and she didn't know what to do. But if she said no, then he would know just how inexperienced she was. He would know she was making a giant internal deal about his hand touching hers, about the possibility of being held against his body. That she felt strange, unnerving sensations skittering over her skin when she looked at him. She was afraid he could see her too clearly.

Isn't this what you wanted? To reach out? To take a chance?

It was. So she did.

She took his hand. She was still acclimating to his heat, to being touched by him, skin to skin, when she found herself pressed flush against his chest, his hand enveloping hers. He wrapped his arm around her waist, his palm hot on her lower back.

She shivered. She didn't know why. Because she wasn't cold. No. She was hot. And so was he. Hot and hard, so much harder than she had imagined another person could be.

She had never, ever been this close to a man before. Had never felt a man's skin against hers. His hand was rough, from all that hard work. What might it feel like if he touched her skin elsewhere? If he pushed his other hand beneath her shirt and slid his fingertips against her lower back?

That thought sent a sharp pang straight to her stomach, unfurling something inside her, making her blood run faster.

She stared straight at his shoulder, at an innocuous spot on his flannel shirt. Because she couldn't bring herself to raise her eyes and look at that hard, lean face, at the raw beauty she had never fully appreciated before.

He would probably be offended to be characterized as beautiful. But he was. In the same way that a mountain was beautiful. Tall, strong and unmoving.

She gingerly curled her fingers around his shoulder, while he took the lead, his hold on her firm and sure as he established a rhythm she could follow.

The grace in his steps surprised her. Caused her to meet his gaze. She both regretted it and relished it at the same time. Because it was a shame to stare at flannel when she could be looking into those dark eyes, but they also made her feel…absolutely and completely undone.

"Where did you learn to dance?" she asked, her voice sounding as breathless as she had feared it might.

But she was curious about this man who had grown up in such harsh circumstances, who had clearly devoted most of his life to hard work with no frills, who had learned to do this.

"A woman," he said, a small smile tugging at the edges of his lips.

She was shocked by the sudden, sour turn in her stomach. It was deeply unpleasant, and she didn't know what to do to make it stop. Imagining what other woman he might have learned this from, how he might have held her…

It hurt. In the strangest way.

"Was she…somebody special to you? Did you love her?"

His smile widened. "No. I've never loved anybody. Not anybody besides my sister. But I sure as hell *wanted* something from that woman, and she wanted to dance."

It took Hayley a while to figure out the meaning behind those words. "Oh," she said, "she wanted to dance and you wanted…" That feeling in her stomach intensified, but along with it came a strange sort of heat. Because he was holding *her* now, dancing with her. *She* wanted to dance. Did that mean that he…?

"Don't look at me like that, Hayley. This," he said, tightening his hold on her and dipping her slightly, his face moving closer to hers, "is just a dance."

She was a tangle of unidentified feelings—knots in her stomach, an ache between her thighs—and she didn't want to figure out what any of it meant.

"Good," she said, wishing she could have infused some conviction into that word.

The music slowed, the bass got heavier. And he matched the song effortlessly, his hips moving firmly against hers with every deep pulse of the beat.

This time, she couldn't ignore the lyrics. About two people and the fire they created together. She wouldn't have fully understood what that meant even a few minutes ago, but in Jonathan's arms, with the heat that burned from his body, fire was what she felt.

Like her nerve endings had been set ablaze, like a spark had been stoked low inside her. If he moved in just the wrong way—or just the right way—the flames in him would catch hold of that spark in her and they would combust.

She let her eyes flutter closed, gave herself over to the moment, to the song, to the feel of him, the scent of him. She was dancing. And she liked it a lot more than she had anticipated and in a way she hadn't imagined she could.

She had pictured laughing, lightness, with people all around, like at the bar she had never been to before. But this was something else. A deep intimacy that grew from somewhere inside her chest and intensified as the music seemed to draw them more tightly together.

She drew in a breath, letting her eyes open and look up at him. And then she froze.

He was staring at her, the glitter in his dark eyes almost predatory. She didn't know why that word came to mind. Didn't even know what it might mean in this con-

text. When a man looked at you like he was a wildcat
and you were a potential meal.

Then her eyes dipped down to his mouth. Her own
lips tingled in response and she was suddenly aware of
how dry they were. She slid her tongue over them, completely self-conscious about the action even as she did
it, yet unable to stop.

She was satisfied when that predatory light in his eyes
turned sharper. More intense.

She didn't know what she was doing. But she found
herself moving closer to him. She didn't know why. She
just knew she had to. With the same bone-deep impulse
that came with the need to draw breath, she had to lean in
closer to Jonathan Bear. She couldn't fight it; she didn't
want to. And until her lips touched his, she didn't even
know what she was moving toward.

But when their mouths met, it all became blindingly
clear.

She had thought about these feelings in terms of fire,
but this sensation was something bigger, something in-
finitely more destructive. This was an explosion. One
she felt all the way down to her toes; one that hit every
place in between.

She was shaking. Trembling like a leaf in the wind.
Or maybe even like a tree in a storm.

He was the storm.

His hold changed. He let go of her hand, withdrew his
arm from around her waist, pressed both palms against
her cheeks as he took the kiss deeper, harder.

It was like drowning. Like dying. Only she didn't want
to fight it. Didn't want to turn away. She couldn't have,
even if she'd tried. Because his grip was like iron, his
body like a rock wall. They weren't moving in time with

the music anymore. No. This was a different rhythm entirely. He propelled her backward, until her shoulder blades met with the dining room wall, his hard body pressed against hers.

He was hard. Everywhere. Hard chest, hard stomach, hard thighs. And that insistent hardness pressing against her hip.

She gasped when she realized what that was. And he consumed her shocked sound, taking advantage of her parted lips to slide his tongue between them.

She released her hold on him, her hands floating up without a place to land, and she curled her fingers into fists. She surrendered herself to the kiss, to him. His hold was tight enough to keep her anchored to the earth, to keep her anchored to him.

She let him have control. Let him take the lead. She didn't know how to dance, and she didn't know how to do this. But he did.

So she let him show her. This was on her list, too, though she hadn't been brave enough to say it, even to herself. To know passion. To experience her first kiss.

She wanted it to go on and on. She never wanted it to end. If she could just be like this, those hot hands cupping her face, that insistent mouth devouring hers, she was pretty sure she could skip the Eiffel Tower.

She felt him everywhere, not just his kiss, not just his touch. Her breasts felt heavy. They ached. In any other circumstances, she might be horrified by that. But she didn't possess the capacity to be horrified, not right now. Not when everything else felt so good. She wasn't ashamed; she wasn't embarrassed—not of the heavy feeling in her breasts, not of the honeyed, slick feeling between her thighs.

This just made sense.

Right now, what she felt was the only thing that made sense. It was the only thing she wanted.

Kissing Jonathan Bear was a necessity.

He growled, flexing his hips toward hers, making it so she couldn't ignore his arousal. And the evidence of his desire carved out a hollow feeling inside her. Made her shake, made her feel like her knees had dissolved into nothing and that without his powerful hold she would crumple onto the floor.

She still wasn't touching him. Her hands were still away from his body, trembling. But she didn't want to do anything to break the moment. Didn't want to make a sound, didn't want to make the wrong move. She didn't want to turn him off or scare him away. Didn't want to do anything to telegraph her innocence. Because it would probably freak him out.

Right, Hayley, like he totally believes you're a sex kitten who's kissed a hundred men.

She didn't know what to do with her hands, let alone her lips, her tongue. She was receiving, not giving. But she had a feeling if she did anything else she would look like an idiot.

Suddenly, he released his hold on her, moving away from her so quickly she might have thought she'd hurt him.

She was dazed, still leaning against the wall. If she hadn't been, she would have collapsed. Her hands were still in the air, clenched into fists, and her breath came in short, harsh bursts. So did his, if the sharp rise and fall of his chest was anything to go by.

"That was a mistake," he said, his voice hard. His words were everything she had feared they might be.

"No, it wasn't," she said, her lips feeling numb, and a little bit full, making it difficult for her to talk. Or maybe the real difficulty came from feeling like her head was filled with bees, buzzing all around and scrambling her thoughts.

"Yes," he said, his voice harder, "it was."

"No," she insisted. "It was a great kiss. A really, really good kiss. I didn't want it to end."

Immediately, she regretted saying that. Because it had been way too revealing. She supposed it was incredibly gauche to tell the guy you'd just kissed that you could have kissed him forever. She tried to imagine how Grant, the youth pastor, might have reacted to that. He would have told her she needed to go to an extra Bible study. Or that she needed to marry him first.

He certainly wouldn't have looked at her the way Jonathan was. Like he wanted to eat her whole, but was barely restraining himself from doing just that. "That's exactly the problem," he returned, the words like iron, "because I *did* want it to end. But in a much different way than it did."

"I don't understand." Her face was hot, and she was humiliated now. So she didn't see why she shouldn't go whole hog. Let him know she was fully outside her comfort zone and she wasn't keeping up with all his implications. She needed stated facts, not innuendo.

"I didn't want to keep kissing you forever. I wanted to pull your top off, shove your skirt up and bury myself inside of you. Is that descriptive enough for you?"

It was. And he had succeeded in shocking her. She wasn't stupid. She knew he was hard, and she knew what that meant. But even given that fact, she hadn't really imagined he wanted... Not with her.

And this was just her first kiss. She wasn't ready for more. Wasn't ready for another step away from the person she had been taught to be.

What about the person you want to be?

She looked at her boss, who was also the most beautiful man she had ever seen. That hadn't been her immediate thought when she'd met him, but she had settled into it as the truth. As certain as the fact the sky was blue and the pine trees that dotted the mountains were deep forest green.

So maybe... Even though it was shocking. Even though it would be a big step, and undoubtedly a big mistake... Maybe she did want it.

"You better go," he said, his voice rough.

"Maybe I don't—"

"You do," he said. "Trust me. And I want you to."

She was confused. Because he had just said he wanted her, and now he was saying he wanted her to go. She didn't understand men. She didn't understand this. She wanted to cry. But a lick of pride slid its way up her spine, keeping her straight, keeping her tears from falling.

Pride she hadn't known she possessed. But then, she hadn't realized she possessed the level of passion that had just exploded between them, either. So it was a day for new discoveries.

"That's fine. I just wanted to have some fun. I can go have it with someone else."

She turned on her heel and walked out of the dining room, out the front door and down the porch steps as quickly as possible. It was dark now, trees like inky bottle brushes rising around her, framing the midnight-blue sky dotted with stars. It was beautiful, but she didn't care. Not right now. She felt...hurt. Emotionally. Physically. The unsatisfied ache between her thighs intensified with the pain growing in her heart.

It was awful. All of it.

It made her want to run. Run back to her parents' house. Run back to the church office.

Being *good* had always been safe.

She had been so certain she wanted to escape safety. Only a few moments earlier she'd needed that escape, felt it might be her salvation. Except she could see now that it was ruin. Utter and complete ruin.

With shaking hands, she pushed the button that undid the locks on her car door and got inside, jamming the key into the ignition and starting it up, a tear sliding down her cheek as she started to back out of the driveway.

She refused to let this ruin her, or this job, or this step she was taking on her own.

She was finding independence, learning new things.

As she turned onto the two-lane highway that would take her back home, she clung to that truth. To the fact that, even though her first kiss had ended somewhat disastrously, it had still shown her something about herself.

It had shown her exactly why it was a good thing she hadn't gotten married to that youthful crush of hers. It would have been dishonest, and not fair to him or to her.

She drove on autopilot, eventually pulling into her driveway and stumbling inside her apartment, lying down on her bed without changing out of her work clothes.

Was she a fallen woman? To want Jonathan like she had. A man she wasn't in love with, a man she wasn't planning to marry.

Had that passion always been there? Or was it created by Jonathan? This feeling. This *need*.

She bit back a sob and forced a smile. She'd had her

first kiss. And she wouldn't dwell on what it might mean. Or on the fact that he had sent her away. Or on the fact that—for a moment at least—she had been consumed with the desire for more.

She'd had her first kiss. At twenty-four. And that felt like a change deep inside her body.

Hayley Thompson had a new apartment, a new job, and she had been kissed.

So maybe it wasn't safe. But she had decided she wanted something more than safety, hadn't she?

She would focus on the victories and simply ignore the rest.

No matter that this victory made her body burn in a way that kept her up for the rest of the night.

CHAPTER FIVE

HE HADN'T EXPECTED her to show up Monday morning. But there she was, in the entryway of the house, hands clasped in front of her, dark hair pulled back in a neat bun. Like she was compensating for what had happened between them Friday night.

"Good morning," he said, taking a sip of his coffee. "I half expected you to take the day off."

"No," she said, her voice shot through with steel, "I can't just take days off. My boss is a tyrant. He'll fire me."

He laughed, mostly to disguise the physical response those words created in him. There was something about her. About all that softness, that innocence, combined with the determination he hadn't realized existed inside her until this moment.

She wasn't just soft, or innocent. She was a force to be reckoned with, and she was bent on showing him that now.

"If he's so bad why do you want to keep the job?"

"My job history is pathetic," she said, walking ahead of him to the stairs. "And, as he has pointed out to me many times, he is not my daddy. My previous boss was. I need something a bit more impressive on my résumé."

"Right. For when you do your traveling."

"Maybe I'll get a job in London," she shot back.

"What's the biggest city you've been to, Hayley?" he asked, following her up the stairs and down the hall toward the office.

"Portland," she said.

He laughed. "London is a little bit bigger."

"I don't care. That's what I want. I want a city where I can walk down the street and not run into anybody that I've ever seen before. All new people. All new faces. I can't imagine that. I can't imagine living a life where I do what I want and not hear a retelling of the night before coming out of my mother's mouth at breakfast the next morning."

"Have you ever done anything worthy of being recounted by your mother?"

Color infused her cheeks. "Okay, specifically, the incident I'm referring to is somebody telling my mother they were proud of me because they saw me giving a homeless woman a dollar."

He laughed. He couldn't help himself, and her cheeks turned an even more intense shade of pink that he knew meant she was furious.

She stamped. Honest to God stamped, like an old-time movie heroine. "What's so funny?"

"Even the gossip about you is good, Hayley Thompson. For the life of me, I can't figure out why you hate that so much."

"Because I can't *do* anything. Jonathan, if you had kissed me in my brother's bar... Can you even imagine? My parents' phone would have been ringing off the hook."

His body hardened at the mention of the kiss. He had been convinced she would avoid the topic.

But he should've known by now that when it came to

Hayley he couldn't anticipate her next move. She was more direct, more up-front than he had thought she might be. Was it because of her innocence that she faced things so squarely? Because she hadn't experienced a whole range of consequences for much of anything yet?

"I wouldn't do that to you," he said. "Because you're right. If anybody suspected something unprofessional had happened between us, it would cause trouble for you."

"I didn't mean it that way." She looked horrified. "I mean, the way people would react if they thought I was… It has nothing to do with you."

"It does. More than you realize. You've been sheltered. But just because you don't know my reputation, that doesn't mean other people in town don't know it. Most people who know you're a good girl know I am a bad man, Hayley. And if anyone suspected I had put my hands on you, I'm pretty sure there would be torches and pitchforks at my front door by sunset."

"Well," she said, "that isn't fair. Because *I* kissed *you*."

"I'm going out on a limb here—of the two of us, I have more experience."

She clasped her hands in front of her and shuffled her feet. "Maybe."

"Maybe nothing, honey. I'm not the kind of man you need to be seen with. So, you're right. You do need to get away. Maybe you should go to London. Hell, I don't know."

"Now you want to get rid of me?"

"Now you're just making it so I can't win."

"I don't mean to," she said, with that trademark sincerity that was no less alarming for being typical of her. "But I don't know what to do with…with this."

She bit her lip, and the motion drew his eye to that

lush mouth of hers. Forced him back to the memory of kissing it. Of tasting her.

He wanted her. No question about it.

He couldn't pretend otherwise. But he could at least be honest with himself about why. He wanted her for all the wrong reasons. He wanted her because some sick, caveman part of him wanted to get all that *pretty* dirty. Part of him wanted to corrupt her. To show her everything she was missing. To make her fall from grace a lasting one.

And that was some fucked up shit.

Didn't mean he didn't feel it.

"Well, after I earn enough money, that's probably what I'll do," she said. "And since this isn't going anywhere... I should probably just get to work. And we shouldn't talk about it anymore."

"No," he said, "we shouldn't."

"It was just a kiss."

His stomach twisted. Not because it disappointed him to hear her say that, but because she had to say it for her own peace of mind. She was innocent enough that a kiss worked her up. It meant something to her. Hell, sex barely meant anything to him. Much less a kiss.

Except for hers. You remember hers far too well.

"Just a kiss," he confirmed.

"Good. So give me some spreadsheets."

THE REST OF the week went well. If well meant dodging moments alone with Jonathan, catching herself staring at him at odd times during the day and having difficulty dreaming of anything except him at night.

"Thank God it's Friday," she said into the emptiness of her living room.

She didn't feel like cooking. She had already made

a meal for Jonathan at his house, and then hightailed it out of there as quickly as possible. She knew that if she'd made enough for herself and took food with her he wouldn't have minded, but she was doing her best to keep the lines between them firm.

She couldn't have any more blurred lines. They couldn't have any more…kissing and other weirdness. Just thinking about kissing Jonathan made her feel restless, edgy. She didn't like it. Or maybe she liked it too much.

She huffed out a growl and wandered into the kitchen, opening the cupboard and pulling out a box of chocolate cereal.

It was the kind of cereal her parents never would have bought. Because it wasn't good for you, and it was expensive. So she had bought it for herself, because she had her own job, she was an adult and she made her own decisions.

Do you?

She shut out that snotty little voice. Yes, she *did* make her own decisions. Here she was, living in her own place, working at the job she had chosen. Yes, she very much made her own decisions. She had even kissed Jonathan. Yes, that had been her idea.

Which made the fallout her fault. But she wasn't going to dwell on that.

"I'm dwelling," she muttered. "I'm a liar, and I'm dwelling." She took down a bowl and poured herself a large portion of the chocolaty cereal. Then she stared at it. She didn't want to eat cereal by herself for dinner.

She was feeling restless, reckless.

She was feeling something a whole lot like desperation. Because of that kiss.

The kiss she had just proposed she wasn't going to think about, the kiss she couldn't let go of. The kiss that made her burn, made her ache and made her wonder about all the mysteries in life she had yet to uncover.

Yeah, *that* kiss.

She had opened a floodgate. She'd uncovered all this potential for passion inside herself, and then she had to stuff it back down deep.

Jonathan Bear was not the only man in the world. Jonathan Bear wasn't even the only man in Copper Ridge.

She could find another guy if she wanted to.

Of course, if she went out, there would be all those gossip issues she and Jonathan had discussed earlier in the week.

That was why she had to get out of this town.

It struck her then, like a horse kicking her square in the chest, that she was running away. So she could be who she wanted to be without anybody knowing about it. So she could make mistakes and minimize the consequences.

So she could be brave and a coward all at the same time.

That's what it was. It was cowardice. And she was not very impressed with herself.

"Look at you," she scolded, "eating cold cereal on a Friday night by yourself when you would rather be out getting kissed."

Her heart started to beat faster. Where would she go?

And then it hit her. There was one place she could go on a Friday night where nobody from church would recognize her, and even if they did recognize her, they probably wouldn't tell on her because by doing so they would be telling on themselves.

Of course, going there would introduce the problem of her older brother. But Ace had struck out on his own when he was only seventeen years old. He was her inspiration in all this. So he should understand Hayley's need for independence.

And that was when she made her decision. It was Friday night, and she was going out.

She was going to one of the few places in town where she had never set foot before.

Ace's bar.

CHAPTER SIX

"I'D LIKE A HAMBURGER," Hayley said, adjusting her dress and trying not to look like she was about to commit a crime.

"Hayley?" Her brother looked at her as if she had grown another head. "What are you doing in my bar?"

"I'm here to have a hamburger. And…a beer."

Ace shook his head. "You don't want beer."

Darn him for being right. She couldn't stand the smell of the stuff, and she'd honestly never even been tempted to taste it.

"No," she agreed. "I want a Coke."

"I will get you a Coke. Are Mom and Dad here?"

She sighed heavily. "No, they're not. I do go places without them. I moved out."

"I know. We talked about it last time Sierra and I went over for dinner."

Hayley's brother had never much cared about his reputation, or about what anyone thought of him. She had been jealous of that for a long time. For years, Ace had been a total hellion and a womanizer, until he'd settled down and married the town rodeo princess, Sierra West. Now the two of them had one child and another on the way, and Ace's position in the community had improved vastly.

"Right. Well, I'm just saying." She traced an imaginary pattern over the bar top with the tip of her finger. "Did I tell you I quit working at the church?"

Ace look surprised by that. "No."

"Well," she said, "I did. I'm working for Jonathan Bear. Helping out with things around the house and in the office."

Ace frowned. "Well, that probably isn't very much fun. He's kind of a grumpy sumbitch."

"I didn't know you knew him all that well."

"He's my future sister-in-law's brother," Ace said, "but no, I don't know him *well*. He's not very sociable. It's not like he comes to the West family gatherings."

"He said he knows you because he buys beer from you."

"That's how everybody knows me," Ace said.

"Except for me."

"You were *trying* to buy beer from me. I'm just not going to sell one to you."

"That's not fair."

"Sure it is," he said, smiling. "Because you don't actually want to buy beer from me. You're just trying to prove a point."

She scowled. She hated that Ace seemed to understand her so well. "Okay, maybe so. I'm kind of proving a point by being here, I guess."

"Well," he said, "it's all right by me."

"Good."

"I kind of wish you would have come on another night, though," he said, "because I have to go. I promised Sierra I would be home early, so I'm about to take off. But I'll tell Jasmine to keep an eye on you."

"I don't need anybody to keep an eye on me."

"Yes," Ace said, laughing, "you do."

Hayley frowned, and plotted how to order a beer when her brother was gone. Ultimately, she decided to stick with Coke, but when the dancing started, she knew that while she might stay away from alcohol, she didn't want to stay seated. She had danced once. And she had liked it.

She was going to do it again.

JONATHAN DIDN'T KNOW what in blazes he was doing at Ace's. Sure, he knew what he'd told himself while getting ready, his whole body restless thanks to memories of kissing Hayley.

He had continued to push those thoughts down while pacing around the house, and then, after a while, he'd decided to go out and find someone to hook up with. He didn't do that kind of thing, not anymore. He had a couple of women he called; he didn't go trawling bars. He was too old for that.

But right now, he was too much of a hazard to his innocent assistant, and he needed to take the edge off.

And it occurred to him that if he went to Ace's bar and found somebody, the news might filter back to Hayley.

Even though she might find it upsetting, it would be beneficial in the long run. She didn't want to mess with a man like him, not really. It was only that she was too innocent to realize the dangers. But she would, eventually, and she would thank him.

That decision made, he'd hauled his ass down to the bar as quickly as possible.

By the time he walked in, his mood had not improved. He had thought it might. The decision to find a willing woman should have cheered him up. But he felt far from cheered. Maybe because an anonymous body was the last thing he wanted.

He wanted *Hayley*.

Whether he should or not. But he wasn't going to have Hayley. So he would have to get the hell over it.

He moved to the bar and then looked over at the dance floor. His chest tightened up. His body hardened. There was a petite brunette in a formfitting dress dancing with no one in particular. Two men hovered nearby, clearly not minding as she turned to and away from each of them, giving them both just a little bit of attention.

She reminded him of Hayley. Out there on the dance floor acting like nothing close to Hayley.

Then she turned, her dark hair shimmering behind her in a stream, a bright smile on her face, and he could barely process his thoughts. Because it was Hayley. *His* Hayley, out there in the middle of the dance floor, wearing a dress that showed off the figure her clothes had only hinted at before. Sure, in comparison to a lot of women, there was nothing flashy about it, but for Hayley Thompson, it was damned flashy.

And he was… Well, he would be damned if he was going to let those guys put their hands on her.

Yeah, he was bad news. Yeah, he was the kind of guy she should stay well away from. But those guys weren't any better. College douche bags. Probably in their twenties, closer to her age, sure, but not the kind of men who knew how to handle a woman. Especially not one as inexperienced as Hayley.

She would need a man who could guide the experience, show her what she liked. A man who could unlock the mysteries of sex, of her body.

Dickwads that age were better off with an empty dorm room and a half bottle of lotion.

And there was no way in hell they were getting their hands on her.

Without ordering, he moved away from the bar and went out on the dance floor. "You're done here," he said to one of the guys, who looked at him as though Jonathan had just threatened his life. His tone had been soft and even, but it was nice to know the younger man had heard the implied threat loud and clear.

Hayley hadn't noticed his approach, or that the other guy had scurried off to the other end of the dance floor. She was too involved with the guy she was currently dancing with to notice. She was shaking her head, her eyes closed, her body swaying to the music. A completely different kind of dancing than the two of them had done last week.

Then her current dance partner caught Jonathan's eye and paled. He slunk off into the shadows, too.

If Jonathan hadn't already found them wanting when it came to Hayley, he would have now. If they were any kind of men, they would have stood up and declared their interest. They would have proclaimed their desire for her, marked their territory.

He still would have thrown punches, but at least he would've respected them a bit.

Not now.

"Mind if I dance with you?"

Her eyes flew open and she looked around, her head whipping from side to side, her hair following suit. "Where are..."

"Tweedledee and Tweedledum had somewhere to be."

"Where?"

"Someplace where I wouldn't beat their asses."

"Why are you going to beat their...butts?"

"What are you doing here, Hayley?"

She looked around, a guilty expression on her face. "I was just dancing. I have to say, when I imagined getting in trouble in a bar, I figured it would be my dad dragging me outside, not my boss."

"I haven't dragged you outside. *Yet*." He added that last bit because at this point he wasn't sure how this night was going to end. "What are you doing?"

She lifted a shoulder. "Dancing."

"Getting ready to have your first threesome?"

Her mouth dropped open. "I don't even know how that would work."

He huffed out a laugh. "Look it up. On second thought, don't."

She rolled her eyes like a snotty teenager. "We were just dancing. It wasn't a big deal."

"Little girl, what you don't know about men could fill a library. Men don't *just want to dance*. And men don't *just want to kiss*. You can't play these kinds of games. You don't know the rules. You're going to get yourself into trouble."

"I'm not going to get myself into trouble. Did it ever occur to you that maybe some men are nicer than you?"

He chuckled, a low, bitter sound. "Oh, I know that most men are a lot nicer than me. Even then, they want in your pants."

"I don't know what your problem is. You don't want me, so what do you care if they do?"

"Hayley, honey, I don't *want* to want you, but that is not the same thing as not wanting you. It is not even close. What I want is something you can't handle."

"I know," she said, looking to the right and then to the left, as though making sure no one was within earshot.

Then she took a step toward him. "You said you wanted to...be inside of me."

That simple statement, that repetition of his words, had him hard as an iron bar. "You better back off."

"See, I thought you didn't want me. I thought you were trying to scare me away when you said that. Because why would you want me?"

"I'd list the reasons, but I would shock you."

She tilted her head to the side, her hair falling over her shoulder like a glossy curtain. "Maybe I want to be shocked. Maybe I want something I'm not quite ready for."

"No," he said, his tone emphatic now. "You're on this big kick to have experiences. And there are much nicer men you can have experiences with."

She bared her teeth. "I was trying! You just scared them off."

"You're not having experiences with those clowns. They wouldn't know how to handle a woman if she came with an instruction manual. And let me tell you, women do not come with an instruction manual. You just have to know what to do."

"And you know what to do?"

"Damn straight," he returned.

"So," she said, tilting her chin up, looking stubborn. "Show me."

"Not likely, babe."

He wanted to. He wanted to pick her up, throw her over his shoulder and drag her back to his cave. He wanted to bury himself inside her and screw them both senseless, breathless. He wanted to chase every man in the vicinity away from her. He wanted to make it known, loud and clear that—for a little while at least—she was his.

But it was wrong. On about a thousand levels. And the fact that she didn't seem to know it was just another bit of evidence that he needed to stay away.

"You're playing with fire," he said.

"I know. When you kissed me, that was the closest to being burned I've ever experienced in my life. I want more of that."

"We're not having this conversation in the middle of a bar." He grabbed her arm and hauled her off the dance floor, steering them both to the door.

"Hayley!"

He turned and saw one of the waitresses standing by the bar with her hands on her hips.

"Is everything all right?" she asked.

"Yes," Hayley responded. "Jasmine, it's fine. This is my boss."

Jasmine arched her brow. "Really?"

Hayley nodded. "Really. Just work stuff."

Then she broke free of him and marched out ahead of him. When they were both outside, she rounded on him, her words coming out on a frosty cloud in the night air.

"You're so concerned about my reputation, but then you wander in and make a spectacle."

"You were dancing with two men when I got there," he said. "And what's happening with that dress?"

"Oh, please," she said, "I wear this dress to church. It's fine."

"You wear that to *church*?" He supposed, now that he evaluated it with more neutrality, it was pretty tame. The black stretch cotton fell past her knees and had a fairly high neckline. But he could see the curves of her breasts, the subtle slope of her waist to her hips, and her ass looked incredible.

He didn't know if hers was the sort of church that did confession, but he would sure as hell need to confess if he were seated in a row behind her during service.

"Yes," she said. "And it's fine. You're being crazy. Because...because you...*like* me. You *like me* like me."

There she went again, saying things that revealed how innocent she was. Things that made him want her even more, when they should send him running.

"I don't have relationships," he said. He would tell her the truth. He would be honest. It would be the fastest way to chase her off. "And I'm betting a nice girl like you wants relationship. Wants romance, and flowers, and at least the possibility of commitment. You don't get any of those things with me, Hayley."

She looked up at him, her blue eyes glittering in the security light. He could hear the waves crashing on the shore just beyond the parking lot, feel the salt breeze blowing in off the water, sharp and cold.

"What would I get?" she asked.

"A good, hard fuck. A few orgasms." He knew he'd shocked her, and he was glad. She needed to be shocked. She needed to be scared away.

He couldn't see her face, not clearly, but he could tell she wasn't looking at him when she said, "That's...that's a good thing, right?"

"If you don't know the answer, then the answer is no. Not for you."

The sounds of the surf swelled around them, wind whipping through the pines across the road. She didn't speak for a long time. Didn't move.

"Kiss me again," she said, finally.

The words hit him like a sucker punch. "What? What did I just tell you about men and kissing?"

"It's not for you," she said, "it's for me. Before I give you an answer, you need to kiss me again."

She raised her head, and the light caught her face. She stared at him, all defiance and soft lips, all innocence and intensity, and he didn't have it in him to deny her.

Didn't have it in him to deny himself.

Before he could stop, he wrapped his arm around her waist, crushed her against his chest and brought his lips crashing down on hers.

CHAPTER SEVEN

SHE WAS DOING THIS. She wasn't going to turn back. Not now. And she kept telling herself that as she followed Jonathan's pickup truck down the long, empty highway that took them out of town, toward his house.

His house. Where she was going to spend the night.

Where she was going to lose her virginity.

She swallowed hard, her throat suddenly dry and prickly like a cactus.

This wasn't what she had planned when she'd started on her grand independence journey. Yes, she had wanted a kiss, but she hadn't really thought as far ahead as having a sexual partner. For most of her life she had imagined she would be married first, and then, when she'd started wavering on that decision, she had at least imagined she would be in a serious relationship.

This was… Well, it wasn't marriage. It wasn't the beginning of a relationship, either. Of that, she was certain. Jonathan hadn't been vague. Her cheeks heated at the memory of what he'd said, and she was grateful they were driving in separate cars so she had a moment alone for a private freak-out.

She was so out of her league here.

She could turn around. She could head back to town, back to Main Street, back to her little apartment where she could curl up in bed with the bowl of cereal she'd left dry and discarded on the counter earlier.

And in the morning, she wouldn't be changed. Not for the better, not for the worse.

She seriously considered that, though she kept on driving, her eyes on the road and on Jonathan's taillights.

This decision was a big deal. She wouldn't pretend it wasn't. Wouldn't pretend she didn't put some importance on her first sexual experience, on sex in general. And she wouldn't pretend it probably wasn't a mistake.

It was just that maybe she needed to make the mistake. Maybe she needed to find out for herself if Jonathan was right, if every experience wasn't necessary.

She bit her lip and allowed herself a moment of undiluted honesty. When this was over, there would be fallout. She was certain of it.

But while it was happening, it would feel really, really good.

If the kissing was anything to go by, it would be amazing.

She would feel…wild. And new. And maybe sex with Jonathan would be just the kind of thing she needed. He was hot; touching him burned.

Maybe he could be her own personal trial by fire.

She had always imagined that meant walking through hard times. And maybe, conventionally, it did. But she was walking into the heat willingly, knowing the real pain would come after.

She might be a virgin, but she wasn't an idiot. Jonathan Bear wasn't going to fall in love with her. And anyway, she didn't want him to.

She wanted freedom. She wanted something bigger than Copper Ridge.

That meant love wasn't on her agenda, either.

They pulled up to the house and he got out of his truck, closing the door solidly behind him. And she...froze. Sitting there in the driver's seat, both hands on the steering wheel, the engine still running.

The car door opened and cool air rushed in. She looked up and saw Jonathan's large frame filling the space. "Second thoughts?"

She shook her head. "No," she said, and yet she couldn't make herself move.

"I want you," he said, his voice rough, husky, the words not at all what she had expected. "I would like to tell you that if you are having second thoughts, you should turn the car around and go back home. But I'm not going to tell you that. Because if I do, then I might miss out on my chance. And I want this. Even though I shouldn't."

She tightened her hold on the steering wheel. "Why shouldn't you?" she asked, her throat constricted now.

"Do you want the full list?"

"I've got all night."

"All right. You're a nice girl. You seem to believe the best of people, or at least, you want to, until they absolutely make it so you can't. I'm not a nice man. I don't believe the best of anyone, even when they prove I should. People like me, we tend to drag people like you down to our level. Unfortunately. And that's likely what's going to happen here. I'm going to drag you right down to my level. Because let me tell you, I like dirty. And I'm going to get you filthy. I can promise you that."

"Okay," she said, feeling breathless, not quite certain how to respond. Part of her wanted to fling herself out of the car and into his arms, while another, not insignificant part wanted to throw the car in Reverse and drive away.

"I can only promise you two things. This—you and me—won't last forever. And tonight, I will make you come. If you're okay with those promises, then get out of the car and up to my room. If you're not, it's time for you to go."

For some reason, that softly issued command was what it took to get her moving. She released her hold on the steering wheel and turned sideways in her seat. Then she looked up at him, pushing herself into a standing position. He had one hand on the car door, the other on the side mirror, blocking her in.

Her breasts nearly touched his chest, and she was tempted to lean in and press against him completely.

"Come on then," he said, releasing his hold on the car and turning away.

The movement was abrupt. It made her wonder if he was struggling with indecision, too. Which didn't really make sense, since Jonathan was the most decisive man she had ever met. He seemed certain about everything, all the time, even if he was sure it was a bad decision.

That certainty was what she wanted. Yeah, she was certain this was a bad decision, too, but she was going for it, anyway.

She had walked into this house five days a week for the past couple weeks, yet this time was different. Because this time she wasn't headed to the office. This time she was going to his bedroom. And she wasn't his employee; he wasn't her boss. Not now.

Her stomach tightened, her blood heated at the idea of following orders. His orders. Lord knew she would need instruction. Direction. She had no idea what she was doing; she was just following her gut instinct.

When they reached the long hallway, they stopped at a different door than usual. His bedroom. She had never been inside Jonathan's bedroom. It was strange to be standing there now. So very deliberate.

It might have been easier if they had started kissing here in the house, and let things come to their natural conclusion… On the floor or something. She was reasonably sure people did it on the floor sometimes.

Yeah, that would have been easier. This was so *intentional*.

She was about to say something about the strangeness of it when he reached out, cupped her chin and tilted her face upward. Then he closed the distance between them, claiming her mouth.

She felt his possession, all the way down to her toes.

He didn't wait for her to part her lips this time. Instead, he invaded her, sliding his tongue forcibly against hers, his arms wrapped tight around her like steel bands. There was nothing gentle about this kiss. It was consuming, all-encompassing. And all her thoughts about the situation feeling premeditated dissolved.

This time, she didn't stand there as a passive participant. This time, she wrapped her arms around his neck—pressing her breasts flush against his chest, forking her fingers through his hair—and devoured him right back.

She couldn't believe this was her. Couldn't believe this was her life, that this man wanted her. That he was hard for her. That he thought she might be a mistake, and he was willing to make her, anyway. God knew, she was willing to make him.

Need grew inside her, prowling around like a restless

thing. She rocked her hips forward, trying to tame the nameless ache between her thighs. Trying to calm the erratic, reckless feeling rioting through her.

He growled, sliding his hands down her back, over her bottom, down to her thighs. She squeaked as he gripped her tightly, pulling both her feet off the ground and picking her up, pressing that soft, tender place between her legs against his arousal.

"Wrap your legs around me," he said against her mouth, the command harsh, and sexier because of that.

She obeyed him, locking her ankles behind his back. He reversed their positions, pressing her against the wall and deepening his kiss. She gasped as he made even firmer contact with the place that was wet and aching for him.

He ground his hips against her, and her internal muscles pulsed. An arc of electricity lanced through her. She gripped his shoulders hard, vaguely aware that she might be digging her fingernails into his skin, not really sure that she cared. Maybe it would hurt him, but she wasn't exactly sure if he was hurting her or not. She was suspended between pleasure and pain, feelings so intense she could scarcely breathe.

And through all that, he continued to devour her mouth, the rhythm of his tongue against hers combining with the press of his firm length between her thighs, ensuring that her entire world narrowed down to him. Jonathan Bear was everything right now. He was her breath; he was sensation. He was heaven and he was hell.

She needed it to end. Needed to reach some kind of conclusion, where all this tension could be defused.

And yet she wanted it to go on forever.

Her face was hot, her limbs shaking. A strange, hollow feeling in the pit of her stomach made her want to cry. It was too much. And it was not enough. That sharp, insistent ache between her legs burrowed deeper with each passing second, letting her know this kiss simply wasn't enough at all.

She moved her hands up from his broad shoulders, sliding them as far as she could into his long, dark hair. Her fingers snagged on the band that kept his hair tied back and she internally cursed her clumsiness, hoping he wouldn't notice. She had enthusiasm guiding her through this, but that was about it. Enthusiasm and a healthy dose of adrenaline that bordered on terror. But she didn't want to stop. She couldn't stop.

Those big, rough hands gripped her hips and braced her as he rocked more firmly against her, and suddenly, stars exploded behind her eyes. She gasped, wrenching her lips away from his as something that felt like thunder rolled through her body, muscles she'd never been aware of before pulsing like waves against the shore.

She pressed her forehead against his shoulder, did her best to grit her teeth and keep herself from crying out, but a low, shaky sound escaped when the deepest wave washed over her.

Then it ended, and she felt even more connected to reality, to this moment, than she had a second ago. And she felt…so very aware that she was pressed against the wall and him, that something had just happened, that she hadn't been fully cognizant of her actions. She didn't know what she might have said.

That was when she realized she was digging her nails into his back, and she had probably punctured his skin. She started to move against him, trying to get away, and he gripped her chin again, steadying her. "Hey," he said, "you're not going anywhere."

"I need to... I have to..."

"You don't have to do anything, baby. Nothing at all. Just relax." She could tell he was placating her. She couldn't bring herself to care particularly, because she needed placating. Her heart was racing, her hands shaking, and that restlessness that had been so all-consuming earlier was growing again. She had thought the earthquake inside her had handled that.

That was when she realized exactly what that earthquake had been.

Her cheeks flamed, horror stealing through her. She'd had... Well, she'd had an orgasm. And he hadn't even touched her. Not with his hands. Not under her clothes.

"I'm sorry," she said, putting her hands up, patting his chest, then curling her hands into fists because she had patted him and that was really stupid. "I'm just sorry."

He frowned. "What are you sorry about?"

"I'm sorry because I—I...I did that. And we didn't..."

He raised one eyebrow. "Are you apologizing for your orgasm?"

She squeezed her eyes tightly shut. "Yes."

"Why?"

She tightened her fists even more, pressing them against her own chest, keeping her eyes closed. "Because we didn't even... You didn't... We're still dressed."

"Honey," he said, taking hold of her fists and drawing them toward him, pressing them against his chest. "You don't need to apologize to me for coming."

She opened one eye. "I...I don't?"

"No."

"But that…" She looked fully at him, too curious to be embarrassed now. "That ruins it, doesn't it? We didn't…"

"You can have as many orgasms as I can give you. That's the magical thing about women. There's no ceiling on that."

"There isn't?"

"You didn't know?"

"No."

"Hayley," he said, his tone grave, "I need to ask you a question."

Oh great. Now he was actually going to ask if she was a virgin. Granted, she thought he'd probably guessed, but apparently he needed to hear it. "Go ahead," she said, bracing herself for utter humiliation.

"Have you never had an orgasm before?"

"Yes," she said, answering the wrong question before he even got his out. "I mean… No. I mean, just a minute ago. I wasn't even sure what it was right when it was happening."

"That doesn't… Not even with yourself?"

Her face felt so hot she thought it might be on fire. She was pretty sure her heart was beating in her forehead. "No." She shook her head. "I can't talk to you about things like that."

"I just gave you your first orgasm, so you better be able to talk to me about things like that. Plus I'm aiming to give you another one before too long here."

"I bet you can't."

He chuckled, and then he bent down, sweeping her up into his arms. She squeaked, curling her fingers around his shirt. "You should know better than to issue challenges like that." He turned toward the bedroom door, kicking it open with his boot before walking inside and kicking it closed again. Then he carried her to the bed and threw her down in the center.

"Wait," she said, starting to feel panicky, her heart fluttering in her chest like a swarm of butterflies. "Just wait a second."

"I'm not going to fall on you like a ravenous beast," he said, his hands going to the top button of his shirt. "Yet." He started to undo the button slowly, revealing his tan, muscular chest.

She almost told him to stop, except he stripped the shirt off, and she got completely distracted by the play of all those muscles. The sharp hitch of his abs as he cast the flannel onto the floor, the shift and bunch of his pectoral muscles as he pushed his hand over his hair.

She had never seen a shirtless man that looked like him. Not in person, anyway. And most definitely not this close, looking at her like he had plans. Very, very dirty plans.

"I'm a virgin," she blurted out. "Just so you know."

His eyes glowed with black fire. For one heart-stopping moment she was afraid he might pick up his shirt and walk out of the room. His eyes looked pure black; his mouth pressed into a firm line. He stood frozen, hands on his belt buckle, every line in his cut torso still.

Then something in his expression shifted. Nearly imperceptible, and mostly unreadable, but she had seen it. Then his deft fingers went to work, moving his belt through the buckle. "I know," he said.

"Oh." She felt a little crestfallen. Like she must have made some novice mistake and given herself away.

"You're a church secretary who confessed to having never had an orgasm. I assumed." He lowered his voice.

"If you hadn't told me outright, I could have had plausible deniability. Which I was sort of counting on."

She blinked. "Did you...need it?"

"My conscience is screwed, anyway. So not really."

She didn't know quite what to say, so she didn't say anything.

"Have you ever seen a naked man before?"

She shook her head. "No."

"Pictures?"

"Does medieval art count?"

"No, it does not."

"Then no," she said, shaking her head even more vigorously.

He rubbed his hand over his forehead, and she was sure she heard him swear beneath his breath. "Okay," he said, leaving his belt hanging open, but not going any further. He pressed his knee down on the mattress, kneeling beside her. Then he took her hand and placed it against his chest. "How's that?"

She drew shaking fingers across his chest slowly, relishing his heat, the satiny feel of his skin. "Good," she said. "You're very...hot. I mean, temperaturewise. Kind of smooth."

"You don't have to narrate," he said.

"Sorry," she said, drawing her hand back sharply.

"No," he said, pressing her palm back against his skin. "Don't apologize. Don't apologize for anything that happens between us tonight, got that?"

"Okay," she said, more than happy to agree, but not entirely sure if she could keep to the agreement. Because every time she moved her hand and his breath hissed through his teeth, she wanted to say she was sorry. Every time she took her exploration further, she wanted to apologize for the impulse to do it.

She bit her lip, letting her hands glide lower, over his stomach, which was as hard and rippled as corrugated steel. Then she found her hands at the waistband of his jeans, and she pulled back.

"Do you want me to take these off?" he asked.

"In a minute," she said, losing her nerve slightly. "Just a minute." She rose up on her knees, pressed her mouth to his and lost herself in kissing him. She really liked kissing. Loved the sounds he made, loved being enveloped in his arms, and she really loved it when he laid them both down, pressing her deep into the mattress and settling between her thighs.

Her dress rode up high, and she didn't care. She felt rough denim scraping her bare skin, felt the hard press of his zipper, and his arousal behind it through the thin fabric of her panties.

She lost herself in those sensations. In the easy, sensual contact that pushed her back to the brink again. She could see already that Jonathan was going to win the orgasm challenge. And she was okay with that.

Very, very okay with that.

Then he took her hem and pulled the cotton dress over her head, casting it onto the floor. Her skin heated all over, and she was sure she was pink from head to toe.

"Don't be embarrassed," he said, touching her collarbone, featherlight, then tracing a trail down to the curve of her breast, to the edge of her bra. "You're beautiful."

She didn't know quite how to feel about that. Didn't know what to do with that husky, earnest compliment. She wasn't embarrassed because she lacked beauty, but because she had always been taught to treasure modesty. To respect her body, to save it.

He *was* respecting it, though. And right now, she felt like she had been saving it for him.

He reached behind her, undoing her bra with one hand and flicking the fabric to the side.

"You're better at that than I am," she said, laughing nervously as he bared her breasts, her nipples tightening as the cold air hit her skin.

He smiled. "You'll appreciate that in a few minutes."

"What will I appreciate?" she asked, shivering. She crossed her arms over her chest.

"My skill level." Instead of moving her hands, he bent his head and nuzzled the tender spot right next to her hand, the full part of her breast that was still exposed. She gasped, tightening her hold on herself.

He was not deterred.

He nosed her gently and shifted her hand to the side, pressing a kiss to her skin, sending electric sensations firing through her. "Don't be shy," he said, "not with me."

She waited for a reason why. He didn't give one, but she found that the more persistent he was—the more hot, open-mouthed kisses he pressed to her skin—the less able she was to deny him anything. Anything at all. She found herself shifting her hands and then letting them fall away.

As soon as she did, he closed his lips over her nipple, sucking deep. She gasped, her hips rocking up off the bed. He wrapped his arm around her, holding her against his hardness as he teased her with his lips and tongue.

Every time she wiggled, either closer to him, or in a moment of self-consciousness, away, it only brought him more in contact with that aching place between her thighs, and then she would forget why she was moving at all. Why she wasn't just letting him take the lead.

So she relaxed into him, and let herself get lost. She was in a daze when he took her hand and pushed it down his stomach, to the front of his jeans. She gasped when his hard, denim-covered length filled her palm.

"Feel that? That's how much I want you. That's what you do to me."

A strange surge of power rocketed through her. That she could cause such a raw, sexual response... Well, it was intoxicating in a way she hadn't appreciated it could be.

Especially because he was such a man. A hot man. A sexy man, and she had never thought of anyone that way in her life. But he was. He most definitely was.

"Are you ready?" he asked.

She nodded, sliding her hand experimentally over him. He moved, undoing his pants and shoving them quickly down, hardly giving her a chance to prepare. Her mouth dried when she saw him, all of him. She hadn't really... Well, she had been content to allow her fantasies to be somewhat hazy. Though reading that romance novel had made those fantasies a little sharper.

Still, she hadn't really imagined specifically how large a man might be. But suffice it to say, he was a bit larger than she had allowed for.

Her breath left her lungs in a rush. But along with the wave of nerves that washed over her came a sense of relief. "You are... I like the way you look," she said finally.

A crooked smile tipped his mouth upward. "Thank you."

"I told you, I've never seen a naked man before. I was a little afraid I wouldn't like it."

"Well, I'm glad you do. Because let me tell you, that's a lot of pressure. Being the first naked man you've ever seen." His eyes darkened and his voice got lower, huskier. "Being the first naked man you've ever touched." He took her hand again and placed it around his bare shaft, the skin there hotter and much softer than she had imagined. She slid her thumb up and down, marveling at the feel of him.

"You're the first man I've ever kissed," she said, the words slurred, because she had lost the full connection between her brain and her mouth. All her blood had flowed to her extremities.

He swore, and then crushed her to him, kissing her deeply and driving her back down to the mattress. His erection pressed into her stomach, his tongue slick against hers, his lips insistent. She barely noticed when he divested her of her underwear, until he placed his hand between her legs. The rough pads of his fingers sliding through her slick flesh, the white-hot pleasure his touch left behind, made her gasp.

"I'm going to make sure you're ready," he said.

She had no idea what that meant. But he started doing wicked, magical things with his fingers, so she didn't much care. Then he slid one finger deep inside her and she arched away, not sure whether she wanted more of that completely unfamiliar sensation, or if she needed to escape it.

"It's okay," he said, moving his thumb in a circle over a sensitive bundle of nerves as he continued to slide his finger in and out of her body.

After a few passes of his thumb, she agreed.

He shifted his position, adding a second finger, making her gasp. It burned slightly, made her feel like she was being stretched, but after a moment, she adjusted to that, too.

That lovely, spiraling tension built inside her again, and she knew she was close to the edge. But every time he took her to the brink, he would drop back again.

"Please," she whispered.

"Please what?" he asked, being dastardly, asking her to clarify, when he knew saying the words would embarrass her.

"You know," she said, placing her hand over his, like she might take control, increase the pressure, increase the pace, since he refused.

But, of course, he was too strong for her to guide him at all. "I need to hear it."

"I need... I need to have an orgasm," she said quickly.

For a moment, he stopped. He looked at her like she mystified him. Like he had never seen anything like her before. Then he withdrew his hand and slid down her body, gripping her hips roughly before drawing her quickly against his mouth.

She squeaked when his lips and tongue touched her right in her most intimate place. She reached down, grabbing hold of his hair, because she was going to pull him away, but then his tongue touched her in the most amazing spot and she found herself lacing her fingers through his hair instead.

She found herself holding him against her instead of pushing him away.

She moved her hips in time with him, gasping for air as pleasure, arousal, built to impossible heights. She had been on the edge for so long now it felt like she was poised on the brink of something else entirely. But right when she was about to break, he moved away from her, drawing himself up her body. He grabbed a small, round packet from the bedspread that she hadn't noticed until now, and tore it open, quickly sheathing himself before moving to position the blunt head of his arousal at her entrance.

He flexed his hips, thrusting deep inside her, and her arousal broke like a mirror hit with a hammer. She gritted her teeth as pain—sharp and jagged—cut through all the hidden places within her. But along with the pain came the intense sensation of being full. Of being connected to another person like she never had been before.

She reached up, taking his heavily muscled arms and holding him, just holding him, as he moved slowly inside her.

He was *inside* her.

She marveled at that truth even as the pain eased, even as pleasure began to push its way into the foreground again.

"Move with me," he said, nuzzling her neck, kissing the tender skin there.

So she did, meeting his every thrust, clinging to him. She could see the effort it took for him to maintain control, and she could see when his control began to fray. When his thrusts became erratic, his golden skin slick with sweat, his breathing rough and ragged, matching her own.

When he thrust deep, she arched her hips, an electric shower of sparks shimmering through her each time.

His hands were braced on either side of her shoulders, his strong fingers gripping the sheets. His movements became hard, rough, but none of the earlier pain remained, and she welcomed him. Opened her thighs wider and then wrapped her legs around his lean hips so she could take him even deeper.

There was no pain. There was no shame. There was no doubt at all.

As far as she was concerned, there was only the two of them.

He leaned down, pressing his forehead against hers, his dark gaze intense as his rhythm increased. He went shallow, then deep, the change pushing her even closer to the edge.

Then he pulled out almost completely, his hips pulsing slightly. The denial of that deep, intimate contact made her feel frantic. Made her feel needy. Made her feel desperate.

"Jonathan," she said. "Jonathan, please."

"Tell me you want to come," he told her, the words a growl.

"I want to come," she said, not wasting a moment on self-consciousness.

He slammed back home, and she saw stars. This orgasm grabbed her deep, reached places she hadn't known were there. The pleasure seemed to go on and on, and when it was done, she felt like she was floating on a sea, gazing up at a sky full of infinite stars.

She felt adrift, but only for a moment. Because when she came back to herself, she was still clutching his strong arms, Jonathan Bear rooting her to the earth.

And then she waited.

Waited for regret. Waited for guilt.

But she didn't feel any of it. Right now, she just felt a bone-deep satisfaction she hoped never went away.

"I…" He started to say something, moving away from

her. Then he frowned. "You don't have a toothbrush or anything, do you?"

It was such a strange question that it threw her for a loop. "What?"

"It doesn't matter," he said. He bent down, pressing a kiss to her forehead. "We'll work something out in the morning."

She was glad he'd said there was nothing to worry about, because her head was starting to get fuzzy and her eyelids were heavy. Which sucked, because she didn't want to sleep. She wanted to bask in her newfound warm and fuzzy feelings.

But she was far too sleepy, far too sated to do anything but allow herself to be enveloped by that warmth. By him.

He drew her into his arms, and she snuggled into his chest, pressing her palm against him. She could feel his heartbeat, hard and steady, beneath her hand.

And then, for the first time in her life, Hayley Thompson fell asleep in a man's arms.

CHAPTER EIGHT

JONATHAN DIDN'T SLEEP. As soon as Hayley drifted off, he went into his office, busying himself with work that didn't need to be done.

Women didn't spend the night at his house. He had never even brought a woman back to this house. But when Hayley had looked up at him like that... He hadn't been able to tell her to leave. He realized that she expected to stay. Because as far as she was concerned, sex included sleeping with somebody.

He had no idea where she had formed her ideas about relationships, but they were innocent. And he was a bastard. He had already known that, but tonight just confirmed it.

Except he had let her stay.

He couldn't decide if that was a good thing or not. Couldn't decide if letting her stay had been a kindness or a cruelty. Because the one thing it hadn't been was the reality of the situation.

The reality was this wasn't a relationship. The reality was, it had been... Well, a very bad idea.

He stood up from his desk, rubbing the back of his neck. It was getting light outside, pale edges beginning to bleed from the mountaintops, encroaching on the velvet middle of the sky.

He might as well go outside and get busy on morning

chores. And if some of those chores were in the name of avoiding Hayley, then so be it.

He made his way downstairs, shoved his feet into his boots and grabbed his hat, walking outside with heavy footsteps.

He paused, inhaling deeply, taking a moment to let the scent of the pines wash through him. This was his. All of it was his. He didn't think that revelation would ever get old.

He remembered well the way it had smelled on his front porch in the trailer park. Cigarette smoke and exhaust from cars as people got ready to leave for work. The noise of talking, families shouting at each other. It didn't matter if you were inside the house or outside. You lived way too close to your neighbors to avoid them.

He had fantasized about a place like this back then. Isolated. His. Where he wouldn't have to see another person unless he went out of his way to do so. He shook his head. And he had gone and invited Hayley to stay the night. He was a dumb ass.

He needed a ride to clear his head. The fact that he got to take weekends off now was one of his favorite things about his new position in life. He was a workaholic, and he had never minded that. But ranching was the kind of work he really enjoyed, and that was what he preferred to do with his free time.

He saddled his horse and mounted up, urging the bay gelding toward the biggest pasture. They started out at a slow walk, then Jonathan increased the pace until he and his horse were flying over the grass, patches of flowers blurring on either side of them, blending with the rich green.

It didn't matter what mess he had left behind at the

house. Didn't matter what mistakes he had made last night. It never did, not when he was on a horse. Not when he was in his sanctuary. The house... Well, he would be lying if he said that big custom house hadn't been a goal for him. Of course it had been. It was evidence that he had made it.

But this... The trees, the mountains, the wind in his face, being able to ride his horse until his lungs burned, and not reach the end of his property... That was the real achievement. It belonged to him and no one else. In this place he didn't have to answer to anyone.

Out here it didn't matter if he was bad. You couldn't let the sky down. You couldn't disappoint the mountains.

He leaned forward to go uphill, tightening his hold on the reins as the animal changed its gait. He pulled back, easing to a stop. He looked down the mountain, at the valley of trees spread out before him, an evergreen patchwork stitched together by rock and river. And beyond that, the ocean, brighter blue than usual on this exceptionally clear morning, the waves capped with a rosy pink handed down from the still-rising sun.

Hayley would love this.

That thought brought him up short, because he wasn't exactly sure why he thought she would. Or why he cared. Why he suddenly wanted to show her. He had never shown this view to anybody. Not even to his sister, Rebecca.

He had wanted to keep it for himself, because growing up, he'd had very little that belonged to him and him alone. In fact, up here, gazing at everything that belonged to him now, he couldn't think of a single damn thing that had truly belonged to him when he'd been younger.

It had all been for a landlord, for his sister, for the future.

This was what he had worked for his entire life.

He didn't need to show it to some woman he'd slept with last night.

He shook his head, turning the horse around and trotting down the hill, moving to a gallop back down to the barn.

When he exited the gate that would take him out of the pasture and back to the paddock, Jonathan saw Hayley standing in the path. Wearing last night's dress, her hair disheveled, she was holding two mugs of coffee.

He was tempted to imagine he had conjured her up just by thinking of her up on the ridge. But if it were a fantasy, she would have been wearing nothing, rather than being back in that black cotton contraption.

She was here, and it disturbed him just how happy that made him.

"I thought I might find you out here," she said. "And I figured you would probably want your coffee."

He dismounted, taking the reins and walking the horse toward Hayley. "It's your day off. You don't have to make me coffee."

Her cheeks turned pink, and he marveled at the blush. And on the heels of that marveling came the sharp bite of guilt. She was a woman who blushed routinely. And he had… Well, he had started down the path of corrupting her last night.

He had taken her virginity. Before her he'd never slept with a virgin in his damn life. In high school, that hadn't been so much out of a sense of honor as it had been out of a desire not to face down an angry dad with a shotgun. Better to associate with girls who had reputations worse than his own.

All that restraint had culminated in him screwing the pastor's daughter.

At least when people came with torches and pitchforks, he would have a decent-sized fortress to hole up in.

"I just thought maybe it would be nice," she said finally, taking a step toward him and extending the coffee mug in his direction.

"It is," he said, taking the cup, knowing he didn't sound quite as grateful as he might have. "Sorry," he conceded, sipping the strong brew, which was exactly the way he liked it. "I'm not used to people being nice. I'm never quite sure what to make of it when you are."

"Just take it at face value," she said, lifting her shoulder.

"Yeah, I don't do that."

"Why not?" she asked.

"I have to take care of the horse," he said. "If you want story time, you're going to have to follow me."

He thought his gruff demeanor might scare her off, but instead, she followed him along the fence line. He tethered his horse and set his mug on the fence post, then grabbed the pick and started on the gelding's hooves.

Hayley stepped up carefully on the bottom rung of the fence, settling herself on the top rung, clutching her mug and looking at him with an intensity he could feel even with his focus on the task at hand.

"I'm ready," she said.

He looked up at her, perched there like an inquisitive owl, her lips at the edge of her cup, her blue eyes round. She was...a study in contradictions. Innocent as hell. Soft in some ways, but determined in others.

It was her innocence that allowed her to be so open—
that was his conclusion. The fact that she'd never really
been hurt before made it easy for her to come at people
from the front.

"It's not a happy story," he warned.

It wasn't a secret one, either. Pretty much everybody
knew his tragic backstory. He didn't go around talking
about it, but there was no reason not to give her what she
was asking for.

Except for the fact that he never talked to the women
he hooked up with. There was just no point to it.

But then, the women he usually hooked up with never
stumbled out of his house early in the morning with cups
of coffee. So he supposed it was an unusual situation all
around.

"I'm a big girl," she said, her tone comically serious. It
was followed by a small slurp as she took another sip of
coffee. The sound should not have been cute, but it was.

"Right." He looked up at her, started to speak and
then stopped.

Would hearing about his past, about his childhood,
change something in her? Just by talking to her he might
ruin some of her optimism.

It was too late for worrying about that, he supposed.
Since sleeping with her when she'd never even kissed
anyone before had undoubtedly changed her.

There had been a lot of points in his life when he had
not been his own favorite person. The feeling was intense
right now. He was a damned bastard.

"I'm waiting," she said, kicking her foot slightly to
signify her impatience.

"My father left when I was five," he said.

"Oh," she said, blinking, clearly shocked. "I'm sorry."

"It was the best thing that had happened to me in all five years of my life, Hayley. The very best thing. He was a violent bastard. He hit my mother. He hit me. The day he left… I was a kid, but I knew even then that life was going to be better. I was right. When I was seven, my mom had another kid. And she was the best thing. So cute. Tiny and loud as hell, but my mother wasn't all that interested in me, and my new sister was. Plus she gave me, I don't know…a feeling of importance. I had someone to look after, and that mattered. Made me feel like maybe I mattered."

"Rebecca," Hayley said.

"Yeah," he replied. "Then, when Rebecca was a teenager, she was badly injured in a car accident. Needed a lot of surgeries, skin grafts. All of it was paid for by the family responsible for the accident, in exchange for keeping everything quiet. Of course, it's kind of an open secret now that Gage West was the one who caused the accident."

Hayley blinked. "Gage. Isn't she… Aren't they… Engaged?"

Familiar irritation surged through him. "For now. We'll see how long that lasts. I don't have a very high opinion of that family."

"Well, you know my brother is married into that family."

He shrugged. "All right, maybe I'll rephrase that. I don't have anything against Colton, or Sierra, or Maddy. But I don't trust Gage or his father one bit. I certainly don't trust him with my sister, any more now than I did then. But if things fall apart, if he ends up breaking off the engagement, or leaves her ten years into the marriage… I'll have a place for her. I've always got a place for her."

Hayley frowned. "That's a very cynical take. If Rebecca can love the man who caused her accident, there must be something pretty exceptional about him."

"More likely, my sister doesn't really know what love looks like," he said, his voice hard, the words giving voice to the thing he feared most. "I have to backtrack a little. A few months after the accident, my mom took the cash payout Nathan West gave her and took off. Left me with Rebecca. Left Rebecca without a mother, when she needed her mother the most. My mom just couldn't handle it. So I had to. And I was a piss-poor replacement for parents. An older brother with a crappy construction job and not a lot of patience." He shook his head. "Every damn person in my life who was supposed to be there for me bailed. Everyone who was supposed to be there for Rebecca."

"And now you're mad at her, too. For not doing what you thought she should."

Guilt stabbed him right in the chest. Yeah, he was angry at his sister. And he felt like he had no damn right to be angry. Shouldn't she be allowed to be happy? Hadn't that been the entire point of taking care of her for all those years? So she could get out from under the cloud of their family?

So she'd done it. In a huge, spectacular way. She'd ended up with the man she'd been bitter about for years. She had let go of the past. She had embraced it, and in a pretty damned literal way.

But Jonathan couldn't. He didn't trust in sudden changes of heart or professions of love. He didn't trust much of anything.

"I'll be mad if she gets hurt," he said finally. "But that's my default. I assume it's going to end badly because I've only ever seen these things end badly. I worked my ass off to keep the two of us off the streets. To make sure we had a roof over our heads, as much food in our stomachs as I could manage. I protected her." He shook his head. "And there's no protecting somebody if you aren't always looking out for what might go wrong. For what might hurt them."

"I guess I can't blame you for not trusting the good in people. You haven't seen it very many times."

He snorted. "Understatement of the century." He straightened, undoing the girth and taking the saddle off the bay in a fluid movement, then draping it over the fence. "But my cynicism has served me just fine. Look at where I am now. I started out in a single-wide trailer, and I spent years working just to keep that much. I didn't advance to this place by letting down my guard, by stopping for even one minute." He shook his head again. "I probably owe my father a thank-you note. My mother, too, come to that. They taught me that I couldn't trust anyone but myself. And so far that lesson's served me pretty well."

Hayley was looking at him like she was sad for him, and he wanted to tell her to stop it. Contempt, disgust and distrust were what he was used to getting from people. And he had come to revel in that reaction, to draw strength from it.

Pity had been in short supply. And if it was ever tossed in his general direction, it was mostly directed at Rebecca. He wasn't comfortable receiving it himself.

"Don't look at me like I'm a sad puppy," he said.

"I'm not," she returned.

He untied the horse and began to walk back into the barn. "You are. I didn't ask for your pity." He unhooked the lead rope and urged the gelding into his stall. "Don't go feeling things for me, Hayley. I don't deserve it. In fact, what you should have done this morning was walked out and slapped me in the face, not given me a cup of coffee."

"Why?"

"Because I took advantage of you last night. And you should be upset about that."

She frowned. "I should be?" She blinked. "I'm not. I thought about it. And I'm not."

"I don't know what you're imagining this is. I don't know what you think might happen next..."

She jumped down from the fence and set her coffee cup on the ground. Then she took one quick step forward. She hooked an arm around his neck and pushed herself onto her tiptoes, pressing her lips to his.

He was too stunned to react. But only for a moment. He wrapped an arm around her waist, pressing his forefinger beneath her chin and urging the kiss deeper.

She didn't have a lot of skill. That had been apparent the first and second times they'd kissed. And when they had come together last night. But he didn't need skill, he just needed her.

Even though it was wrong, he consumed her, sated his hunger on her mouth.

She whimpered, a sweet little sound that only fueled the driving hunger roaring in his gut. He grabbed her hair, tilting her head back farther, abandoning her mouth to scrape his teeth over her chin and down her neck, where he kissed her again, deep and hard.

He couldn't remember ever feeling like this before. Couldn't remember ever wanting a woman so much it was beyond the need for air. Sure, he liked sex. He was a man, after all. But the need had never been this specific. Had never been for one woman in particular.

But what he was feeling wasn't about sex, or about lust or desire. It was about her. About Hayley. The sweet little sounds she made when he kissed the tender skin on her neck, when he licked his way back up to her lips. The way she trembled with her need for him. The way she had felt last night, soft and slick and made only for him.

This was beyond anything he had ever experienced before. And he was a man who had experienced a hell of a lot.

That's what it was, he thought dimly as he scraped his teeth along her lower lip. And that said awful things about him, but then so did a lot of choices in his life.

He had conducted business with hard, ruthless precision, and he had kept his personal life free of any kind of connection beyond Rebecca—who he was loyal to above anyone else.

So maybe that was the problem. Now that he'd arrived at this place in life, he was collecting those things he had always denied himself. The comfortable home, the expansive mountains and a sweet woman.

Maybe this was some kind of latent urge. He had the homestead, now he wanted to put a woman in it.

He shook off that thought and all the rest. He didn't want to think right now. He just wanted to feel. Wanted to embrace the heat firing through his veins, the need stoking the flame low in his gut, which burned even more with each pass of her tongue against his.

She pulled away from him, breathing hard, her pupils dilated, her lips swollen and rounded into a perfect O. "That," she said, breathlessly, "was what I was thinking might happen next. And that we might… Take me back to bed, please."

"I can't think of a single reason to refuse," he said—a lie, as a litany of reasons cycled through his mind.

But he wasn't going to listen to them. He was going to take her, for as long as she was on offer. And when it ended, he could only hope he hadn't damaged her too much. Could only hope he hadn't broken her beyond repair.

Because there were a couple things he knew for sure. It would end; everything always did. And he would be the one who destroyed it.

He just hoped he didn't destroy her, too.

CHAPTER NINE

IT WAS LATE in the afternoon when Hayley and Jonathan finally got back out of bed. Hayley felt… Well, she didn't know quite what she felt. Good. Satisfied. Jonathan was… Well, if she'd ever had insecurities about whether or not she might be desirable to a man, he had done away with those completely. He had also taught her things about herself—about pleasure, about her own body—that she'd never in her wildest dreams conceived of.

She didn't know what would happen next, though. She had fallen asleep after their last time together, and when she'd awoken he was gone again. This morning, she had looked for him. She wasn't sure if she should do that twice.

Still, before she could even allow herself to ponder making the decision, she got out of bed, grabbed his T-shirt from the floor and pulled it over her head. Then she padded down the hallway, hoping he didn't have any surprise visitors. That would be a nightmare. Getting caught wearing only a T-shirt in her boss's hallway. There would be a lot of questions about what they had just spent the last few hours doing, that was for sure.

She wondered if Jonathan might be outside again, but she decided to check his office first. And was rewarded when she saw him sitting at the computer, his head lowered over the keyboard, some of his dark hair falling over his face after coming loose from the braid he normally kept it in.

Her heart clenched painfully, and it disturbed her that her heart was the first part of her body to tighten. The rest of her followed shortly thereafter, but she really wished her reaction was more about her body than her feelings. She couldn't afford to have feelings for him. She wasn't staying in Copper Ridge. And even if she were, he wouldn't want her long-term, anyway.

She took a deep breath, trying to dispel the strange, constricted feeling that had overtaken her lungs. "I thought I might find you here," she said.

He looked up, his expression betraying absolutely no surprise. He sneaked up on her all the time, but of course, as always, Jonathan was unflappable. "I just had a few schematics to check over." He pushed the chair away from the desk and stood, reaching over his head to stretch.

She was held captive by the sight of him. Even fully dressed, he was a beautiful thing.

His shoulders and chest were broad and muscular, his waist trim. His face like sculpted rock, or hardened bronze, uncompromising. But she knew the secret way to make those lips soften. Only for her.

No, not only for you. He does this all the time. They are just softening for you right now.

It was good for her to remember that.

"I'm finished now," he said, treating her to a smile that made her feel like melting ice cream on a hot day.

"Good," she said, not quite sure why she said it, because it wasn't like they had made plans. She wondered when he would ask her to leave. Or maybe he wanted her to leave, but didn't want to tell her. "It's late," she said. "I could go."

"Do you need to go?"

"No," she said, a little too quickly.

"Then don't."

Relief washed over her, and she did her best not to show him just how pleased she was by that statement. "Okay," she said, "then I won't go."

"I was thinking. About your list."

She blinked. "My list?"

"Yeah, your list. You had dancing on there. Pretty sure you had a kiss. And whether or not it was on the list… you did lose your virginity. Since I helped you with those items, I figured I might help you with some of the others."

A deep sense of pleasure and something that felt a lot like delight washed through her. "Really?"

"Yes," he said, "really. I figure we started all of this, so we might as well keep going."

"I don't have an official list."

"Well, that's ridiculous. If you're going to do this thing, you have to do it right." He grabbed a sheet of paper out of the printer and settled back down in the office chair. "Let's make a list."

He picked up a pen and started writing.

"What are you doing? I didn't tell you what I wanted yet."

"I'm writing down what we already did so you have the satisfaction of checking those off."

Her stomach turned over. "Don't write down all of it."

"Oh," he said, "I am. All of it. In detail."

"No!" She crossed the space between them and stood behind him, wrapping her arms around his broad shoulders as if she might restrain him. He kept on writing. She peered around his head, then slapped the pen out of his hand when she saw him writing a very dirty word. "Stop it. If anybody finds that list I could be…incriminated."

He laughed and swiveled the chair to the side. He wrapped his arm around her waist and pulled her onto his lap. "Oh no. We would hate for you to be incriminated. But on the other hand, the world would know you spent the afternoon with a very firm grip on my—"

"No!"

He looked at her and defiantly put a checkmark by what he had just written. She huffed, but settled into his hold. She liked this too much. Him smiling, him holding her when they had clothes on as if he just wanted to hold her.

It was nice to have him want her in bed. Very nice. But this was something else, and it was nice, too.

"Okay, so we have dancing, kissing, sex, and all of the many achievements beneath the sex," he said, ignoring her small noises of protest. "So what else?"

"I want to go to a place where I need a passport," she said.

"We could drive to Canada."

She laughed. "I was thinking more like Europe. But… Could we really drive to Canada?"

"Well," he said, "maybe not today, since I have to be back here by Monday."

"That's fine. I was thinking more Paris than Vancouver."

"Hey, they speak French in Canada."

"Just write it down," she said, poking his shoulder.

"Fine. What next?"

"I feel like I should try alcohol," she said slowly. "Just so I know."

"Fair enough." He wrote *get hammered*.

"That is not what I said."

"Sorry. I got so excited about the idea of getting you drunk. Lowering your inhibitions."

She rolled her eyes. "I'm already more uninhibited with you than I've ever been with anyone else." It was true, she realized, as soon as she said it. She was more herself with Jonathan than she had ever been with anyone, including her family, who had known her for her entire life.

Maybe it was the fact that, in a town full of people who were familiar with her, at least by reputation, he was someone she hadn't known at all until a couple weeks ago.

Maybe it was the fact that he had no expectations of her beyond what they'd shared. Whatever the case, around him she felt none of the pressure that she felt around other people in the community.

No need to censor herself, or hide; no need to be respectable or serene when she felt like being disreputable and wild.

"I want to kiss in the rain," she said.

"Given weather patterns," he said slowly, "we should be able to accomplish that, too."

She was ridiculously pleased he wanted to be a part of that, pleased that he hadn't said anything about her finding a guy to kiss in the rain in Paris. She shouldn't be happy he was assuming he would be the person to help her fulfill these things. She should be annoyed. She should feel like he was inserting himself into her independence, but she didn't. Mostly because he made her independence seem...well, like *more*.

"You're very useful, aren't you?"

He looked at her, putting his hand on her cheek, his

dark gaze serious as it met hers. "I'm glad I can be useful to you."

She felt him getting hard beneath her backside, and that pleased her, too. "Parts of you are very useful," she said, reaching behind her and slowly stroking his length.

The light in his eyes changed, turning much more intense. "Hayley Thompson," he said, "I would say that's shocking behavior."

"I would say you're responsible, Jonathan Bear."

He shook his head. "No, princess, you're responsible for this. For all of this. This is you. It's what you want, right? The things on your list that you don't even want to write down. It's part of you. You don't get to blame it all on me."

She felt strangely empowered by his words. By the idea that this was her, and not just him leading her somewhere.

"That's very… Well, that's very… I like it." She furthered her exploration of him, increasing the pressure of her touch. "At least, I like it with you."

"I'm not complaining."

"That's good," she said softly, continuing to stroke him through the fabric of his pants.

She looked down, watched herself touching him. It was…well, now that she had started, she didn't want to stop.

"I would be careful if I were you," he said, his tone laced with warning, "because you're about to start something, and it's very likely you need to take a break from all that."

"Do I? Why would I need a break?"

"Because you're going to get sore," he said, maddeningly pragmatic.

And, just as maddeningly, it made her blush to hear him say it. "I don't really mind," she said finally.

"You don't?" His tone was calm, but heat flared in the depths of his dark eyes.

"No," she replied, still trailing her fingertips over his hardening body. "I like feeling the difference. In me. I like being so…aware of everything we've done." For her, that was a pretty brazen proclamation, though she had a feeling it paled in comparison to the kinds of things other women had said to him in the past.

But she wasn't one of those other women. And right now he was responding to her, so she wasn't going to waste a single thought on anyone who had come before her. She held his interest now. That was enough.

"There's something else on my list," she said, fighting to keep her voice steady, fighting against the nerves firing through her.

"Is that so?"

She sucked in a sharp breath. "Yes. I want to… That is… What you did for me… A couple of times now… I want to… I want to…" She gave up trying to get the words out. She wasn't sure she had the right words for what she wanted to do, anyway, and she didn't want to humiliate herself by saying something wrong.

So, with unsteady hands, she undid the closure on his jeans and lowered the zipper. She looked up at him. If she expected to get any guidance, she was out of luck. He just stared at her, his dark eyes unfathomable, his jaw tight, a muscle in his cheek ticking.

She shifted on his lap, sliding gracefully to the floor in front of the chair. Then she went to her knees and turned to face him, flicking her hair out of her face.

He still said nothing, watching her closely, unnervingly so. But she wasn't going to turn back now. She lifted the waistband of his underwear, pulling it out in order to clear his impressive erection, then she pulled the fabric partway down his hips, as far as she could go with him sitting.

He was beautiful.

That feeling of intimidation she'd felt the first time she'd seen him had faded completely. Now she knew what he could do, and she appreciated it greatly. He had shown her so many things; he'd made her pleasure the number one priority. And she wanted to give to him in return.

Well, she also knew this would be for her, too.

She slid her hands up his thighs, then curled her fingers around his hardened length, squeezing him firmly. She was learning that he wasn't breakable there. That he liked a little bit of pressure.

"Hayley," he said, his voice rough, "I don't think you know what you're doing."

"No," she said, "I probably don't. But I know what I want. And it's been so much fun having what I want." She rose up slightly, then leaned in, pressing her lips to the head of his shaft. He jerked beneath her touch, and she took that as approval.

A couple hours ago she would have been afraid that she'd hurt him. But male pleasure, she was discovering, sometimes looked a little like pain. Heck, female pleasure was a little like pain. Sex was somewhere between. The aching need to have it all and the intense rush of satisfaction that followed.

She shivered just thinking about it.

And then she flicked her tongue out, slowly testing this new territory. She hummed, a low sound in the back of her throat, as she explored the taste of him, the texture.

Jonathan Bear was her favorite indulgence, she was coming to realize. There was nothing about him she didn't like. Nothing he had done to her she didn't love. She liked the way he felt, and apparently she liked the way he tasted, too.

She parted her lips slowly, worked them over the head, then swallowed down as much of him as she could. The accompanying sound he made hollowed out her stomach, made her feel weak and powerful at the same time.

His body was such an amazing thing. So strong, like it had been carved straight from the mountain. Yet it wasn't in any way cold or unmovable; it was hot. His body had changed hers. Yes, he'd taken her virginity, but he had also taught her to feel pleasure she hadn't realized she had the capacity to feel.

Such power in his body, and yet, right now, it trembled beneath her touch. The whisper-soft touch of her lips possessed the power to rock him, to make him shake. To make him shatter.

Right now, desire was enough. She didn't need skill. She didn't need experience. And she felt completely confident in that.

She slipped her tongue over his length as she took him in deep, and he bucked his hips lightly, touching the back of her throat. Her throat contracted and he jerked back.

"Sorry," he said, his voice strained.

"No," she said, gripping him with one hand and bringing her lips back against him. "Don't apologize. I like it."

"You're inexperienced."

She nodded slowly, then traced him with the tip of her tongue. "Yes," she agreed, "I am. I've never done this for any other man. I've never even thought about it before." His hips jerked again, and she realized he liked this. That he—however much he tried to pretend he didn't—liked that her desire was all for him.

"I think you might be corrupting me," she said, keeping her eyes wide as she took him back into her mouth.

He grunted, fisting his hands in her hair, but he didn't pull her away again.

The muscles in his thighs twitched beneath her fingertips, and he seemed to grow larger, harder in her mouth. She increased the suction, increased the friction, used her hands as well as her mouth to drive him as crazy as she possibly could.

There was no plan. There was no skill. There was just the need to make him even half as mindless as he'd made her over the past couple days.

He had changed her. He had taken her from innocence… to this. She would be marked by him forever. He would always be her first. But society didn't have a term for a person's experience after virginity. So she didn't have a label for the impact she wanted to make on him.

Jonathan hadn't been a virgin for a very long time, she suspected. And she probably wasn't particularly special as a sexual partner.

So she had to try to make herself special.

She had no tricks to make this the best experience he'd ever had. She had only herself. And so she gave it to him. All of her. Everything.

"Hayley," he said, his voice rough, ragged. "You better stop."

She didn't. She ignored him. She had a feeling he was close; she recognized the signs now. She had watched him reach the point of pleasure enough times that she had a fair idea of what it looked like. Of what it felt like.

His whole body tensing, his movements becoming less controlled.

She squeezed the base of him tightly, pulling him in deeper, and then he shattered. And she swallowed down every last shudder of need that racked his big body.

In the aftermath, she was dazed, her heart pounding hard, her entire body buzzing. She looked up at him from her position on the floor, and he looked down at her, his dark eyes blazing with…anger, maybe? Passion? A kind of sharp, raw need she hadn't ever seen before.

"You're going to pay for that," he said.

"Oh," she returned, "I hope so."

He swept her up, crushed her against his chest. "You have to put it on my list first," she said.

Then he brought his mouth down to hers, and whatever she'd intended to write down was forgotten until morning.

CHAPTER TEN

SOMETIME ON SUNDAY afternoon Hayley had gone home. Because, she had insisted, she wasn't able to work in either his T-shirt or the dress she had worn to the bar on Friday.

He hadn't agreed, but he had been relieved to have the reprieve. He didn't feel comfortable sharing the bed with her while he slept. Which had meant sleeping on the couch in the office after she drifted off.

He just… He didn't sleep with women. He didn't see the point in inviting that kind of intimacy. Having her spend the night in his bed was bad enough. But he hadn't wanted to send her home, either. He didn't want to think about why. Maybe it was because she expected to stay, because of her general inexperience.

Which made him think of the moment she had taken him into her mouth, letting him know he was the first man she had ever considered doing that for. Just the thought of it made his eyes roll back in his head.

Now, it was late Monday afternoon and she had been slowly driving him crazy with the prim little outfit she had come back to work in, as though he didn't know what she looked like underneath it.

Who knew he'd like a good girl who gave head like a dream.

She had also insisted that they stay professional during

work hours, and it was making it hard for him to concentrate. Of course, it was always hard for him to concentrate on office work. In general, he hated it.

Though bringing Hayley into the office certainly made it easier to bear.

Except for the part where it was torture.

He stood up from his chair and stretched slowly, trying to work the tension out of his body. But he had a feeling that until he was buried inside Hayley's body again, tension was just going to be the state of things.

"Oh," Hayley said, "Joshua Grayson just emailed and said he needs you to go by the county office and sign a form. And no, it can't be faxed."

For the first time in his life, Johathan was relieved to encounter bureaucracy. He needed to get out of this space. He needed to get his head on straight.

"Great," he said.

"Maybe I should go with you," she said. "I've never been down to the building and planning office, and you might need me to run errands in the future."

He gritted his teeth. "Yeah, probably."

"I'll drive my own car." She stood, grabbing her purse off the desk. "Because by the time we're done it will be time for me to get off."

He ground his teeth together even harder, because he couldn't ignore her double entendre even though he knew it had been accidental. And because, in addition to the double meaning, it was clear she intended to stay in town tonight and not at his place.

He should probably be grateful she wasn't being clingy. He didn't like to encourage women to get too attached to him, not at all.

"Great idea," he said.

But he didn't think it was a great idea, and he grumbled the entire way to town in the solitude of his pickup truck, not missing the irony that he had been wanting alone time, and was now getting it, and was upset about it.

The errand really did take only a few minutes, and afterward it still wasn't quite time for Hayley to clock out.

"Do you want to grab something to eat?" he asked, though he had no earthly idea why. He should get something for himself and go home, deal with that tension he had been pondering earlier.

She looked back and forth, clearly edgy. "In town?"

"Yes," he returned, "in town."

"Oh. I don't... I guess so."

"Calm down," he said. "I'm not asking you to Beaches. Let's just stop by the Crab Shanty."

She looked visibly relieved, and again he couldn't quantify why that annoyed him.

He knew they shouldn't be seen together in town. He had a feeling she also liked the casual nature of the restaurant. It was much more likely to look like a boss and employee grabbing something to eat than it was to look like a date.

They walked from where they had parked a few streets over, and paused at the crosswalk. They waited for one car to crawl by, clearly not interested in heeding the law that said pedestrians had the right-of-way. Then Jonathan charged ahead of her across the street and up to the faded yellow building. A small line was already forming outside the order window, and he noticed that Hayley took pains to stand slightly behind him.

When it was their turn to order, he decided he wasn't having any of her missish circumspection. They shouldn't be seen together as anything more than a boss and an assistant.

But right now, hell if he cared. "Two orders of fish and chips, the halibut. Two beers and a Diet Coke."

He pulled his wallet out and paid before Hayley could protest, then he grabbed the plastic number from the window, and the two of them walked over to a picnic table positioned outside the ramshackle building. There was no indoor seating, which could be a little bracing on windy days, and there weren't very many days that didn't have wind on the Oregon coast.

Jonathan set the number on the wooden table, then sat down heavily, looking up at the blue-and-white-striped umbrella wiggling in the breeze.

"Two beers?"

"One of them is for you," he said, his words verging on a growl.

"I'm not going to drink a beer." She looked sideways. "At least not here."

"Yeah, right out here on Main Street in front of God and everybody. You're a lot braver in my bedroom."

He was goading her, but he didn't much care. He was… Well dammit, it pissed him off. To see how ashamed she was to be with him. How desperate she was to hide it. Even if he understood it, it was like a branding iron straight to the gut.

"You can't say that so loud," she hissed, leaning forward, grabbing the plastic number and pulling it to her chest. "What if people heard you?"

"I thought you were reinventing yourself, Hayley Thompson."

"Not for the benefit of…the town. It's about me."

"It's going to be about you not getting dinner if you

keep hiding our number." He snatched the plastic trian-
gle from her hands.

She let out a heavy sigh and leaned back, crossing
her arms. "Well, the extra beer is for you. Put it in your
pocket."

"You can put it in your own pocket. Drink it back at
your place."

"No, thanks."

"Don't you want to tick that box on your list? We
ticked off some pretty interesting ones last night."

Her face turned scarlet. "You're being obnoxious, Jonathan."

"I've been obnoxious from day one. You just found it
easy to ignore when I had my hand in your pants."

Her mouth dropped open, then she snapped it shut
again. Their conversation was cut off when their food
was placed in front of them.

She dragged the white cardboard box toward her and
opened it, removing the container of coleslaw and setting it to the side before grabbing a french fry and biting
into it fiercely. Her annoyance was clearly telegraphed
by the ferocity with which she ate each bite of food. And
the determination that went into her looking at anything
and everything around them except for him.

"Enjoying the view?" he asked after a moment.

"The ocean is very pretty," she snapped.

"And you don't see it every day?"

"I never tire of the majesty of nature."

His lips twitched, in spite of his irritation. "Of course
not."

The wind whipped up, blowing a strand of dark hair
into Hayley's face. Reflexively, he reached across the

table and pushed it out of her eyes. She jerked back, her lips going slack, her expression shocked.

"You're my boss," she said, her voice low. "As far as everyone is concerned."

"Well," he said, "I'm your lover. As far as I'm concerned."

"Stop."

"I thought you wanted new experiences? I thought you were tired of hiding? And here you are, hiding."

"I don't want to…perform," she said. "My new experiences are for me. Not for everyone else's consumption. That's why I'm leaving. So I can…do things without an audience."

"You want your dirty secrets, is that it? You want me to be your dirty secret."

"It's five o'clock," she said, her tone stiff. "I'm going to go home now."

She collected her food, and left the beer, standing up in a huff and taking off down the street in the opposite direction from where they had parked.

"Where are you going?"

"Home," she said sharply.

He gathered up the rest of the food and stomped after her. "You parked the other way."

"I'll get it in the morning."

"Then you better leave your house early. Unless this is you tendering your resignation."

"I'm not quitting," she said, the color heightening in her face. "I'm just… I'm irritated with you."

She turned away from him, continuing to walk quickly down the street. He took two strides and caught up with her. "I see that." He kept pace with her, but she seemed bound and determined not to look at him. "Would you care to share why?"

"Not even a little bit."

"So you're insisting that you're my employee, and that you want to be treated like my employee in public. But that clearly excludes when you decide to run off having a temper tantrum."

She whirled around then, stopping in her tracks. "Why are you acting like this? You've been...much more careful than this up till now." She sniffed. "Out of deference to my innocence?"

"What innocence, baby? Because I took that." He smiled, knowing he was getting to her. That he was making her feel as bad as he did. "Pretty damn thoroughly."

"I can't do this with you. Not here." She paused at the street corner and looked both ways before hurrying across the two-lane road. He followed suit. She walked down the sidewalk, passed the coffeehouse, which was closing up for the day, then rounded the side of the brick building and headed toward the back.

"Is this where you live?" he asked.

"Maybe," she returned, sounding almost comically stubborn. Except he didn't feel like much was funny about this situation.

"Here in the alley?" he asked, waving his hand around the mostly vacant space.

"Yes. In the Dumpster with the mice. It's not so bad. I shredded up a bunch of newspaper and made a little bed."

"I suspect this is the real reason you've been spending the night at my place, then."

She scowled. "If you want to fight with me, come upstairs."

He didn't want to fight with her. He wanted to grab her, pull her into his arms and kiss her. He wanted to stop talking. Wanted to act logical instead of being wounded by something he knew he should want to avoid.

It didn't benefit him to have anyone in town know what he was doing with Hayley. He should want to hide it as badly as she did.

But the idea that she was enjoying his body, enjoying slumming it with him in the sheets, and was damned ashamed of him in the streets burned like hell.

But he followed her through the back door to a little hallway that contained two other doors. She unlocked one of them and held it open for him. Then she gestured to the narrow staircase. "Come on."

"Who's the boss around here?"

"I'm off the clock," she said.

He shrugged, then walked up the stairs and into an open-plan living room with exposed beams and brick. It was a much bigger space than he had expected it to be, though it was also mostly empty. As if she had only half committed to living there.

But then, he supposed, her plan *was* to travel the world.

"Nice place," he said.

"Yeah," she said. "Cassie gave me a deal."

"Nice of her."

"Some people are nice, Jonathan."

"Meaning I'm not?" he asked.

She nodded in response, her mouth firmly sealed, her chin jutting out stubbornly.

"Right. Because I bought you fish and french fries and beer. And I give you really great orgasms. I'm a monster."

"I don't know what game you're playing," she said, suddenly looking much less stubborn and a little more wobbly. And that made him feel something close to guilty. "What's the point in blurring the lines while we walk through town? We both know this isn't a relation-ship. It's…it's boxes being ticked on a list."

"Sure. But why does it matter if people in town know you're doing that?"

"You know why it matters. Don't play like you don't understand. You do. I know you do. You know who I am, and you know that I feel like I'm under a microscope. I shared all of that with you. Don't act surprised by it now."

"Well," he said, opting for honesty even though he knew it was a damned bad idea. "Maybe I don't like being your dirty secret."

"It's not about you. Any guy that I was… Anyone that I was…doing this with. It would be a secret. It has to be."

"Why?"

"Because!" she exploded. "Because everyone will be…disappointed."

"Honey," he said, "I don't think people spend half as much time thinking about you as you think they do."

"No," she said. "They do. You know Ace. He's the pastor's son. He ran away from home, he got married, he got divorced. Then he came back and opened a bar. My parents…they're great. They really are. But they had a lot of backlash over that. People saying that the Bible itself says if you train up a child the way he should go, he's not going to depart from it. Well, he departed from it, at least as far as a lot of the congregants were concerned. People actually left the church." She sucked in a sharp breath, then let it out slowly. "I wanted to do better than that for them. It was important. For me to be…the good one."

Caring about what people thought was a strange con-cept. Appearances had never mattered to Jonathan. For him, it had always been about actions. What the hell did Rebecca care if he had been good? All she cared about was being taken care of. He couldn't imagine being bound by rules like that.

For the first time, he wondered if there wasn't some kind of freedom in no one having a single good expectation of you.

"But you don't like being the good one. At least, not by these standards."

Her eyes glittered with tears now. She shook her head. "I don't know. I just… I don't know. I'm afraid. Afraid of what people will think. Afraid of what my parents will think. Afraid of them being disappointed. And hurt. They've always put a lot of stock in me being what Ace wasn't. They love Ace, don't get me wrong. It's just…"

"He made things hard for them."

Hayley nodded, looking miserable. "Yes. He did. And I don't want to do that. Only…only, I was the good one and he still ended up with the kind of life I want."

"Is that all?" Jonathan asked. "Or are you afraid of who you might be if you don't have all those rules to follow?"

A flash of fear showed in her eyes, and he felt a little guilty about putting it there. Not guilty enough to take it back. Not guilty enough to stay away from her. Not guilty enough to keep his hands to himself. He reached out, cupping her cheek, then wrapped his arm around her waist and drew her toward him. "Does it scare you? Who you might be if no one told you what to do? I don't care about the rules, Hayley. You can be whoever you want with me. Say whatever you want. Drink whatever you want. Do whatever you want."

"I don't know," she said, wiggling against him, trying to pull away. "I don't know what I want."

"I think you do. I just think you wish you wanted

something else." He brushed his thumb over her cheekbone. "I think you like having rules because it keeps you from going after what scares you."

He ignored the strange reverberation those words set off inside him. The chain reaction that seemed to burst all the way down his spine.

Recognition.

Truth.

Yeah, he ignored all that, and he dipped his head, claiming her mouth with his own.

Suddenly, it seemed imperative that he have her here. In her apartment. That he wreck this place with his desire for her. That he have her on every surface, against every wall, so that whenever she walked in, whenever she looked around, he was what she thought of. So that she couldn't escape this. So that she couldn't escape him.

"You think you know me now?" she asked, her eyes squinting with challenge. Clearly, she wasn't going to back down without a fight. And that was one of the things he liked about her. For all that she was an innocent church secretary, she had spirit. She had the kind of steel backbone that he admired, that he respected. The kind of strength that could get you through anything. But there was a softness to her, as well, and that was something more foreign to him. Something he had never been exposed to, had never really been allowed to have.

"Yeah," he said, tightening his hold and drawing her against his body. "I know you. I know what you look like naked. I know every inch of your skin. How it feels, how it tastes. I know you better than anybody does, baby. You can tell yourself that's not true. You can say that this, what we have, is the crazy thing. That it's a break from your real life. That it's some detour you don't want anyone in town to know you're taking. But I know the truth. And I think somewhere deep down you know it, too. This isn't the break. All that other stuff…prim, proper church girl. That's what isn't real." He cupped her face, smoothing his thumbs over her cheeks. "You're fire, honey, and together we are an explosion."

He kissed her then, proving his point. She tasted like anger, like need, and he was of a mind to consume both. Whatever was on offer. Whatever she would give him.

He was beyond himself. He had never wanted a woman like this before. He had never wanted anything quite like this before. Not money, not security, not his damned house on the hill.

All that want, all that need, paled in comparison to what he felt for Hayley Thompson. The innocent little miss who should have bored him to tears by now, had him aching, panting and begging for more.

He was so hard he was in physical pain.

And when she finally capitulated, when she gave herself over to the kiss, soft fingertips skimming his shoulders, down his back, all the way to his ass, he groaned in appreciation.

There was something extra dirty about Hayley exploring his body. About her wanting him the way she did, because she had never wanted another man like she wanted him. By her own admission. And she had never had a man the way she'd had him, which was an admission she didn't have to make.

He gripped her hips, then slipped his hands down her thighs, grabbing them and pulling her up, urging her legs around his waist. Then he propelled them both across the living room, down onto the couch. He covered her, pressing his hardness against the soft, sweet apex of her thighs. She gasped as he rolled his hips forward.

"Not so ashamed of this now, are you?" He growled, pressing a kiss to her neck, then to her collarbone, then to the edge of her T-shirt.

"I'm not ashamed," she said, gasping for air.

"You could've fooled me, princess."

"It's not about you." She sifted her fingers through his hair. "I'm not ashamed of you."

"Not ashamed of your dirty, wrong-side-of-the-tracks boyfriend?"

Her eyes flashed with hurt and then fascination. "I've never thought of you that way. I never... *Boyfriend?*"

Something burned hot in his chest. "Lover. Whatever."

"I'm not ashamed of you," she reiterated. "Nothing about you. You're so beautiful. If anything, you ought to be ashamed of me. I'm not pretty. Not like you. And I don't even know what I'm doing. I just know what I want. I want you. And I'm afraid for anybody to know the truth. I'm so scared. The only time I'm not scared is when you're holding me."

He didn't want to talk anymore. He consumed her mouth, tasting her deeply, ramping up the arousal between them with each sweet stroke of his tongue across hers. With each deep taste of the sweet flavor that could only ever be Hayley.

He gripped the hem of her top, yanking it over her head, making quick work of her bra. Exposing small, perfect breasts to his inspection. She was pale. All over. Ivory skin, coral-pink nipples. He loved the look of her. Loved the feel of her. Loved so many things about her that it was tempting to just go ahead and say he loved *her*.

That thought swam thick and dizzy in his head. He

could barely grab hold of it, didn't want to. So he shoved it to the side. He wasn't going to claim that. Hell no.

He didn't love people. He loved *things*.

He could love her tits, and he could love her skin, could love the way it felt to slide inside her, slick and tight. But he sure as hell couldn't love *her*.

He bent his head, taking one hardened nipple into his mouth, sucking hard, relishing the horse sound of pleasure on her lips as he did so. Then he kissed his way down her stomach, to the edge of her pants, pulling them down her thighs, leaving her bare and open.

He pressed his hand between her legs, slicked his thumb over her, teased her entrance with one finger. She began to whimper, rolling her hips under him, arching them to meet him, and he watched. Watched as she took one finger inside, then another.

He damn well watched himself corrupt her, and he let himself enjoy it. Because he was sick, because he was broken, but at least it wasn't a surprise.

Everyone in his life was familiar with it.

His father had tried to beat it out of him. His mother had run from it.

Only Rebecca had ever stayed, and it was partly because she didn't know any better.

Hayley didn't know any better, either, come to that. Not really. Not when it came to men. Not when it came to sex. She was blinded by what he could make her body feel, so she had an easy enough time ignoring the rest. But that wouldn't last forever.

Fair enough, since they wouldn't last forever, anyway. They both knew it. So there was no point in worrying about it. Not really.

Instead, he would embrace this, embrace the rush. Embrace the hollowed out feeling in his gut that bordered on sickness. The tension in his body that verged on pain. The need that rendered him hard as iron and hot as fire.

"Come for me," he commanded, his voice hoarse. All other words, all other thoughts were lost to him. All he could do was watch her writhing beneath his touch, so hot, so wet for him, arching her hips and taking his fingers in deeper.

"Not yet," she gasped, emitting little broken sounds.

"Yes," he said. "You will. You're going to come for me now, Hayley, because I told you to. Your body is mine. You're mine." He slid his thumb over the delicate bundle of nerves there.

And then he felt her shatter beneath his touch. Felt her internal muscles pulse around his knuckles.

He reached into his back pocket, took out his wallet and found a condom quickly. He tore it open, then wrenched free his belt buckle and took down the zipper. He pushed his jeans partway down his hips, rolled the condom on his hard length and thrust inside her, all the way to the hilt. She was wet and ready for him, and he had to grit his teeth to keep from embarrassing himself, to keep it from being over before it had begun.

She gasped as he filled her, and then grabbed his ass when he retreated. Her fingernails dug into his skin, and he relished the pain this petite little thing could inflict on him. Of course, it was nothing compared to the pain he felt from his arousal. From the great, burning need inside him.

No, nothing compared to that. Nothing at all.

He adjusted their positions, dragging her sideways on the couch, bringing her hips to the edge of the cushion, going down on his knees to the hardwood floor.

He knelt there, gripping her hips and pulling her tightly against him, urging her to wrap her legs around him. The floor bit into his knees, but he didn't care. All he cared about was having her, taking her, claiming her. He gripped her tightly, his blunt fingertips digging into her flesh.

He wondered if he would leave a mark. He hoped he might.

Hoped that she would see for days to come where he had held her. Even if she wouldn't hold his hand in public, she would remember when he'd held her hips in private, when he'd driven himself deep inside her, clinging to her like she might be the source of all life.

Yeah, she would remember that. She would remember this.

He watched as a deep red flush spread over her skin, covering her breasts, creeping up her neck. She was on the verge of another orgasm. He loved that. Another thing he was allowed to love.

Loved watching her lose control. Loved watching her so close to giving it up for him again, completely. Utterly. He was going to ruin her for any other man. That was his vow, there and then, on the floor of her apartment, with a ragged splinter digging into his knee through the fabric of his jeans. She was never going to fuck anyone else without thinking of him. Without wanting him. Without wishing it were him.

She would go to Paris, and some guy would do her with a view of the Eiffel tower in the background. And she would wish she were here, counting the familiar beams on her ceiling.

And when she came home for a visit and she passed

him on the street, she would shiver with a longing that she would never quite get rid of.

So many people in his life had left him. As far as he'd known, they had done it without a backward glance. But Hayley would never forget him. He would make sure of it. Damn sure.

His own arousal ratcheted up to impossible proportions. He was made entirely of his need for her. Of his need for release. And he forgot what he was trying to do. Forgot that this was about her. That this was about making her tremble, making her shake. Because he was trembling. He was shaking.

He was afraid he might be the one who was indelibly marked by all this.

He was the one who wouldn't be able to forget. The one who would never be with anyone else without thinking of her. No matter how skilled the woman was who might come after her, it would never be the same as the sweet, genuine urging of Hayley's hips against his. It would never be quite like the tight, wet clasp of her body.

He had been entirely reshaped, remade, to fit inside her, and no one else would do.

That thought ignited in his stomach, overtook him completely, lit him on fire.

When he came, it was with her name on his lips, with a strange satisfaction washing through him that left him only hungrier in the end, emptier. Because this was ending, and he knew it.

She wasn't going to work for him forever. She wasn't going to stay in Copper Ridge. She might hold on to him in secret, but in public, she would never touch him.

And as time passed, she would let go of him by inches,

walking off to the life of freedom she was so desperate for.

Walking off like everyone else.

Right now, she was looking up at him, a mixture of wonder and deep emotion visible in her blue eyes. She reached up, stroking his face. Some of his hair had been tugged from the leather strap, and she brushed the strands out of his eyes.

It was weird how that hit him. How it touched him. After all the overtly sexual ways she'd put her hands on him, why that sweet gesture impacted him low and deep.

"Stay with me," she said, her voice soft. "The night. In my bed."

That hit even harder.

He had never slept with her. He didn't sleep with women. But that was all about to change. He was going to sleep with her because he wanted to. Because he didn't want to release his hold on her for one moment, not while he still had her.

"Okay," he said.

Then, still buried deep inside her, he picked her up from the couch, brought them both to a standing position and started walking toward the door at the back of the room. "Bedroom is this way?"

"How did you know?"

"Important things, I know. Where the bedroom is." He kissed her lips. "How to make you scream my name. That I know."

"Care to make me scream it a few more times?"

"The neighbors might hear."

It was a joke, but he could still see her hesitation. "That's okay," she said slowly.

And even though he was reasonably confident that

was a lie, he carried her into her bedroom and lay down on the bed with her.

It didn't matter if it was a lie. Because they had all night to live in it. And that was good enough for him.

CHAPTER ELEVEN

WHEN HE WOKE up the next morning he was disoriented. He was lying in a bed that was too small for his large frame, and he had a woman wrapped around him. Of course, he knew immediately which woman it was. It couldn't be anyone else. Even in the fog of sleep, he wasn't confused about Hayley's identity.

She smelled like sunshine and wildflowers. Or maybe she just smelled like soap and skin and only reminded him of sunshine and wildflowers, because they were innocent things. New things. The kinds of things that could never be corrupted by the world around them.

The kinds of things not even he could wreck.

She was that kind of beautiful.

But the other reason he was certain it was Hayley was that there was no other woman he would have fallen asleep with. It was far too intimate a thing, sharing a bed with someone when you weren't angling for an orgasm. He had never seen the point of it. It was basically the same as sharing a toothbrush, and he wasn't interested in that, either.

He looked at Hayley, curled up at his side, her brown hair falling across her face, her soft lips parted, her breathing easy and deep. The feeling carved out in his chest was a strange one.

Hell, lying there in the early morning, sharing a toothbrush with Hayley didn't even seem so insane.

He sat up, shaking off the last cobwebs of sleep and extricating himself from Hayley's hold. He groaned when her fingertips brushed the lower part of his stomach, grazing his insistent morning erection. He had half a mind to wake her up the best way he knew how.

But the longer the realization of what had happened last night sat with him, the more eager he was to put some distance between them.

He could get some coffee, get his head on straight and come back fully clothed. Then maybe the two of them could prepare for the workday.

He needed to compartmentalize. He had forgotten that yesterday. He had let himself get annoyed about something that never should have bothered him. Had allowed old hurts to sink in when he shouldn't give a damn whether or not Hayley wanted to hold his hand when they walked down the street. She wasn't his girlfriend. And all the words that had passed between them in the apartment, all the anger that had been rattling around inside him, seemed strange now. Like it had all happened to somebody else. The morning had brought clarity, and it was much needed.

He hunted around the room, collecting his clothes and tugging them on quickly, then he walked over to the window, drew back the curtains and tried to get a sense of what time it was. She didn't have a clock in her room. He wondered if she just looked at her phone.

The sky was pink, so it had to be nearing six. He really needed to get home and take care of the horses. He didn't want to mess up their routine. But he would come back. Or maybe Hayley would just come to his place on time.

Then he cursed, realizing he had left his car at the other end of Main Street. He walked back to the living room, pulled on his boots and headed out the door, down the stairs. His vision was blurry, and he was in desperate need of caffeine. There were two doors in the hallway, and he reached for the one closest to him.

And nearly ran right into Cassie Caldwell as he walked into The Grind.

The morning sounds of the coffee shop filled his ears, the intense smell of the roast assaulting him in the best way.

But Cassie was staring at him, wide-eyed, as were the ten people sitting inside the dining room. One of whom happened to be Pastor John Thompson.

Jonathan froze, mumbled something about coming in through the back door, and then walked up to the counter. He was going to act like there was nothing remarkable about where he had just come from. Was going to do his very best to look like there was nothing at all strange about him coming through what he now realized was a private entrance used only by the tenant upstairs. It didn't escape his notice that the pastor was eyeballing him closely. And so was Cassie. Really, so was everybody. Damn small town.

Now, he could see why Hayley had been so vigilant yesterday.

If only he could go back and be vigilant in his door choice.

"Black coffee," he said, "two shots of espresso."

Cassie's gaze turned hard. "I know."

"I came through the wrong door," he said.

She walked over to the espresso machine, wrapped a damp cloth around the wand that steamed the milk and twisted it, a puff of steam coming out as she jerked the cloth up and down roughly, her eyes never leaving his. "Uh-huh."

"I did."

"And it's just a coincidence that my tenant happens to live upstairs. My tenant who works for you." She said that part softly, and he was sure nobody else in the room heard it.

"That's right," he said. "Just a coincidence."

Suddenly, the door to the coffee shop opened again, and Hayley appeared, wearing a T-shirt and jeans, her hair wild, like she had just rolled out of bed.

Her eyes widened when she saw her father. Then she looked over at the counter and her eyes widened even further when she saw Jonathan.

"Good morning," he said, his voice hard. "Fancy meeting you here before work."

"Yes," she said. "I'm just gonna go get ready."

She turned around and walked back out of the coffee shop, as quickly as she had come in. So much for being casual. If he hadn't already given it away, he was pretty sure Hayley's scampering had.

"You were saying?" Cassie said, her tone brittle.

"I'm sorry," he said, leaning in. "Is she your sister?"

"No."

"Best friend?"

"No."

"Is she your daughter? Because I have a feeling I'm about to catch hell from the reverend here in a few minutes, but I'm not really sure why I'm catching it from you."

"Because I know her. I know all about you. I am friends with your sister, and I know enough through her."

"Undoubtedly all about my great personal sacrifice and sparkling personality," he said.

Cassie's expression softened. "Rebecca loves you. But she's also realistic about the fact that you aren't a love-and-commitment kind of guy. Also, I do believe Ms. Hayley Thompson is younger than your sister."

"And last I checked, I wasn't committing any crimes. I will just take the coffee. You can keep the lecture."

He was not going to get chased out of the coffee shop, no matter how many people looked at him. No matter how much Cassie lectured him.

He was not the poor kid he'd once been. He was more than just a boy who had been abandoned by both parents. He was a damned boon to the town. His business brought in good money. *He* brought in good money. He wasn't going to be treated like dirt beneath anybody's shoe.

Maybe Hayley was too good for him, but she was sleeping with him. She wanted him. So it wasn't really up to anybody to say that she shouldn't.

When he turned around after Cassie gave him his coffee, the pastor stood up at his table and began to make his way over to Jonathan.

"Hello. Jonathan, right?" the older man said, his voice shot through with the same kind of steel that Jonathan often heard in Hayley's voice. Clearly, she got her strength from her father. It was also clear to Jonathan that he was not being spoken to by a pastor at the moment. But by a fairly angry dad.

"Pastor John," Jonathan said by way of greeting.

"Why don't you join me for a cup of coffee?"

Not exactly the words Jonathan had expected, all things considered. He could sense the tension in the room, sense the tension coming off Hayley's father.

People were doing their very best to watch, without appearing to do so. Any hope Jonathan had retained that they were oblivious to what it meant that he had come down from the upstairs apartment was dashed by just how fascinated they all were. And by the steady intent on Pastor John's face.

If the old man wanted to sit him down and humiliate him in front of the town, wanted to talk about how Jonathan wasn't fit to lick the dust off Hayley's boots, Jonathan wouldn't be surprised. Hell, he welcomed it. It was true, after all.

"I think I will," Jonathan said, following the other man back to his table.

He took a seat, his hand curled tightly around his coffee cup.

"I don't think we've ever formally met," John said, leaning back in his chair.

"No," Jonathan said, "we wouldn't have. I don't recall darkening the door of the church in my lifetime. Unless it was to repair something."

Let him know just what kind of man Jonathan was. That's where this was headed, anyway. Jonathan had never met a woman's parents before. He had never been in a relationship that was serious enough to do so. And this wasn't serious, either. But because of this damn small town and Hayley's role in it, he was being forced into a position he had never wanted to be in.

"I see," the pastor said. "Hayley has been working for you for the past couple of weeks, I believe."

He was cutting right to the chase now. To Jonathan's connection to Hayley, which was undeniable. "Yes."

"I've been very protective of Hayley. Possibly overprotective. But when my son, Ace, went out on his own, he didn't find much but heartbreak. I transferred some of my fear of that happening again onto Hayley, to an unfair degree. So I kept her close. I encouraged her to keep working at the church. To live at home for as long as possible. You have a sister, don't you?"

Damn this man and his ironclad memory for detail. "I didn't think it was Christian to gossip. But I can see that you've certainly heard your share about me."

"I do know a little something about you, yes. My son is married to one of Nathan West's children, as I'm sure you know. And your sister has a connection to that family, as well."

Jonathan gritted his teeth. "Yes. My sister is with Gage. Though only God knows why. Maybe you could ask Him."

"Matters of the heart are rarely straightforward. Whether it's in the case of romantic love, or the love you feel for your children, or your sister. It's a big emotion. And it is scary at times. Not always the most rational. What you feel about Rebecca being with Gage I suppose is similar to the concerns I have about Hayley."

"That she's with a bastard who doesn't deserve her?"

The pastor didn't even flinch. "That she's involved deeply enough that she could be hurt. And if we're going to speak plainly, I suppose the question I could ask you is whether or not you would think any man was good enough for Rebecca, or if you would be concerned—no matter who it was—that he wouldn't handle her with the care you would want."

Jonathan didn't have much to say about that. Only because he was trying to be angry. Trying to take offense at the fact that the older man was questioning him. Trying to connect this conversation to what he knew to be true—everybody looked at him and saw someone who wasn't worthy. He certainly didn't deserve kindness from this man, not at all. Didn't deserve for him to sit here and try to forge some kind of connection.

Jonathan had taken advantage of Hayley. Regardless of her level of experience, she was his employee. Even if she had been with a hundred men, what he had done would be problematic. But, as far as he was concerned, the problem was compounded by the fact that Hayley had been innocent.

So he waited. He waited for that hammer to fall. For the accusations to fly.

But they didn't come. So he figured he might try to create a few.

"I'm sure there's a certain type of man you would prefer your daughter be with. But it's definitely not the guy with the bad reputation you'd want stumbling out of her apartment early in the morning."

John nodded slowly, and Jonathan thought—with a certain amount of triumph—that he saw anger flicker briefly in the older man's eyes.

"I told you already that I feel very protective of her," Pastor John said. "But I wonder if, by protecting her as much as I did, I shielded her too effectively from the reality of life. I don't want her to get hurt." He let out a long, slow breath. "But that is not within my control."

"Is this the part where you ask me about my intentions toward your daughter? Because I highly doubt we're ever going to sit around a dinner table and try to make small talk. This isn't that sort of thing." With those words, Jonathan effectively told Hayley's father that all he was doing was fooling around with her. And that wasn't strictly true. Also, he hated himself a little bit for pretending it was.

For saying that sort of thing to her father when he knew it would embarrass her.

But in a way, it would be a mercy. She cared what people in town thought about her. She cared about her father's opinion. And this conversation would make it so much easier for her to let Jonathan go when the time came.

She was always going to let you go. She has traveling to do, places to see. You were her dirty detour along the way. You're the one who needs distance. You're the one who needs to find a way to make it easier.

He ignored that voice, ignored the tightening in his chest.

"Why isn't it that sort of thing?" The question, issued from Hayley's father, his tone firm but steady, reached something deep inside Jonathan, twisted it, cracked it.

It couldn't be anything more than temporary. Because of him. Because of what he was. Who he was. That should be obvious. It would have been even more obvious if Pastor John had simply sat down and started hurling recriminations. About how Jonathan was beneath the man's pure, innocent daughter. About why a formerly impoverished man from the wrong side of the tracks could never be good enough for a woman like her.

It didn't matter that he had money now. He was the same person he had been born to be. The same boy who had been beaten by his father, abandoned by his mother. All that was still in him. And no custom home, no amount of money in his bank account, was ever going to fix it.

If John Thompson wouldn't look at him and see that, if he wouldn't shout it from across a crowded coffee shop so the whole town would hear, then Jonathan was going to have to make it clear.

"Because it's not something I do," he returned, his voice hard. "I'm in for temporary. That's all I've got."

"Well," John said, "that's a pretty neat lie you've been telling yourself, son. But the fact of the matter is, it's only the most you're willing to give, not the most you have the ability to give."

"And you're saying you want me to dig down deep and find it inside myself to be with your daughter forever? Something tells me that probably wouldn't be an ideal situation as far as you're concerned."

"That's between you and Hayley. I have my own personal feelings about it, to be sure. No father wants to believe that his daughter is being used. But if I believe that, then it means I don't see anything good in you, and that isn't true. Everybody knows how you took care of your sister. Whatever you think the people in this town believe about you, they do know that. I can't say you haven't been mistreated by the people here, and it grieves me to think about it."

He shook his head, and Jonathan was forced to believe the older man was being genuine. He didn't quite know what to do with that fact, but he saw the same honesty shining from John that he often saw in Hayley's eyes. An emotional honesty Jonathan had limited experience with.

The older man continued. "You think you don't have the capacity for love? When you've already mentioned your concern for Rebecca a couple of times in this conversation? When the past decade and a half of your life was devoted to caring for her? It's no secret how hard you've worked. I may never have formally met you until this moment, but I know about you, Jonathan Bear, and what I know isn't the reputation you seem to think you have."

"Well, regardless of my reputation, you should be concerned about Hayley's. When I came through that door this morning, it was unintentional. But it's important to Hayley that nobody realizes what's happening between us. So the longer I sit here talking to you, the more risk there is of exposing her to unnecessary chatter. And that's not what I want. So," he said, "out of respect for keeping it a secret, like Hayley wants—"

"That's not what I want."

CHAPTER TWELVE

HAYLEY WAS SHAKING. She had been shaking from the moment she had walked into The Grind and seen Jonathan there, with her father in the background.

Somehow, she had known—just known—that everyone in the room was putting two and two together and coming up with sex.

And she also knew she had definitely made it worse by running away. If she had sauntered in and acted surprised to see Jonathan there, she might have made people think it really was coincidental that the two of them were both in the coffeehouse early in the morning, coming through the same private door. For reasons that had nothing to do with him spending the night upstairs with her.

But she had spent the past five minutes pacing around upstairs, waiting for her breath to normalize, waiting for her heart to stop beating so hard. Neither thing had happened.

Then she had cautiously crept back downstairs and come in to see her father sitting at the table with Jonathan. Fortunately, Jonathan hadn't looked like he'd been punched in the face. But the conversation had definitely seemed tense.

And standing there, looking at what had been her worst nightmare not so long ago, she realized that it just… wasn't. She'd never been ashamed of Jonathan. He was…

the most determined, hardworking, wonderful man she had ever known. He had spent his life raising his sister. He had experienced a childhood where he had known nothing but abandonment and abuse, and he had turned around and given love to his sister, unconditionally and tirelessly.

And, yeah, maybe it wasn't ideal to announce her physical affair with him at the coffee shop, all things considered, but…whatever she had expected to feel… She didn't.

So, it had been the easiest thing in the world to walk over to their table and say that she really didn't need to keep their relationship a secret. Of course, now both Jonathan and her father were looking at her like she had grown a second head.

When she didn't get a response from either of them, she repeated, "That's not what I want."

"Hayley," Jonathan said, his tone firm. "You don't know what you're saying."

"Oh, please," she returned. "Jonathan, that tone wouldn't work on me in private, and it's not going to work on me here, either."

She took a deep breath, shifting her weight from foot to foot, gazing at her father, waiting for him to say something. He looked… Well, it was very difficult to say if John Thompson could ever really be surprised. In his line of work, he had seen it all, heard it all. While Protestants weren't much for confession, people often used him as a confessional, she knew.

Still, he looked a little surprised to be in this situation.

She searched his face for signs of disappointment. That was her deepest fear. That he would be disappointed in her. Because she had tried, she really had, to be the child Ace wasn't.

Except, as she stood there, she realized that was a steaming pile of bull-pucky. Her behavior wasn't about being what Ace hadn't been. It was all about desperately wanting to please people while at the same time wishing there was a way to please herself. And the fact of the matter was, she couldn't have both those things. Not always.

That contradiction was why she had been hell-bent on running away, less because she wanted to experience the wonders of the world and more because she wanted to go off and do what she wanted without disappointing anyone.

"Jonathan isn't just my boss," she said to her dad. "He's my… Well, I don't really know. But…you know." Her throat tightened, tears burning behind her eyes.

Yes, she wanted to admit to the relationship, and she wanted to live out in the open, but that didn't make the transition from good girl to her own woman any easier.

She wanted to beg her dad for his approval. He wasn't a judgmental man, her father, but he had certainly raised her in a specific fashion, and this was not it. So while he might not condemn her, she knew she wasn't going to get his wholesale approval.

And she would have to live with that.

Living without his approval was hard. Much harder than she had thought it might be. Especially given the fact that she thought she'd accepted it just a few moments ago. But being willing to experience disapproval and truly accepting it were apparently two different things.

"Why don't you have a seat, Hayley," her father said slowly.

"No, thank you," she replied. "I'm going to stand, because if I sit down... Well, I don't know. I have too much energy to sit down. But I—I care about him." She turned to Jonathan. "I care about you. I really do. I'm so sorry I made you feel like you were a dirty secret. Like I was ashamed of you. Because any woman would be proud to be involved with you." She took a deep breath and looked around the coffee shop. "I'm dating him," she said, pointing at Jonathan. "Just so you all know."

"Hayley," her father said, standing up, "come to dinner this week."

"With him?"

"If you want to. But please know that we want to know about your life. Even if it isn't what we would choose for you, we want to know." He didn't mean Jonathan specifically. He meant being in a physical relationship without the benefit of any kind of commitment, much less marriage.

But the way he looked at her, with nothing but love, made her ache all over. Made her throat feel so tight she could scarcely breathe.

She felt miserable. And she felt strong. She wasn't sure which emotion was more prominent. She had seen her father look at Ace like this countless times, had seen him talk about her brother with a similar expression on his face. Her father was loving, and he was as supportive as he could be, but he also had hard lines.

"I guess we'll see," she said.

"I suppose. I also imagine you need to have a talk with him," he said, tilting his head toward Jonathan, who was looking uncertain. She'd never seen Jonathan look uncertain before.

"Oh," she said, "I imagine I do."

"Come home if you need anything."

For some reason, she suddenly became aware of the tension in her father's expression. He was the pastor of Copper Ridge. And the entire town was watching him. So whether he wanted to or not, he couldn't haul off and punch Jonathan. He couldn't yell at her—though he never had yelled in all her life. And he was leaving her to sort out her own circumstances, when she could feel that he very much wanted to stay and sort them out for her.

Maybe Jonathan was right. Maybe she had never put a foot out of line because the rules were easier. There were no rules to what she was doing now, and no one was going to step in and tell her what to do. No one was going to pull her back if she went too far. Not even her father. Maybe that had been her real issue with taking this relationship public. Not so much the disappointment as the loss of a safety net.

Right now, Hayley felt like she was standing on the edge of an abyss. She had no idea how far she might fall, how bad it might hurt when she landed. If she would even survive it.

She was out here, living her potential mistakes, standing on the edge of a lot of potential pain.

Because with the barrier of following the rules removed, with no need to leave to experience things... Well, it was just her. Her heart and what she felt for Jonathan.

There was nothing in the way. No excuses. No false idea that this could never be anything, because she was leaving in the end.

As her father walked out of the coffeehouse, taking with him an entire truckload of her excuses, she realized exactly what she had been protecting herself from.

Falling in love. With Jonathan. With a man who might

never love her back. Wanting more, wanting everything, with the man least likely to give it to her.

She had been hiding behind the secretary desk at the church, listening to everybody else's problems, without ever incurring any of her own. She had witnessed a whole lot of heartbreak, a whole lot of struggle, but she had always been removed from it.

She didn't want to protect herself from this. She didn't want to hide.

"Why did you do that?" Jonathan asked.

"Because you were mad at me yesterday. I hurt your feelings."

He laughed, a dark, humorless sound. "Hayley," he said, "I don't exactly have feelings to hurt."

"That's not true," she said. "I know you do."

"Honey, that stuff was beaten out of me by my father before I was five years old. And whatever was left… It pretty much dissolved when my mother walked away and left me with a wounded sister to care for. That stuff just kind of leaves you numb. All you can do is survive. Work on through life as hard as you can, worry about putting food on the table. Worry about trying to do right by a kid who's had every unfair thing come down on her. You think you being embarrassed to hold my hand in public is going to hurt my feelings after that?"

She hated when he did this. When he drew lines between their levels of experience and made her feel silly.

She closed the distance between them and put her fingertips on his shoulder. Then she leaned in and kissed him, in full view of everybody in the coffeehouse. He put his hand on her hip, and even though he didn't enthusiastically kiss her back, he made no move to end it, either.

"Why do I get the feeling you are a little embarrassed to be with *me*?" she asked, when she pulled away from him.

He arched his brow. "I'm not embarrassed to be with you."

Maybe he wasn't. But there was something bothering him. "You're upset because everyone knows. And now there will be consequences if you do something to hurt me."

"When," he said, his tone uncompromising. "*When* I do something. That's what everyone is thinking. Trust me, Hayley, they don't think for one second that this might end in some fairy-tale wedding bullshit."

Hayley jerked back, trying to fight the feeling that she had just been slapped in the face. For whatever reason, he was trying to elicit exactly that response, and she really didn't want to give it to him. "Fine. Maybe that is what they think. But why does it matter? That's the question, isn't it? Why does what other people think matter more than what you or I might want?

"You were right about me. My choices were less about what other people might think, and more about what might happen to me if I found out I had never actually been reined in." She shook her head. "If I discovered that all along I could have done exactly what I wanted to, with no limit on it. Before now, I never took the chance to find out who I was. I was happy to be told. And I think I've been a little afraid of who I might be beneath all of these expectations."

"Why? Because you might harbor secret fantasies of shoplifting doilies out of the Trading Post?"

"No," Hayley said, "because I might go and get myself hurt. If I had continued working at the church, if I'd kept on gazing at the kind of men I met there from across the room, never making a move because waiting for them to do it was right, pushing down all of my desires because it was lust I shouldn't feel… I would have been safe. I wouldn't be sitting here in this coffee shop with you, shaking because I'm scared, because I'm a little bit turned on thinking about what we did last night."

"I understand the turned on part," he said, his voice rough like gravel. He lifted his hand, dragging his thumb over her lower lip. "Why are you afraid?"

"I'm afraid because just like you said… There's a very low chance of this ending in some fairy-tale wedding… nonsense. And I want all of that." Her chest seized tight, her throat closing up to a painful degree. "With you. If you were wondering. And that is… That's so scary. Because I knew you would look at me like that if I told you."

His face was flat, his dark eyes blazing. He was…well, he was angry, rather than indifferent. Somehow, she had known he would be.

"You shouldn't be afraid of not getting your fairy tale with me. If anything, you should be relieved. Nobody wants to stay with me for the rest of their life, Hayley, trust me. You're supposed to go to Paris. And you're going to Paris."

"I don't want to go," she said, because she wanted to stay here, with him. Or take him with her. But she didn't want to be without him.

"Dammit," he said, his voice like ground-up glass. "Hayley, you're not going to change your plans because of me. That would last how long? Maybe a year? Maybe two if you're really dedicated. But I know exactly how that ends—with you deciding you would rather be anywhere but stuck in my house, stuck in this town."

"But I don't feel stuck. I never did. It was all…me

being afraid. But the thing is, Jonathan, I never wanted anything more than I wanted my safety. Thinking I needed to escape was just a response to this missing piece inside of me that I couldn't put a name to. But I know what it is now."

"Don't," he bit out.

"It was you," she said. "All of this time it was you. Don't you see? I never wanted anyone or anything badly enough to take the chance. To take the risk. To expose myself, to step out of line. But you... I do want you that badly."

"Because you were forced to take the risk. You had to own it. Yesterday, you didn't have to, and so you didn't. You pulled away from me when we walked down the street, didn't want anyone to see."

"That wasn't about you. It was about me. It was about the fact that...basically, everybody in town knows I've never dated anybody. So in my case it's a little bit like announcing that I lost my virginity, and it's embarrassing."

Except now she was having this conversation with him in a coffeehouse, where people she knew were sitting only a few feet away, undoubtedly straining to hear her over the sound of the espresso machine. But whatever. She didn't care. For the first time in her life, she really, really didn't care. She cared about him. She cared about this relationship. About doing whatever she needed to do to make him see that everything she was saying was true.

"I'm over it," she added. "I just had to decide that I was. Well, now I have. Because it doesn't get any more horrifying than having to admit that you were having your first affair to your father."

"You see," he said. "I wouldn't know. Nobody was all that invested in me when I lost my virginity, or why.

I was fifteen, if you were curious. So forgive me if your concerns seem foreign to me. It's just that I know how this all plays out. People say they love you, then they punch you in the face. You take care of somebody all of their damn life, and then they take off with the one person you spent all that time protecting them from. Yeah, they say they love you, and then they leave. That's life."

Hayley's chest tightened, her heart squeezing painfully. "I didn't say I loved you."

He looked stricken by that. "Well, good. At least you didn't lie to me."

She did love him, though. But he had introduced the word. Love and its effects were clearly the things that scared him most about what was happening between them.

Love loomed large between them. Love was clearly on the table here. Even if he didn't want it to be, there it was. Even if he was going to deny it, there it was.

Already in his mind, in his heart, whether she said it or not.

She opened her mouth to say it, but it stuck in her throat.

Because he had already decided it would be a lie if she spoke the words. He was so dedicated to that idea. To his story about who Jonathan Bear was, and who he had to be, and how people treated him. His behavior was so very close to what she had been doing for so long.

"Jonathan—"

He cut her off. "I don't love people," he said. "You know what I love? I love things. I love my house. I love my money. I love that company that I've spent so many hours investing in. I love the fact that I own a mountain, and can ride a horse from one end of my land to the other, and get a sense of everything that can never be taken from me. But I'll never love another person, not again." He stood up, gripping her chin with his thumb and forefinger. "Not even you. Because I will never love anything I can't buy right back, do you understand?"

She nodded, swallowing hard. "Yes," she said.

His pain was hemorrhaging from him, bleeding out of every pore, and there was nothing she could do to stop it. He was made of fury, of rage, and he was made of hurt, whether he would admit it or not.

"I think we're done then, Hayley."

He moved away from her, crossing the coffeehouse and walking out the door. Every eye in the room was on her, everybody watching to see what she would do next. So she did the only thing she could.

She stood up and she ran after Jonathan Bear for the entire town to see.

JONATHAN STRODE DOWN the street. The heavy gray sky was starting to crack, raindrops falling onto his head. His shoulders. Good. That was just about perfect.

It took him a few more strides to realize he was headed away from his car, but he couldn't think clearly enough to really grasp where he was going. His head was pounding like horse hooves over the grass, and he couldn't grab hold of a thought to save his life.

"Jonathan!"

He turned, looking down the mostly empty street, to see Hayley running after him, her dark hair flying behind her, rain flying into her face. She was making a spectacle of herself, right here on Main, and she didn't seem to care at all. Something about that made him feel like he'd been turned to stone, rooted to the spot, his heart thundering heavily in his chest.

"Don't run from me," she said, coming to a stop in front of him, breathing hard. "Don't run from us."

"You're the one who's running, honey," he said, keeping his voice deliberately flat.

"We're not done," she said. "We're not going to be done just because you say so. You might be the boss at your house, but you're not the boss here." Her words were jumbled up, fierce and ferocious. "What about what I want?"

He gritted his teeth. "Well, the problem is you made the mistake of assuming I might care what you want."

She sprang forward, pounding a closed fist on his shoulder. The gesture was so aggressive, so very unlike Hayley that it immobilized him. "You do care. You're not a mountain, you're just a man, and you do care. But you're awfully desperate to prove that you don't. You're awfully desperate to prove you have no worth. And I have to wonder why that is."

"I don't have to prove it. Everyone who's ever wandered through my life has proved it, Hayley. You're a little bit late to this party. You're hardly going to take thirty-five years of neglect and make me feel differently about it. Make me come to different conclusions than I've spent the past three decades drawing."

"Why not?" she asked. "That's kind of the point of knowing someone. Of being with them. They change you. You've certainly changed me. You made me...well, more me than I've ever been."

"I never said I needed to change."

"That's ridiculous. Of course you need to change. You live in that big house all by yourself, you're angry at your sister because she figured out how to let something go when you can't. And you're about ready to blow this up—to blow us up—to keep yourself safe." She shivered, the rain making dark spots on her top, drops rolling down her face.

"There's no reason any of this has to end, Hayley." He gritted his teeth, fighting against the slow, expanding feeling growing in his chest, fighting against the pain starting to push against the back of his eyes. "But you have to accept what I'm willing to give. And it may not be what you want, what you're looking for. If it's not, if that makes you leave, then you're no different from anyone else who's ever come through my life, and you won't be any surprise to me."

Hayley looked stricken by that, pale. And he could see her carefully considering her words. "Wow. That's a very smart way to build yourself an impenetrable fort there, Jonathan. How can anyone demand something of you, if you're determined to equate high expectations with the people who abandoned you? If you're determined to believe that someone asking anything of you is the same as not loving you at all?"

"You haven't said you loved me." His voice was deliberately hard. He didn't know why he was bringing that up again. Didn't know why he was suspended between the desire for her to tell him she didn't, and the need—the intense, soul-shattering need—to hear her say it, even if he could never accept it. Even if he could never return it.

"My mistake," she said, her voice thin. "What will you do if I tell you, Jonathan? Will you say it doesn't matter, that it isn't real? Because you know everything, don't you? Even my heart."

"I know more about the world than you do, little girl,"

he said, his throat feeling tight for some reason. "Whatever your intentions, I have a better idea of what the actual outcome might be."

She shocked him by taking two steps forward, eliminating the air between them, pressing her hand against his chest. His heart raged beneath her touch, and he had a feeling she could tell.

"I love you." She stared at him for a moment, then she stretched up on her toes and pressed a kiss to his lips. Her lips were slick and cold from the rain, and he wanted to consume her. Wanted to pretend that words didn't matter. That there was nothing but this kiss.

For a moment, a heartbeat, he pretended that was true.

"I love you," she said again, when they parted. "But that doesn't mean I won't expect something from you. In fact, that would be pretty sorry love if I expected to come into your life and change nothing, mean nothing. I want you to love me back, Jonathan. I want you to open yourself up. I want you to let me in. I want you to be brave."

He grabbed hold of her arms, held her against his chest. He didn't give a damn who might see them. "You're telling me to be brave? What have you ever faced down that scared you? Tell me, Hayley."

"You," she said breathlessly.

He released his hold on her and took a step back, swearing violently. "All the more reason you should walk away, I expect."

"Do you know why you scare me, Jonathan? You make me want something I can't control. You make me want something I can't predict. There are no rules for this. There is no safety. Loving you... I have no guarantees. There is no neat map for how this might work out. It's not a math equation, where I can add doing the right things with saying the right things and make you change. You have to decide. You have to choose this. You have to choose us. The rewards for being afraid, or being good, aren't worth as much as the reward for being brave. So I'm going to be brave.

"I love you. And I want you to love me back. I want you to take a chance—on me."

She was gazing at him, her eyes blazing with light and intensity. How long would it take for that light to dim? How long would it take for him to kill it? How long would it take for her to decide—like everyone else in his life—that he wasn't worth the effort?

It was inevitable. That was how it always ended.

"No," he said, the word scraping his throat raw as it escaped.

"No?" The devastation in her voice cut him like a knife.

"No. But hey, one more for your list," he said, hating himself with every syllable.

"What?"

"You got your kiss in the rain. I did a lot for you, checked off a lot of your boxes. Go find some other man to fill in the rest."

Then he turned and left her standing in the street.

And in front of God and everybody, Jonathan Bear walked away from Hayley Thompson, and left whatever remained of his heart behind with her.

CHAPTER THIRTEEN

THIS WAS HELL. Perhaps even literally. Hayley had wondered about hell a few times, growing up the daughter of a pastor. Now, she thought that if hell were simply living with a broken heart, with the rejection of the person you loved more than anything else echoing in your ears, it would be pretty effective eternal damnation.

She was lying on her couch, tears streaming down her face. She was miserable, and she didn't even want to do anything about it. She just wanted to sit in it.

Oh, she had been so cavalier about the pain that would come when Jonathan ended things. Back in the beginning, when she had been justifying losing her virginity to him, she had been free and easy about the possibility of heartbreak.

But she hadn't loved him then. So she really hadn't known.

Hadn't known that it would be like shards of glass digging into her chest every time she took a breath. Hadn't known that it was actual, physical pain. That her head would throb and her eyes would feel like sandpaper from all the crying.

That her body, and her soul, would feel like they had been twisted, wrung out and draped over a wire to dry in the brutal, unfeeling coastal air.

This was the experience he had talked about. The one that wasn't worth having.

She rolled onto her back, thinking over the past weeks with Jonathan. Going to his house, getting her first job away from the church. How nervous she had been. How fluttery she had felt around him.

Strangely, she felt her lips curve into a smile.

It was hard to reconcile the woman she was now with the girl who had first knocked on his door for that job interview.

She hadn't even realized what all that fluttering meant. What the tightening in her nipples, the pressure between her thighs had meant. She knew now. Desire. Need. Things she would associate with Jonathan for the rest of her life, no matter where she went, no matter who else she might be with.

He'd told her to find someone else.

Right now, the idea of being with another man made her cringe.

She wasn't ready to think about that. She was too raw. And she still wanted him. Only him.

Jonathan was more than an experience.

He had wrenched her open. Pulled her out of the safe space she'd spent so many years hiding in. He had shown her a love that was bigger than fear.

Unfortunately, because that love was so big, the desolation of it was crippling.

She sat up, scrubbing her arm over her eyes. She needed to figure out what she was going to do next.

Something had crystallized for her earlier today, during the encounter with Jonathan and her father. She didn't need to run away. She didn't need to leave town, or gain anonymity, in order to have what she wanted. To be who she wanted.

She didn't need to be the church secretary, didn't need to be perfect or hide what she was doing. She could still go to her father's church on Sunday, and go to dinner at her parents' house on Sunday evening.

She didn't have to abandon her home, her family, her faith. Sure, it might be uncomfortable to unite her family and her need to find herself, but if there was one thing loving Jonathan had taught her, it was that sometimes uncomfortable was worth it.

She wasn't going to let heartbreak stop her.

She thought back to how he had looked at her earlier today, those black eyes impassive as he told her he wouldn't love her back.

Part of her wanted to believe she was right about him. That he was afraid. That he was protecting himself.

Another part of her felt that was a little too hopeful. Maybe that gorgeous, experienced man simply couldn't love his recently-a-virgin assistant.

Except…she had been so certain, during a few small moments, that she had given something to him, too. Just like he had given so much to her.

For some reason, he was dedicated to the idea that nobody stayed. That people looked at him and saw the worst. She couldn't understand why he would find that comforting, and yet a part of him must.

It made her ache. Her heart wasn't broken only for her, but for him, too. For all the love he wouldn't allow himself to accept.

She shook her head. Later. Later she would feel sorry for him. Right now, she was going to wallow in her own pain.

Because at the end of the day, Jonathan had made the choice to turn away from her, to turn away from love.

Right now, she would feel sorry for herself. Then maybe she would plan a trip to Paris.

"Do you want to invite me in?"

Jonathan looked at his sister, standing on the porch, looking deceptively calm.

"Do I have a choice?"

Rebecca shook her head, her long dark hair swinging behind her like a curtain. "Not really. I didn't drive all the way out here to have this conversation with moths buzzing around me."

It was dark out, and just as Rebecca had said, there were bugs fluttering around the porch light near her face.

"Come in, then," he said, moving aside.

She blinked when she stepped over the threshold, a soft smile touching her lips. The scar tissue on the left side of her mouth pulled slightly. Scar tissue that had been given to her by the man she was going to marry. Oh, it had been an accident, and Jonathan knew it. But with all the pain and suffering the accident had caused Rebecca, intent had never much mattered to him.

"This is beautiful, Jonathan," she said, her dark eyes flickering to him. "I haven't been here since it was finished."

He shrugged. "Well, that was your choice."

"You don't like my fiancé. And you haven't made much of an effort to change that. I don't know what you expect from me."

"Appreciation, maybe, for all the years I spent taking care of you?" He wanted to cut his own balls off for saying that. Basically, right about now he wanted to escape his own skin. He was a bastard. Even he thought so.

He was sitting in his misery now, existing fully in the knowledge of the pain he had caused Hayley.

He should never have had that much power over her. He never should have touched her. This misery was the only possible way it could have turned out. His only real defense was that he hadn't imagined a woman like Hayley would ever fall in love with a man like him.

"Right. Because we've never had that discussion."

His sister's tone was dry, and he could tell she was pretty unimpressed with him. Well, fair enough. He was unimpressed with himself.

"I still don't understand why you love him, Rebecca. I really don't."

"What is love to you, Jonathan?"

An image of Hayley's face swam before his mind's eye. "What the hell kind of question is that?"

"A relevant one," she said. "I think. Particularly when we get down to why exactly I'm here. Congratulations. After spending most of your life avoiding being part of the rumor mill, you're officially hot small-town gossip."

"Am I?" He wasn't very surprised to hear that.

"Something about kissing the pastor's daughter on Main Street in the rain. And having a fight with her."

"That's accurate."

"What's going on?"

"What it looks like. I was sleeping with her. We had a fight. Now we're not sleeping together."

Rebecca tilted her head to the side. "I feel like I'm missing some information."

"Hayley was working for me—I assume you knew that."

"Vaguely," she said, her eyes glittering with curiosity.

"And I'm an asshole. So when I found out my assistant was a virgin, I figured I would help her with that." It was a lie, but one he was comfortable with. He was comfortable painting himself as the villain. Everybody would, anyway. So why not add his own embellishment to the tale.

"Right," Rebecca said, sarcasm dripping from her voice. "Because you're a known seducer of innocent women."

Jonathan turned away, running his hand over his hair. "I'm not the nicest guy, Rebecca. We all know that."

"I know *you* think that," Rebecca said. "And I know we've had our differences. But when I needed you, you were there for me. Always. Even when Gage broke my heart, and you couldn't understand why it mattered, why I wanted to be with him, in the end, you supported me. Always. Every day of my life. I don't even remember my father. I remember you. You taught me how to ride a bike, how to ride a horse. You fought for me, tirelessly. Worked for me. You don't think I don't know how tired you were? How much you put into making our home…a home? Bad men don't do that. Bad men hit their wives, hit their children. Abandon their daughters. Our fathers were bad men, Jonathan. But you never were."

Something about those words struck him square in the chest. Their fathers *were* bad men.

He had always known that.

But he had always believed somewhere deep down that he must be bad, too. Not because he thought being an abusive bastard was hereditary. But because if his father had beaten him, and his mother had left him, there must be something about him that was bad.

Something visible. Something that the whole town could see.

He thought back to all the kindness on Pastor John Thompson's face, kindness Jonathan certainly hadn't deserved from the old man when he was doing his absolute damnedest to start a fight in the middle of The Grind.

He had been so determined to have John confirm that Jonathan was bad. That he was wrong.

Because there was something freeing about the anger that belief created deep inside his soul.

It had been fuel. All his life that belief had been his fuel. Gave him something to fight against. Something to be angry about.

An excuse to never get close to anyone.

Because underneath all the anger was nothing but despair. Despair because his parents had left him, because they couldn't love him enough. Because he wasn't worth...anything.

His need for love had never gone away, but he'd shoved it down deep. Easier to do when you had convinced yourself you could never have it.

He looked at Rebecca and realized he had despaired over her, too. When she had chosen Gage. Jonathan had decided it was just one more person who loved him and didn't want to stay.

Yeah, it was much easier, much less painful to believe that he was bad. Because it let him keep his distance from the pain. Because it meant he didn't have to try.

"What do you think love is?" Rebecca asked again, more persistent this time.

He didn't have an answer. Not one with words. All he had were images, feelings. Watching Rebecca sleep after a particularly hard day. Praying child services wouldn't come by to check on her while he was at work, and find her alone and him negligent.

And Hayley. Her soft hands on his body, her sweet surrender. The trust it represented. The way she made him feel. Like he was on fire, burning up from the inside out. Like he could happily stay for the rest of his life in a one-room cabin, without any of the money or power he had acquired over the past few years, and be perfectly content.

The problem was, he couldn't make her stay with him.

This house, his company, those things were his. In a way that Hayley could never be. In a way that no one ever could be.

People were always able to leave.

He felt like a petulant child even having that thought. But he didn't know how the hell else he could feel secure. And he didn't think he could stand having another person walk away.

"I don't know," he said.

Rebecca shook her head, her expression sad. "That's a damn shame, Jonathan, because you show me love all the time. Whether you know what to call it or not, you've given it to me tirelessly over the years, and without you, without it, I don't know where I would be. You stayed with me when everybody else left."

"But who stayed with me?" he asked, feeling like an ass for even voicing that question. "You had to stay. I had to take care of you. But the minute you could go out on your own you did."

"Because that's what your love did for me, you idiot."

"Not very well. Because you were always worried I thought of you as a burden, weren't you? It almost ruined your relationship with Gage, if I recall correctly."

"Yes," she said, "but that wasn't about you. That was my baggage. And you did everything in your power to help me, even when you knew the result would be me going back to Gage. That's love, Jonathan." She shook her head. "I love you, too. I love you enough to want you to have your own life, one that doesn't revolve around taking care of me. That doesn't revolve around what happened to us in the past."

He looked around the room, at the house that meant so much to him. A symbol of security, of his ability to care for Rebecca, if her relationship went to hell. And he realized that creating this security for her somehow enabled him to deny his own weaknesses. His own fears.

This house had only ever been for him. A fortress to barricade himself in.

Wasn't that what Hayley had accused him of? Building himself a perfect fortress to hide in?

If everybody hated him, he didn't have to try. If there was something wrong with him, he never had to do what was right. If all he loved were things, he never had to risk loss.

They were lies. Lies he told himself because he was a coward.

And it had taken a virginal church secretary to uncover the truth.

She had stood in front of him and said she wanted love more than she wanted to be safe. And he had turned her down.

He was afraid. Had been all his life. But before this very moment, he would have rather cut out his own heart than admit it.

But now, standing with his sister looking at him like

he was the saddest damn thing she'd ever seen, a hole opened in his chest. A hole Hayley had filled.

"But doesn't it scare you?" he asked, his voice rough. "What if he leaves?"

She reached out, putting her hand on his. "It would break my heart. But I would be okay. I would have you. And I would…still be more whole than I was before I loved him. That's the thing about love. It doesn't make you weak, Jonathan, it makes you stronger. Opening yourself up, letting people in…that makes your life bigger. It makes your life richer. Maybe it's a cliché, but from where I'm standing you need to hear the cliché. You need to start believing it."

"I don't understand why she would want to be with me," Jonathan said. "She's…sweet. And she's never been hurt. I'm…well, I'm a mess. That's not what she deserves. She deserves to have a man who's in mint condition, like she is."

"But that's not how love works. If love made sense, if it was perfectly fair, then Gage West would not have been the man for me. He was the last man on earth I should have wanted, Jonathan. Nobody knows that more than me, and him. It took a miracle for me to let go of all my anger and love him. At the same time… I couldn't help myself.

"Love is strange that way. You fall into it whether you want to or not. Then the real fight is figuring out how to live it. How to become the person you need to be so you can hold on to that love. But I'm willing to bet you are the man she needs. Not some mint condition, new-in-the-box guy. But a strong man who has proved, time and time again, that no matter how hard life is, no matter how intensely the storm rages, he'll be there for you.

And more than that, he'll throw his body over yours to protect you if it comes to that. That's what I see when I look at you, Jonathan. What's it going to take for you to see that in yourself?"

"I don't think I'm ever going to," he said slowly, imagining Hayley again, picturing her as she stared up at him on the street. Fury, hurt, love shining from her eyes. "But…if she sees it…"

"That's a start," Rebecca said. "As long as you don't let her get away. As long as you don't push her away."

"It's too late for that. She's probably not going to want to see me again. She's probably not going to want me back."

"Well, you won't know unless you ask." Rebecca took a deep breath. "The best thing about love is it has the capacity to forgive on a pretty incredible level. But if there's one thing you and I both know, it's that it's hard to forgive someone leaving. Don't make that the story. Go back. Ask for forgiveness. Change what needs to be changed. Mostly…love her. The rest kind of takes care of itself."

CHAPTER FOURTEEN

HAYLEY HAD JUST settled back onto her couch for more quality sitting and weeping when she heard a knock at her door.

She stood up, brushing potato chip crumbs off her pajamas and grimacing. Maybe it was Cassie, bringing up baked goods. The other woman had done that earlier; maybe now she was bringing more. Hayley could only hope.

She had a gaping wound in her chest that could be only temporarily soothed by butter.

Without bothering to fix her hair—which was on top of her head in a messy knot—she jerked the door open.

And there he was. Dark eyes glittering, gorgeous mouth pressed into a thin line. His dark hair tied back low on his neck, the way she was accustomed to seeing him during the day.

Her heart lurched up into her throat, trying to make a break for it.

She hadn't been expecting him, but she imagined expecting him wouldn't have helped. Jonathan Bear wasn't someone you could anticipate.

"What are you doing here?"

He looked around. "I came here to talk to you. Were you…expecting someone else?"

"Yes. A French male prostitute." He lifted his brows. "Well, you told me to find another man to tick my boxes."

"I think you mean a gigolo."

"I don't know what they're called," she said, exasperated.

The corner of his mouth twitched. "Well, I promise to be quick. I won't interrupt your sex date."

She stepped to the side, ignoring the way her whole body hurt as she did. "I don't have a sex date." She cleared her throat. "Just so you know."

"Somehow, I didn't think you did."

"You don't know me," she grumbled, turning away from him, pressing her hand to her chest to see if her heart was beating as hard and fast as she felt like it was.

It was.

"I do, Hayley. I know you pretty damn well. Maybe better than I know myself. And…I think you might know me better than I know myself, too." He sounded different. Sad. Tired.

She turned around to face him, and with his expression more fully illuminated by the light, she saw weariness written there. Exhaustion.

"For all the good it did me," she said, crossing her arms tightly in a bid to protect herself. Really, though, it was too late. There wasn't anything left to protect. He had shattered her irrevocably.

"Yeah, well. It did me a hell of a lot of good. At least, I hope it's going to. I hope I'm not too late."

"Too late for what? To stick the knife in again or…?"

"To tell you I love you," he said.

Everything froze inside her. Absolutely everything. The air in her lungs, her heart, the blood in her veins.

"You…you just said… Don't tease me, Jonathan. Don't

play with me. I know I'm younger than you. I know that I'm innocent. But if you came back here to lie to me, to say what you think I need to hear so you can…keep having me in your bed, or whatever—"

Suddenly, she found herself being hauled forward into his arms, against his chest. "I do want you in my bed," he said, "make no mistake about that. But sex is just sex, Hayley, even when it's good. And what we have is good.

"But here's something you don't know, because you don't have experience with it. Sex isn't love. And it doesn't feel like this. I feel…like everything in me is broken and stronger at the same time, and I don't know how in the hell that can be true. And when you told me you loved me… I knew I could either let go of everything in the past or hold on to it harder to protect myself." He shook his head. "I protected myself."

"Yeah, well. What about protecting me?"

"I thought maybe I was protecting you, too. But it's all tangled up in this big lie that I've been telling myself for years. I told you I didn't love people, that I love things. But I said that only because I've had way too much experience with people I love leaving. A house can't walk away, Hayley. A mountain can't up and abandon you. But you could.

"One day, you could wake up and regret that you tied your future to me. When you could have done better… When you could have had a man who wasn't so damn broken." He cupped her cheek, bent down and kissed her lips. "What did I do to earn the love of someone like you? Someone so beautiful…so soft. You're everything I'm not, Hayley Thompson, and all the reasons I love you make perfect sense to me. But why do you love me? That's what I can't quite figure out."

Hayley looked into his eyes, so full of pain, so deeply wounded. She would have never thought a man like him would need reassurance from anyone, least of all a woman like her.

"I know I don't have a lot of experience, Jonathan. Well, any experience apart from you. I know that I haven't seen the whole world. I haven't even seen the whole state. But I've seen your heart. The kind of man you are. The change that knowing you, loving you, created in me. And I know…perfect love casts out all fear.

"I can't say I haven't been afraid these past couple of days. Afraid I couldn't be with you. That things might not work out with us. But when I stood on Main Street… I knew fear couldn't be allowed to win. It was your love that brought me to that conclusion. Your love was bigger than the fear inside me. I don't need experience to understand that. I don't need to travel the world or date other men for the sake of experience. I need you. Because whether or not you're perfect, you're perfect for me."

"*You're* perfect," he said, his voice rough. "So damned perfect. I want…to take you to Canada."

She blinked. "Well. That's not exactly an offer to run off to Vegas."

"You want to use your passport. Why wait? Let's go now. Your boss will let you off. I'm sure of it."

Something giddy bubbled up in her chest. Something wonderful. "Right now? Really?"

"Right the hell now."

"Yes," she said. "Yes, let's go to Canada."

"It's not the Eiffel Tower," he said, "but I will take you there someday. I promise you that."

"The only thing I need is you," she said. "The rest is negotiable."

His lips crashed down on hers, his kiss desperate and intense, saying the deep, poetic things she doubted her stoic cowboy would ever say out loud. But that was okay. The kiss said plenty all on its own.

EPILOGUE

JONATHAN HATED WEARING a suit. He'd never done it before, but he had come to a swift and decisive conclusion the moment he'd finished doing up his tie.

Hayley was standing in their bedroom, looking amused. The ring on her left hand glittered as bright as her eyes, and suddenly, it wasn't the tie that was strangling him. It was just her. The love on her beautiful face. The fact she loved him.

He still hadn't quite figured out why. Still wasn't sure he saw all the things in himself that Rebecca had spoken of that day, all the things Hayley talked about when she said she loved him.

But Hayley did love him. And that was a gift he cherished.

"You're not going to make me wear a suit when we do this, are you?" he asked.

"I might," she said. "You look really hot in a suit."

He wrapped his arm around her waist and pulled her to his chest. "You look hottest in nothing at all. Think we could compromise?"

"We've created enough scandal already without me showing up naked to my wedding. Anyway, I'm wearing white. I am a traditional girl, after all."

"Honey, you oughta wear red."

"Are you calling me a scarlet woman?"

He nodded. "Yes, and I think you proved your status earlier this morning."

She blushed. She still blushed, even after being with him for six months. Blushed in bed, when he whispered dirty things into her ear. He loved it.

He loved *her*.

He couldn't wait to be her husband, and that was something he hadn't imagined ever feeling. Looking forward to being a husband.

Of course, he was looking forward to the honeymoon even more. To staying in a little apartment in Paris with a view of the Eiffel Tower.

For him, trading in a view of the mountains for a view of the city didn't hold much appeal. But she wanted it. And the joy he got from giving Hayley what she wanted was the biggest thing in his world.

Waiting to surprise her with the trip was damn near killing him.

"You have to hurry," she said, pushing at his shoulder. "You're giving the bride away, after all."

Jonathan took a deep breath. Yeah, it was time. Time to give his sister to that Gage West, who would never deserve her, but who loved her, so Jonathan was willing to let it go. Willing to give them his blessing.

Actually, over the past few months he'd gotten kind of attached to the bastard who would be his brother-in-law. Something he'd thought would never be possible only a little while ago.

But love changed you. Rebecca had been right about that.

"All right," he said. "Let's go then."

Hayley kissed his cheek and took his hand, leading him out of the bedroom and down the stairs. The wedding guests were out on the back lawn, waiting for the event to start. When he and Hayley exited the house, they all turned to look.

He and Hayley still turned heads, and he had a feeling they always would.

Jonathan Bear had always been seen as a bad boy. In all the ways that phrase applied. The kind of boy no parent wanted their daughter to bring home to Sunday dinner. And yet the pastor's daughter had.

He'd definitely started out that way. But somehow, through some miracle, he'd earned the love of a good woman.

And because of her love, he was determined to be the best man he could possibly be.

* * * * *

We hope you enjoyed reading

Joshua and The Cowgirl

by *New York Times* bestselling author
SHERRYL WOODS

and

Seduce Me Cowboy

by *New York Times* bestselling author
MAISEY YATES

Originally HQN Books and
Harlequin® series stories!

From passionate, suspenseful and dramatic
love stories to inspirational or historical,
Harlequin offers different lines to
satisfy every romance reader.

New books in each line
are available every month.

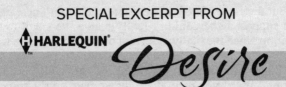
She was going to be interviewing Isaiah's potential wife.

The man she had been in love with since she was a
teenage idiot, and was still in love with now that she was
an idiot in her late twenties.

There were a whole host of reasons she'd never, ever
let on about her feelings for him.

She loved her job. She loved Isaiah's family, who were
the closest thing she had to a family of her own.

She was also living in the small town of Copper Ridge,
Oregon, which was a bit strange for a girl from Seattle,
but she did like it. It had a different pace. But that meant
there was less opportunity for a social life. There were
fewer people to interact with. By default she, and the
other folks in town, ended up spending a lot of their free
time with the people they worked with every day. There
was nothing wrong with that. But it was just…

Mostly there wasn't enough of a break from Isaiah on
any given day.

But then, she also didn't enforce one. Didn't take one. She supposed she couldn't really blame the small-town location when the likely culprit of the entire situation was her.

"Place whatever ad you need to," he said, his tone abrupt. "When you meet the right woman, you'll know."

"I'll know," she echoed lamely.

"Yes. Nobody knows me better than you do, Poppy. I have faith that you'll pick the right wife for me."

With those awful words still ringing in the room, Isaiah left her there, sitting at her desk, feeling numb.

The fact of the matter was, she probably could pick him a perfect wife. Someone who would facilitate his life, and give him space when he needed it. Someone who was beautiful and fabulous in bed.

Yes, she knew exactly what Isaiah Grayson would think made a woman the perfect wife for him.

The sad thing was, Poppy didn't possess very many of those qualities herself.

And what she so desperately wanted was for Isaiah's perfect wife to be her.

But dreams were for other women. They always had been. Which meant some other woman was going to end up with Poppy's dream.

While she played matchmaker to the whole affair.

Don't miss what happens when Isaiah decides it's Poppy *who should be his convenient wife in*
Want Me, Cowboy *by USA TODAY bestselling author Maisey Yates, part of her Copper Ridge series!*

Available November 2018 wherever Harlequin® Desire books and ebooks are sold.

www.Harlequin.com

HARLEQUIN® *Desire*

Family sagas…scandalous secrets…burning desires.

Save **$1.00**
on the purchase of ANY
Harlequin® Desire book.

Available wherever books are sold,
including most bookstores, supermarkets,
drugstores and discount stores.

Save $1.00
on the purchase of any Harlequin® Desire book.
Coupon valid until February 28, 2019.
Redeemable at participating outlets in the U.S. and Canada only.
Not redeemable at Barnes & Noble stores. Limit one coupon per customer.

52616147

5 65373 00076 2 (8100)0 12401

HARLEQUIN

Presents®

Coming next month—a tale of innocence and desire!

In *The Spaniard's Untouched Bride* by Maisey Yates,
brooding Matias *must* marry to inherit the Navarro fortune.
So when his ruthless brother kidnaps his fiancée,
Matias is left without a bride. Will heiress Camilla
agree to be his convenient wife?

Camilla Alvarez refuses to abandon her beloved horses when
formidable tycoon Matias Navarro acquires her family's
renowned rancho. Instead, she disguises herself as his stable
boy! Yet when Camilla's charade is discovered, Matias offers
her an even more shocking role—his wife! Innocent Camilla is
transformed into a bride deserving of his diamonds, but their
convenient marriage is transformed by the scorching heat of
their wedding night…

The Spaniard's Untouched Bride
Available January 2019